continued . . .

Titles by Mike Lupica

. . .

NONFICTION

FICTION

RED ZONE

Mike Lupica

BERKLEY BOOKS, NEW YORK

THE BERKLEY PUBLISHING GROUP
Published by the Penguin Group
Penguin Group (USA) Inc.
375 Hudson Street, New York, New York 10014, USA
Penguin Group (Canada), 10 Alcorn Avenue, Toronto, Ontario M4V 3B2, Canada
(a division of Pearson Penguin Canada Inc.)
Penguin Books Ltd., 80 Strand, London WC2R 0RL, England
Penguin Group Ireland, 25 St. Stephen's Green, Dublin 2, Ireland (a division of Penguin Books Ltd.)
Penguin Group (Australia), 250 Camberwell Road, Camberwell, Victoria 3124, Australia
(a division of Pearson Australia Group Pty. Ltd.)
Penguin Books India Pvt. Ltd., 11 Community Centre, Panchsheel Park, New Delhi—110 017, India
Penguin Group (NZ), Cnr. Airborne and Rosedale Roads, Albany, Auckland 1310, New Zealand
(a division of Pearson New Zealand Ltd.)
Penguin Books (South Africa) (Pty.) Ltd., 24 Sturdee Avenue, Rosebank, Johannesburg 2196,
South Africa

Penguin Books Ltd., Registered Offices: 80 Strand, London WC2R 0RL, England

This is a work of fiction. Names, characters, places, and incidents either are the product
of the author's imagination or are used fictitiously, and any resemblance to actual persons,
living or dead, business establishments, events, or locales is entirely coincidental.

RED ZONE

A Berkley Book / published by arrangement with the author

PRINTING HISTORY
G. P. Putnam's hardcover edition / October 2003
Berkley mass-market edition / October 2004

Copyright © 2003 by Mike Lupica.

ISBN: 0-425-19875-8

BERKLEY®
Berkley Books are published by The Berkley Publishing Group,
a division of Penguin Group (USA) Inc.,
375 Hudson Street, New York, New York 10014.
BERKLEY is a registered trademark of Penguin Group (USA) Inc.
The "B" design is a trademark belonging to Penguin Group (USA) Inc.

PRINTED IN THE UNITED STATES OF AMERICA

10 9 8 7 6 5 4 3 2 1

For my wife,

TAYLOR

The one we all dream about.
The one who walks into the room
and changes everything.

Acknowledgments

Ralph Iannelli, who gave me the business.
Thomas J. O'Neill, who let me borrow his life, again.

RED ZONE

RED ZONE

PART ONE

Scratch

1

Let's get something straight right from the start: Whoever said it was better to have loved and lost than never to have loved at all can kiss my ass.

I assume it was one of those English poets deeper than Dr. Phil. Though it actually sounds lame enough to have come from some sports columnist trying to show everybody what a Real Writer he is. Or one of the guys doing the smirkfest that currently passes for sports broadcasting, where they can't seem to give you a goddamn score without throwing in a couple of rim shots first.

You know the drill: We just want to know if the Yankees beat the Red Sox, but they think it's open-mike night at the comedy club.

If I sound hot about my former friends in the media, maybe it's because they had so much fun at my expense after I did the whole love-and-lost deal with my football team, the New York Hawks. I wasn't the first to find out how fast it can turn around on you when you're not on top anymore, in sports or anything else. But I'd actually convinced myself that the media actually liked me for my adorable self, not all the checks I picked up, parties I threw, slow news days I got them through, or Very Bad Girls I fixed them up with on the road.

"Clear something up for me," I said to Gil Spencer of the *Daily News.* "I screwed up with the Hawks, right? I didn't dump Martha Stewart's stock for her?"

"You're smart enough to figure it out, Jack," Spencer said. "Bad shit makes really good copy."

"Even when it happens to one of the good guys?"

"*Especially* when it happens to one of the good guys," he said.

It happened to me the way it did, the whole thing in lights, because it was New York, and the Hawks had become the most glamorous pro football team in the world. It happened because of all the things I'd ever said—me, Jack Molloy—about how a Molloy would always be in charge of the Hawks, the same way idiots would always be in charge of network television.

It happened because I didn't have just the coolest team in sports but the single most valuable property, even more than the Yankees—they owned their own network, but I owned my own stadium—and blew it, gave it away like some dumb goober trusting my pension to my CEO and Arthur Andersen.

I had the best job in sports, and walked away from it, like one of those dumb-ass jocks who thinks retiring with the trophy is all that matters, then finds out differently once the goddamn games go on without him.

You ever watch one of those plays in football where it seems like everybody on the field is fighting for the ball after somebody fumbles it and the refs nearly have to use the Jaws of Life to pry the players apart?

This is how you end up on the bottom of a pile like that a year after thinking you were cute enough to be hanging on to the front of the boat and yelling that you were king of the world.

But why wouldn't I think that way? I'd been estranged from my old man, Big Tim Molloy, for five years before his heart gave out at a Hawks preseason game one night. If I was in his will at all, I was supposed to be in the footnotes section at the end. But the old man had always told me that the only thing better than a good entrance was a good exit. And he had always loved a good surprise. The surprise was that he left the football side of the operation to me.

The last line of the will was scrawled in what was left of his Catholic school handwriting.

You're up, Molloy is what it said.

Molloy being what he had always called me—when we were talking, anyway—and what I had always called him.

And what happened next was this: In my one and only season running the Hawks, with a little bit of the old man's flair and a lot of tricky moves I think he would have appreciated, I beat the game. My twin sibs, Ken and Babs, didn't want me to succeed; neither did a prospective buyer for the Hawks named Allen Getz; neither did my frisky stepmother, Kitty Drucker-Cole Molloy. My fellow owners wanted me around about as much as they wanted Jews in their country clubs. And ultimately they did what a lot of people, at least those outside Las Vegas, where I'd made my chops as Billy Grace's right-hand man, had done throughout what had passed for my adult life:

Underestimated me.

As Casey Stengel, one of the old man's drinking buddies, used to say, You could look it up.

I had finally outscammed the owners who were trying to scam me, including the Christian hard-on who ran the Ownership Committee; beat back Getz; made peace in the family; won the damn Super Bowl, the first the Hawks had ever won; then handed over the day-to-day running of the team to my brother.

You remember our win over the Los Angeles Bangers. Everybody does, mostly because it was acknowledged to be the most exciting finish to an NFL championship game since the Colts–Giants sudden-death game in 1958, the day Johnny Unitas basically invented pro football, at least on television.

It was at that point that I decided I had pretty much conquered pro football, and Annie Kay and I left for Paris. I was actually starting to think about marrying her at that point, even though Billy Grace used to say there were two things he never expected to hear me say.

One was that I really was getting married.

Two was "Could I get another one of those fruity drinks over here, please? With an umbrella?"

I didn't even bother to hang around for the Hawks' victory parade that went down Fifth Avenue, across Central Park South, then up Central Park West, past the old man's last New York City apartment, ending with the party at Tavern on the Green where our defensive end, Raiford (Prison Blues) Dionne, and veteran offensive tackle Elvis Elgin had that unfortunate episode where they confused one of the female cops sent to quiet the festivities with the kind of strippers often used at bachelor parties. They'd eventually taken her into the chef's office to see what kind of bad underwear she had on underneath her NYPD blues. It was then that they found out Badge No. 362054 was actually the real thing and not part of her costume.

I turned the Hawks over to my brother, because he had wanted to run them his whole life, most of which had been spent kissing up to the old man. He wanted to be there every day. He wanted to be the boss over the long haul. And as much fun as I'd had that first season running with the big dogs, I didn't want to be there over the long haul, just because I didn't want to be anywhere over the long haul.

Or so I told myself.

Big Tim Molloy, the bookmaker's son who'd done it all and seen it all, who'd talked George Steinbrenner into buying the Yankees and sat at the same table with every big-city big guy from Rockefeller to Paley to Trump, had been a born boss. The same with Billy Grace. But I wasn't like them, even if I'd kidded myself into believing I was, at least in the short run. I didn't want to sit in draft meetings and listen to a bunch of bullshit about the salary cap, I didn't want to cut players I knew and liked, even if Pete Stanton, my general manager and chief back-watcher, did the actual cutting.

I didn't want to suck around agents or have them suck around me. I wanted to sit on league committees as much as I wanted to sit through *The Nutcracker.* Or have my own nuts caught in one.

All this I told myself as I said goodbye to the Hawks.

Annie and I holed up at The Ritz, in a suite directly above the Hemingway Bar. And what was supposed to have been a month in Europe turned out to become a lot more than that. It was fine with Annie, who was switching television jobs at the time and had to wait for her contract with Fox Sports to expire before she could start at CBS. She would remind me every couple of days that she wasn't abandoning her network dreams by becoming my full-time sex slave—the dreams involved becoming Diane Sawyer someday, once Diane went to the home—she was just putting them temporarily on hold.

"I've got to decide whether I'm really in love with you," she said, "or just going through a who's-your-daddy? phase."

I was about twenty years older than she was, but liked to think I kept myself up.

"I just don't want this to be one of those gross deals down the road where I look like I'm the one kissing Clint Eastwood in the movies," she said.

I thanked her, as always, for her refreshing honesty and told her to pass the Viagra.

We went from Paris to Lake Como, one of your romance capitals of Italy. We went to Spain, and I got drunk enough to lose a bet to a bartender, which is how I ended up running with both the schmucks and the bulls at Pamplona. We did a month at the Hotel du Cap in the south of France that ended up costing me more than the second war against Saddam. Finally, we settled into a flat in London that I had borrowed from one of Billy Grace's Hollywood friends, a screenwriter who got a couple of million per movie and half that for what Hollywood called "polishes," which the screenwriter said involved cleaning up the punctuation on the polish that came right before yours, and punching the whole thing up with jokes even studio executives could understand.

"The original screenplays and adaptations support Heather and the children and the therapists and trainers and yoga teachers and plastic surgeons," the screenwriter told me one night at Billy's casino, Amazing Grace. "The polishes are for gambling and the girls from the escort service."

Annie and I spent two months at the place at Lennox Gardens, hard by Beauchamp Place and a five-minute walk from Harrod's. We ate at all the best restaurants, and occasionally made short trips to Scotland when Annie would get it into her head that she needed another Mary, Queen of Scots fix. I was a good sport about all of it. I had never done any real time in Europe, I was flush for the first time in my life, and, best of all, I wasn't required to be anywhere. I certainly wasn't on the kind of twenty-four-hour call Billy used to tie me to in the old days, back when I was his casino host and go-to guy, known as the Jammer, in charge of making sure our high rollers felt more love than the rest of the Strip's high rollers.

If what they were experiencing during their stay at Amazing Grace was anything close to real love, I was supposed to make sure they sure as shit didn't get caught at it.

And this almost-wedded bliss might have lasted until the end of Annie's Fox contract, if Bubba Royal hadn't shown up for a visit.

He was still in a walking cast, having busted his knee on the last play of the Super Bowl against the Bangers, after throwing the crucial block on Bobby Camby's sweep

around left end. It was a daring call by Bubba, my old
UCLA teammate, since by the time Camby finally got to
the end zone, time had expired, officially wiping out any
chance for the short field goal by our kicker, Benito Siragusa, that would have won the game a lot more easily than
Camby's play.

Of course, a field goal would not have enabled the
Hawks to cover the point spread, and thus win the bet
Bubba had made on himself through the sports book at
Amazing Grace the night before the game.

Afterward, there were some questions about why Bubba
had risked everything at the end of the game, but even
the NFL commissioner, Wick Sanderson, stood up and
dismissed them, praising Bubba's ability to make game-
winning decisions on the fly, and what he actually called
Bubba's "gambling spirit."

Wick still wanted to believe that everybody in America
bet NFL games, *except* NFL players.

"Right," Bubba liked to say. "And those are everybody's
real tits in the movies."

I fronted him the money for the bet, by the way.

In addition to the walking cast, Bubba also showed up
wearing a flight attendant named Brittany with whom he'd
fallen in love on the overnight Virgin Atlantic from Kennedy.

"Just for the record, Jack," he said. "The virgin part? It
don't mean her."

I told him I had sort of figured that out on my own.

This was after he and Brittany had spent most of the day
in Bubba's suite at The Dorchester, and finally came downstairs about six o'clock to meet Annie and me in the bar.

"Tell me something," Bubba said. "What're the odds of
me meeting somebody like this before our plane even sets
down at that Hedgerow Airport of theirs?"

"No disrespect meant to your date," I said. "But you
could meet girls in a maximum-security facility."

"Nah," he said. "I mean the odds on her name, man.
Brittany. As in Great Brittany!"

He arranged his bad leg under the table and said, "Let's order up some drinks and tell 'em to make sure and put ice in 'em. Goddamn jet lag's already got me by the balls."

Annie smiled brilliantly at him and at Brittany, whose right hand had disappeared from the table as soon as she sat down. "And not just jet lag, apparently," Annie said, in her perky TV voice.

The first time Brittany, who looked like every big-haired, big-breasted, small-brained blonde Bubba had ever known, got up to use what she actually called the loo, I asked him if she might possibly have a last name.

"What is this, Jack," he said, "a fuckin' grand jury?"

Bubba, his football career officially over, no training camp to worry about for the first time in his adult life, stayed in London for a month. Annie ended up leaving before he did. It was after one of those nights when Bubba and I never came home, and she said it was just one too many. But I had seen it coming for a long time before, even as we went through the motions of being the happy couple, never running out of tourist things to do and trying to break all existing world screwing records in our downtime.

Annie Kay being the nearly perfect woman in this sense:

She liked sports *and* sex.

"Bottom line, Jack?" she said that day. "I'm ready to go back to work. And you show absolutely no signs of ever wanting to go back to work."

"Maybe when the season starts."

She said, "Right."

I said, "I can explain about last night, by the way."

She kissed me sweetly on the forehead, right before picking up the phone to call British Airways.

"Jack," she said, "no one in all of recorded history has ever been able to explain last night better than you can."

Much later, Annie would admit that her agent, Skipper, had called the day before with the news that someone Annie had always referred to as "that *Survivor* bitch" had dropped out of the running at *The NFL Today*. All of a sudden, Annie Kay wasn't first runner-up anymore, she was the one who was going to sit with Jim Nantz and Boomer Esiason and Deion Sanders on Sundays.

"Skipper was as excited that day as I'd ever heard him," Annie would tell the TV columnist from *Sports Illustrated*. "He said CBS had decided to go in a bold new direction: tight outfits and actual knowledge of pro football."

So we had one more night on the town, a full-out Great Brittany dinner at Rules, a restaurant near the theater district that had been around since Robin Hood, then a farewell drink at the bar of The Connaught Hotel. We took a cab home and sat for a while on a bench in the gated park across from the flat, holding hands and promising each other this wasn't the end for us, even if we both knew better.

"Look on the bright side," Annie said. "You can go back to doing what you do best."

Which was?

"Ordering another round and saying, 'What was your name again, honey?' "

When I woke up in the morning, she was gone, having left behind one more of her famous notes:

Dear Jack,
    You have pretty much everything you need now, with the exception of me and Sundays in the fall.
    Love,
    Annie

    P.S. It really was just a yeast infection, I swear.

She meant Sundays at Molloy Stadium, which the old man had somehow managed to get built with his own money at a time when sports owners all over the country were holding up city governments for new ballparks the way Bonnie and Clyde used to hold up banks. It was just slightly south of where Yonkers Raceway used to be on the

Major Deegan, modeled after the old Polo Grounds, where Big Tim Molloy had first watched the Giants play in the old days, and had what I considered to be the best single view of sports anywhere:

Mine. From my personal luxury box, Suite 19, which happened to be my old UCLA number. Suite 19 had also become my New York apartment when I was running the Hawks. It was another thing the columnists and TV assholes had loved about me when they still loved me, back when I was the colorful bad boy acting as if he'd taken over the principal's office.

I had told myself all along that when I got tired of Europe, I'd just show up unannounced at Suite 19 one day, probably just in time for the first game of the next season, surround myself with a bunch of old pals, and start up the party all over again. I'd let Ken continue to run the show with the help of Pete and Liz Bolton, the team president and an old flame of mine (that was before I found out that she'd gone to the West Coast to take a job as Vice President of Programming for Oversexed Teens on the WB network). I'd let Babs run marketing and promotions and the handing out of comp tickets to celebrity assholes. I'd do my best to stay out of the way of both of them.

Except I never came back that season.

I stayed at Lennox Gardens. I kept in touch with Pete Stanton by e-mail, signing off on the big stuff even while Ken thought he was the one signing off on the big stuff, basically empowering Pete to do whatever he needed to do to see if we could somehow repeat, even though injuries would start hammering us in the preseason and never really stop.

About a month after Annie left, I started up with an actress appearing in the new Tom Stoppard play. About the same time, I made a sizable investment in an upscale gambling club around the corner from The Connaught, and began showing up a few nights a week in a tuxedo and imagining myself as Billy Grace on training wheels. Thinking, way in the back of my mind, that I might go back to Vegas someday, when Billy was finally ready to retire, see if I could run with the big dogs there.

Maybe then I'd be ready to be a full-time boss.

It turned out that while I was screwing around with all this civilized Bond, James Bond, shit in London, the New York Hawks staggered into the playoffs as a 9–7 wild-card team and won three straight upset games on the road in the playoffs. Then, in the Super Bowl, which was played at the new Joe's Stone Crab Stadium in downtown Miami, Benito Siragusa just missed the forty-seven-yard field goal—wide fucking right—against the 49ers that would have made it two Super Bowls in a row.

Now it was the first Sunday in April, a couple of days after Sarah, the actress, had announced that she was leaving both Tom Stoppard and me.

She'd informed me that she was up for the part in a new Fox sitcom, one about an English nanny who goes to work for a gangster in the Federal Witness Protection Program named Gus (The Goat) Triano, tentatively called *Goat's Nanny.*

"I've seen the script," Sarah said. "I do so much bending over in the pilot, I'm afraid your people back home might think it's one of their exercise shows."

I said, "You trained at the Royal Academy. Now you're going to do tits-and-ass comedy in the States?"

"I'll be wearing lots of the same outfits you're always asking me to wear. Think of it that way."

"Field hockey uniform?"

Sarah said, "Episode three."

I had a half-dozen Sunday papers spread out around me in the living room and was trying to root my favorite soccer team, Tottenham Hotspur, home against somebody, when

Ken Molloy called from New York to say that he and Babs had decided to sell their half of the Hawks and how was merry old England, by the way?

"Excuse me?"

"Dick Miles has made us a fabulous offer, and we've decided to take it."

I said, "Dick Miles wants to buy half of our team?"

"Actually, he wants it all, Jack."

"Fuck him, he can't have it all."

"I told him you'd say something like that."

I shut down the sound on the television, walked across the room to the screenwriter's wet bar, poured myself a shot of Dewar's, and drank some.

"Jack, are you there?" my brother said.

"Sonofabitch," I said when I'd cleared the Scotch. "Dick Miles. Captain Commerce himself. Even used to chase some of the same properties the old man did about a hundred years ago. Him and his partner, what's his name, died not too long ago?"

"Bill Francione," Ken said. "The parent company is actually called MF, Inc. Cute, right? Francione was Mr. Inside, Dick was Mr. Outside. When Francione died, *Business Week* said they were the greatest team since Johnson met Johnson."

"Weren't they supposed to be buying NBC?" I said. "Or maybe it was CBS. Whose stock is more in the toilet?"

"Anytime anything big goes on the market, they're supposed to be a big player—sports teams, airlines, networks, the *L.A. Times,* you name it. There's never been a hot property Dick Miles didn't want. He was always the hustler, Francione was always the one putting one foot in front of the other. But Dick tells me they'd agreed to go after the Hawks just before Francione died. Just as a way of having Dick deal with his sports jones once and for all."

"His Jerry Jones," I said.

"He says he's craved action his whole life, and that we've got the best kind in the whole wide world."

"How much?"

"Action?"

"Jesus Christ, Ken. How much is he willing to pay?"

"Half a billion."

"No shit. Now you really can tell him to go fuck himself. That midget who owns the Saints, Bobby Finkel, paid eight hundred million, and that was nearly ten years ago."

There was a pause at the other end of the line. I was standing at the front window, looking across the street to the beautifully manicured park, where a big redhead was walking an English cocker spaniel small enough to fit inside her handbag. She looked up suddenly, as if I'd trained a searchlight on her, and smiled. I smiled back.

"I meant for our half," Ken said.

"Half a billion for your *half?*"

"Kind of gets your attention, doesn't it?"

"Let me get this straight. Miles is willing to be the guy who finally pays one billion dollars for *one* football team?"

"This is a great country, isn't it? Even if England has better museums."

Then Ken said, "Daddy always said you couldn't put a price on what it meant to own the Hawks, and I always thought he was right. Until now."

"Five hundred million to you guys," I said. "And the same to me?"

"I might have missed something while you were doing the math," Ken said. "But what happened to *fuck him?*"

2

I had always thought of Dick Miles as Jack Welch, just slightly less horny.

You remember Welch. He sometimes looked like the brightest of all the bright boys of the '80s and early '90s, making fortune after fortune for GE, retiring with all the championship belts, getting standing ovations every time he showed his bald head and famous smile. Then he had a long lunch one day with a female business reporter, went straight from there to the good parts, got caught by his lawyer wife shortly thereafter, and ended up paying a couple of hundred million extra on his divorce.

At the time, my friend Mo Jiggy said that he thought the slogan for GE was supposed to be we bring good things to life, not back to the two-bedroom suite at your hotel.

Dick Miles had come out of Newark, the son of a car salesman at Central Cadillac and Oldsmobile in Newark; his personal website was heavy on details like that. He attended Barringer High in Newark, went from there to Rutgers, graduated with a degree in business administration, came out of there and hit Wall Street running. Started out as a trainee with a big firm of the '40s and '50s, Valerio, Cowen and Saunders. After a few years, he and Bill Francione started MF, Inc. An in-your-face name for an in-your-face team. They started out financing car dealerships and midsized manufacturing companies. They were never the biggest or the flashiest, but they held their own with the big boys, and never got taken out of their offices with raincoats over their heads by the U.S. Attorney. Then, in the '80s and '90s, they hit and hit big. Miles and Francione were two of the first guys to understand about using leverage and junk bonds to finance companies that the mainstream, white-shoe Wall Street companies wouldn't touch at first and sometimes not ever, and it made them disgustingly rich.

The rest of it I knew, just because everybody knew Miles, even if Francione preferred to stay in the background. He was the flashy one, the out-front one, the gambler, and not just in business; Miles loved Vegas and loved Atlantic City, and had done as much time being the kind of player we called a "whale" in Vegas as any high-profile guy around. He seemed to win as much as he lost, and had a hell of a time.

Then he'd fly back to New York, and he and Bill Francione would make another pile of money for themselves. In the late '80s and '90s, they managed to survive the crash of the dot-coms, then ran around the telecommunications business picking up equipment and semiconductors for pennies on the dollars.

I remembered reading about Francione's stroke when it happened, a big obit in *The Times* of London not long after Annie and I arrived in town. I hadn't known as much about Francione as I did Miles, because that's the way Francione had wanted it. I knew the last sports team they were supposed to be interested in buying was the Arizona Cardinals.

I also knew Dick Miles was known as Bottom Line Miles to his money guys, the ones who'd gotten rich just by going along with him and Francione for their wild ride across the '80s and '90s, into the new millennium. He was The Dick in the tabloids, and, presumably, with a couple of younger trophy wives. But even when he divorced them, everybody seemed chummy afterward, and he never ended up on the front page the way guys like Welch did.

"I owe it to my two best friends in the world, Pre and Nup," he told *Forbes* one time, in a special issue about current hot guys in business that actually included me.

In addition to the wide path he'd cut through business, he was also known far and wide as America's number one sports fan, a jock sniffer of both national and international acclaim. He had two celebrity-row seats next to Spike Lee at Knick games. He had a box at Yankee Stadium behind the Yankee dugout—Miles said he wanted to be downstairs with the real fans, he didn't need to watch baseball in some suite with what he called whorehouse decor. When they took a shot of the gallery at the Masters, there was Dick Miles eating a pimento and cheese sandwich. There he was at the Winter Olympics, waiting along with the rest of us to see which figure-skating judges were going to screw the American team. There he was in the Royal Box at Wimbledon, the only one in there who didn't look cryogenically frozen.

And now that he'd divorced Mrs. Miles number three or four—you could lose track of marriages with him, like with Jennifer Lopez—he'd usually have somebody next to him who looked like Miss Tennessee.

Now he'd decided all that wasn't enough, he wanted to get out of the stands and into the game.

With my team.

About an hour after I got off the phone with my brother, now working on my third Dewar's of the afternoon, Dick Miles called the flat at Lennox Gardens and said that he'd asked Ken if it would be all right for him to call me directly, and he'd said, sure, why not?

"What if he'd said no?"

Dick Miles barked out a laugh. "What the hell kind of language is *no*, Jack?"

I marveled again at how good a connection you could get on a transatlantic phone call, and mentioned that to Dick Miles.

Miles said, "The two of us need to have about nine thousand drinks and talk some things out."

"Maybe when I get back to New York. If I do get back there one of these days."

"I meant tonight," he said.

"I think I just figured out why you sound as if you're practically across the street."

"I'm stompin' at The Savoy, son," he said. "Meet me here for a drink and then we'll go eat some of that English food that tastes like fax paper."

Not asking. Telling.

"Just so we understand each other," I said. "Whatever deal you're making with my sibs, I'm not selling the Hawks completely out of the family. It would be like selling the old man out."

"I'm going out for a run," Dick Miles said. "Leave a message with the desk about where we're meeting and what time," and he dial-toned me before I got the chance to tell him, *My Fair Lady*–like, all that would be loverly.

We ate at Wilton's. It was across from Turnbull & Asser on Jermyn Street, had its own oyster bed, the best Dover sole in all of London, drinks served in big-boy glasses. Even though most of the grannies serving you looked older than Queen Elizabeth, one of them always seemed to show up with a fresh Scotch before you were even sure you wanted one.

Dick Miles was shorter than I expected, just because he'd come across so big when I'd seen him on television. He was one of those guys who look like they'd just as soon arm-wrestle you as shake your hand. He wore a cashmere blue blazer with some sort of elaborate phony-ass crest on it, an open-necked shirt the color of flamingos, the shirt tight enough to show off his upper body. He was designer bald, his hairline way back from his forehead, what hair he had on the sides looking as if it had been shaved down in some kind of slick hundred-dollar way. And he had the kind of deep tan that looked professional as well, as if he stopped at the tanning parlor after the gym and before his massage. Bright blue eyes that he trained on you like laser dots. He looked younger than whatever he was, which was in his late sixties at least, even if everything about his face, especially around the blue eyes, looked a little too tight.

Even the famous jaw that everybody always talked and wrote about looked as if it'd had more work done on it than Mount Rushmore.

"I hope they don't require ties at this fish joint you're taking me to," he said. "I hate ties. Never even wore one when I was working. You practically have to put a gun on me to make me wear one now."

I told him dress was fairly casual at Wilton's.

"Ties always felt like choke collars on me," he said. "Goddamn, the only thing worse than a Windsor knot is whatever knot's in second place. And, Jesus H. Christ, don't get me started on trying to tie the frigging bow tie on your tuxedo."

I told him I didn't want to get off on the wrong foot or anything, but what signal was I giving off that I gave a shit about whether he liked ties or not?

"Wait a second," he said. "Not everything I say is fascinating?"

Through drinks at The Savoy and through the smoked salmon appetizers at Wilton's, we'd managed to talk about everything except the Hawks. English football, which meant soccer. Which one you thought was duller, BBC1 or BBC2? Which prince was more likely to end up marrying a slutty gold digger, Harry or William? Like we were on a first date and we were talking all around the only thing we really wanted to be talking about, which was whether or not anybody was going to get laid tonight.

Finally, Dick Miles said, "You ready to get down to it?"

I said, "I was worried that I might have to act interested about where we are with the Eurodollar."

Miles laughed. Affable big guy. The same part he'd been playing for the last hour and a half. And the thirty or forty years before that.

"Let me tell you something from the jump," he said. "I didn't just like your father and enjoy the hell out of his company. I *respected* him. And believe me when I tell you, Jack, I know how proud he would have been of how you handled yourself around the Hawks, starting with when you had the stones to fire that prick Vince Cahill."

Cahill had been the Hawks' coach when I took over the team. That was before he made the mistake a lot of people in sports make: He thought the guy cashing the checks was on some sort of equal footing with the guy signing the checks. I fired his fat ass a few weeks into the season. He was on one of the pregame shows now, where every ex-coach except Pop Warner seemed to find a safe place to land.

"The old man used to tell me that blood was thicker than water," I said. "Even Dewar's and water."

"He was a smart bastard, wasn't he?"

"Almost always."

"Except with women," Dick Miles said. "I mean, the ones that came after your beautiful mother passed. That Kitty he married retired the trophy for bad trophy wives. Shouldn't even have been mentioned in the same breath with Katherine Molloy, if you ask me."

"I'll drink to that."

We both did.

"What's Kitty doing now, by the way?"

"Far as I know," I said, "she's still doing Allen Getz."

"Hey," he said. "Weren't we about to get down to it?"

"This is where you officially make your pitch and I tell you I'm flattered, I really am, but no dice. Even if you did fly over here on spec."

"That's my style, Jack, you have to know that. Did you read my book?"

Now I laughed. "Fuck, no."

"It was on the best-seller list for about sixteen weeks."

"I vaguely remember reading a couple of reviews. I believe they said you took credit for inventing everything except search engines and oral sex."

"If you were one of the suckers who paid twenty-four ninety-five for the wit and wisdom of Dick Miles," he said, "you would have at least walked away knowing I don't screw around when I want something."

"Stop it," I said, "you're going way too fast for me."

"You know what I'm saying, Jack. You don't wait around once the market opens. You know who told me that one time? An old girlfriend. She thought she was in line to be the second Mrs. Miles after my first wife, Sale, died in that tragic helicopter accident in Aspen. But before anybody knew it, I'd up and married Kirsten, Sale's funeral planner, about six weeks after the fact. Anyway, the girlfriend called up and told me she'd learned a valuable lesson with guys like me—next time she was coming to the goddamn wake."

"Good story," I said. "I'm not selling."

"You know what I always thought a line like that was, Jack? Foreplay."

"Listen," I said. "I understand what my brother and sister are doing. I'm a little more surprised about Ken, just because I thought being The Man was going to float his boat more than it obviously has. But at the end of the day, neither one of them ever loved running the Hawks as much as they loved the *idea* of running the Hawks. Now, Babs can break more records for charity committees, and hump all the tennis pros she wants around organizing church socials. I'm not so sure about Ken. He's always loved to do a lot of political shit on the side. Maybe he can buy Gracie Mansion someday the way Bloomberg did."

"You're saying it was different with you."

"I loved football. I loved it the way the old man did. When I was a kid, the only thing better than the games was standing on the field with the old man before the games. And you want to know something? The only teams he ever loved as much as the Hawks were the ones I played on, at least until my knee turned into a special effect at UCLA. So, yeah, I was different. Ken and Babs were in it for the money, even though neither one of them would ever admit that—they still say their hearts belong to daddy. Now they're getting out for the money. The old man and me, we were in it for the action."

Miles said, "I'm the one who needs new action. More than I thought, to tell you the truth. I'm tired of the goddamn boardroom, Jack. And I don't want to be in the goddamn boardroom when I crap out, the way Billy Francione did."

"At least my father was getting ready to watch a Hawks game when he checked out."

"I do everything I can to stay young. But the juice you get from something you're really passionate about, that's the real Fountain of Youth, Jack."

I grinned. "Maybe I will buy that book."

Miles said, "I know all about your career on the Strip, back when you were the Jammer. So answer me a Vegas-type question: Why does somebody walk away from the table when he's got a sky-high stack of chips in front of him?"

Blue eyes brighter than ever all of a sudden.

We both knew he wouldn't have asked the question if he didn't already know the answer.

"Because he doesn't want to play anymore," I said.

"Pay the man!" he said, slapping the table as he did.

"It still doesn't mean I want to sell."

Miles leaned in. "Listen to me, Jack. I've been on the line for more than forty years in one way or another. I've made fortunes that everybody knows about, and lost some that only Bill and I knew about. You know what my good friend Lee Trevino said about pressure once, right? Real pressure is playing for five bucks when you've got two in your fucking pocket. I've been there, okay, even when people thought I was rolling in it. Been this close to being tapped out when the only ones who knew were Bill and me." He put his thumb and forefinger about a quarter-inch apart. "This close, and then got out of it. Was it about the money? Hell, yes. But with me, it was about the *getting* of the money. Or the getting out of it. Which meant it was about the action. And now, at my advanced age, after going everywhere and doing everygoddamnthing, I've decided that the kind of action you've got, getting to put it on the line every Sunday, is the best kind around."

"You're preaching to the choir."

"The bottom line? From old Bottom Line Miles? You've got something I want. But I've got something you want just as much."

"And what would that be?" I asked.

"I've got rich," he said.

We ended up back in the bar at The Savoy. Dick Miles had suggested a retro place over in Covent Garden called Dead Rock Stars, where he said you could run into the kind of girls who took their shirts off on Page Three of the *Sun*. I told him I'd pass, I'd decided I already knew enough girls. He said, fine, said he had to make one phone call, came back a few minutes later and joined me at the same table in the corner we'd had before dinner.

By now, Dick Miles had consumed enough Scotch to stage the Henley Regatta, but he didn't seem to be showing any signs of being drunk. Or getting tired. He ordered a Hennessy, and I said I'd join him and then I'd be out of there, we'd been spinning our wheels for a while now and it was probably time to wrap this shit up for the night.

"We keep coming back to the same thing," I said. "With as much money as we're talking about here, I can't see at least some part of this football team not being in the Molloy family somewhere."

"Peter O'Malley sold the Dodgers to Murdoch after he nearly sold it to me, and as far as I can tell, the earth kept spinning on its axis."

"We both know O'Malley regretted it as soon as the ink was dry. At least that's what he told my friend Billy Grace one time."

We were in the smoking section of the bar. Miles lit a cigar. I told the John Gielgud waiting on us to bring me whatever kind of cigarette the bartender was smoking.

"You smoke?" Miles said.

"I quit for a year," I said. "I know I've got it licked now."

We smoked and sipped brandy at another old place in a city that was the capital of old. By now, it had been a long enough night that I fit right in. Miles waited through a silence, as hard as I could see that was for him. Then he came right at me again, telling me that there is no way I would have left if I still loved the Hawks the way I said I did, that I sounded like somebody giving him a bunch of bullshit about amicable breakups.

"I thought you were the king of amicable breakups," I said.

"Like I said, bullshit," Miles said. "There's no such thing."

He blew a nifty smoke ring toward the ceiling. "I love it when I hear them saying they still love each other as much as they ever did, how the love will always be there," he said. "My ass it will."

"You're saying I'm like that with the Hawks now?"

"You said your brother and sisters were more in love with the idea of running the team instead of running the fucking thing? You're in love with this whole notion that the team is still the great love of your life, instead of that knockout from TV you've been going out with. But let's be honest, Jack, it's that time of the night: If you still wanted to be there, you'd be there."

He looked at his watch, one of those Rolex deals with the blue-and-red around the outside that I knew cost more than my whole wardrobe. "I know you're tired, so let's really wrap this up. I've got a friend dropping by." Miles grinned. "And I can't wait to find out what her name is."

"It sounds like the beginning of something magical," I said. "I can't ever keep track. Are you married now or not?"

"Extremely not. I recently divorced Mrs. Miles number three. She turned out to be a dangerous combination. Way too young and way too smart."

I waited, sure there was one more pitch coming before we called it a night.

There was.

Dick Miles said, "What if there was a way for you to sell me, say, half of your half? You could stay around the team, the Hawks would still be in the family, we'd all walk away from the deal happy."

"I'm listening."

Miles leaned forward, completely happy, even here, at this time of night, to be negotiating. He seemed more excited about closing in for the kill with me than about the hookup on her way over to The Savoy.

"I buy half of your half *and* you stay on as team president for a year, at least. If we haven't tried to kill each other by then, you can stay on. Or you sell me the other twenty-five percent and move on."

"Who's in charge?"

"We're in charge."

I said, "You want to be in the football business this much?"

"I do," he said. "But I want to be in business with you, too. I never got to do a deal with your father. So now I'll do one with you."

"If I get the money and the title, it seems like I'm getting the better of it."

"Because I'm not looking to come in and start changing things, Jack. We're talking about a team that nearly won two Super Bowls in a row. I'm looking to maintain. For quality control. The best person to help me with that is you."

"I haven't said yes yet."

"But we've moved a good distance from all that *no* shit."

"No shit," I said.

"Someday you'll be my age," he said. "And maybe you'll be the one they're talking about like you're already as dead as Billy Francione. Like there's no way you could ever possibly top yourself. They sit up there in the crowd and say, Shit, he's got it made in the shade, somebody stop and give that guy the game ball. But I need a new game, Jack. Maybe my partner up and dying on me has made me realize that. The best game is being *alive*. The rest of it is just waiting to die."

Miles paused and said, "I'm telling you something as a guy who knows a little something about business, Jack. Jump on this one."

I shook my head, smiling at him.

Liking him.

"What's so funny?" he said.

"I was just thinking about how much of my life I've spent fading guys exactly like you. The bigger the better. First in Vegas, then the NFL. So why do I sit here and feel as if it's the other way around now, that I'm being faded by you?"

"I'm not looking to fade you," he said. "I'm looking for a partner."

He threw a pile of funny English money on the table as a tip, stood up, put his hand out. I shook it.

"Trust me," he said.

I told myself it was probably just my imagination that it sounded a lot more like, bend over.

3

I left it this way with Miles: I'd give him my answer as soon as I knew what the hell it was. He said we both knew what the answer was going to be already.

Then I walked a long time in the London night, even colder than usual for a cold London spring, walking along Hyde Park, thinking about everything we'd talked about, trying to go over all the good points Miles had made.

Always coming back to the money.

A quarter of a billion when we closed the deal. Nearly the same amount later if I decided to get out for good.

I had action he wanted, he had rich.

I walked and smoked a little more and felt my head start to clear from all the Scotch, and tried not to think too much about what the old man would have thought about Dick Miles swooping in for the kill this way.

I loved the Hawks, I wasn't bullshitting Miles or myself about that. It didn't mean I loved them the way Big Tim Molloy had, just because no one could.

The last thing I told Miles in front of The Savoy was that I couldn't do anything until I talked to my people.

Miles said he didn't think I was the type that had people.

A couple, I said.

One was Billy Grace, who had turned into my second father without us ever really talking about it.

He'd only had the one daughter with his first wife, though Billy rarely talked about Jade anymore. She'd moved to Beverly Hills as a teenager, finally married the lead singer of a band called Fourth Level of Hell. The last time her name had come up in conversation, Billy had vaguely mentioned she was trying "one of those Melissa Etheridge, sperm-bank-baby deals." When I'd first moved to Vegas, feeling too much pressure from the old man to become Little Tim Molloy and run the Hawks before I was ready, Billy had basically adopted me. I'd find out much later that my real father had asked him to do it.

I couldn't ever do the math on East Coast time in relation to London time, whether we were five hours ahead or six hours, so Las Vegas time was out of the question. I finally just called Billy's house off the eighteenth hole of his golf course, God's Acre, figuring he was somewhere between winning his last thousand-dollar nassau and his first cocktail of the day with his current sweetie, Oretha Keeshon.

Oretha was the ex-wife of former Hawks wide receiver A.T.M. (Automatic Touchdown Maker) Moore, now a star football commentator for ESPN on all their pre- and postgame shows, and the host of his own half-hour talk show, *Bitch Slap*.

When he'd called London to tell me about his new career in show business, I'd told him the title of the show sounded a little racy for ESPN, which was owned by the Disney Corporation, but A.T.M. had said that as far as he could tell, that practices and standards shit had a way of adjusting itself when ratings started to drop faster than dead rappers.

The union between Billy and Oretha had made A.T.M. almost as happy as Billy and Oretha had made each other.

"Let somebody else take care of the variable needs of Miss High Maintenance" is the way A.T.M. put it when he first saw them making out at our post–Super Bowl party at the Arizona Biltmore.

Oretha picked up on the first ring, and I told her it was the old matchmaker calling from London.

"Well, well, well," she said in her throaty voice. "If it isn't the black sheep of the family."

I pictured her in some kind of skimpy summer outfit, long legs, killer body, Tyra Banks looks, just Tyra with shorter hair and a little more weight to her, good weight, all of it wrapped up in attitude and sass and this basic message: You're right, you're not man enough.

"Thought *you* were the black sheep of the family now."

She said, "It's a funny thing. The longer I stay with my hunky man, the whiter I seem to get. Billy keeps talkin' about sittin' me right smack dab in the middle of the Junior League."

"Promise me something," I said.

"Anything for you, babe, you know that. You moved me into the high-rent district once and for all."

"Your first meeting of the Junior League? Take me with you."

Billy sounded out of breath after Oretha yelled at him to pick up, as if he'd just done his forty-five minutes on the treadmill while having dirty thoughts about Jennifer Garner on *Alias*.

"What do you need?" he said. Force of habit.

Just a couple of minutes, I said. He said, sure, he and Oretha were eating in and watching *The Sopranos* episode they usually taped because *Alias* was on at the same time.

"You still like *The Sopranos*?"

"I can't lie to you, Jammer," he said. "Some of that shit, God, it takes you back." Then: "So what's up?"

I told him then about the twins selling, about Dick

Miles, about the deal he finally put on the table at The Savoy. The way he kept bringing it back to me having walked away from the Hawks already.

All that.

"Schmuck," he said when I was finished.

"That's it? Schmuck. Not, I see how he gave you a lot to think about? Not that you can hear in my voice how conflicted I am?"

"Schmuck," Billy Grace said.

"Would you care to elaborate?"

I heard a snorting sound. "You are getting more smoke blown up your ass than from a jet engine. You must've majored in song girls at UCLA, because you certainly didn't major in math. Because if he's got the seventy-five percent and you've got the twenty-five percent, you're not his partner, you're his caddie, no matter how much he's paying you to carry his fucking bag. Jesus, didn't I teach you better than that?"

"It's a lot of money," I said in a nice, level voice. "And I get to keep my hand in. He's not going to have me around just for show."

"Yeah," Billy said, "that's exactly what he's going to do."

"Did I mention that it's a shitload of money?"

"I forget," he said. "When was it that we were in this for the fucking money? Did I miss the memo on that? If you just wanted the money, you didn't have to get your hands dirty in the first place, you could have folded right away and sold to the little lab rat who was popping your stepmommy at the time. Getz."

I didn't say anything. I could hear Billy drinking something, most likely a martini strong enough to use as a heat shield. If it was gin, he was just getting warmed up.

"If memory fucking serves, this was supposed to be about your father and doing something on your own for once. And football, for Chrissakes. Those of us cheering you on from the sidelines assumed this was about you finally proving you were as smart as you think you are. I don't mean to sound like one of those candy-ass shrinks on the radio, but there it is. Only now you call up and give me this shit about Dick Miles. You want to talk yourself into believing you're something more than a hand puppet for him, go right ahead. Just leave me the fuck out of it."

"You done?"

"Temporarily."

"You can't see how I would think of this as the best of both worlds?"

Knowing how lame that sounded.

"That's what everybody says right before they sell out," Billy Grace said.

I kept the portable phone to my ear and walked over and looked out at the park, brightly lit at night because the little neighborhood watch group had made sure of that. I said to Billy, "There's no talking to you when you get like this."

He said, "Like what? Like the one of us who still knows you better than you know yourself?" And hung up on me, just like that.

I put the phone down and went over to the screen-writer's fancy sound system, one that I'd needed Annie to figure out for me, and put on a CD of Miles Davis playing around with John Coltrane, remembering as I did so a story Mo Jiggy had told me about them, because Mo Jiggy seemed to have stories about everybody who'd ever been big in the music business. Mo told about Coltrane going off on a riff one time, for ten or fifteen minutes, flying and scatting and bebopping from here to heaven. When it was finally over, he said to Miles, "I don't know how to stop, man. Tell me how to stop, Miles." And Miles had said, "Try takin' the fuckin' horn out of your mouth." Then I fixed my-self one last brandy, even though I knew I'd already had more than enough, and went back to the window and looked out some more, wondering again why I'd come to love Lon-don this much. I was a New York kid and had gone to college in Los Angeles and had had the most fun of my life in Vegas, even after the city fathers had done everything humanly possible to turn the place into some kind of theme park except put mouse ears on the hookers.

At least the ones who weren't already being asked to wear them.

Only now I'd settled in here. Everything somehow slowed down a little bit here. Or maybe I was the one slowing down. For the first time in my life, I actually liked going to the theater, which in New York only happened if I was afraid somebody was going to withhold sexual favors. I liked walking around—aimlessly, my best thing—in the afternoon, Piccadilly or Charing Cross Road, or over to see my man Lord Nelson, whom I thought of as the maître d' of Trafalgar Square.

I loved being on the floor of the gambling club at night—I'd renamed it Scratch—feeling like a swell, watching rich old Brits gamble away heart-stopping sums of the funny money, so many of them with young girls on their arms, the girls trying to look glam themselves, sounding glam with their accents, trying to look interested in the games the old men were playing, but watching with their dead showgirl eyes.

The old man told me once, "You had style even before you could afford it, Molloy."

Now I was going to be able to afford it for the rest of my life, and still have a part of his football team, and what was so fucking bad about that?

The next CD in the stack was Miles going it alone, starting with my all-time favorite version of "Blue Haze."

Big fucking deal, I thought, I'd left on my own. But what about before that, when I threw everything I had at all the people trying to take the Hawks away from me? Billy didn't want to talk about that, he just wanted to make it sound as if I were getting ready to pimp the Hawks out. Except this wasn't some cheap hustler I was thinking about selling to, it was Dick Miles. If you were going to put your business into somebody's hands, who better than him? Everything he'd ever touched had turned to gold.

Hadn't it?

Whatever Billy said, I really did feel as if Miles wanted to go partners on this with me. And Miles wasn't getting into this to lose, or to look like some kind of amateur, that wasn't ever his play. He hadn't made all his money and gotten as goddamn famous as he was taking over successful companies and fucking them up like they were the Democratic Party.

Had he?

I opened the window and let some of the night noise come into the quiet room, decided to make one more call to the States.

Annie.

When she heard it was me, she said, "Shouldn't you be staring down somebody's dress while her husband Reggie decides whether or not to hit on seventeen?"

"Not tonight, dear," I said. "And how are you?"

"I'm sitting here watching some ESPN rerun. Now they've got some show where they put guys up on a split screen so they can yell at each other from different cities while the host keeps score."

"That's what we need," I said. "More shows with guys arguing about sports."

"Why are you calling me?" Annie said.

"Would you believe because I miss you?"

"What happened to the little pinched-face no-talent who my sources say is a dead ringer for Reba McEntire?"

"Who told you about her?"

"You forget how many friends I have at CNN, Jack. Inquisitive friends, Jack. Powerful friends. And I can't even begin to explain why the gossip columnist at the *Daily Mail* took such a shine to me."

"You're not allowed to be bitchy. You broke up with me, remember?"

"I wasn't being bitchy, I was asking what happened to the little bitch. There's a difference."

"Oh," I said.

"Why are you calling me?" she said.

I took a deep breath, let it out away from the receiver, and said, "I might be thinking about, like, you know, maybe selling the team."

"You can't," she said. "Uh-uh. No way. Don't be stupid, which means more stupid about certain things than you already are. It's good that you called and asked me to make up your mind for you. No sale."

"It's certainly open-minded of you."

"I'm here for you, bud. All you say is that the New York Hawks are not for sale today, not in this lifetime, thanks for the interest, I have to go chase red-haired bitches now."

"Aren't you even a little curious about who it is?"

"I already know it's Dick Miles, Jack. *Duh.* It was in the papers two days ago that the former evil twins are looking to cash out. But I don't care who it is, your Dick or the next one in line. If you sell to anybody, you will hate yourself for the rest of your life more than I will hate you for the rest of your life."

"He wants me to be his partner."

"Right. Oh, right, Jack. You know what they always said about old Steinbrenner, right? Back in the old days, before the Yankees started winning again and he reinvented himself as Grandpa Walton? There's nothing more limited than one of his limited partners."

"You sound like Billy."

"Maybe that's because we're the two people in the whole stupid world who love you the most."

I smiled, just at the whole thought of her. Even though she'd dumped me. Even though she was all the way on the other side of the ocean.

"I know this is slightly off point," I said, "but what are you wearing right now?"

Annie said, "Take some time to think this through, Jack. And then do not do it."

"What's so wrong with getting the money and still getting to be president of the team? People are barely going to know anything has changed."

There was a long pause, and then she said in a quiet voice, "You're the one who's changed—back into the frat boy who doesn't give a shit. Now let me hear you hang up the phone. It always makes me feel bad when I have to hang up on you."

"Do you really love me as much as Billy does?"

"I can't believe what I'm hearing," Annie said. "Or not hearing. God, you're really going to do this, aren't you?"

"I honestly don't know yet."

"You are, aren't you?"

"I won't do anything without talking to you again, I promise."

"I have to be honest with you, Jack. Promises haven't always been your strong suit."

"This time I really promise."

"Hang up the phone, Jack."

I did.

4

I **waited a** few weeks, drinking almost every night with Bubba, who was visiting Brittany again. He had pointed out that the longer the two of them could keep up with what he called this bicoastal shit, the longer his relationship might actually last. "I should have gone foreign instead of domestic a long time ago" is the way he put it. We mostly drank at Dead Rock Stars, at least on the nights Brittany was flying. When I finally got around to telling him about Dick Miles and what Miles had on the table, Bubba actually supported my decision to sell, and that was before he'd reached the point in the evening when his friend Grey Goose did most of the talking for him.

"You and me is like brothers," he said. "Always have been, always will be."

I raised my glass to that.

"So you know all's I know is football," he said. "And here's what I mostly know about football: This shit will break your fuckin' heart eventually. Even on the best day I ever had, the best day of my whole damn life, you know what football did for me? Ripped through my knee the way my wives used to rip through my checking. But now that I've had a little time to step back and reflect on life and whatnot, know what I finally decided? It was for the best, Jack. On account of, it was time for me to call for the check. It was just time. Maybe it's time for you the way it was for me. Sellin' the man all of it or a piece of it, that's your business. But there ain't no shame in takin' the man's money and then goin' to the bar."

He finally left London a few days later, saying that when his leg was healed up enough, to call him on his new star-satellite cell, he'd be someplace foreign where the fish were biting and the girls spoke as little English as possible.

"I see myself sittin' in some little bar someplace doin' a lot of *no habla español,* but could you bring me another margarita there, Maria?"

I hugged him on the street before he arranged his bad leg inside the cab, and told him I might be joining him sooner than he thought.

"I was almost one of them didn't know when to leave, Jack," he said. "Don't you be one of them yourself."

I sat up most of that night, doing more thinking than Scotch, coming up with all sorts of reasons I was doing this that had nothing to do with the money. The one where I was a bad boss. The one where I'd never been tied down to a desk in my life, since I'd never considered my Jammer duties a real desk job for a minute, I was having too much fucking fun, arranging what needed to be arranged, fixing what needed to be fixed. Once, I'd set up a poker game between a sitting president of the United States and the reigning world poker champion. On the lowdown, of course. Another time, it was a golf game between the emperor of Japan and Michael Jordan.

When I told Jordan about the poker game, he said, "Next time, let the President play golf and let me play cards."

I told him all he had to do was call. If I could fix him up, I would. That was the real fun of the job sometimes, figuring out what you could give to guys who already had everything.

That was the life.

Now Dick Miles was in my life.

Now Miles, somebody else who had everything, wanted my team, and was willing to pay me what he was willing to pay me, and still let me run with the ball.

Jump on this one, he'd said.

I called my brother the next day and told him I was doing it.

He said he'd tell Babs, and call the league office, and have our in-house lawyers draft some sort of letter of agreement and send it over to Dick Miles. He said the next time the owners on the Finance Committee got together was in early May, a couple of weeks before the start of minicamps, which were like a one-week version of spring training in pro football, a month or so before the real training camps opened. Ken also informed me that even if the Finance Committee approved the sale and allowed Miles to take over operation of the Hawks, the sale wouldn't become official until they voted again after the season; if he passed then, the committee would send it to the full ownership, all thirty-two owners. But everybody knew that would be a formality with Miles the way it had been with me; the full ownership never went against the recommendations of the Finance Committee.

In the interim, which in this case meant the season, it was the same for Miles as for any other prospective owner: He had to put up five percent of the total he would eventually pay out. If for some reason he was voted out at the end of one season, the original owners of the team got to keep the down payment—in Miles's case, and with what he was willing to pay for seventy-five percent of the Hawks, it worked out to thirty-seven-point-five million, which meant twelve and a half apiece for Ken, Babs, and me—and the team reverted back to them. Then they could change their minds and keep it, or sell to somebody else.

It just showed the kind of hoops even somebody like Miles was willing to jump through to get into the club.

It hadn't worked this way even a couple of years ago after I'd inherited the football side of the Hawks. I wasn't trying to buy in at the time; I still had to be approved, whatever the old man said in his will. Even if a team stayed in the family, they treated you like a new owner. In my case, the last preseason meeting of owners had been held right before Big Tim Molloy pitched forward into a tray of hot and cold appetizers in his own suite at Molloy Stadium before an exhibition game. So I'd had to wait until Super Bowl Week before the Finance Committee approved me; the rest of the owners went along the next day.

But now, after an emergency meeting at the last Super Bowl in Miami, the Finance Committee, chaired these days by Bangers owner Vito Cazenovia, had changed the process, implementing what were unofficially known around the league as the Maurie Grubman Rules.

Maurie had been the rookie owner of the San Diego Chargers, having purchased them the year before from Bitsy Aguilera, the former showgirl who'd inherited them when her husband Emilio had died in a mysterious boating accident. It turned out Bitsy hadn't liked being a boss babe nearly as much as she thought she would, and discovered that the business of running a pro football team, no matter how much delegating you did, took way too much time away from what she considered her true calling in life: personal trainers.

So she'd sold the Chargers to Maurie Grubman, a former venture capitalist who'd landed in Hollywood as a producer of teen movies that dealt with a crazed phys ed teacher, a hunky hero vampire, and what seemed to be a repertory company of half-naked Reese Witherspoon blondes.

But it hadn't taken long for people to figure out that

Maurie Grubman had three basic problems when it came to professional football:

1. He had about as much respect for coaches and players as he did for directors and actors.

2. Cocaine.

3. Crack cocaine.

By the end of his first season with the Chargers, he had gone through three head coaches, turned over half the team's roster, and been fined more than three million dollars for a constant stream of derogatory comments about NFL referees, and for violating the restraining order that one of them, a head linesman, had had to take out against him after Maurie had published the man's home address and home phone on Yahoo.com.

But the granddaddy of them all for Maurie came in the Chargers' second-to-last game of what would eventually be a disastrous 3–13 season, when his team actually had the chance to pull off a huge upset against the heavily favored New England Patriots. The Chargers' quarterback, Ratchett Upshaw, seemed to have thrown a sixty-three-yard touchdown pass to win the game for the Chargers. But while Ratchett and the rest of the Chargers were celebrating in the end zone, the play was being called back because of a holding penalty. The ball was moved back ten yards, Ratchett was sacked on the next play, and the Chargers lost.

Maurie ran from the sidelines, where he liked to watch games and also chat up Charger Girls, jumped the back judge from behind, and began beating him with the closest yard marker, until the yellow windbreakers from stadium security finally pulled him off. Before leaving the field, he demanded to be hooked up to the public address system, and did a fifteen-minute-long rant for the benefit of the home crowd.

I remember reading accounts of the incident, and I had

decided that my favorite line from the poor, drugged-out bastard was this:

"Forget erectile dysfunction. We all know what the three scariest f——ing words are in the English language: Late f——ing flag!"

A month later, at that emergency Super Bowl meeting, the first of its kind ever called, the Grubman Rules were put into effect. From then on, there would be a probation period on any new owner. No one officially became a card-carrying member of the Old Boys Club of NFL owners until the second vote, which came right before the start of the playoffs, no matter who he was or how much money he'd paid.

Not even someone like Dick Miles, everybody's All-American.

But as long as I was good to go, my brother had said to me, we were going to start the process. He asked if I planned to come back for the inevitable press conference he was sure Miles would want to hold. I told Ken I'd let everybody know.

You're sure you're going to be all right when the time comes? Ken asked. Standing next to all of us and smiling at the camera?

I reminded my brother that no one could fake sincerity better than I could.

Ken and Miles and the league office finally concluded all the paperwork a few days before the Finance Committee met at Vito Cazenovia's new resort, Veni Vidi Vito, in San Juan. Anticipating approval, Dick Miles scheduled a press conference for the following Monday in New York.

I celebrated this news at Scratch.

The only reason I'd been allowed to purchase a stake in a gambling club in the first place, which was normally against league rules, was that (a) it was located outside North America, and (b) I was no longer involved in the day-to-day running of the Hawks. I'd told Wick Sanderson, the commissioner, that I must have missed the part about foreign casinos in the bylaws, and he'd informed me that it was one of the subparagraphs in the secondary clauses about special exceptions as deemed necessary by what he described as the "discretionary powers of the commissioner's office." I'd said, what discretionary powers? He'd said the discretionary powers as they related to someone—me—who had brought so much happiness into his life these last couple of years.

He was referring to his longtime girl-on-the-side, Carole Sandusky, known to all in Las Vegas who loved her as Hollywood Tits. Then I'd introduced her to the commissioner, who'd moved her to New York and into an apartment with a river view in the United Nations Plaza.

I'd thought I might have to sell Scratch now that I was returning to be president of the Hawks under Dick Miles, but my lawyer, Oscar Berkowitz, had cleared things with the league. Oscar wanted to know if I thought the business would continue to show the kind of growth it had since I'd become involved, and I told him the guy running it could start running Amazing Grace or The Bellagio or The Mirage in Vegas tomorrow, he was that good.

His name was Neville Hayward. He was in his early thirties, a tall, handsome sonofabitch, a former hustler, former model, former actor, a world-class mimic and role player his whole life—all in all a character out of *Oliver Twist,* one strong enough and tough enough to escort people who'd forgotten their manners out to the street himself—and a total homosexual.

One night at the bar, a big guy we didn't know and who clearly didn't know Neville started to get into it with him. I watched, fascinated, as Neville transformed himself into this cool wise-guy, even throwing in a bit of a Jersey accent, until the guy completely backed down, paid his check, and left.

"That was my *consigliere,*" he said afterward. "With a little badda-bing thrown in just for giggles."

The first time I'd seen him nearly break somebody's arm just by putting his right hand on it above the elbow, I'd said, "Are you absolutely certain you like boys?"

Neville said, "Pretty much since that first night at the Home for Wayward Teens in Chelsea."

"And you never wanted to try it with a girl?"

He said, "You never wanted to try a wanker up your—"

I told him to back off, he'd made his point.

It was after midnight now, quiet in the back bar even as the action outside on the floor was just starting to pick up, as it always did at this time of night. Now Neville was the one asking why I was walking away from things I loved, only he meant London and Scratch, in that order.

It was the two of us and our new hostess, Fiona, a tiny, black-haired beauty who had played her way off the roulette wheel about the same time she'd started dating me. My first date with her had actually been a double date with Bubba and Brittany. Fiona had been acting as proper and British as a proper British girl could act, right up until either her third or fourth margarita at Dead Rock Stars, at about the same time in the evening that the female patrons in the place were invited to get up on the bar and dance.

Fiona, who had been wearing a tight black evening dress, proceeded to be the first up, and then to engage in a combination of striptease and dirty boogie that Bubba would say later had nearly moved him to tears, even before he saw the fire-engine-red thong she was wearing, the one showing off the discreet tattoo of the Union Jack on her creamy bottom.

"You keep an eye on that one, Jack," he said. "Because that there is a girl who wants to better herself."

At Scratch now, Fiona said, "You're really fixing to leave all this for a bloody football team?"

I thought she meant the club until I noticed that when she said "all this" she was staring down at her own cleavage.

"It's only going to be for about six months," I said. "I

just feel like I owe it to myself and the old man to give it one more season just to make sure things are squared away."

"What if they're not?"

That was Neville. Staring at me like I was trying to count cards at blackjack.

"They will be," I said.

"You're sure of that, sweetie?"

Neville didn't go serious on me very much, he wasn't the type, he preferred to play things over-the-top most of the time, or at least Noël Coward. But when he did get serious, he didn't let you up, and he stayed with you.

"If you had to bet on somebody to take good care of the Hawks, and the money to fix them if anything went wrong, you'd probably go with Dick Miles before you'd go with me."

Neville said, "I doubt that," and sipped some of his champagne. Then he stood up, made sure there wasn't any kind of crease or speck of anything marring the immaculate look of his new Armani tuxedo, and said he had a late date.

"I'm actually tying up the entire evening here, if you think about it."

"How so?"

"It's a football player I'm meeting. From Manchester United, actually."

He gave us the guy's name, which even I knew.

"Our new middie is queer?" I said.

"Queenier than the queen of hearts," Neville said, adjusting the rose in his lapel.

He looked at me and said, "I am going to say this to you just this once, and then never say it again. If you get back over there and find you need anything—and I mean any bloody thing—you call and I will be there straightaway."

"Just watch my back here," I said. "If my luck holds, I won't need you over there."

"One of these days, dear Jack, your luck is going to run out," he said, and walked away.

A few minutes later, after I'd made one last tour of the floor, Fiona finished her drink and told me to drink up, too, she was tired of everybody else playing games on tables.

In the end, I skipped Dick Miles's press conference, held in the Grand Ballroom, third floor, Waldorf-Astoria, let him have his big moment on his own without me getting in the way. I just asked that he read the statement I'd e-mailed to Brian Goldberg, the Hawks' public relations man, who had spent the last few weeks calling me the kind of scummy turncoat weasel you found in most government agencies.

The statement read this way:

After much soul-searching—meaning I managed to locate mine—I've decided to sell enough of my share of the Hawks so that my friend Dick Miles can have a controlling interest, and run the team the way he sees fit. But rather than deprive the people who will really be running the Hawks—the New York media—of all their fun, I'm going to hang around for a while as team president and primary off-the-record quote. And if Mr. Miles hasn't mentioned it already, he's picking up the tab for the open bar after the press conference. God Bless You, and God Bless America. John Francis Molloy.

I didn't even watch the press conference, despite knowing that ESPN International was showing it live. I also didn't return phone calls from ESPN; WNUT, the Hawks' flagship radio station; WFAN in New York; the five thousand or so other sports-talk radio stations from around the country who'd somehow managed to get my London telephone number; or any American sportswriter except Gil Spencer of the *Daily News,* and I only talked to him on the rather shaky assumption that we were still buds.

He began the interview by asking me what the fuck I was thinking.

I told him I was like the Robert Redford character at the end of *The Sting,* one of my favorite movies. Paul Newman, who's really organized the whole con, asks Redford if he is going to hang around to get his cut now that they've scammed the bad guy, Robert Shaw. Redford says, nah, he'd only blow it.

"Guys like me, running family-owned businesses, you know we're a dying breed in sports," I said. "Guys like Dick Miles are supposed to own teams the way they own everything else in the frigging world."

The next day, Spencer would write that I actually sounded as if I might possibly believe that shit, even if he didn't put it exactly that way in the newspaper. Then he felt it necessary to point out that the name of Redford's character in the movie is "Hooker."

His kicker?

"The old joke about hookers goes something like this: We've established who everybody is here, now we're just quibbling about price. Jack Molloy didn't even quibble. But to make him more comfortable with the whole transaction, the *Daily News* has learned that Dick Miles did leave the money for Molloy on the dresser."

I told Dick Miles my plan was to be back for the opening of training camp.

I ended up going back sooner.

A month after the press conference, right after the end of minicamp, Brian Goldberg called to tell me that Pete Stanton was taking early retirement and that Josh Blake, our coach, had decided against signing the contract extension that had been sitting in his desk drawer all season, and was going to Green Bay as general manager and coach instead, replacing the man who'd previously held the two jobs there, Zip Kahn.

I had missed it in the *International Herald Tribune*, but Zip had died suddenly of a heart attack the previous weekend, during the last show of the night at the only topless dance club in Green Bay, Wisconsin.

It seems he'd reached forward to stick one more hundred-dollar bill in the G-string of his favorite dancer, a former Packers cheerleader wearing one green tassle and one yellow—the team colors—on her breasts. At that point, Zip had fallen backward from the stage, clutching his chest. The people closest to him had thought he was just the same enthusiastic patron he'd always been, until even the dancer's big finish with the replica of the Vince Lombardi Trophy had failed to revive him.

It wasn't until I returned to New York that I saw what had already become a famous front-page headline in the *Milwaukee Journal Sentinel*:

STRIPPER FELLS ZIPPER

Somehow in the first twenty-four hours after Zip was pronounced dead by the paramedics, the Packers had contacted Josh's agent, flown both of them to Green Bay on the fucking Cheeseheads' private plane, then closed the deal that made Josh, at thirty-eight, the youngest man since George Halas to be calling all the shots with an NFL team.

So now the general manager who'd picked our championship players was gone, and so was the coach who'd coached them.

Other than that, Dick Miles was pretty much leaving things with the Hawks as he'd found them.

5

I took the first morning plane to New York.

When Brian had called the night before, a little before midnight London time, he said Josh had already flown to Green Bay for the press conference that would formally introduce him as the Packers' boss at Kraft Cheese–Lambeau Field. I told Brian to let me talk to Pete. He said Pete wasn't taking any calls and hadn't been taking any calls and, as far as he knew, might never be taking calls ever again.

"Not even from me?"

"Especially not from you."

I told Brian that I didn't want to put him out or anything, but could he possibly make sure that no other key goddamn Hawks personnel went over the wall before my return.

He said he had kind of a full plate, but he'd see what he could do.

"By the way," I said, "are you thinking about bailing out on me, too?"

"Funny you should ask. There does seem to be a sudden opening for assistant general manager in Green Bay."

"Would me doubling your salary and expanding your duties be a funny way of changing your mind?"

"We'll talk," he said, and then said he had to go, too, the beat guy from the *Post* was nosing around in the locker room, but that I should call and leave a message on his cell what flight I'd be taking, he'd have somebody meet me.

Somebody turned out to be Susan Burden, Pete's assistant. Susan: wearing the kind of smart suit smart women still wore to work, this one black, her silver-blond hair cut a little shorter than usual, generally looking the way any sixty-year-old woman in her right mind would kill to look. She was about five-eleven, thin as she'd always been, without looking as if she needed a hot meal. She was still a knockout at her age, even though I knew she'd give me a good slap for feeling the need to add the part about *her age*. She'd never been the type to get a lift, she didn't do Botox, she didn't have her lips blown up like floats in the Macy's parade. She just hadn't ever been the type. There were women all over New York City, all ages, who just wouldn't give up. Susan wasn't one of them, and never had been.

She had been working in the English Department at Spence, one of the best private schools in Manhattan, when Big Tim Molloy had met her at a teachers' conference for Babs. Susan spent very little time that night talking about Babs's writing style, which she'd describe to me much later with these two words: Gidget's Diary. But she did spend the rest of the conference explaining to him why the Hawks going back to a 4-3 defense was dumber than the Giants and Jets leaving New York for a mob burial ground on the wrong side of the Hudson, and telling him that it was time to think about going to a more vertical passing game like the Raiders'. The old man offered her a job as his personal assistant that night. She went to work for him when school was out, and pretty much ran his life until the day he died; ran interference for him, too, cleaning up his grammar, knowing which calls he should return and which assholes to blow off, doing everything humanly possible to keep him from marrying Kitty Drucker-Cole, mostly because Susan Burden was always in love with the old man herself, even if he never seemed to pick up on that. Or wasn't interested if he did. After he died, she went to work for Pete; by then the Hawks were all the family she had.

I hugged her for a long time after I made it through Customs, and told her the carry-on was all I had, mostly because a carry-on was all I ever had, unless I was traveling with Annie Kay, whose idea of packing just the essentials involved half the luggage department at Bergdorf-Goodman.

She said the Lincoln Town Car that Mr. Miles would be paying for was parked illegally out front.

As soon as we were moving toward the airport exit, I asked her what the hell was going on with the Hawks, starting with the outgoing general manager.

"You better ask the outgoing general manager," she said.

"I tried after Brian called me last night, but was informed that he was unreachable."

"In more ways than you know," she said, staring out the window at either an airport hotel or a tall, ugly airplane hangar—it was often difficult to tell at Kennedy.

The driver slid open the window separating us from him and said, where to?

I told him the Sherry-Netherland, then said to Susan, "I'm not ready to go to the office yet. I have to decide how I want to play this before I do something stupid."

Susan said, "I see that as growth."

"By the way, is Suite Nineteen still intact, or did Miles turn it into a you-know-what pad?"

She patted my knee. "Thank you so much for not saying fuck, dear."

She had always been one of those women, maybe because of her regal looks, who could talk dirty and carry it off.

"So Miles hasn't changed the locks on me?"

"It's pretty much as you left it—I checked before I came

out here. Don't worry, the lights go down low if you even start to think dirty thoughts. Ultimate bachelor pad, ultimate bachelor view. For my sweet, dear ultimate and perennial bachelor." She turned, her eyebrow cocked in the way women can. "Annie?"

"She finally wised up."

"I have this feeling it was slightly more complicated than that."

"I'll tell you about it later," I said. "Where's Pete right this minute?"

"He was already cleaning out his office when I arrived at work this morning. He was gone when I called a few minutes ago. But one of the temps said he was leaving, so I'm assuming he's on his way to his apartment."

"Doesn't he have a cell phone with him?"

"Pete Stanton? He'd carry a machete first."

For some reason, this was the first time in all recorded history that there wasn't unspeakably bad gridlock leaving Kennedy, so we were cruising up the Van Wyck. The driver said, tunnel or Triborough, the 59th Street Bridge was a beast at this time of day. I told him to take the Triborough, it was still the first look at the big town I liked best.

I said to Susan, "Would you mind telling me, in your own words of course, what's been happening the last few days?"

She waited a long time before saying, "I'm not going to beat you up about selling, Jack. I'm sure you've gotten that from enough people already. You're a grown man, you're as headstrong as Tim . . . your father . . . was. You have a right to live your life any way you choose."

"That's not what you said in your letter."

"I've calmed down since then. That was the kind of letter you're supposed to put in the desk for a few days and then rip into tiny little shreds before it ever makes it into an envelope."

It was the handwritten letter she'd sent to London after

she'd found out what I was doing with Dick Miles, the one telling me that she would call me a bastard, but that would imply I had at least some of my father in me.

"What's done is done," she said now. She was still staring out the window, the lighting of the gray day somehow making her look younger instead of older, a sad look on her face. Sometimes in the old days, when she didn't know I was watching her, I would see the same expression when she looked at my father. When she wasn't smiling at him.

Christ, I thought, maybe all Molloy men were total morons about women. I let Annie walk, and the old man chose a maxed-out credit card like Kitty over Susan Burden.

"I can fix this," I said. "It's what I do. I fix things."

"Even after you sold, you led everyone to believe you were going to be involved." She turned to me now, her face sad. "You stayed away too long, Jack."

"But that's what I'm trying to tell you. I'm back now."

"But Pete is gone and Josh is gone and . . ."

"What?"

"I'm going with them," she said. "I'll be leaving at the end of the month myself. I guess you should know that."

"I'll let them take out the goalposts before I let you leave."

"I've already handed in my letter to Mr. Miles."

"I'm sure it was beautifully written, like all of your correspondence. But I'm not accepting it."

"I love you, Jack," she said. "I've loved you since you were fifteen years old, the way I loved your father. All those years when you were estranged from your father? It broke my heart as much as it did his. But I knew something he didn't: You'd be back someday. And even though it happened after he was gone, it was all right, or so I told myself. Because I still felt you two had somehow made peace. Finally you were running the Hawks the way he always wanted you to. The way he believed in his heart you could. Then you left after the Super Bowl. And that was all right, too—you were in love, you had a right to go off and be in love. I wish I had found somebody like that. . . ." She waved a hand, as if shooing a fly out of the way. "But I always assumed you'd come back." She closed her eyes, opened them, said, "Only now this has happened. I'm sorry about all the other terrible things I said in that letter, but the truth is, all of this has happened because you allowed it to happen. The Hawks don't belong to the Molloys anymore, they belong to Dick Miles." She sighed. "This is the long way of telling you that you can't accept or reject my resignation letter, one I did leave in my desk for a couple of days and then mailed anyway. You don't call the shots here anymore, that's pretty plain to all of us. That was your choice. Our choice—mine, Pete's, Josh's, probably Brian's eventually—is to leave."

It was the longest speech of her life, at least in my presence, all the way back to when I was a kid. When she finally finished, nobody said anything for four slow avenue blocks and then three blocks downtown on Fifth.

She dropped me off at the big clock in front of the Sherry. I told her to at least hang in there until I talked to Pete. She said that if her letter said she'd be around until the end of the month, she'd be around until the end of the month, dammit. When she said the last part, I thought she might start to cry.

I leaned over and kissed her on the cheek, her perfume smelling like soap, and said, "I need you."

"That's what somebody else in the family told me once," she said. "Right before he went off and needed somebody else more."

I told the woman at the front desk that I'd like an inside suite, I already knew what the park looked like, then I went upstairs and tried Pete's apartment. No answer, again. Then I called Dick Miles's office at the stadium. A woman who identified herself in a thick Irish accent as Ms. Thorpe said that Mr. Miles was flying back from a business meeting in the Midwest, but would be calling in for messages.

"You're with . . . ?" she said.

"I'm with the band."

"Beg your pardon, sir."

"Just tell Mr. Miles his soon-to-be-not-so-silent partner Mr. Jack Molloy called."

"And he'll know what that is in regard to?"

I hung up on Ms. Thorpe, tried Pete again. Still no answer. I decided to walk over to his apartment on Fifty-sixth and Second and just wait for him in the lobby until he showed up. I knew he was in the same small two-bedroom he'd had for years, having moved in there after the divorce from Pam, his first and only wife. Pam Stanton had finally decided, not long after the Memphis Marauders of the old American Football League became the New York Hawks of the National Football League, that she was tired of organizing her marriage and her life around the watching of game tapes, the attending of combine meetings, the scouting trips to college football games on Saturday, and Sundays with the Hawks that always seemed to be about thirty-six hours long, both home and away.

Before Pete had gotten into football full-time as the old man's Memphis p.r. man, he'd been a sportswriter. He'd married Pam while doing that.

"I can't say sports hasn't been fun," Pam said to Pete the day they'd signed the official divorce papers. "But I think from here, I'll just go and take in that movie we've been talking about for fifteen goddamn years."

Other than that, she said, she'd take the condo in Jupiter, Florida, and he could have the remote from the big-screen.

I was sitting in the lobby at 300 East Fifty-sixth, reading all about Pete's retirement and Josh's sudden decision to replace Zip Kahn, all the speculation about who was going to replace both of them, when I saw Pete Stanton come shuffling through the revolving doors carrying two large Orvis duffel bags, a laptop case hanging from his shoulder.

He looked older than the last time I'd seen him, his black hair finally showing some gray in it, and seemed to have lost some weight, which made him look even older. I had never figured out how that worked, older guys dropping weight and adding years as they did, telling themselves they were getting all healthy even as their skin started to hang on them and look as if you could pull it like putty.

He was wearing the same navy blue V-neck sweater and open-collar blue shirt he always wore, underneath what I knew was a Brooks Brothers blazer. The doorman said something to him, nodded in my direction. When Pete saw me, he smiled.

"Oh boy," he said, "is this going to be some fun retirement home or what."

"I'm here to save Private Ryan," I said, taking the duffel bag out of his right hand.

"I saw that movie," he said. "The good guys who didn't die in the beginning just about all died in the end."

Pete said he had Scotch or Scotch. I said Scotch would be fine. He poured me a glass of Dewar's and water that was as dark as a tabletop and did the same for himself. We sat in the small living room dominated by the big-screen TV. There was one bookshelf, ceiling to floor, next to it. The cassettes, neatly labeled, were all of Hawks games from the last several seasons. Just about all of the books were either NFL media guides or thick blue school binders that contained scouting reports of draft-eligible college kids. All of the pictures on the walls were from Pete's football life: Pete with the old man. Pete with me. Pete with Bubba Royal and A.T.M. Moore. Pete with Butterball Morton, our star offensive tackle and the first player in NFL history to cop to actually weighing more than 400 pounds.

"You start lying about how much you weigh in at," Butterball had told me in the training room one time, "before long you're lying about all the important shit in your life.

The bitches you got on the side. How many cars you got. The size of your business. All like that."

It is worth pointing out that by "business," Butterball did not mean the Chevy dealership he owned in Yonkers.

There was one picture of Pete and Pam Stanton on their wedding day, on the beach in Honolulu. He'd arranged it with the *Baltimore Sun,* the newspaper he was working for at the time, that they could get married the day after the Pro Bowl, then stay over for their honeymoon. It was one of the reasons Pam always called it a marriage of convenience from the start.

"If he'd been working in Memphis by then," she said, "I assume the ceremony would have taken place on the front steps of Graceland."

As we sipped our drinks in silence, both of us wondering who was going to make the first move, I tried to guess how old Pete was. Just going by the arc of his career, he had to be in his early sixties by now. But I knew he had never acted his age or thought his age or indicated that he felt his age. When I'd walked into the Hawks' offices the day after the reading of the old man's will, most of the people there had looked at me as if I were there to steal laptops off their desks. But that had all changed as soon as Pete Stanton, the most respected guy in the building, had made it clear he was riding shotgun for me, and now what, assholes?

And now he was leaving.

"Okay," I said. "Let me get this straight: You and Josh nearly win back-to-back Super Bowls despite more casualties than a *Terminator* movie, and now he's leaving for the fucking Arctic Circle of football and you're going . . . where? You're not enough of a phony to get a gig on one of the pregame shows."

"What, you don't think I could yuck it up with those guys?" he said. "Hell, I used to laugh at you."

I sipped my drink, close enough to finishing it that I was already feeling ice on my teeth.

"Why?" I said.

"Me, or Josh?"

"Start with Josh. We'll work our way up to the main event."

"You knew his contract was up when the season was over, which meant right after the Super Bowl, right?"

"I *gave* him the fucking contract, remember? I'm the one who *made* him head coach."

"And he appreciated that. And he loved you being his boss. He even liked an old columnist like me being his immediate boss, even though we both knew *he* already knew more about this game than I do. It was a dream setup, and everybody was sure things were going to stay the way they were, at least until I packed it in." He took a healthy swallow of Scotch. "Understand something, Jack: There was never any problem with this. Between him and you, him and Ken, him and me. We had always planned to sit down after the Super Bowl, him and Ken and me, and he was going to sign his new five-year deal, and away we'd go. But then Ken postponed the first meeting we had scheduled, after we got back from Miami. Then he put it off a couple more times. Even then I'm not worried. But then I start hearing about Dick Miles. Now I'm worried. Then it comes out that not only is Miles buying the twins' half, but he might get enough from you to take over the running of the team, and the day that shit is in the papers, I get a call from Josh at seven-thirty in the morning, telling me not to get crazy or anything, but he's decided to review his options. I said to him, 'What options?' He says, 'The Cowboys are about to open up again.' Which happened to be true. Jerry Jones was just waiting to fire Rashid once he was officially off probation."

I said, "Was Rashid the shoplifter they hired right after Parcells, or was he the one with the high school senior from Fort Worth?"

"Shoplifter. The one with the prom queen was their old strong safety, Charlie Bonaparte. He was the one who swore he thought the girl's voter registration card was legit."

"Oh, yeah, I remember now. I have to say, she did seem very mature that one time I saw her on *Access Hollywood*."

Pete made a sighing sound that was like a rush of cold air coming through a vent. "Anyway," he said, "I went to Mr. Miles right away and told him there might be a problem with the coach. He hit me with his big smile, big-voiced me, and said, ho ho ho, he had made a career in business off other people's problems. Said he'd talk to Josh first thing. But when he finally did—I get this from Josh—he said he would never stand in the way of one of his top managers exploring all opportunities and having the chance to better himself. Which would have been fine, except that Josh hadn't even mentioned wanting to explore other opportunities."

"He's young, he's black, hell, he was Tyrone Willingham before Willingham invented being a young black coach at Notre Dame," I said. "He's won a Super Bowl and nearly stole another one. And Miles is telling him—no, *encouraging* him—to become a free agent?"

Pete's phone made a chirping sound from the kitchen. He walked in there, picked up the receiver, placed it back down, hanging up on whoever it was, not even bothering to let the machine get it. He came back with a new bottle of Dewar's and a pitcher of ice water. The perfect host. I was in the room's one chair, Pete's recliner. He was on the couch. He put the bottle on the coffee table between us. "Must have been a wrong number," he said.

"Why didn't you call me? Why didn't either *one* of you call me, for Chrissakes?"

"Jack, we talked the whole thing to death when you were trying to decide whether to sell or not. Josh was with me in my office one day, we must have talked an hour with you on the speakerphone. I couldn't talk you out of doing that, why was I going to let you talk me out of doing this? Now, that was me. Josh was different, he's not anywhere near the end like I am, I couldn't let him walk away, especially knowing the Packers were going to come after him as soon as Zip died in one last titty bar. So I went to Mr. Miles and told him that at least I had to get you into the loop. He said he understood how I felt but there was really no point, he had to move on this himself, and he hoped *I* understood *that*. Said that while you were still a valuable and trusted part of the organization, he was going to have to start calling the shots sooner or later, and now was as good a time as any."

"And you let him handle it."

Pete studied his new drink as if there were a goldfish swimming in it, then drank some.

"You know him by now. He's a pretty charming SOB, and very persuasive. I can see why he is who he is and how he did everything he did. He has this way of getting you on his side even when you're not sure you want to play."

"You sound pretty sweet on a guy who just convinced you it was gold watch time."

"I'm just trying to explain to you how I got there," Pete said. "We—Miles and me—talked about a lot of stuff that day. The guy does his homework, I'll give him that. He knows how far over the salary cap we are. You know the deal—that's usually the price tag for winning the big game. Or even coming close nowadays. He knows the tough decisions we're going to have to make, some of the good guys we're going to have to let go. I'm talking about guys who've won for us. And he actually asked a good question that day, asked me if I'd be able to take sentiment out of it and make the right choices so we could go forward. Get back on top. Told me he'd made them plenty of times, and it took a certain element of cruelty to get it right, and asked me if I had that in me, especially with people I considered friends."

"Coming right at you with hard stuff."

"Tell me about it," he said. "I had to tell him, no, maybe I couldn't take sentiment out of it, any more than your old man used to take sentiment out. Miles said, 'I understand Tim Molloy used to be real sentimental about things, when the Hawks weren't winning a goddamn thing.' Then he talked about how Josh and I had been a great team, but that sometimes you had to change the team to keep it great."

"And you bought that?"

"He told me to take some time, think everything over," he said. "By the time I got back to my office, I realized I'd walked in there with the guy to talk about Josh leaving, and now I was the one who wanted to leave."

He told me that the more he thought about it, the more what Miles said made sense to him. That he'd loved the old man and loved the Hawks and loved being one of the few guys in history to move out of the sports section and p.r. and become someone who'd built a champ. But that he wasn't one of those guys who was going to work until he died, who'd run around to the television shows someday saying boo-fucking-hoo, they fired me because I was too old.

"I even thought about giving it another shot with Pam," he said.

"I thought she remarried."

"She did," he said. "Older guy. Orthopedic surgeon. Heart attack. I think it was actually the erect-o pills did him in."

The phone started to chirp again, and this time Pete walked in and unplugged it. When he sat back down, he said, "And that, boys and girls, is how Josh and I became a package deal."

"Goddammit!" I said. I was pacing now in front of the bookshelves, Pete's personal NFL Book-of-the-Month Club. "You were supposed to stay around as long as you wanted, and Josh was supposed to be here longer than Shula's jaw in Miami. Miles shouldn't have been the one saying he'd handle this shit, it should have been me."

"You were the go-to guy here," Pete said. "But that was when you were here."

He was standing, too, his back to me, staring out at his terrace, his downtown view of Second Avenue. "Then you weren't here, Jack. No one knew for sure when you were coming back. So all of a sudden, I didn't have a go-to guy and neither did Josh." He turned around and now Pete Stanton looked his age, whatever his age was. "I always remember something Parcells told me. Remember how he left the Giants after they won their second Super Bowl? It was right about this time of year, actually. Parcells quit and said it was time. That was his whole explanation. It was time. And at the time, everybody just thought he was setting himself up to take his next job, at least after he sat out a year."

"He nearly went to Tampa, right?"

"He was always nearly going to Tampa. He never took the Bucs job, but he spent enough time interviewing there that he could have joined a lawn bowling league. Then he shocked the shit out of everybody and went to Dallas, right before he put together that group to buy the Bengals."

"He's the only New York coach who was ever better than Josh."

"No shit," Pete said. "But here's the deal with him. He didn't leave because it was time, or because he was sick of coaching the Giants, the team he'd loved his whole life. It was that Tim Mara sold his half of the team to old man Tisch. And even though Parcells loved Well Mara, the other owner, he knew Well would always side with George Young, the general manager. Young was the guy who'd drafted Lawrence Taylor, drafted Simms, hired Parcells in the first fucking place, got the Giants back in play. Well Mara was always going to take his side. But that had always been all right, because Parcells had Timmy. On the big stuff, Timmy was Parcells's go-to guy. One time, Phil Simms was holding out and Parcells called him and said, fuck negotiating, what kind of money was it gonna take to get a deal done? Simms told him. Parcells called Timmy. Timmy said done. That was the end of the holdout. Only then Timmy was gone, just like that. The way you're gone, now that you've sold a piece of your piece." He shrugged. "Josh and I are just as gone."

"But now I'm back."

Pete forced a smile, but it was like he was trying to push a piano across the room. "Yeah," he said. "Jack is back."

"I'm going to tell you what I just told Susan: You can't quit."

"I never thought you would, not after you'd had a taste."

"Let me talk to Miles. I know it's too late to do anything about Josh. But you're not going anywhere. What would the old man say?"

"I've got some this-just-in news for you, Jack. This ain't your old man's football team anymore."

6

I told Pete Stanton not to leave town.

"Does that mean I'm still a suspect?" he said.

"Just don't, okay?"

"It's over, Jack."

"Not until the fathead sings."

"Which fathead?"

"Me."

I walked back to the Sherry, smoking like death row from the emergency pack of Winston Ultra Lights I'd bought at a newsstand on Fifty-seventh and Third. I checked for messages at the desk, not even waiting to go upstairs. Nothing from The Dick. Maybe he was still traveling. Or hadn't been to Florida at all and Ms. Thorpe of the IRA was just bullshitting me. Or maybe she hadn't given him my snippy message at all.

I had been back only a few hours. It already felt like a month. I got on the king-sized bed, thinking I would close my eyes for a few minutes, empty out my head the way the yoga sissies tell you to.

I woke up four hours later, in the dark, groggy enough from jet lag and Scotch to think I was back at Lennox Gardens. I considered giving Annie a call, but after Susan and Pete, my ass was worn out already with I-told-you-sos. It was eight o'clock, too late for anybody to be at Molloy unless Dick Miles was holed up in his office, figuring out his next move. And suddenly his next move—hiring a new coach or general manager, entirely on his own—was making me almost as paranoid as the ones he'd made already.

I called Brian Goldberg, always the best inside guy in the whole operation, on his cell.

"Where's Miles?" I said.

"I don't know."

"Or you know and you're not telling your old boss."

"If this place were like that shitty *Mole* show on TV, I'd win the lying and cheating and betraying events every time. So I can't tell you that I *would* tell if I did know where Miles is, now that he's the one paying me. But I don't know. So I can't."

"The surprising thing is, I actually followed that."

"It was always as if we could read each other's mind, darling."

I said, "At least give me your best guess on this: Is he interviewing people already?"

"I've been asking that question today myself, since nobody has seen him. The guy flies around a lot and still manages to spend a lot of time here—I'm not actually sure how he pulls that off. There's no inner circle here, unless you count Bitch Face, his secretary, and she doesn't confide in the little Jew."

"What are you doing for dinner?"

"Nothing."

"Where do you want to go? Beef?"

It was a combination of The Palm and a high-end strip joint, all the way downtown in the meatpacking district, owned by Mo Jiggy, who was not just a rap star and sports agent and man about town, but now a restaurateur as well.

Beef was what I imagined would happen if one of those ESPN Zone restaurants met Hooters.

"Closed for remodeling while Mo's on his world tour for his new CD. You heard the new single? 'Holding Cell'? It's fun. Very uplifting and upbeat."

"What's it about?"

"All the timeless themes. Keepin' it real. Puttin' it down. Bitches and hos."

"You pick a place."

"A.T.M. just opened a place on Eighty-fourth and Third. Just to give our kids an option until the grand reopening of Beef."

"Name, please?"

"I'll give you one hint: It's named after his absolute favorite thing in the whole world."

"Yum," I said.

"Meet you at nine," Brian said.

I had spent more time in bars than I cared to think about, from the time I got my first fake ID from one of Babs's dirty-haired boyfriends at the age of fifteen. I had always liked the conversation in bars, whether you were talking to the guys or some girl you just met. I liked the lighting in bars, at least the ones that got it right, which meant the place was lit slightly better than West Virginia coal mines, but not much better. I liked the attitudes of good bartenders, the ones who knew how to listen and how not to be eavesdropping, who could actually make you believe they gave a shit about your problems as much as they did the game they were trying to watch. I liked the smoke in bars, at least until the anti-tobacco Nazis had banned cigarette and cigar smoking, even from the bars that said they would hold the line forever on smoking, and fuck the fine. I had bartended in bars and owned pieces of New York City bars myself and had pretty much designed all of Billy

Grace's bars at Amazing Grace when I was still in my previous incarnation as the Jammer. I had fallen in love plenty of times in bars, fallen out of love, closed them at six in the morning and opened them six hours later at a time of day I always thought of as Bloody Mary.

As soon as A.T.M. showed me the restaurant area and bar area of Yum, I could see it had a chance to be one of the dream places of all time. And told him so.

"Believe you mean wet dream," he said. He made a gesture with one of the huge hands that had terrorized defensive backs for years and said, "What we've done here, Jack, is *raised* the damn bar."

There were no girls walking around without clothes on, the way they did at Beef. But it didn't matter, because the clothes the waitresses *were* wearing came from Victoria's Secret. A.T.M.'s new management group had somehow cut a deal with the people from Victoria's Secret to have their up-and-coming models, prospects who hadn't made the catalogue and the television specials yet, work part-time at Yum, modeling bad-girl, see-through lingerie at the same time.

When I took my first wonderful look around at all the lace in the front room, I asked A.T.M. how his female patrons liked having models like this serve them while dressed the way they were dressed.

"It's like all of life," he said. "You either want to compete or you don't."

The bar area was actually in the building next door; A.T.M. said that's the way a lot of what he called uptempo New York places were doing it these days. The restaurant itself looked like any hot, big-ticket restaurant, Daniel or Café Boulud or Kraft or Town. Just with a constant parade of legs and hair and bodies and black lace and white lace and killer smiles.

And high heels.

Lots and lots of high heels.

"Everything over here is strictly regulation," A.T.M.

said. "If the girls want to go next doors when they off, what kind of boss would discourage them? You know what they say, Jack."

"What's that?"

"The horny customer is always right."

"Okay, other than the bar, what else is next door?"

"The sports-watching room in the back. Then there's the upstairs gots-to-be-a-member room, which me and the boys just think of as the spa."

A.T.M.—known as Ahmad Taj Majal Moore until he had his name legally changed to Automatic Touchdown Maker—still looked fit enough to run an old-fashioned hitch-and-go down the sideline for Bubba Royal, the quarterback with whom he'd made so much New York football history. But he had decided to retire after the Hawks' Super Bowl win, over the Bangers; he'd been inspired, he explained at the time, by the success his golf buddy Charles Barkley was having on television. "The money was close enough, that was the key," he told *TV Guide*. "We run the numbers and figured out that I didn't have to give up none of my toys, or lay off none of my boys."

Historically, there were enough guys in A.T.M.'s posse for them to qualify as a small black college.

Brian Goldberg had faxed me the article at the time, which included the quote that I took as A.T.M.'s farewell to pro football.

"Let the rest of them m——f——ers go over the m—— f——ing middle from now on."

He went to work for ESPN not long after that, ESPN having won the bidding war with the other football networks for his services; nearly matched his TV income with endorsements; and wrote a fast, funny autobiography with Gil Spencer, called *What Is, Is: How I Walked Away with Every Damn Thing I Ever Wanted 'Cept Halle Berry's Phone Number,* which did twelve weeks on the *New York Times* best-seller list. Two months earlier, he'd opened Yum.

Tonight he wore a tangerine-colored cashmere pullover that looked soft enough to wrap the baby in, baggy black slacks, Jesus sandals, and a diamond-studded earring in the shape of a bank card, from the days when his touchdown dance involved him going through the motions of punching in his ATM number and withdrawing cash. He had a new haircut, with a high fade in the front and the sides nearly shaved to his gleaming skull.

"We'll go upstairs later, I'll show you around the spa," he said.

I told him I was already counting the minutes.

I said, "You're going to let me be a special member?"

"And get an early look at next year's catalogue," he said, and then said come on, Brian was waiting for me next door with some of the Hawks who stayed over in town after minicamp.

"The players pissed at me?" I said.

"Some of the veterans got issues," he said. "That includes some of the fat boys over in the sports-watching room."

He stopped and whispered something to a six-foot-tall redhead carrying a tray of drinks and wearing what appeared to be an outfit made entirely of white stockings.

I said, "What do you think about what's going on with the team?"

A.T.M. leaned over, kissed the redhead behind her ear, turned to me, and said, "I got out on account of I was tired of getting my dick knocked around backwards, Jack. What was your sissy-pants damn excuse?"

My first reaction to the group at Brian Goldberg's table:

Pro football had gotten a hell of a lot fatter in just the one year I'd been away.

Butterball Morton, our right offensive tackle, had been a rookie on our practice squad when we'd won our Super

Bowl. But once he'd shown Josh Blake he was as interested in winning football games as he was the all-you-can-eat deal at Denny's, he'd become an All-Pro; that was in addition to being the league's first official 400-pound man. He had a constantly red face, as if just moving himself around required a Herculean effort, and hair that he'd bleached blond, the part closest to his skull still dark, the top part looking as if it had been spray-painted a hooker shade of platinum.

When Brian stood up and said, "You guys all know our former leader, Mr. Molloy," Butterball nodded at me and then belched.

"Good to see you, too, Butter," I said.

To his left was Zeke Widger, our center, a head shorter than Butterball, but nearly as wide now. I couldn't remember what his official weight had been when I left, but he seemed to have put on another fifty pounds since I'd seen him last. He was a funny, white, bald cracker from Crackerville, Georgia, a proud near-graduate of the University of Georgia, sitting there now at Yum with an industrial-sized plate of nachos in front of him, and a half-dozen eight-ounce bottles of Classic Coke that appeared to be guarding the nachos like little toy soldiers.

Zeke wiped his right hand across the bib he was wearing over his gray Hawks T-shirt, extended it to me, and said, "That guy pay you as much as the papers said?"

"Pretty much."

Zeke looked up at the blond waitress standing next to him and said, "Start a new tab for him and bring us more of everything. And tell the cook to give me some goddamn beef to go with all the green shit next time around."

The last guy to greet me was one of my all-time favorite New York Hawks, Elvis Elgin, who'd moved from right tackle to right guard so that Butterball could play his normal position. Elvis had been a star with the Hawks from the first day he'd shown up from Iowa State, one of those guys from the sticks who'd arrived in New York knowing all the moves, how to get around, who to know, who to bribe, where the best girls were, the best hip-hop, and, most important of all, the best ribs. He had a posse even bigger than A.T.M.'s and was on his way to the Pro Football Hall of Fame in Canton. Tonight he was dressed in a black shirt, black tie, all of that setting off a rather incredible amount of jewelry: earrings in both ears, two gold necklaces—one long, one short—one Super Bowl ring heavy enough and sturdy enough to use as a doorstopper.

He came around the table, smiling at me, and gave me a bear hug that seemed to indicate he thought I was choking to death on a chicken bone.

"My, son," I said, after I could feel the oxygen coming back into my lungs, "how you've grown."

"Was Butter gave me my sense of empowerage," he said. "Him crackin' the four hundred the way he did was like whatever English boy it was cracked the four-minute mile back in the day."

"And it's all muscle, right?"

"Hell, yeah," Elvis said. "I owe it all to what the sportswriters call my tireless work in the weight room. And the diet supplements, of course."

"Where's the rest of our stellar offensive line? A.T.M. said the whole gang was here."

Butterball belched again and said, "They already started they spa days."

Brian Goldberg made room for me between him and Elvis. When the blonde came back with Zeke's nachos, I told her I'd like a light Dewar's and water. She leaned close to me and said, "Would you like to munch on anything?"

I told her a drink would be just fine but that I had a tendency to get hungrier as the evening wore on.

She had short hair and a low-cut version of the sweatshirt Butterball was wearing, her breasts almost as big as his. Her green eyes reminded me of Annie's. She said, "Are you really the owner of the team?"

"Part."

"I'll bet it's a good part," she said in a husky voice, and then headed off for the bar.

Brian said, "Well, would you look at that—the same people skills as always."

There were television sets everywhere you looked in the room, a half-dozen lined up on the walls, one at each end of the bar, smaller screens attached to the recliner chairs over in the smoking section. Most of them were showing various baseball games from various cities. Some of them were showing a replay of the Hawks–Bangers Super Bowl. There were a few more Hawks scattered around the room, and what seemed like a squadron of off-duty Victoria's Secret girls.

"You know why they're showin' this much baseball?" Elvis said.

"I was wondering about that."

Elvis said, "'Cause they's games, and they's on."

I told him that was as good a definition of America as I'd ever heard.

We made small talk until Kim the friendly waitress brought more drinks. Then Elvis said, "We ain't none of us too fuckin' happy about recent events."

I said, "Neither am I."

Zeke Widger said, "Losin' Pete is one thing. Losin' Josh, on the other hand, that right there is a whole separate sack of shit."

Butterball belched again, as if punctuating the thought, or at least the alliteration.

"I got to tell you, Jack," Elvis said, "I always had it in my mind to be one of them played his whole career with one team. . . ." He let the thought drift away, like smoke. "But now, I just don't know."

"You got the money," Butterball said. "We get stuck with the fuckin' bill."

There were little buzzers in front of each player at the table, the kind they gave you at restaurants to let you know your table was ready. Zeke Widger's began to vibrate now, flashing red lights. He stuck it in his pocket, drank one more Coke in one loud swallow, and left.

"Don't tell me," I said to Brian. "Spa?"

"You don't want to lose your slot," he said. "Some nights they get stacked up down here like planes over La Guardia."

I said to Elvis and Butterball, "Were you guys at the stadium working out today?"

They both nodded.

"Either one of you hear any rumblings about who the next coach is going to be?"

"No names," Elvis said. "But the new strength coach? Harm Battles? He said he thinks Miles might go college."

I said, "New strength coach? What happened to Ernie?"

Ernie Heinz had been one of the first strength and conditioning coaches in the league, one of the old man's brainstorms, going all the way back to when the Hawks were still the Memphis Marauders.

"Ernie retired," Brian said. "I thought you knew. Couple of weeks after Miles took over. That's when we hired Harm Battles away from Notre Dame."

"Why him?" I said.

Brian said, "Miles is one of those guys who practically wets his pants when he hears the fight song. Apparently, he played golf one time with Lou Holtz in a charity golf tournament and never got over it."

Butterball said, "He hasn't come right out and said it yet, but his mission statement, far as we can tell, is bigger, faster, stronger, more drugs."

"Comes on like a hopped-up little dude himself," Elvis said. "One of those guys who makes coffee nervous."

"And he thinks Miles is going to hire a guy out of college to coach the Hawks? Should I be worried he's going back to South Bend?" I turned to Brian. "Who's the guy who replaced Willingham after he went to the Rams?"

"Jerry O'Rourke," Brian said. "But it ain't happening. Bobby Finkel actually made a call last month, but whatever priest he talked to told him to do something I'm pretty sure is a sin in your faith."

Now Elvis's buzzer went off at the same time Butterball Morton's did. They got up at the same time, as if pulling out for a sweep. It was like watching some kind of tidal wave rise up right in front of you.

"Before we go upstairs, tell us somethin', boss," Elvis Elgin said. "Your new tax bracket—is it ringin' your bell so far?"

When A.T.M. finally made it next door and saw it was just Brian and me left at the table, he asked if we wanted to move up on the spa list, past the Jets linebackers who'd wandered in about a half hour before. A.T.M. said old habits were hard to break, but Christ, he still hated the Jets.

"By the way, your server girl?" A.T.M. said. "I had her one time upstairs. Ask her about that hot rock thing she does. It's her specialty."

I told him there wasn't one signal she'd given off in the last two hours that made me doubt that for a second.

"Your type, too," A.T.M. said.

"Because she looks a little like Annie, you mean?"

" 'Cause she had your table."

I told him I'd been drinking Scotch off and on all day since I'd landed in America, so just a check would be fine, thank you. A.T.M. said it was already covered. I told him that wasn't necessary. He reminded me that I'd introduced Oretha to Billy and gotten her out of his damn situation once and for all.

"You know," I said, "Billy's about half in love with your ex and probably fixing to marry her. And I have to tell you, I've gotten along great with her since I met her that time at the Super Bowl, when she ambushed you with the television crew and started calling you all the bad names."

A.T.M. gave me a look so sad I thought he was about to tell me the dog had died.

"You've got a few years on me, am I right, Jack?"

"Right on," I said.

"Huh?" A.T.M. said.

"It's an expression guys my age used once."

"Well," he said, "as old as you are, you shoulda figured out a long time ago the difference between the way they are when they want you and the way they are after they gots you."

He said he was going back over to the restaurant now, which was starting to close up, to see which girls might be catching their second wind.

Brian stood with me on the street while I smoked a cigarette. I told him I'd be at Molloy Stadium bright and early, he could count on that. Brian said he'd be at his desk when I got there. Long fucking day, I said. Brian said that's the only kind he was having all of a sudden. Goddamn, I'm tired, I said. He grinned at me and said he wasn't just tired, he felt as old as A.T.M. just said I was. I asked if he wanted to take the first cab and he said, no, he still thought of me as the boss, I should take it.

"Or," I said, "we could head over to Suite Nineteen and keep drinking till we pass out."

Brian Goldberg said, "I was afraid you'd never ask."

He had all his keys with him, so we went in through the gate nearest the players' parking lot, on the back side of the stadium, away from the Major Deegan. We walked down the long ramp from there, past the Hawks' locker room, past the visitors' locker room and the X-ray room and the new weight room, past the rows of golf carts that the coaches sometimes used if we were working out on the practice field with artificial turf next door, or the bubble next to that.

When we passed the entrance to the field, I stopped, said "Wait" to Brian, and then walked into Molloy Stadium for the first time since I'd left for London more than a year earlier.

Walked through the goalposts where the Hawks came out on Sunday, walked from the south end of the field toward the north, walked between the hash marks like I was stepping off a penalty, looking at the royal-blue seats closest to the field, the lighter color of blue in the mezzanine, the navy ones that looked almost black in the half-lit stadium in the upper deck. Looking at the way the arc lights that had been turned on reflected off the tall windows of the luxury boxes, mine included, Suite 19, square on the fifty-yard line in what I'd always thought of as Big Tim Molloy Stadium.

The place I'd always thought of as the goddamn capital of pro football, whatever the Cheeseheads who'd stolen my coach thought about the charms of Kraft Cheese–Lambeau Field.

I turned when I got to the forty-yard line and saw Brian watching me from the mouth of the tunnel, hands in his pockets. I made a signal to him that meant, one minute. He nodded.

Finally I was standing on our logo at midfield, the hawk flying across the city's skyline, noticing the change they'd made after 9/11, a red-white-and-blue ribbon across where the Twin Towers had been.

Stood there now, alone, closed my eyes, and then I could see the old man standing next to me when most of this was just piles of dirt and heavy equipment and the skeleton for the stadium, the old man seeing so much more than that, of course, the old man telling me he could see it all, what was going to be his masterpiece, all its possibilities. I always loved him the most in moments like that, the dreamer in him winning out over the robber baron and bullshitter every time, the dreamer explaining how the place really was going to look like the old Polo Grounds, where Frankie Molloy, *his* old man, had first taken him to Giants games, before the Giants moved over to Yankee Stadium in the '50s, when he first started to be crazy in love with Gifford and Conerly and Kyle Rote, my godfather, Pat Summerall, old Number 88, and Big Red Webster and all the rest of them.

The old man in his camel topcoat and blue hard hat, pointing here and there and everywhere and finally to the sky.

"You're aware they said I couldn't raise the money on my own, Molloy," he said.

Me in my McBurney letter jacket and feeling like a donkey in my own hard hat.

I knew him well enough by then to know he hadn't really asked a question and didn't really expect an answer, it was all part of the game we played with each other, the dance we always danced, him leading and me following every move he made.

"Not only couldn't I raise the money but I most *certainly* couldn't get the place built in a year and a half, not dealing with the various thieves in politics and real estate and construction in our fair city."

I was about sixteen at the time, and enough of a smart mouth to point out that he sometimes bragged at the dinner table about *being* one of those thieves.

"A figure of speech, Molloy. A figure of speech. You know what it really is? Vision, son. And you've got to be born with that sort of vision. It's not something you can learn, it's something the Good Lord either gives you or He doesn't. It doesn't matter whether it's the sport of football we're talking about, or the business of football, or any kind of football. It's life, you see. When nobody thought I could even get a foot in the door with your mother, God rest her soul, when there were suitors with much better prospects than my own competing for her affections, I could already see myself married to her. Whatever it took to get her hand. Just because I've always been a whatever-it-takes guy, Molloy. Did I ever tell you the story about what happened to her boyfriend's distributor cap the night of the spring dance?"

I told him it was one of my favorites.

"Anyway," he said, "the point I'm makin' is that it's a gift some of us have, the ability to see things that're meant to be."

He'd even get more Irish in his voice than usual when he made this speech, Irishing himself up real good. It was a speech I'd heard before and he knew I'd heard before. Before long he was telling me other things I already knew, about talking Paley into helping back *My Fair Lady,* and the dinner in Chinatown with Ed Koch where he first told Koch he was bringing the Memphis Marauders to New York, about telling Warren Buffett to go back home, he could get rich any damn place, about backing John Lindsay when nobody thought Lindsay had a chance, and convincing Steinbrenner to go after Reggie. When the old man used to get revved like that, I kept waiting for him to tell me how he beat the Indians out of Manhattan.

"Stop me if I've told you all this," he'd say, knowing I'd never stop him, that him talking this way and me listening was the rock-bottom core of who we were.

"And who said there could be three football teams in New York?" he'd say in a voice big enough to be heard over the heavy equipment. "No one, that's who. And who said we could bring the NFL back to the city itself, inside the city limits I'm talking about, where it always belonged?"

"Only you, Molloy."

Right on cue. Good boy.

"Exactly," he said.

"Whatever it takes," I said.

"Sometimes you have to raise a little holy hell," he said.

And then he told me that day that he was going to show them all over again with Molloy Stadium.

He showed them.

And now I had shown them, hadn't I?

I walked straight back down the field, looking straight ahead now, not looking up at the halo the lights made in the

night sky, walking fast, to where Brian Goldberg was waiting for me.

"Fuck it," I said. "We're out of here."

Tell me about it, Brian said.

We let ourselves out the same way we'd come in.

It was about six hours later, before I had even begun any
meaningful hangover management, that some holy hell began to break loose at Molloy Stadium.

PART TWO

Jackass Molloy

7

I **woke up** about eight, having set the clock radio and CD player next to the bed for my wake-up music from Counting Crows. Annie had hooked me up with them when we were in London, played *Hard Candy* for me and then laughed her head off the next day when I went out and bought everything they'd ever done, like it was Liverpool in the '60s and I'd discovered the Beatles.

"But this is a good thing," she said. "This is something we've been needing to do for quite some time."

I'd asked what she meant by that, exactly, and Annie had said, "I'm very fond of you, Jack. And have shown that, over time, in more ways than either one of us could ever count. But you have the musical taste of an elevator at the MGM Grand."

"What about jazz?" I said. "What about Miles and Coltrane and Ben Webster and the rest of our love music?"

"Rock and roll," she said. "*Current* rock and roll. Think about it."

"Okay, but no rap," I said. "I'm not doing rap."

"What about Mo Jiggy's stuff? I know you listen to that sometimes, even though you won't admit it."

"That's just me showing a good friend that I'm able to get down with my bad self."

"Oh," Annie said.

So the first thing I heard through the thick walls of my hangover was "Mr. Jones." The next was a wake-up call from Miss Susan Burden.

"Are you awake?"

"Yes and no."

"You need to get over here."

"Here meaning Molloy?"

"Where the fun never stops," Susan said.

"What kind of fun are we talking about now?"

"He's scheduled a press conference for noon, and the general atmosphere, already, is 'calling all cars.'"

"It's gotta be a new coach."

"One would assume."

"Who is it? Somebody must know."

"Still a state secret."

"Even Brian doesn't know?"

"I haven't seen him all morning. He's either bunkered down with Miles, or he's on the run."

"You tried his cell?"

"Five after eight, voice mail is already full."

"I know it's insanely early, but has Pete heard anything?"

"No. I called him right before I called you. And don't feel insulted, dear. I was just going alphabetically through the list of people who used to have something to say around here."

"Wait a second," I said. "If you were doing it that way, you would've called me first."

Susan said, "Well, you've got me there, don't you?"

"I'll be there in half an hour."

There was a brief silence on her end, then the sound of her other line ringing. Then Susan Burden said, "Some-

times when the other shoe falls, it can end up in a whole
pile of something, right?"

I said, "Thank you for not saying shit, dear."

Ms. Karla Thorpe, Miles's secretary, sat outside what
used to be my office, and the old man's office before that,
somehow giving off the general air that the entire area, and
maybe the entire Molloy Stadium complex, had been in *her*
family for as long as they'd all been getting weepy over
"Danny Boy."

But it wasn't hers, of course.

It was Dick Miles's.

His art on the walls now, not the old man's. His antique
furniture, all of it looking as if it had been transferred from
the Union Club, or maybe the New York Public Library.
His.

Karla Thorpe was a pretty snappy dish, I had to admit
that. Long hair somewhere between red and brown, splash
of freckles across the bridge of her nose, green eyes, black-
framed glasses that somehow worked for her, fit the size and
shape of her face, the kind of glasses a person with bad sex
thoughts always running through his head could imagine
her whipping off as she locked the door behind her and gave
the long hair a toss as you said to her, "Ms. *Thorpe . . .*"

I gave my head a shake, trying to clear it, and only felt a
quick wave of dizziness, and a reminder of how much I'd
actually had to drink in less than twenty-four hours back in
town.

When she got off the call she was on, I said, "Jack Molloy to see the boss."

"Oh," she said. "Oh, yes. Mr. Molloy."

"Call me Jack."

"Well, then, *Jack.*" She had real Irish in her voice, not
the old man's made-up kind, you could hear her trying to
soften it rather than play it up. "I'm terribly sorry we got
off on the wrong foot the other day. Yesterday, actually. You

must forgive me, I'm still puttin' names with faces, so on and so forth. Now I've got a face to put with your fine old-country name, which I certainly should have known in the first place, sittin' where I'm sittin' and all."

I knew she wasn't being this nice or this apologetic on her own, despite being this close to the devastating Molloy charm. Miles must have put a choke collar on her after she'd told him about our snippy exchange on the phone.

"No harm, no foul," I said.

She looked at me as if I'd suddenly started speaking hip-hop. "I'm sorry?"

"Forget it. Is he in?"

"He's expecting you."

Miles hadn't just come in and moved me out; he'd called me in London and asked if I'd mind taking a converted conference room down the hall—more space! he'd said on the phone—and I said, sure. Now he had an even bigger antique desk than Karla Thorpe's. He'd added television screens where the old man's bookcases had been. And the walls in here were a trip down memory lane for Dick Miles now, not Big Tim Molloy. He'd even framed the front-page headline the *Post* went with after his press conference at the Waldorf:

WE GET DICK

He'd also expanded the room, making it slightly bigger than before, making it L-shaped, opening it out to your left as you came through the door. So I didn't notice until Miles came charging around the big old desk to shake my hand, tell me it was damn good to see me, ask me how the hell I'd been, that there were two other men sitting over there to our left, on a long leather couch.

One was a stocky, square-faced blond guy, hair perfect, perfect tan, wearing a turtleneck sweater and houndstooth tweed jacket, pale blue eyes staring at me through rimless glasses, as much warmth in the look as you'd get from somebody impounding your car.

This was Borden Skiles, the most famous and most successful sports agent in the business, the one most universally despised by owners in all the major sports, beginning with football, where he had the most clients; and generally the kind of well-dressed weasel who made all other weasels question who they really were and where they were going with their lives.

I nodded in his direction. "Nice to see you again, Borden."

He said "Jack" without moving his thin lips that really didn't look like lips at all, just speed bumps around his mouth.

And he didn't move to get up off the couch, or show anything that indicated that we had made actual human contact. I could get that out of him, I knew, but only if I threw a twenty on the carpet.

But I wasn't as interested in Borden Skiles as I was in the man sitting next to him, the guy with hair spilling nearly into his eyes, wearing faded jeans and worn cowboy boots and a suede jacket. I was staring at Bobby Bullard and hoping that he was in New York—that he and Borden Skiles were in New York—only because the two of them had taken the wrong fucking plane.

If they hadn't, it meant that Bullard, ex-coach of the Texas Tech Red Raiders, ex-coach of the Houston Texans, ex-coach of Mississippi State, currently the homespun, aw-shucks, dad-gummit color commentator for ABC's main college football game on Saturdays, was the new coach of the New York Hawks.

Bobby (Bet the Over) Bullard.

When he saw me staring, Dick Miles said, "Jack, I don't suppose I have to introduce the most innovative damn offensive mind since Bill Walsh, do I?"

I whipped my head around and said, "Is Spurrier here?"

Bullard let out a big haw.

"Everybody told me before I got up here to the big city that you were about three loads of smart-ass," Bullard said.

He did get up and walk over and shake hands as if he was glad to see me.

Borden Skiles stayed where he was, watching the three of us in the middle of the room mill around like it was a freshman mixer.

Miles said, "I suppose you can figure out why Borden and Bobby are here."

I looked at Skiles and said, "You've decided to put them in your will."

Bullard laughed again, though not as loudly as before.

"Jack," he said, "gettin' the chance to work with you is gonna be more fun than drawin' those squiggly little ball plays of mine."

"One big happy family," Skiles said from across the room.

Miles cleared his throat in an almost operatic way and said, "This is a great day for the Hawks, that's what this is."

He went back around his desk and sat down. Bullard went back to the couch. I stayed where I was, hands in my pockets, staring past Miles, out his window, staring at the upper deck across the way, not thinking dirty thoughts about Miles's secretary anymore but imagining myself silhouetted there above the top row of seats, standing on top of the redbrick wall behind them, throwing each one of these bastards into Parking Lot C, one by one. . . .

I felt myself smiling at the image as I said to Miles, "Great."

"He's a persuasive sonofabuck, your Mr. Miles," Bullard said, brushing his hair out of his eyes, giving me his famous sideline grin, the one that actually reminded you of someone squinting into a big sun.

"Isn't he?" I said.

Miles rubbed his hands together like a kid. "Who

would've bet I could get Bobby to come out of the television booth and take one more shot at the title?"

"If you did bet, I hope you took the over," I said, moving around to Miles's left, my back nearly to the rest of them, so I could get a better look at the field.

They called him Bet the Over because he'd run up the score at Texas Tech every chance he got. The over-under number, if you're one of the fans who actually love the NFL for its own true self and not because they can bet on it with both hands, is what Vegas says will be the total number of points two teams in a game will score. Once the number is established, you can either bet the over or the under. If anybody ever bet the under with Bobby Bullard's Red Raiders, it must have been because a nor'easter blew through Texas that looked like something out of a Russian winter.

"Ever-body's got their vices," he said once, in a famous quote they used on the cover of *Sports Illustrated*. "Mine just happens to be touches."

It's what he called touchdowns.

He'd won one national championship at Texas Tech, was on probation twice for recruiting violations, had been married even more than Dick Miles, from what I remembered. Somehow he had escaped firing from the chancellor when his second or third wife turned out to be the Red Raider Homecoming Queen, Becky Lynn Shrake, who was dating the sure-handed tight end in his spread offense at the time.

He'd cried with Becky Lynn on *Larry King Live* and said, "I don't have to tell you that love can be harder'n third and long, Larry—hell, you've had more wives than Brigham Young," immediately pointing out to Larry that he didn't mean the high-flying Cougars of the Western Athletic Conference.

Bobby Bullard had a home in Las Vegas, I knew that, and when he was in town spent more time in the high-end casinos than the slot machines did. It only made him fall further into disfavor with the people running the NCAA, who would rather have star players riding around campus in expensive foreign cars than college coaches being associated with any kind of gambling, legal or otherwise. But other than getting married or engaged, Bullard's three favorite hobbies had always been these: gambling at casinos; gambling on golf (he was a three handicap); and gambling on thoroughbred racehorses, which in his case meant the ones he owned and everybody else's.

"I just don't frankly wanna live in a world where you're praised for bein' a gamblin' man on the road against the Texas Longhorns, but not with the feature race at Hollywood Park" is the way he once explained his philosophy on leisure time.

There were always plenty of opportunities for him to go pro, just about every January after the college season was over; the best offers generally came when he was on probation. But every time he was supposed to be on his way to the Lions or Patriots or Falcons, people would dismiss the rumors, saying ol' Bobby could never make the move to the NFL, they actually had a salary cap up there.

He finally did leave Tech (after it was discovered that thanks to an enthusiastic Tech alum, the team's star tailback, Boo Hanley, had more Viacom stock than a lot of high-profile chief executives), becoming the second coach of the Houston Texans, at a contract worth more than six million a year; it meant he was making more than his rival Steve Spurrier—with whom he'd knocked heads and come away a loser in a couple of big bowl games—had gotten when he'd left the University of Florida for the Redskins.

Bobby had endeared himself to Wick Sanderson at his initial press conference by informing America that he was getting ready to score more often than some of those hooker-girls did in Vegas.

He left after two years.

During that time the Texans were in the top three in the NFL in scoring, the bottom three in defense, had a record of sixteen wins and sixteen losses, made the playoffs once as a wild card. They lost games in which they had scored forty or more points four different times, which explained why Bullard also hired and fired four defensive coordinators while in Houston. Bullard was also the Texans' general manager, even though the rumor was that Borden Skiles made most of the personnel decisions—most of those decisions, not coincidentally, involving Borden Skiles clients.

His marriage to Becky Lynn had ended abruptly when one of the Houston television stations broke the news that he was having an affair with the wife of his last defensive coordinator with the Texans, Vance Hopewell, Jr., who went all the way back to Texas Tech with Bullard, and had served as best man at two of his weddings.

Bullard had cried again while explaining that one, blubbering at a press conference that letting Vance go was the toughest dad-gummit decision of his entire football career. He said Vance had always been a good friend, not to mention a loyal assistant. But that once he realized he had to choose between the woman he now knew was his true soul mate and a guy whose 3-4 defense couldn't keep the Cowboys from scoring four touches in the fourth quarter of the Texans' last regular-season game, he knew his path was clear.

"Bottom line, boys?" he said that day. "Bobby Lee Bullard needs a better damn playbook for the game of life."

He resigned suddenly a month later to take the Mississippi State job, won another national championship there, then said he was retiring from coaching for good. You could take that sucker to the damn bank, he said, his next official function as a football coach would be the day they inducted his ass into Cooperstown.

Bullard apparently confusing the National Baseball Hall of Fame with the one for college football.

For the last three years, he had been delivering his folksy wisdom for ABC, and turning himself into the redneck version of John Madden, falling into a lucrative gig as the commercial spokesperson for Jimmy Dean's Pure Pork

Sausages, writing a couple of how-to-watch-football books geared to all the Bubbas in his audience, and even playing himself in a sitcom that ran for seven weeks on ABC, in the coveted time slot before *The Bachelor*.

"So this is the medium to which I am devoting my hopes and dreams," Annie said one Saturday afternoon while we were watching a Florida–Georgia game in Suite 19. "One in which a guy can become a star for saying things like 'That call was tastier'n a honey-glazed ham at Christmas.' The critics are right. He's a comic genius, speaking the true language of the common man."

"But only if the common man is wearing bib overalls," I pointed out.

"Dad-gummit all to Grandma's house, you're right," Annie said.

I told her I actually liked it better when he said, Hey there, Brent, these two teams are going at it like they was in heat.

"Whoa, pards!" she said, using another of his trademark expressions.

Now he had his shitkicker boots up on Miles's coffee table, one that looked made for shitkicker boots, low and solid and old, as if it had come from some Old West ranch-house. Or, knowing New York, some design house in the Village.

"You just got to hang with me, Jack," Bullard said. "We might do it a little different than you're used to, throw it around a little more, confuse 'em with some of my old ball plays. But Borden and me didn't come here to have some-body else take the pretty girl back to the dorm. And don't you think otherhow."

What I was actually thinking was this: Please shoot me now.

Instead of saying that out loud, I turned to Dick Miles. "The star search to replace Josh certainly didn't take long."

"It's like I told you in London," Miles said. "When I see something I want, I get after it."

"You never call anymore," I said. "You never write."

"I called Bobby," Miles said. "And when I did, he told me that he'd just gotten off the phone with Jerry Jones. I told him don't answer the phone, I was calling Borden. We did the deal on the phone, by the time Jones called back, it was that line . . . what's that line you used from TV, the one when you think the game's officially over, Bob?"

"The hay is in the barn."

"That's what he told Jerry."

I said, "And the hay being in the barn this way explains why I didn't even get a call?"

"When you lose a star, you replace him with a star, at least if one's available. As far as I'm concerned, those are just the fundamentals, and nothing you were going to say was going to change my mind on them. Once we lost Josh, we had to move, done deal. It's why as soon as Bobby and Borden said yes, I cranked up the old Dick Jet and told the pilot to point it toward Vegas. We signed the papers at Bobby's house and flew back last night." He leaned back, put his hands behind his head, gave me a smug look, and said, "That's my story and I'm sticking to it."

"Maybe later you could give me the story on how Josh ended up in Green Bay."

"All in due time, Jack. All in due time. Not only will I fill you in on that one, but on a few more tricks I've got planned."

"Tricks like the kind hooker-girls turn?" I said.

Bobby Bullard seemed to think it was funny.

8

Miles said he was going to take Bullard and Borden Skiles down to the Hawks' locker room; Brian Goldberg was waiting there with our photographer to take posed pictures of Bullard that I knew we'd use immediately on our website, and for the p.r. blitz I could see coming like a huge storm front.

Before they all left, Miles asked where I'd be when he finished and I told him my office. I told Bobby Bullard maybe I'd see him at the press conference later.

"Or maybe we could set up some time this week, throw some of your big-city whiskey down our throats, and you could kind of point me in the right direction."

"I actually do know a couple of real estate agents who won't try to steal everything except your Blockbuster card."

"I meant, point me towards the best titty bars," Bullard said.

Dick Miles had been telling the truth about the size of my new office in relation to his: Mine was bigger. Susan Burden must have handled the move, because somehow everything looked pretty much the same to me, including one of the game balls Josh Blake had given me after the Bangers game, eventually signed by the whole team. It was at the front of my desk in its ornate stand, acting like some kind of hood ornament.

There were all my pictures of the old man on the walls; the pictures of the old man and me; my old powder-blue No. 19 from UCLA, still caked with dirt from the field at the Rose Bowl and more dried blood than I actually remembered, the uniform mounted and framed. And she'd added some new items, from after the Super Bowl win over the Bangers. Me with my arm around Pete. Me trying to hug Josh Blake and the Lombardi Trophy at the same time. Bubba and me under the goalposts at Charles Keating Stadium, Bubba with the crutch he'd used to get from one postgame ceremony to another. There was the one they'd used with the sidebar they'd done on me in the special commemorative issue of *Sports Illustrated* they sold in New York City, the full-page shot showing me kissing Annie in one of the end zones, fireworks above us in the sky.

There was the one I liked best of all: the black-and-white of the old man and me, one I'd never seen before, shot from behind, him in the camel topcoat I still had hanging from a hook on the back of my door, me as a skinny kid in some kind of long dark coat of my own, the Molloy Stadium scoreboard in the distance reflecting what had to be a bright winter sun and saying that the Hawks were getting ready to play the Giants.

Him probably giving me his favorite gameday line: Let all the other bastards have the rest of the week, all he wanted was Sunday afternoon.

I got up and walked over and took the camel coat off the hook and hung it inside a garment bag in the closet and closed the door. I could look at all these pictures and remember everything. The coat was different. The coat was the old man and his Sunday afternoons here, when it was his team and his place. Sometimes when the weather would get cold, I would wear it down on the field before the game and imagine he was standing there with me.

Never again, I thought.

It was Dick Miles's team now, Dick Miles's place. His Sundays.

I walked over and did something I did quite frequently when I was on the premises:

Talked to Big Tim Molloy.

"Tell me something, Molloy," I said, my voice sounding as loud as it always did when I was alone with him like this. "You used to tell me you had all the answers, all the questions, most of the follow-ups. So you tell me now how I should play this, now that I seem to be the one who's gotten played."

He didn't say anything, because he'd died too soon, died before we could square things between us. He just stayed where he was in the picture, staring up at that scoreboard, his head full of what I was sure was blue sky, full of his dreams and schemes, wondering what to do next in a big-town life that was always so full of big fun, and adventure.

I went over and sat down at my desk, Susan having stacked today's New York papers to one side. Sat there and wondered what would be a good time of the morning to show up here in the future, sketching out what my workday would be like in my new office, trying to plot out a late arrival and an early lunch and then where I wanted to be in Manhattan when the cocktail hour began, out there with other swells who didn't have enough to do, when I heard a knock on the door and saw Dick Miles's head pop through it.

"You wanted to see me, Mr. Molloy?" he said.

From the time I'd left Miles's office, I'd convinced myself there was no point in having a meltdown when it was the two of us alone. Because for all the smiley, "Hey, pards" shit we'd exchanged in his office, Bullard and Skiles sitting there watching us, I knew that was exactly what Dick Miles was expecting me to do.

I was going to remain calm, is what I was going to do, honestly try to get his side of the story, his version of everything that had happened over the past seventy-two hours or so, with Pete and Josh, Bullard and Skiles, what Big Tim Molloy used to call the whole caper.

Act like a grown-up, basically.

That was the ticket.

Then he was inside the door, right there in front of me, strutting because he couldn't help himself. Saying, did you want to see me, like an office intern, and the next thing I knew I was grabbing my Super Bowl game ball and throwing it as hard as I could at Dick Miles.

The ball would have clipped him on the side of the head if he hadn't shown pretty good agility for a guy his age, and ducked it at the last second.

"Hey!" he said. "What the *hell* do you think you're doing, Jack?"

I felt calmer than anger-management class all of a sudden.

"Actually, that's my line," I said. "I've sort of been wondering what the hell you think *you're* doing, *Dick.*" Leaning on his name pretty hard. "And I'd like a straight answer and not the kind of you-and-me-against-the-world bullshit you spoon-fed me in London."

Miles didn't say anything, just retrieved the ball from where it had landed near the door, walked across the room, and placed it carefully back in its stand, even spinning it so the laces and NFL logo were facing me. Then he sat down across from me, put out both hands in a settle-down motion, and said, "Take it easy, Jack."

I said, "I'm not the one who needs to take it easy. No shit, what's the new policy around here? If you don't turn over the entire front office in thirty minutes, my fucking pizza is free?"

Miles said, "I hear you, okay? I hear you." I studied him and wondered if it was the same blazer he'd worn in London, with the same dopey patch, or if he had a closet full of them. Today's shirt was lavender. When he crossed his legs, I could see the shirt matched his socks. "I know things are moving pretty fast for you. Hell, they're moving fast for me, too. But when I realized after talking to both Pete and Josh that I had to move, I felt pretty sure I knew what your response was going to be. So I did what I always do, what I've been doing in business for forty years: trusted my gut, took my shot, waited for the hit."

"Don't tell me," I said. "It's from your book."

"Whole chapter, actually. About how if you don't understand that all of business is a contact sport, don't even take off your warm-up jacket."

I told Dick Miles at least I understood why this was going to be such a beautiful friendship between him and his new coach—the two of them could sit around quoting each other *to* each other.

"Let me ask you a question," I said. "Do you actually believe—having been around football for as long as you have, of course—that you can replace Josh Blake with this rhinestone-cowboy peckerwood?"

"Yes."

Like he was saying, back at you.

I said, "That's rich."

"Not as rich as you."

"Let me make sure I understand something: Do you plan to rich-slap me every time I even suggest you might be full of shit on something?"

Miles said, "I know Josh is your guy, Jack, you're the one who hired him. But it's not as if anybody was humping him for Coach of the Year *last* year. I know, I was at every game. I heard what the fans around me were saying, I read the papers, I even listened to the radio, God help me. And it was fairly well documented that the Hawks needed an awful lot of luck down the stretch to even make the playoffs, much less make it back to the Super Bowl."

I started to say something, but he held up a hand to stop me. "You're still allowed to think he's a boy genius, by the way. But me? I'm allowed to look at a young guy who's coached a total of about thirty games in the league, one who inherited a team built to win by Pete Stanton and Vince Cahill, whatever kind of prick Cahill turned into later. Then, when that same young guy was asked to do it again, he couldn't."

"We lost half our starters on defense," I said, "and if Benito makes the kick, we still win it all."

He gave me his lean-in now. His stare-down. "I know a little bit about reading people, Jack, especially when they're signing on to be top managers with me. I could tell as soon as I sat down with him that he didn't want to be here. I told him that you and I were going to be partners on this—"

"Why do I keep forgetting we're partners?"

"—but he clearly wasn't buying that—"

"I can't imagine why not."

"—and so I finally just told him that if he had it in his heart to leave, I wasn't going to stand in his way."

Miles stood up then, walked over to the wall to my right, the one that had the most space for pictures, stopping in front of the one of my father and mother when they were students at Fordham.

"He was one smart bastard, wasn't he?"

"Better yet," I said, "he always did what he said he was going to do."

Miles said, "I get it, okay? I get that you want to do more right now than just whip a ball at me. Do some bad-ass thing to *my* balls, maybe. But let me say one more thing about Josh Blake, even if it's going to piss you off more: Send up a fucking flare if he ever sniffs the big game from out there in Frozen Tundra, Wisconsin."

"But we're not going to miss a beat playing Bobby-Ball."

"No," Dick Miles said, "we're not. The guy's won everywhere he's been except with the Texans, and he didn't have time to get his own players in there. On top of that, he was in a bad place, personally."

"Too far from The Mirage?"

"I'm asking you to trust me on this."

"That again."

"Bobby Bullard is going to give us the kind of change we need. And the *charge* we need. Didn't everybody think the Rams were crazy when they brought Dick Vermeil back after he'd been in television all those years? How'd that go in St. Louis?"

I didn't have a snappy comeback for that, so instead of saying anything, I rearranged the newspapers, putting the *Times* on top of the *Post* and *Daily News*.

The old ad-libber.

When I spoke again, I knew I sounded as tired as I felt, like we were both coming to the end of the kind of pitch meeting that used to wear my ass out at Amazing Grace, some agent selling me a singer, or comic or even lion tamer. "What about Pete?" I said.

"I don't know what he told you, but Pete's the one who thinks it's time to call it quits. Can you honestly sit here and tell me you can't see that yourself?" Putting his big blues on me.

Now I put *USA Today* on top of the pile and said, "No, I can't."

"I know you love Pete, how loyal you two are to each other. But there's something else you need to know about him: He did a god-awful job with the cap last year. Even the guys in the nosebleed seats know you're not supposed to be twenty fucking million over the salary cap with a team that went nine and seven during the regular season. It's why we've got some tough player decisions coming up this summer, ones I can't trust to somebody who's more interested in getting his ex-wife back than getting us back to the Super Bowl."

"You'd rather trust the job to a cheap hustler like Borden Skiles?"

"Borden is many, many things, Jack. Cheap isn't one of them, believe me."

"You know what I'm saying."

"Bobby's the general manager, not Borden, I made that clear to both of them. He has a right to do what they wouldn't let him do in Houston, bring in guys to play his kind of ball. But he'll have to run it by you, and then I'll sign off on everything, the way my friend Jerry does in Big D."

"Things didn't work out so great for him after Jimmy Johnson left until he went and hired another real coach in Parcells."

Miles said, "Jerry won with Barry Switzer after Jimmy left, don't forget that. And would have won more if Barry didn't start showing that one flaw after he did win."

"That being?"

"He turned lazier than my housekeeper."

"You've done your homework."

"For the last time, Jack: I didn't spend this kind of money to blow the goddamn franchise. Do I want to make it about me as much as possible along the way? Hell yes! It's the only way for guys like me to really feel like the guys on the field. But first and foremost, I want to win."

"I have to ask you one more thing," I said. "What happened to: I'm not going in trying to change things, I'm into quality control, I'm just looking to maintain?"

"Sometimes you've got to change the maintaining," he said.

"Call me next time before you decide to rock the house."

"Press conference is at noon sharp," he said. "It's your call whether you show up or not."

"I might wander by."

"Sonofabitch," Dick Miles said in the doorway. "I hired myself a goddamn coach today. Did you get this kind of rush when you fired Cahill that time and hired Josh?"

I told Dick Miles I still got goose bumps just thinking about it.

They had set up the kind of stage you see on the field after the Super Bowl. The scoreboards at each end of the stadium said, "Howdy, Bobby." There was a podium with our flying City Hawk on the front of it, the same one from the logo painted into the field, folding chairs for Miles, Bullard, Skiles, Brian Goldberg. One for me, if I wanted it.

By the time I got down there at about a quarter to twelve, most of the seats, which stretched in neat rows from midfield all the way back to the twenty-yard line, were filled. I recognized most of the usual suspects, the beat guys from the papers and the sports radio stations, columnists from all the papers, reporters from the New York television stations in addition to Fox Sports, the Madison Square Garden network, ESPN, and the city's own cable news channel, Channel 1.

I had come the long way to the field so I could avoid all my media friends, especially the ones who had done everything after the sale except fillet me. I was hanging back in the shadows in the tunnel at the east end of Molloy Stadium, watching the whole thing organize. Dick Miles was with Brian near the stage, pointing at the paper Brian had in his hands. I saw Bobby Bullard with Vicky Dunne, a television reporter who'd been with Fox Sports when I'd left town but had moved over to ESPN, according to Annie. Annie explained it by saying that Vicky had slept up as far as she could at Fox, so it was time to broaden her horizons. Annie had once been Vicky's intern, and the two were not close. When Annie got the job at *The NFL Today,* she'd e-mailed me that the only person who hadn't called to congratulate her was Vicky, but that was probably because she still hadn't taken her head out of the oven.

When I'd first taken over the Hawks, it was an open secret around the team and the New York media that Vicky was having a rather warm coach-reporter relationship with Vince Cahill. Now I saw her laughing at whatever Bobby said. Then he laughed at whatever she said. Then she was touching his arm. Then he was leaning over to brush a hair out of her eyes. She'd been a redhead before. Now her hair was the color of coal. It was just simple math to figure out she had to change, there were only so many shades of red and orange.

A female voice behind me said, "I hope she's not making you jealous, big boy."

I turned around and there was Annie, in her CBS blazer, in a skirt short enough to show off legs that belonged in a high-kicking chorus line, hair long, longer than it had been at Lennox Gardens, eyes full of intelligence and wit and fun and all the other very cool things that cool women like Annie had going for them.

"I don't think I'm her type," I said.

Annie said, "Are you kidding? Everybody's her type."

"She and our new coach really do seem to be getting along."

"Always remember something with Vicky," Annie said. "With her, undercover journalism actually means under-the-covers."

She walked over to me and put her arms around me and held me for a minute, somehow making me feel worse than I already did. Other than one unfortunate drunken episode upstairs when she'd found me studying more than film with Liz Bolton, still our team president in those days, all we'd ever known here were good times. Down here on the field, upstairs in Suite 19.

Even sneaking into our new high-tech video room one time and showing what I considered to be film-school creativity with Josh Blake's projector.

"You're covering this," I said.

"They like season number one so much they're already putting me on the *Evening News* sometimes," she said.

"Very cool."

"For network guys, yeah, they are pretty cool."

"I meant you."

She ducked her head a little, the way she did with compliments. Another shot to the heart. "They've even had some talks with Skipper about me cohosting their morning show from time to time."

I said, "You might be the first person to actually get people to watch it."

"Don't try being nice to me," she said. "I still hate you for selling."

"Join the club. I'm starting to hate me for selling."

"Selling out," she said.

I told her that was Billy Grace's line.

On the field, Brian Goldberg was doing a mike check at the podium. Vicky Dunne noticed Dick Miles coming down the steps from the stage and moved away from Bobby Bullard as if the old coach had pulled a knife on her. Borden Skiles was already in his seat behind Brian, his head probably full of incentive clauses.

Annie said, "If Miles is out there, that tells me you didn't choke the life out of the bastard when you found out he'd hired Bobby Bull."

"How do you know I wasn't in the old loop on this one?"

"Because you wouldn't hire this guy to broadcast your games, much less coach them. Plus, it's been my experience that you only allow yourself one monumental life-altering fuckup per month."

"Technically, I believe I finalized my end of the sale last month."

I felt her looking at me. "Are you actually going to be part of this circus today?"

"I was pondering that exact same question when you ambushed me here in my little hidey-place."

"Don't do it," she said, and nearly smiled. "Especially dressed like that."

I looked down at myself. I was wearing my usual work clothes: blazer, blue shirt, khakis, New Balance cross-trainers, just in case somebody needed me to go out for a couple of passes.

"I could borrow a shirt from Dick and pretend I'm a peacock."

Annie said, "I hear this is just the beginning with this guy."

"I'm not sure I can take any more good news today."

"Think about it, Jack. The team's capped out to the outer reaches of the galaxy. There's a lot of decisions to be made around here, on both sides of the ball, starting with the fact that there doesn't seem to be much of a backup plan at backup quarterback if Tucker can't do the job."

Tucker O'Neill was the Boy Scout who'd finally replaced Bubba Royal at quarterback, after years of praying before every single game that this was the Sunday when Bubba would finally be too old, or get sacked and have his liver explode. Or have the kind of career-ending injury he'd had in the Super Bowl.

But when he did get his chance to be first string, he'd thrown more interceptions than touchdown passes, and if Bobby Camby hadn't had the season of his life rushing the ball, coming up just short of two thousand yards, the magic number for ball carriers in the NFL, we wouldn't even have made the playoffs.

"Mr. Miles considers himself a cap expert already," I said to Annie.

"Jack, guys like Miles always think they're experts about everything in sports when they buy the team. They think it's going to be like their other businesses. Only it's not. Then all these guys—*most* of these guys—who've been told what geniuses they are start acting like the dumbest caller to the radio."

"Wow," I said. "I feel better already."

Out at the fifty, Brian and Miles and Bullard were walking up the steps.

Annie put a hand on my arm. "I'm going out there to get with my crew. You stay here."

"I had some very clever material prepared. Plus a short prayer."

"I mean it," she said. "You'll look like you're flacking for him."

Over the sound system, I heard Brian Goldberg yell, "Whoa, pards!"

Annie pulled me all the way into the shadows, almost into some kind of John Deere thing they used on our new grass, the two of us knocking over a plastic garbage can. She put a hand on each shoulder, gave me the kind of look smart people give you sometimes, the one that says they know all about you, don't even think about trying to bull-shit them.

"Dad-gummit," Brian Goldberg said from the podium, "we've gone and got Bobby Lee Bullard out of the booth and back on the damn field where he belongs."

"What are you going to *do*, Jack?" Annie said.

Make a phone call, I said.

9

Billy Grace and Oretha arrived in the Amazing Grace jet at Teterboro Airport over in Jersey about eight that night. He had told me on the phone that he was bringing along the two bodyguards who enjoyed New York City the most at this time of year, Vinny One and Johnny Angel. Vinny also drove the rented stretch limo that was waiting for them on the tarmac, Billy having that kind of relationship with the car company from East Rutherford, one called Getaway Cars.

The first time Billy had ever informed the owner of Getaway Cars that he wanted to have one of his people drive, he had been told that there was a company policy prohibiting that.

"But upon reflection, they decided that maybe it was time to change that particular policy," Billy said. "At least that's how it worked out once Vinny had that talk with them in *his* car."

Billy called from The Regency, a few blocks east of the Sherry-Netherland, at Sixty-first and Park, and said we'd worry about dinner later, I should walk over and have a drink with him and Oretha in the suite.

When Oretha let me into their two-bedroom, I said, "I thought you guys always stayed at The Four Seasons."

From the living room, Billy, in his white complimentary robe, said, "Booked."

"For *you?*" I said.

"Don't worry, I would've had them unbook in the old days," he said. "But my big girl has got me into letting shit go. Less control of shit giving you more."

"See there, big man," she said. "This here is progress, not sending Vinny and Johnny over to talk to the man."

"We'll just continue to take it case by case," Billy said. "May that fag manager over there rest in peace."

"Now, don't go backslidin' on me, baby," she said. "Don't backslide on me now."

Oretha was wearing a white T-shirt and blue jeans, and still looked as if she could walk into any room in New York tonight dressed as simply as that and turn every head in the place, male or female. She *was* Billy's big girl, nearly six feet tall in bare feet, her hair currently in tight, short curls. The white shirt made her skin look darker than it really was. Didn't matter one way or the other. Oretha Keeshon was one of the most beautiful women, of any race, color, creed, sports allegiance, or political party, I had ever known.

"Sorry about the mess you're in," she said, hooking an arm around my waist. "But it did give us a nice excuse to come east. Billy and I are going shopping together on Fifth Avenue first thing in the morning. First time we've ever done that together. I told him it's gonna be like getting to play a round of golf with Tiger."

Billy said, "She says she's even gonna do that Tiger fist pump every time they run my Visa Gold through."

He was over at the bar, fixing himself a martini. "Two hundred and fifty million he walks away with for being in this mess," he said. "Boo fucking hoo."

"I don't get the real money until the sale goes through

after the season," I said. "All I've got in the bank is a down payment."

"Boo fucking hoo," he said again.

"I missed you, too," I said. "And you look good, by the way."

He did. Oretha was the best thing that had happened to Billy, at least outside of the casino business, in all the years since I'd first gone to work for him. She was making him take care of himself better than he ever had, making him want to look and act younger the way I wanted to with Annie, even though I wasn't ever going to admit that to her.

Grace wasn't his real name, I could never remember his real name, just that it sounded like a whole sentence in Italian. But he was almost as dark as Oretha, with thick black hair, constantly heavy beard. He came at you behind what looked like an old guy's barrel chest, but one you found was hard as the side of a building when he'd demand that you give it a good whack.

He had grown up as a semi-mobbed kid in an Italian section of the South Bronx, a runner mostly, and had been smart enough to figure out early that while the bad guys he'd been running for could be good to know, you didn't want to make a career out of working for them. So he'd never been arrested, at least outside some nickel-and-dime stuff with bookies, he'd never done any time; finally ended up in Las Vegas in the early '60s when it was starting to go legit, when it was all Frank and Dean and Sammy and the Rat Pack, and ring-a-ding-ding, and when was the last show at The Sands? He even got a job at The Sands eventually, as the kind of Jammer I'd be with him later on, a go-to guy, somebody who could handle himself with the girls, the pit bosses, the high rollers. And the wise guys. He worked his way up and ended up second-in-command, never properly explaining to me how he showed up in town as broke as he was and got as rich as he did as fast as he did.

But that's exactly what Billy Grace did.

"A slight case of amazing grace," a friend of his said to

him one time, describing the lightning-fast move he'd made up The Strip, and that became the name of his casino when he got enough backing to take his shot.

That was twenty years ago. Now in Las Vegas, it was Billy Grace one, and all those Kirk Kerkorians and Steve Wynns fighting it out for the silver medal.

And when we were together, as we were now, it didn't matter to him that I'd inherited the Hawks, or won a Super Bowl with them; that I was about to inherit a small fortune—for me, anyway—once this sale went through. It was the same as it had always been between the two of us.

He was still the big man.

I was still the Jammer.

In the suite now, he said, "I didn't want to bruise your delicate feelings and not fucking drop everything to fly across the country and hold your hand." He toasted me with his martini and said, "Drink?"

It was a couple of hours later. Oretha was on the other side of the living room, watching a re-air of A.T.M. Moore's interview show on ESPN, frequently talking back to the television set.

Somehow when she even imagined herself in the presence of her ex-husband, she streeted down her speech, and frankly seemed to come up a little short herself when it came to letting shit go.

"That's it, bitch," she was saying, munching on her microwave popcorn. "Fool 'em into thinking that's a brain what *works*."

"Oh, shit, don't drop that paper you're holdin'," she said. "On account that's where somebody wrote up actual *ideas* for your sorry-ass self couldn't get through all those colleges without me."

She leaned forward now, cupped a hand to her ear.

"What's that?" she said. "Got to collect your thoughts? Shit, that won't take long."

Billy and I were over near the fireplace. He was still in the white robe and tennis sneakers he'd been wearing when I came in, mostly listening while I told him the whole story about Miles, from the beginning, going over some parts he already knew, all the way to Annie asking me before the press conference what I was going to do and me going back to the office and calling him on his hot-line number, telling him I needed a favor. He said on the phone, You got it. I said, I didn't tell you what the favor is, and Billy said, Sonofabitch, you're right.

Then I told him I needed to see him, it would be no problem for me to go out to Kennedy and catch the next Air West to Vegas. He told me it was easier for him to go get on his jet and fly to New York. Give his sweet girl a little change of scenery.

Now here he was, like he'd instant-messaged himself across the country.

Billy said, "We don't either one of us have to go back over the parts where you were warned this was going to happen, do we?"

I said, "Only if it makes you feel big and important kicking a man when he's down."

From the other side of the room Oretha said, "Uh-oh, now you been asked a question back." She sipped some white wine and then made a whoop-whoop noise, like a ship's alarm sounding. "Mayday, Mayday, monkey boy's got to think for hisself now."

Billy smiled in her direction. "I gotta tell you, this is one cute kid you hooked me up with."

"Oops," she said to the television. "No smart comeback written down on your little paper? Wait, I got it, Snap, why don't you pretend you're talkin' to one of your little hos?"

Oretha stood up, saying she needed more Butch Cassidy popcorn with the extra butter, that sometimes watching A.T.M. was more fun than one of those Harry Hobbit, Lord of the Secret Ring movies.

"Back to your situation," Billy said.

"I never leave it for long."

"You got two choices as I see it," he said. "One is, you just hang around on the sidelines until the end of the season, get the rest of your money, then officially become the playboy of the Western world you always saw yourself being." He tasted some of the espresso the room-service waiter had brought a few minutes ago. "But if that's the way you decide to go, you gotta get all the way out. And after you're all the way out, you stop watching pro football forever. Because there won't be a single game you'll watch the rest of your life doesn't make you sick."

Oretha came back in with her popcorn, kissed Billy, gave her ass a little shake for both of us as she walked back to the television.

Billy made a biting motion with his teeth.

"That's one option," I said. "What's the other?"

"No comment on the first?"

"You know you're right. I'd have to find myself another sport."

"Only in your mind, there ain't no other sport, and never has been, at least not since you were tearing up the playing fields for McNugget High."

"McBurney."

"Whatever."

I said, "I could buy an NBA team and bounce around like a cheerleader the way the guy in Dallas does."

"Or a baseball team," Billy said. "Isn't half that goddamn sport always for sale?"

"Now you're really depressing me."

"Okay, this is two: You go back to England, think of that gambling place you're running as finishing school, then when you're ready, you sell it, take that and what you're gonna get from Miles, and become my partner at my joint." He held up a thick finger. "And when I say partners, I mean you buy in."

"You mean it?"

It was the future neither one of us had ever discussed.

The one that would officially make me his kid in every way except blood. As big as Billy Grace was on blood. The old man always had his dream about me running the Hawks. Maybe this was Billy's tough-guy dream, finally on the table between us.

"No, I'm just being a cutup here," he said. "I just flew three thousand miles because I'm such an impulsive, romantic bastard. Of course I mean it, you dumb shit. Somewhere down the road, I was gonna have to decide whether to die running the place, which is not such an attractive option, frankly. Or sell it. Or leave it to Sabrina, the Teenage Witch."

His daughter, Jade.

"She's not a teenager anymore."

"Tell her that."

"Am I supposed to be the kind of limp-dick partner Dick Miles wants me to be?"

"What do you think?"

He poured himself more espresso. "Now, there is one more option."

"You said there were only two."

"What are you, the goddamn gaming commission?"

"Sorry."

He folded his arms in front of him, all business now. As if everything else had just been an opening act. I knew the body language, knew the look.

"Option three: You stay and fight. You fight behind enemy lines, which is where you are now, no matter how well-intentioned this asshole says he is, or how much he says he wants to win, or how much he keeps telling you the two of you are in this together. He's gonna lie about that because guys like Miles lie without knowing they're lying. And they don't think they mean anything by doing it. You know Arum's line, right?"

He meant Bob Arum, the boxing promoter, with whom we both went way back in Vegas. Arum got caught in some kind of lie once, and when the sportswriters called him on it, he shrugged and said, "Yesterday I was lying, today I'm telling the truth."

I told Billy, of course I knew Arum's line.

"It's Miles's way with the Hawks now, not yours. That's just the way it is. But that doesn't mean you can't still do some good for your team. So you show up, you sit in as many meetings as you can take, you pick your fights, knowing you're going to lose most of them but maybe not all of them. You understand?"

"Yeah."

"This you are going to do for yourself, your father, your team."

Going to do.

I said, "The first two options really weren't options, were they?"

"Not so's you'd notice," Billy Grace said.

We did room service in the suite after that. Billy and I told stories Oretha had heard before about the old days, she told a few about A.T.M. I'd never heard, we all laughed a lot. When we finished, I hugged Oretha first, then Billy, walked back to the Sherry, packed my stuff, checked out, took a cab up to Molloy Stadium, checked back into Suite 19.

10

Over the next two months, right up until the Falcons beat us, 31–13, for our fourth straight preseason loss, here was Dick Miles's version of not being like those other guys.

Meaning one of those rich guys who decided they had invented the two-deep zone as soon as they attended their first league meeting:

- He brought in the league's first dietary supplement coach as an assistant to Harm Battles, his hand-picked strength coach from the Fighting Irish.

   I'd finally met Battles my second morning back on the job, when I was in the weight room working out with a couple of the fat boys from the offensive line.

   Battles came bouncing in like a drum majorette, wearing a blue Hawks T-shirt and matching sweat-pants, about five-six, built like a Triple-A battery, hair buzzed down to his scalp. He called out greetings to Elvis and Butterball. Butterball greeted him back with a belch. Elvis ignored Harm Battles and continued flipping through some kind of soul-sister skin magazine while riding the room's one stationary bike, which looked like a tricycle underneath him.

Battles came over and stood next to where I was doing some arm curls with hand weights.

"Are you on any kind of program?" he asked.

I looked over my shoulder, as if he had to be talking to somebody else. "Me? On an actual conditioning program?"

"I meant a vitamin program." Harm pulling out a bottle with brightly colored pills that reminded me of Skittles.

"I assume those all check out with the chemists at the league," I said.

Battles shrugged and said, "You bet, dude!" and went over to chat with Butterball.

His assistant, the dietary supplement coach, was Hans Nowitzky, an East German until the Wall fell, one who had worked in the '70s and '80s with a squadron of East German athletes who (a) had won a ton of gold medals and (b) were all now permanently banned from international competition.

"What's his specialty?" I asked Elvis Elgin.

"Masking agents."

Hans Nowitzky spent most of our practices working on soccer-style field goals and showing off what I thought was a pretty good leg.

I asked him one day how he liked American football as opposed to, say, the 400 medley relay.

"Hans's swimmers," he said, "are never asking so many questions about is this really a B_{12} shot," and then put another one through the uprights from forty-two yards away.

• Brought in his new top accountant, Manny (Mandrake the Magician) Katzenberg, Miles saying just wait, Manny was going to turn himself into the salary cap wizard of the entire National Football League.

It didn't take me long to figure out what Manny's specialty was really going to be:

A second set of books.

Miles and I were on the field the day before the Falcons game, watching Bobby Bullard walk through a couple of new trick plays, when I pointed out to him that as loose as Wick Sanderson could be about some things, he tended to get pretty cranky about salary cap cheats.

"If Manny got caught," Miles said, "Manny wouldn't be with me."

• That same week, between our first and second pre-season games, Miles accepted the resignation of Brian Goldberg, making it a clean sweep of the three guys I'd trusted the most around the Hawks:

Pete. Josh. Brian.

The only ally in the front office I had left was Susan Burden, who after a lot of begging and groveling from me had allowed her notice to somehow get lost in the system, and set up shop outside my office as my new executive assistant.

Brian stopped by Suite 19 the night he officially announced he was on his way to Green Bay as Josh's assistant general manager, a big step toward becoming a real general manager someday. I could see right away there was no point in trying to talk him out of it, it was too big a shot for him, the chance to do it the way Pete Stanton had, prove that you didn't have to move up through the ranks as a personnel wonk if you wanted to run a team, you just needed passion and brains and something the old man used to describe with one of his favorite words, moxie.

"Plus," Brian said, "it gets less and less creatively challenging making sure the backup tight end calls the radio station on time."

"We both know your job description is a hell of a lot more than that around here."

"Yeah," he said, "I know, too. But it already feels like two jobs, remembering what I'm supposed to know and what I'm not supposed to do, spinning unspinnable stuff for the papers." He was pacing in the middle of the big room where we watched the games on Sunday. "You want to start drinking soon?"

I told him to get the ice, I'd get the bottle. He said he'd prefer to start with one of the Red Stripe beers from Jamaica I'd turned him onto, as a way of easing into getting as shitfaced as he planned.

"And that's not the worst part," he said. "The worst part is acting as if I like working for this guy."

I handed him a beer and he clicked it off my glass.

"You have to stay," he said. "I don't."

I asked him what made him so sure I was going to stay.

"Because we know that lost causes are your secret passion," he said. "Them and Hope and Crosby *Road* movies."

"Me and Miss Susan will be around until the last plane out of Saigon."

"Remember how they used to call the Yankees the Bronx Zoo in the bad old days?" Brian said.

"I grew up here, remember?"

"Well," he said, "technically we're in the Bronx, too."

• Miles replaced Brian with a kid who'd been overseeing p.r. for the whole Miles empire, Jeff Brewer. And it was clear from the day he moved into

Brian's old office, about three doors down from my new one, that he had a lot more responsibility than just football p.r., and more access to Dick Miles than anybody in the building.

Brewer was good-looking, still only thirty, wore expensive clothes he tried to make look casual, had long hair that looked messy every day but I figured required as much work as it did styling gel, drove a Jag, had one of those air filters installed in his office that sucked in the smoke from his imported Bolivar cigars, was about my size and built like a jock, had all the lines and all the moves, whether bullshitting with the players in the locker room or trying to charm every person in every room, male or female.

"I know all about Jack Molloy," he said when he came into my office and introduced himself. "I've always thought there should be a course guys like me should take on guys like you."

"You don't have to do all your sucking up at once," I said to Brewer. "If you know so much about me, you know I prefer to pace myself."

He ran a hand through his thicket of dark hair, gave me his secretary smile, and said, "I probably shouldn't tell you this. But some of my friends even call me Jammer."

- Dick Miles fired our defensive coordinator, Fred Burrell, after our second preseason loss, 51–42, to the Giants at Giants Stadium.

That was the first game Miles decided to watch from the sidelines, mostly standing at the thirty-yard line on the home side of the field, cheering the team on when something good happened, posing the rest of the time with his arms crossed, a move he'd apparently learned from his friend and role model Jerry Jones. He even put in a request with the league office to wear his own headset and microphone, but Wick Sanderson himself called back and informed Miles that there was a league rule prohibiting anybody but the coaches from communicating that way during games.

"I don't want to actually call plays," Miles said. "I just want to hear whether they're talking their X's and O's bullshit, or discussing some broad one of them met the night before."

Off the record, Wick Sanderson told me there wasn't an actual rule about owners and headsets on the books, but there should be, the way there should be one about keeping them up in their luxury boxes where they belonged.

"I can't stop these assholes from being down there," Sanderson said. "But I can sure as hell do everything in my power to stop them from playing dress-up."

So Miles didn't wear a headset during the Hawks–Giants game, but he did give television—and the next day's newspapers—a wonderful picture in the last minute of the first half. It was right after the Giants' quarterback, Malik-El Mathers, hit his Pro Bowl wide receiver, Alibay Rippman, for a seventy-two-yard touchdown pass.

It was here that Miles left his post at the thirty-yard line and went over to where Fred Burrell was watching the game and began gesturing wildly at him, as if he were a limo driver who'd been slow bringing the car around.

What only the players in the area could hear—and an enterprising soundman from NFL Films—was the following exchange:

Miles: "I know I'm new to this, so just tell me when these Soul Train dancers of yours actually start covering people—the regular season?"

Burrell: "This is the time of year when we try different shit out."

Miles: "This is the *Giants.* This is *New York.* You're embarrasing me in front of the *mayor.*"

Burrell: "This is the *preseason.* This is *New Jersey.* Which mayor are you talking about, the one from Moonachie?"

It is worth mentioning that Fred Burrell had been the toughest and meanest middle linebacker to come out of the Big Ten since Dick Butkus, and had ten ferocious seasons with the Chiefs until the steroids caught up with him and his teammates convinced him his penis was half the size it had been when he came into the league.

But anybody who had ever played with or for Fred Burrell—or just knew him the way I'd come to know him—was well aware he wouldn't take shit from a weapon of mass destruction.

On the sidelines that night, Miles concluded by saying, "Well, focus, goddammit!"

Burrell took off his headset at this point, grabbed the back of Dick Miles's blazer, pulled Miles's head down until his face was pretty close to what Fred swore was no longer an anabolically challenged penis, and said, "Focus on *this,* little man."

Miles fired him after the game and announced he was replacing him with Vance Hopewell, Jr., the coordinator Bobby Bullard had fired—and cuckolded—at Texas Tech.

"Women come and go," Bullard explained to the media the next day. "Football is forever. Football and some of those sex rashes you pick up."

- That same night, in the second half, we all watched our quarterback, Tucker O'Neill, scramble out of the pocket and foolishly try to dive for the last few yards that would have meant a first down, instead of folding up into the fetal position the way quarterbacks were taught, breaking his right arm and tearing up his shoulder in the process.

The next morning, while Tucker was still in surgery, Miles called and asked if I could come down to his office. Bobby Bullard and Jeff Brewer were already there.

Miles informed me that he'd put Borden Skiles on the Dick Jet even before the game was over last night, and that he was already flying back from Texas with Bullard's old Tech quarterback, Ty Moranis. And that Moranis would work out for us as soon as he landed.

"Ty Moranis?" I said, trying to keep my voice calm. "Doesn't he still have some obligations with the prison all-star team?"

Miles said, "He's been out more than a year, Jack. Did all his community service, too."

I started to say something, but Bobby Bullard cut me off. "I know what you're thinking, Jack. I know the boy's had more than his share of trouble. But he's always been like a son to me. And he still has an arm's as good as a gun."

"If I'm not mistaken," I said, "it's the only one he's ever actually had a permit for."

"He knows my system," Bullard said.

"About as well as he knows *the* system."

Ty Moranis had come out of Texas Tech ten years ago as the No. 1 pick in the NFL draft, and there wasn't a scout anywhere who didn't think he was going to be the greatest quarterback of them all. He was going to make everybody forget Elway's arm, Marino's release. When Michael Vick came along later, they compared his speed to the speed Ty Moranis had shown as a kid. He had been programmed to be a pro quarterback by his semicrazed father, Art Moranis, who'd briefly played for the Raiders before going off to kill enough Vietcong as a Green Beret that he was sure he'd made the John Wayne Hall of Fame. Art married late, but from the time Ty was old enough to hold a midget football in his right hand, his whole life was football. When the boy was a little older, the father basically sold him off into football the way parents of gymnasts sell off their undernourished dancing pixies to coaches from former Communist countries who are supposed to turn them into Olympians. It started with the private school with the best junior-high-level football team in southern California, even though the Moranises were living in Oakland at the time. Father and son had then moved to Austin, because Art had done some checking and found there was a coach at Austin High who was running the closest thing to a pro-style offense in the whole country. Ty flourished in it, even made the cover of *Sports Illustrated* his senior year. He just never found the time to have a real childhood around football camps in the summer, football season in the fall, the workouts with the quarterback coach Art had hired for him the rest of the year. But Ty went on to become an All-America as a freshman at Texas Tech, won the Heisman his junior year, decided to leave college early and become the No. 1 draft choice of the league and the Arizona Cardinals.

And somehow he managed to keep all the crazy anger he felt toward his father, all the resentment he had in him, relatively in check, until he got to the pros.

It was then that the Cardinals, and the five teams he would play for after that, found out about his fondness for booze, drugs, parties, hookers, busting up bars, high-speed chases. And guns.

Guns of all shapes, sizes, calibers.

Asked recently who his heroes were, the reporter from the *Arizona Republic* meaning his quarterback hero, Ty said, "Tupac. Biggie Smalls. Like that."

"Anybody living," the reporter said, "somebody like Eminem maybe?"

"Talk to me when he finally eats some lead, dog," Ty said.

He lasted two years in Arizona, until his interpretation of dunking the coach in Gatorade involved stuffing an empty bucket over the head of offensive coordinator Angie Loguidice with three minutes left in the first quarter of a Cardinals–Cowboys game because of a third-down play Angie had just sent in from the sidelines, a pass in the flat that had resulted in a Cowboys interception.

"Wasn't no different from his usual view of things," Ty said to the media. "Head up his own ass."

The Chargers picked him up on waivers, but let him go the week the regular season ended when a routine traffic stop in La Jolla after he'd run a red light resulted in the police finding an arsenal of automatic weapons underneath a blanket in the back of his Chevy Suburban.

He told the cops he'd gotten an anonymous tip about a possible home invasion at his condo in Carlsbad.

One of the cops said, "An invasion by who, North Korea?"

It was when he was with the Bears the season before last that he finally got himself real jail time, on the night when he decided to settle all his lingering grudges against Art Moranis once and for all. Ty got drunk at a strip club in San Francisco, drove over the Bay Bridge, and attempted to burn down Art's house in Oakland with Art sitting in his den, wearing his old Red Raiders warm-up and watching a tape of the Texas Tech–Miami national championship game in the Sugar Bowl from Ty's junior year on his big-screen Sony.

As Ty lit the gasoline trail leading to his father's front door, a neighbor heard him yell out, "Hey, Dad, did I mention that I really didn't want to leave my friends and move to fucking Austin?"

His lawyers invented a football-abuse defense, the first of its kind, and he was able to plead down from attempted murder to arson, finally doing eight months in Lompoc.

I actually remembered watching on CNN International when he was released from jail, and the correspondent waiting to interview him asked what he'd learned behind bars.

"Prison tats are cooler," Ty Moranis said.

At the time, everybody assumed he was finished with pro football, even though he was still just thirty-one years old, but every team in the league had stayed away from him.

Until now.

"We feel good about this," Bobby Bullard told me. "Ty's daddy's living in some undisclosed location in, like, Militiaville, Idaho. Or maybe it's Montana. We feel like that's gonna go a long way toward keepin' the boy's general shit in check."

I stood near the visitors' bench with the fat boys from the offensive line, Elvis, Butterball, Zeke Widger, and our 398-pound rookie from Ohio State, Sloppy Thurston, who Elvis said just didn't have the courage to admit to 400 yet.

"It's a variation of that AA deal you read about," Elvis said. "There's a lot of gravy between admittance and acceptance."

We were watching Ty Moranis loosen up his arm, soft-tossing to Sultan McCovey, the free agent wide receiver we'd signed away from the Cowboys after A.T.M. retired.

Elvis had just informed us that Sultan had announced in

the locker room that he wanted his name pronounced Sul-*tan*—like suntan—from now on.

"By the way," Butterball asked Elvis, "why do you guys have to jack around with your names the way you do?"

"You guys?" Elvis said, smiling.

"Dudes."

"Black dudes," Elvis said.

Butterball grunted. "Sometimes you spend more time on your names than you do gardening around with your hair."

Elvis kept smiling as Butterball said, "If you're not turning Sultan into Sul*tan,* you're pulling that Ahmad shit."

Now Elvis Elgin just laughed.

On the field, Moranis sent Sultan long, and threw one sixty yards on a line, dead-cold spiral, with a flick of his wrist, his arm coming forward in such a streak it was like the flash of a camera. Moranis wasn't wearing a helmet, just a Mets cap turned around on his head, Oakley sunglasses. There were so many tats on his arm, prison and otherwise, he seemed to be wearing a long-sleeved shirt of some kind of floral design.

I said to Elvis and the other fat boys, "You ever see anything go like that?"

Elvis said, "Yeah, baby, but I believe it was one of them spud missiles."

They stopped after about half an hour, the last throw of the day on a rollout, Moranis sprinting to his right, stopping right before he got to the sideline, not even getting his feet set before he threw one to Sultan in the corner of the end zone.

Sultan did one of his most popular touchdown dances, an elaborate three-step process that included a variation of the moonwalk Michael Jackson used to do when he still had a nose, going from that right into a backward somersault, finally dropping to one knee and throwing his arms out before pointing to Jesus.

Probably giving thanks for being a wide receiver instead of a leaper in the chorus.

Ty Moranis just nodded his head as if it were all strictly routine, then juked his shoulders from side to side as if listening to some kind of hip-hop. Maybe there'd been other players in the league who wanted to be black as much as he did. I just couldn't recall any offhand.

Bullard waved me over to where he and Moranis stood on the other side of the field.

"Touchdown Ty," Bullard said, "meet one of your new bosses, Mr. Jack Molloy."

When I put my hand out, Moranis leaned into me with something that was half hug and half chest bump.

"Dog," he said.

I always thought my response to that should be *Woof, woof.*

"It's like I told you, Jack," Bullard said. "There ain't ever been a chucker like this."

I said to Moranis, "I guess once you have the arm, you never lose it?"

He gave me a bored look and said, "Evidently."

"Well," I said, "I hope this works out for both of us."

"Dog," Moranis said, nodding again, as if that explained everything.

Then he turned to Bullard and said, "We need to go chill somewheres and get straight on the chips." Started bopping his head from side to side and said, "The cheese."

Now he juked off toward the runway down the field to his left, the fat boys joining him as if they were a rolling pocket, making it look as if Moranis were surrounded by all the New England states, the Mets cap all that I could see of him, still bopping to the beat.

"He's going to get something to eat?" I said.

"Chips and cheese are money in Ty's language," Bullard said.

"Dog," I said.

I had plans to meet Pete Stanton that night at The Last Good Year, a bar we both liked not far from his apartment, owned by an insane Yankee fan and all-around top New York guy named Joe Healey. When I ran into Annie at the late-afternoon press conference Jeff Brewer had pulled together to announce the signing of Ty Moranis to an incentive-laden one-year contract, I invited her to join us.

"Not as a date," she said.

"Agreed."

"We're no longer dating," she said. "Plus . . ."

"Plus what?"

"Nothing," she said. "We're not dating."

"I was sort of hoping that one of these days you might explain why," I said. "Now that I'm back from overseas."

We were in Suite 19, Annie having finished her work downstairs, including a one-on-one with Moranis that she said involved her asking probing questions about his troubled past, and him mostly grunting while he stared at her breasts.

"One of the reasons we're no longer dating," she said now, "is that you don't even *know* why we're no longer dating."

I said, "That's one of those girl traps you guys set. Just come by and have a sociable drink and let me whine about what a disaster this season is going to be."

"You mean now that you've got John Dillinger playing quarterback for the old blue?"

"Among other reasons."

"Okay," she said, "I'll come, but on one condition."

"Name it."

"Tell me the incentives in Ty's contract, I hear they're pretty funny."

I gave her what I knew:

- On top of his base salary of $500,000, he got an-
  other half-million at the end of the regular season

if he had not been officially charged with a crime, arrested for one, indicted, or convicted.

- Another half-million on top of that, also paid out at the end of the regular season, if he had not been found in violation of his parole or the league's drug policy. I told Annie that Bobby Bullard didn't seem overly concerned about the drug clause, saying, "Ol' Hans will handle that one."

At our postworkout meeting in Dick Miles's office, Moranis had turned to me during the conversation about drugs and said, "This include weed?"

I said, "The last time I checked, marijuana was still illegal."

Moranis had given me a sad look and said, "Don't you think that's, like, *sick*?"

- No public nudity of any kind.

Jeff Brewer had done a background check, and it turned out that one of Ty Moranis's favorite things when he got drunk enough was dancing on bars and taking all his clothes off.

- During games, he wasn't allowed to come within fifty feet of our new offensive coordinator, Phil Bondy, even though we all knew Bobby Bullard would be calling most of the plays.

The last one, I informed Annie, was actually Borden Skiles's idea.

"What's one more restraining order?" Skiles said. "My feeling is, better safe than sorry."

- Finally, I told Annie, the contract featured a more rigorous policy about firearms than you had at most airports. Which meant no guns in his apartment. No guns in the car. No guns on his person.

Moranis fought that one the hardest.

"Man, you don't understand," he said. "I *got* to pack."

I told him not to worry, the crime rate in New

York had kept going down while he was in the big house.

In Suite 19, Annie Kay looked over her notes and said, "What about hookers?"

I told her he was about to dig in on that one until I told him about a little place uptown I knew called Yum.

11

Pete Stanton called to say he was flying to Florida, a spur-of-the-moment thing, to see Pam, he didn't know how long he'd be away, or when he might be in touch, but for me to hang in there. When I got off with Pete, Susan Burden told me that Annie had called to say she couldn't make it either, she was tied up.

"And she asked me to clarify just one point," Susan said.

"Which one?"

Susan read it off her message pad. "She said to tell you not *that* kind of tied up, you poor repressed Catholic boy."

So that's how I ended up sitting by myself at the bar at The Last Good Year, sipping a Scotch, half-watching a Mets game on the television above me, listening to Eamonn, the bartender, bitch about a new round of antismoking ordinances, when she sat down next to me.

She being the one you always hope will take the empty seat next to you at the bar. Or to sit down in Seat 3B on the American to L.A. when you've just gotten yourself set up in 3A.

I turned my head and smiled at her. She smiled back, then ordered a white wine from Eamonn. I kept looking at her, because she clearly had it all over any baseball that had ever been played. She was no kid, maybe in her mid-thirties, maybe even what I'd always considered the real f-word, forty. But with her it didn't matter. Short black hair, but not too short. Dark eyes, dark, flawless skin, a few wrinkles around the eyes, tiny beauty mark to the right of her mouth. Loose summer sweater, pink, sleeves rolled up to her elbows. Short black skirt. Great legs. No jewelry of any kind, earrings, rings, watch, necklace.

Eamonn put a napkin down in front of her. She took a sip of her wine, gave him a dazzling smile, said "Perfect" to him, turned to me again, and said, "And good evening to you, Mr. Molloy."

I asked if I could have just one second, pointed to the sky the way Sultan did after a touchdown, said, "Thank you, God."

She smiled at me now, put out her hand, and said, "I'm Carey."

I shook her hand. "First name or last name?"

"First."

"Okay, then," I said. "So I'm already at first base with you."

"Not exactly," she said. She put out her hand. "Carey Nash. Pleased to meet you."

"The pleasure, Carey Nash, is all mine."

"I was hoping to find you here, as opposed to some of the alternatives," she said. "Because I have to say, for a well-known man-about-town, you don't show up at many places where the female help wears clothes."

"You can't fault a guy for liking order in his life."

She recrossed her legs, a move I thought should have been accompanied by a blast from the horn section, and took another sip of wine.

"I guess I'm saying that finding you didn't require a lot of surveillance."

I looked down and said, "Legwork is the key."

Carey said, "Isn't it, though?"

"Obviously this isn't a chance meeting in the night," I said. "Unless, on a much more optimistic note, you're stalking me."

"It isn't," she said. "A chance meeting. Not the stalking thing."

I said, "Then why don't we go into the back room and get a quiet table and then we can talk about whatever you want to talk about, and then I can talk about my growing midlife crisis."

"Sounds delightful."

"My midlife crisis?"

"A quiet table."

I put a ten on the counter for Eamonn and told him we were moving to the back. Carey and I walked through the front-room mob, the noise level growing exponentially as the place got more crowded, the early-dinner people now three-deep in front of Eamonn with the after-work people. I saw Myron Bolitar, a sports agent I knew, an investigative reporter named Peter Finley, who had his own *60 Minutes*– type show on HBO now, a couple of NYPD detectives, an anchorman from Channel 2 who'd just finished the six o'clock news, an actress from the new Office Depot commercials that I was fairly certain I had dated before I moved to Vegas. The Office Depot girl in deep conversation with the owner, Joe Healey, who must have thought he was going good with her, because he didn't even give Carey Nash a second look when we walked past him.

Little John, the little Scot who'd moved up to maître d' of the back room, showed us to my favorite table, the one Healey called Table 50, his personal homage to the old Stork Club and the table where Winchell and Runyon and the owner, Sherman Billingsley, used to hold court.

When Carey and I sat down, I said, "Why *are* you here?"

"Think of it as a fact-finding mission," she said, "to see if we might be able to help each other out."

"You first," I said, and drank more of my drink.

"I'm also here, out of the goodness of my heart, to warn you that you're in way over your head with Dick Miles, even though you probably don't think you are."

"And how you do you happen to know that?"

"I was in over my head with him once when I didn't think I was," she said. "At least until he fired me."

We had been there a couple of hours, occasionally ordering another appetizer instead of dinner, drinking our drinks, Carey saying she wanted to hear about me first, we'd get around to the Hawks later.

So I told her about how I'd always wanted to play for the Hawks, not run them, at least until I tore up my knee at UCLA. I told her about how I'd owned places like this, and fooled around in television, about Billy Grace and Vegas, and a lot of stuff that never made the papers about how I managed to hold on to the team that first season. She was a good listener, and kept asking the right questions to keep me talking.

But then, there'd never been a pretty woman I'd met in my life I didn't think was smarter than Sandra Day O'Connor.

Finally I said, "Which company of Miles's did you get fired from, by the way?"

"We'll get to that," she said. "Besides, my story's not nearly as colorful as yours."

"Yeah, that's me," I said. "A colorful guy."

"A guy having second thoughts."

I said, "And thirds."

"Our Dick can be very persuasive when he sees something he wants."

"You bet!" I said, trying to sound as peppy as Miles's. "It's right there in his book!"

"I was still around when he was writing it," Carey said. "He thought it was going to sell like *Tuesdays with Morrie*. I told him, only if he died in the end."

Table 50 was big enough to seat eight people, more than that if we pushed the chairs on the outside together. Carey and I were in the booth part, backs against the wall, facing the rest of the room. She had situated herself just close enough to me that every so often I could feel the brush of her leg against mine. Every time she did, it made me hotter than the time before.

But then, Annie had always said that the Gross National Product could make me hot.

Carey asked me how much Miles was around the office.

"Somehow he's around a lot and away a lot," I said, "as if he doesn't sleep."

"He thinks there should be some kind of medal you get for amount of time sleeping, lowest score wins. Like golf."

"But he sure is busy when he's around."

"Where does he go when he isn't around?"

"Only Karla, his assistant, knows for sure, and she doesn't talk."

Carey said, "Talking isn't one of Karla's specialties."

"You know Karla?"

"I've known a lot of Karlas," she said.

"You seem to know a lot, period."

She said, "I know something you should know: Nothing can ever be Dick's fault. He's fine when things are going good, takes all the credit and all the bows. But when they even start to go bad, he's like one of the rich guys dressing like a woman to get off the *Titanic*."

"Somebody else takes the fall."

"Not somebody, Jack. *You.* It's why he wants you around. You're one of his fallback positions if the regular season turns to shit like the preseason."

"You know this for a fact."

"I learned the hard way about Dick Miles," she said. "Now I could teach a course about him."

"And now you're warning me because . . . Tell me again why you're warning me?"

"Maybe I'm just a girl with a heart as big as all outdoors. Who thinks your game might be part of some bigger game for him."

She waved at Little John for two more drinks. Before I could ask her what bigger game, she said, "You're starting to wish you hadn't sold, aren't you?"

"I'm way out of the starting gate by now, believe me."

"I know this won't make you feel any better, but you're not the first. To sell something to Dick Miles and then want to unsell."

"Oh, he's got me, all right."

"By the balls, Jack. Doing what he does with just about everybody in his life, which means controlling them with money."

"I don't even have the money yet, that's the funny part."

"Except nobody's laughing," she said. "Are they?"

"This bigger game you mentioned," I said, "does it involve you?"

There was a cheer from the front room, and we both looked up at the television closest to us in the back, where a Met was circling the bases.

"It might," she said. "Indirectly."

"So you're not looking out for me as much as for yourself."

"I told you," she said, "there's a way we might be able to look out for each other."

She finally told me she'd started working for Miles at his cell phone company, You Talkin' To Me, moving out of marketing there and eventually fast-tracking her way to the job of vice president, corporate affairs, for MF, Inc., not too far down the corporate ladder from Miles and Francione. She said that Bill Francione used to call her their vice president in charge of vision. When I asked what happened after that to get her terminated, she gave me a light kiss on the cheek, told me all in due time, said she had to go to the ladies' room.

When she came back, she waved at Little John again, this time for a check.

"We're leaving?" I said. "There's still so much I don't know about you that you probably have no intention of telling me."

"You're too tense, Jack," she said. "We need to get you somewhere and relax."

When I grabbed for my check, she said it was on her, reached into her small black purse, pulled out a hundred-dollar bill, threw it on the table, then led the way toward the front door. Healey was at the waiters' stand at the end of the bar when I passed by there. I leaned over and said in a quiet voice, "If Annie happens to call or stop by . . ."

"You think I don't know the drill by now?" Joe Healey said, looking up at the television screen over the bar, which he'd had switched over to the Yankee game. "Who's Annie? And while we're on the subject, who the fuck are you?"

It turned out Carey had an apartment in a building one block east from Pete Stanton's, a two-bedroom on the thirty-fifth floor of 400 East Fifty-sixth, one that had a terrific view of the East River and a lot of neon lights over in Queens. She sat me down in the L-shaped living room and put on one of my favorite CDs, Carol Sloane singing duets with Clark Terry, making me think that Carey the mystery woman had even had me checked out for my taste in music.

When she came out of the kitchen, she was carrying a bottle of Moët & Chandon and two glasses.

"I should warn you," I said. "Mixing Scotch and champagne has a way of breaking down my inhibitions."

"Our research," she said, "indicates that you don't have any inhibitions, Jack." She handed me my glass and said, "Follow me."

We stood on her terrace and watched a tugboat move slowly north toward the 59th Street Bridge and listened to the big old city below us, at the same time listening to Carol Sloane through the door she'd left open.

I told her that it was time for her to start talking, even if

I wasn't always the greatest listener in the world, and had the fucking papers from the sale of the Hawks to prove it.

"I'm not so sure about that," Carey said. "The listening part, I mean. You've been telling me all night you didn't listen enough to your father, but you seem to remember everything he ever told you."

"I meant I should have listened better when he was still in the room."

Nobody said anything now. I stole a look at her in profile. She'd taken off her shoes and was still almost as tall as I was. "So what about you?" I said. "Where are you from?"

"Here," she said. "Born, raised, schooled, all the way through Columbia. Then Harvard Business. Actually started out in the casino business in Atlantic City, at least on the corporate side. Went with Trump Corp. for a while. Met Dick Miles at some fund-raiser one night at the Met. The rest is my own little personal corporate history."

"Romantic history?"

"One marriage," she said. "Other boys, before and after. Mostly good boys. Some bad ones. The bad ones were more fun." I got another smile. "Or at least much more interesting projects."

"Am I a project?"

She said, "Within a bigger project, maybe."

"Like a game within a game."

"Now you're starting to catch on."

"You think?"

Now she placed her champagne glass on the table behind us, took mine out of my hands, put her arms around my neck, gave me a long look with eyes that were black in the night, and kissed me.

After she kissed me again, she said, "Wait here."

She walked through the living room in the semidarkness and disappeared into what had to be her bedroom. I drank more champagne and tried to figure out where the old *Daily News* printing plant used to be across the river, down somewhere to my right.

A light went on behind me, at the end of her long couch, and when I turned around, there was Carey, the oversized New York Hawks T-shirt she was wearing barely covering an area Bubba had always called "America's real most wanted."

She came back through the terrace doors and said, "You don't have to worry about me, Jack. I'm a team player."

"Remember what the coaches say," I said. "There's no *I* in team."

She got close to my ear and said, "But there is *me*."

Then she started to work on the buttons of my blue shirt.

"Maybe we ought to go inside," I said.

"What in the world for?" Carey Nash said.

When I woke up in the morning, not sure where I was at first, I noticed she had left a copy of the *Post* at the end of her old four-poster bed.

I turned it over to read the back page first, and got popped between the eyes by one of their typically clever back-page headlines.

Which I probably would have found much more amusing if it didn't happen to be about me.

MILES TO MOLLOY:
YOU DON'T KNOW JACK

Underneath was a picture of Dick Miles and me shaking hands and smiling for the cameras at practice one day. The long caption underneath said that these were obviously happier days for both of us around the Hawks, now that Miles was privately blaming me for the mess the team was currently in, the player moves and bonuses I had signed off on last year, some aging players I was fighting him on releasing this year.

There was even the suggestion that it was me, not Miles, who'd encouraged Josh Blake to leave New York for the Green Bay job.

The article inside was written by their new Hawks beat reporter, a kid I'd seen around practice, Ken Verdi. But unless Verdi was one of the great computer hackers of modern times, he'd had inside help on this one, his big exclusive quoting one e-mail after another I'd sent Pete Stanton from London last season.

"The old man used to say all the time you only get so many chances to win," one of them said. "Fuck the salary cap."

That part was true, the old man did used to say that and I had told Pete to fuck the salary cap.

Pete was unavailable for comment, Verdi said.

So was Liz Bolton, our former team president.

I didn't think Pete would have talked to this asshole. Liz I wasn't so sure about; I'd have to give her a call in Hollywood later.

Miles was unavailable for comment, even though I knew most of the blind quotes in the article had to come from him or from Jeff Brewer, his version of Robin the Boy Wonder.

The article said that even though Miles, with his controlling interest, could do whatever the hell he pleased, he was trying to be respectful of me and the Molloy family by allowing me input on player personnel decisions, but that I had fought him on moving some aging players on both offense and defense, fought him on the firing of Fred Burrell.

All bullshit.

Down near the bottom, Verdi said that the *Post* had made repeated attempts to reach me the night before—it was a dodge I knew, waiting until the last minute to give the condemned man a chance to defend himself—but that I had been unavailable for comment.

I was sure there were probably voice mail messages on my office phone and at Suite 19. I didn't own a cell phone.

When I finished rereading the article, I slam-dunked the newspaper on the bed and said, "Sonofabitch."

"Are you talking about yourself," Carey said from the doorway, "or the new owner of the team?"

I looked at her, in a pale blue robe, hair wet from a shower, carrying two mugs of coffee, said to her, "Well, you were right."

"I just didn't expect to be right this soon." She came over and handed me my coffee and said, "Now you've got to get out there and defend your honor, and I've got a plane to catch."

"Where to?"

"Another fact-finding mission," she said. "One that might be productive for both of us."

"More mystery."

"Not for very much longer."

"You knew he was going to pull something like this."

"Are you kidding?" Carey leaned over, kissed me lightly on the forehead. "I was married to the sonofabitch."

12

I changed clothes when I got to Suite 19 about 8:30, remembered to check my messages before going downstairs to see if Dick Miles was in yet. Or Jeff Brewer. Or both. Borden Skiles, I knew, was on the West Coast, trying to steal the Clippers' new seven-five center from Mozambique, Cornelio Camus, away from David Falk or Scott Boras or one of the other superweasels.

There were three new messages on the machine, two of them from Ken Verdi, both saying the same thing, Verdi practically whispering that he needed to talk to me as soon as possible, to please call him back at the number at his office he gave me, or on his cell.

The other one was from Annie Kay, the machine's voice telling me that it had come in at 7:01 A.M.

"Did you see that rag . . . Wait a second. . . . Why aren't you picking up? . . . You better be in the shower, buster, or out running the stadium steps. . . . Because if you're not, then I cannot *believe* I was worried about you. . . . So here's my message: If you're not a slutball, meaning not a slutball *last night,* call me back."

When I arrived at Miles's office, Karla Thorpe informed me that her boss was in Hilton Head, at the annual two-day retreat he had for all his top managers, and she didn't even know if he'd be calling in for messages before tomorrow. She asked if I wanted to leave a message and I said, no, it could wait. She said, are you sure? Sure am, I said.

I thought about mentioning that I'd run into Carey, figuring that would get him out of whatever early-morning sensitivity session they were having down there. I also wanted to see what reaction that would get out of Miss Karla. But I decided against it, figuring it was a card I could play later, if I wanted to play it at all.

"Do you happen to know if Jeff's in?" I said.

"Mr. Jeff, he likes to beat the coaches in."

Jeff Brewer didn't have a secretary; he thought it made him look more regular, like just another drone. He kept his door open most of the time—unless he was smoking one of his Cubans—and answered his own phone.

He told just about everybody that he answered his own phone, as if the rest of us would find that fascinating.

Like his boss hating fucking ties.

When I walked into his office now, he was facing stage right, waving both hands in the air, like a ref signaling for an incomplete pass, and saying into the little microphone attached to his headset, "Uh-uh, Gil. Not playing. Not responding to your theory. In fact, I'm flattering it by calling it a theory instead of the load of crap that it is. Nothing for me there. We had nothing to do with this."

You couldn't see the headset in his hair. If the microphone had been on the other side of his head, it would have looked as if he were talking to himself.

"Huh-loooo," he said. "What part of 'we had nothing to do with this' is tripping you up here?"

I said, "I need to talk to you. Now."

Brewer turned, saw me on the other side of his desk. He put up one finger. "Gil, for the last time, you're on the wrong path here." Nodded. "Trust me.

"Hey, Jammer—"

"Point number one," I said, still standing. "Don't call me Jammer. My friends call me Jammer."

"Sorry, Jack—"

"Point number two," I said. "If you and your boss ever try anything like this shit in the *Post* again, I will knock you on your ass."

Jeff Brewer, in his white shirt and khaki slacks and scuffed penny loafers, got up from behind his desk, left plenty of space between us as he walked across the room and shut his door.

"Wait, what about the famous open-door policy?" I said.

Brewer said, "I don't want everybody to think recess has started early." He went over to the coffeemaker set on a table underneath his high-definition television screen, poured himself some, gestured at me with his mug. I shook my head.

When he sat back down, I said, "I'm here to clear something up, kid. If you lined up everybody you know, the very last one you'd want to fuck with this way is me."

"I didn't do this, Jack. Dick didn't do this."

"Really."

"Call Ken Verdi if you want. Ask him if it came from us. He'll tell you that the first time he's talked to me all week is when I called him at six-thirty this morning, as soon as I read the piece. And if he's being truthful, he'll tell you that I read him the riot act because he *didn't* call me before he went with it."

"Ass-Covering 101," I said.

"My job is to cover everybody's ass here. Including yours."

He ran an agitated hand through his messy-cool hair, like some move he'd learned watching Hugh Grant movies.

"I was told by somebody close to Dick," I said, "that accountability isn't one of his strong suits when things start turning to sludge."

"We're all accountable here," Brewer said. "Because we're all on the same team."

"One that certainly has a lot of unnamed sources on it."

"And I'm going to find out who they are, don't worry," he said.

"Your boss see the story online? Or did Verdi give it to him last night so he could proofread it before the copy editors got their hands on it?"

"I e-mailed it to him first thing. I don't know whether he received it yet or not. He's in Hilton Head, you know—"

"Retreating."

"It's the same weekend every year, Jack."

I said, "Let me ask you something: A one-day shitstorm like this, one that will lead every sportscast in town tonight and be on the goddamn radio all day—what's really in it for you guys?"

"Nothing," he said. "Because we had nothing to do with it."

"Is it that important to deflect attention away from the way the team has been playing?"

"Jack, for the last time, I know my limitations. I don't have the game to outhustle you. I'm out of my weight class, okay? I was talking about that with Annie last night."

He came at me with it like it was nothing more than a throwaway line, then sipped some of his coffee.

"Were you?" I said.

"Now hold on, okay? We were having an innocent drink after I got her a few minutes with Ty after this appearance he had to do at the ESPN Zone for their magazine. He's on next week's cover, you know."

"Be still my heart."

"We walked over a couple of blocks and had a drink at the Algonquin."

"Work-related, of course."

"I'm trying to get to know the people I'm going to *need*

to know," he said. "And Annie Kay of *The NFL Today* certainly falls into that category."

"Sometimes," I said, "I feel like she defies category. Right now, for instance."

"Anyway, are you surprised that part of the conversation was about you? For most people, you're still as much the face of the organization as anybody."

"Let me ask you another question, Jeff: You think any of this bullshit is actually working with me?"

"I want to work with you, Jack. Not against you."

"Right," I said.

We sat there smiling at each other.

Finally, I said, "I used to work for Billy Grace."

Brewer said that, hell, everybody knew that.

"And since my old man died," I said, "he's sort of become like a second dad to me. The way I imagine Dick Miles is with you."

"And your point being?" Brewer said, still smiling at me, like I was a cute secretary who was supposed to go all weak at the knees.

I was over at the door by now.

"My dad can beat up your dad," I said.

I went back to my office, and when Miss Susan Burden came back from the ladies' room I asked her to find out everything she could, as soon as she could, about Carey Nash Miles. Do that bad, Google.com thing she liked to do on her desktop.

"The most recent ex," she said. "Former top manager for him and all-around up-and-comer. Very pretty."

"You've met her?"

"A name, and a face, from the gossip columns, nothing more," she said. "Can I ask why you're suddenly so interested in her?"

"I ran into her last night."

"I see," she said, giving me one of those Mona Lisa half-smile looks they all like to use on you when they know they've nailed you on something but don't want to come right out and say it.

"No, you don't see, actually. I ran into her at The Last Good Year, is all."

"I see," she said again, and went to start tap-tap-tapping away on her computer.

I waited until ten-thirty, New York time, to call Billy Grace, trying to get him before he and Oretha went out for their power walk on the back nine at God's Acre, knowing the two of them liked to get their hour in before the first golfers on Billy's course made the turn.

He picked up himself, first ring. I got right to it, asking him to find out if some top-secret business thing might be going on with Dick Miles. I told Billy I couldn't see it, him laying out big change on something else, knowing the kind of payout he had to make to the twins and me after the season. But maybe, I said, Billy could ask around anyway, dig up something that hadn't been reported yet on one of those ticker channels.

"Ask some of your banker pals," I said. "Bankers love you, right?"

"Yeah, they love me for myself," he said in a low voice, so Oretha couldn't hear, "like the girls around here used to." Then: "Can I ask why you are interested in a matter such as this?"

I told him what Carey Nash had said about a game within a game.

"Jesus, please tell me you're not popping Miles's wife."

"Ex-wife."

"Jammer," he said with a loud sigh. "Once a wife, always a wife."

He said he'd call when he got something, if there was anything to get.

I had already told Susan that if any of my friends in the media called wanting a reaction to the *Post* article, to tell them I was in meetings all day.

"And you," she'd said, "usually the outgoing one."

I thought about tracking down Mo Jiggy on the road, because not only did he have as much common sense as anybody I knew, including Billy, he could also do this: Take whatever problems you thought you had, analyze them in a motherfucker- and cocksucker-laced way, make fun of them with all the shuck and jive-ass he had in him, and finally make them small enough to either laugh at or just flush.

I sat there instead in the new office that was so much roomier than the old one. Even though I liked the old office just fine. The office I had when I was the one running the Hawks. When I was the one doing sleight-of-hand in the media.

Before I turned into a brand-new character:

Jackass Molloy.

Wondering how I could even figure out a bigger game with Dick Miles, if there was such a thing, when I couldn't even hold my own in the one currently being played around the Hawks.

Wondering about ex-wives and ex-girlfriends and young Jammers and exclusives about me in the *New York Post.*

Sitting there drinking another coffee that I didn't need and smoking a cigarette I certainly didn't need and really wondering this:

How much worse things might get around here when the real season started for the New York Hawks.

Not knowing at the time that I'd be wrong about that, the start of the season, the way I'd been wrong about just about every other fucking thing so far.

On account of this, as Billy Grace would say.

On account of Dick Miles's Hawks were about to start out 4–0.

13

I was watching Bobby Bullard roll up the score on the Patriots as if he were back with the Texas Tech Red Raiders, back in the days when he would keep the starters in against some weak-sister team from Deliverance State, trying to make some early-season statement to the pollsters that he had the biggest and baddest college football team in the land.

It was 41–13 for the Hawks with just over four minutes to go, and the Patriots had just turned it over to us on downs at their forty-eight yard line. It seemed like a perfect spot for our backup second-year quarterback from the University of Hawaii, Don Lo Malufalu, known to his teammates as Down Low. Bullard, I thought, could give Down Low a few snaps and some valuable game experience on the chance that Ty Moranis got hurt sometime before the end of the season, or, more likely, ended up back behind bars.

Except when our offense came back on the field, here came Ty and Sultan McCovey and Bobby Camby and the rest of the first-stringers. And on first down, when we should have been running the ball and running some clock, here was Ty throwing one over the middle to Sultan for fifteen yards, Sultan miraculously holding on to the ball after the Patriots' safeties, Acie Dobbs and Caldwell Barker, put simultaneous wrecking-ball hits on him, Dobbs coming from behind him and Caldwell Barker from the side.

"Yo, that's the ticket," A.T.M. said from the theater seat next to me in Suite 19. "Hang it up over the middle so the free and strong can take out they issues on the boy's bony ass."

Sultan, we both saw, was still down on the field, being attended to by a couple of our trainers, plus Harm Battles and Hans Nowitzky, Hans making Sultan take a swig of something pink from the plastic bottle he produced from his Hawks windbreaker as soon as they got him into a sitting position.

A.T.M. said, "Bobby Bull still puttin' it down on the over-under?"

"Looks like," I said. "But I don't see why he'd have to, with the money Miles is paying him."

"Yeah," A.T.M. said, "considerations like that certainly slowed down Bubba's bookie cravings in the old days."

Behind us, from the living room area of the suite, another cheer came from the friends A.T.M. had asked if he could bring with him from Yum for the game: Kristi, Kammi, Emerald, and two other precious stones I'd forgotten since they'd all shown up for the four o'clock game at about one and immediately began drinking mimosas. Once they'd lost interest in Hawks vs. Patriots, something that happened after it was 35–6 for us at halftime, they'd announced they could do a much better job leading cheers than what they called skanks and what the organization called the Hawk Girls. Ever since, the girls of Suite 19 had been doing their own pretty nifty combination of lap dancing and push-em-back, push-em-way-back cheers for an audience that included Commissioner Wick Sanderson, the new weekend anchor of the *NBC Nightly News,* the sales manager from our flagship radio station, WNUT, and our injured quarterback Tucker O'Neill, who'd gotten divorced while I was in London and apparently put his whole Jesus deal on hold.

The commissioner was willing to let his hair down a little because:

a. he'd just concluded a difficult and protracted collective bargaining agreement with the NFL Players Association; and

b. his sweetie, Carole Sandusky, was out in Los Angeles for "work," Sanderson making little brackets with his fingers around "work."

"I, uh, thought she'd retired from the business," I said to Wick Sanderson.

"No, not that kind of work," he said. "Just the annual tune-up on her breasts."

At the moment, Emerald was on the commissioner's lap, making his head disappear between amazing breasts of her own as she made a motion that reminded me of a ref signaling for delay of game.

Just to be on the safe side, I went over and made sure the door to the suite was double-locked, came back to where I was sitting with A.T.M. just in time to see Ty Moranis sell a beautiful play fake to Bobby Camby and then throw one down the sideline to our veteran fullback Redford Newman, Newman running into the end zone untouched and giving Moranis his fifth touchdown pass of the game.

Redford Newman was cool about everything; he was one of the few guys left who didn't think scoring a touchdown meant getting in touch with your inner Four Top.

The problem was Ty Moranis.

While Redford was handing the ball to the back judge, Moranis was running in front of the Patriots bench as if carrying some kind of automatic weapon on his hip, machine-gunning the players and coaches closest to him on the sideline, one by one.

A.T.M. said, "Aw shit, baby, that's not what we're lookin' for," just as about half the Patriot team rushed Moranis, causing the Hawks to come running from the home side of the field, and creating a scene that looked exactly like hooligan time at English soccer.

I noticed that Wick Sanderson had somehow disengaged from Emerald's T-shirt and was standing behind A.T.M. and me.

"Well, fuck," he said, straightening his glasses with one hand and his rep tie with the other. "There goes the postgame party with the girls."

It took half an hour of real time to separate the players, then have the lead official read the names of the ones who'd been ejected from the last two minutes and twenty seconds of a game we ended up winning 55–13, our last touchdown an interception return by our free safety, Nike Evans.

Before I stopped by the locker room, I stood in back of the interview room and watched Bobby Bullard aw-shucks and hot-damn and whoa-pards his way through his postgame press conference, mostly fielding questions about why he'd had the Hawks run it up on the Patriots.

Bullard kept acting surprised anybody not wearing panties could think that way.

"Aw hell, all those boys of ours did was put an old-fashioned speed limit on 'em," Bullard said. "But now you boys—and ladies—are actin' as if we put a turd in the damn punch bowl."

Gil Spencer raised a hand.

"But you have to admit that if you don't throw the last touchdown pass, then Ty can't put their faces in it that way," Spencer said. "Then there's no brawl."

Bullard said, "Hell, Gil, that weren't no brawl." He grinned. "The sides got to be even for a brawl. And how can the sides be even when the other side can't even give us a damn *game*?"

"Comments like that," Ken Verdi said, "and games like today aren't going to make you very popular with your fellow coaches."

Another grin from Bobby Bull. "The opinions of my fellow coaches," he said, "matter about as much to me as the ones used to come out the smart mouths of my ex-wives."

Jeff Brewer turned Bobby's mike off at that point, so there'd be some debate afterward whether Bullard actually muttered, "They's nothing but bitches, anyways," as he stepped down from the podium.

When I got to the locker room, the consensus on the fight was that our fat boys were better than theirs.

Butterball said, "It wouldn't've been anything more than hugging and farting if Ty would've just stopped carrying on like he was having some kind of epi-lectric seizure."

"Have to say, though," Elvis said from the locker next to him, "even I didn't know there was that many variations of fag out there."

Zeke Widger said, "Twenty years of organized ball, I thought I'd heard them all—least until Ty got going today."

Elvis said, "I still say he made up 'cross-eater.'"

Butterball said, "Then, after he run out of homo names, he just starts talking all his white smack-rap and threatening to blow away their nickel defense."

I said, "I thought he was off guns."

Elvis said, "Yeah, them and pussy."

I said to the fat boys, "Is he really as good as he's looked so far?"

Ty Moranis already had one thousand passing yards, fourteen touchdown passes, just two interceptions, and had even run for two touchdowns.

"Playing like he was s'posed to," Elvis Elgin said, "'fore he turned into Rambo."

On the other side of the room, Dick Miles was practically sprinting from locker to locker, high-fiving everybody in sight. When he saw me with the fat boys, he waved me over.

•

"How 'bout them Hawks!" he said, turning his voice cornpone the way he did any time Bullard was in the general vicinity. "Didn't I tell you we'd be there when the damn bell rang?"

"Is that what you told me?" I said.

"Bet your ass," he said. "Four-and-oh, partner. And this was supposed to be the hard-on part of our schedule. Wasn't it?"

I said that's what the experts in the media had said and, golly, they were never wrong, were they?

"C'mon, admit it, Jack," he said. "I'm not the football-challenged dink you thought I was going to be."

"It's a long season," I said.

"Christ-o-mighty, Jack," Dick Miles said. "You sound like a fucking sportswriter."

Then he laughed and gave me one of those open-handed shots to the back, like I was a soft-drink machine he couldn't get to work. Like we were buddies again. And as far as most of the media guys watching us were concerned, that's exactly what we were. Miles had spent enough time convincing them that we'd kissed and made up the day the story in the *Post* had appeared; formed what A.T.M. described as a "separation peace," as if that was somehow tied in with the separation he used to create with cornerbacks coming off the line of scrimmage.

When Miles had come back from hugging corporate vice chairmen and comptrollers and beating tom-toms in Hilton Head, done the touchy-feely Andrew Weil routine he endorsed in his books, he flew back to New York and came straight to the stadium without even stopping at the apartment he kept at the Waldorf, the one that used to belong to Sinatra when he was in town.

Blew Susan Burden a kiss as he walked past her, walked into my office, and said, "I didn't do it, get over it."

I said, "If you didn't do it, Jeff your loyal golden retriever did."

"Nope. Not our style."

Arms crossed in the middle of the room. Toy general.

"Not what I heard," I said. "About your style. Or lack thereof."

"You heard wrong, then. You want me to call a press conference and deny it, I will. You want me to take out an ad in the papers, you got it. Just tell me what I have to do to get us past this."

I said, "Let it go. You've done more than enough already."

"I'll find out who the leak is."

"How about we just do this," I said. "How about we just continue to build our relationship on a lack of trust?" Trying to smile my way through the bullshit the way the old man had taught me. The way I always had in Vegas.

Big Tim Molloy used to say that you always saved your best fuck-you smile for the biggest prick in the room.

That day in the office, Miles said, "You're going to learn to love me, Jack. Everybody does eventually, they can't help themselves."

In the locker room now, he went over to the area I'd just left, where all the fat boys were, and said in a loud voice, "Phil Simms said on TV you ate up their front four like it was a rib-eating contest!"

I wandered through the locker room and then down the hall to where Bobby Bullard's office was, found the coach sitting with his chair tipped back, lucky cowboy boots, ones that looked soft as slippers, up on his desk, Hawks visor still on his head, drinking a Budweiser out of a bottle. Borden Skiles was in a chair to Bullard's right, flipping through the game stats as if there were a profit margin in there someplace. Or a treasure map.

Bullard looked up at me and said, "Where's all them New York football experts said Bobby Bull was in over his damn head?"

Without looking up from his reading, Borden Skiles said, "Getting ready to run you for mayor, I imagine. Like all the other front-runners"—now he looked up over his rimless reading glasses, directly at me—"who didn't think you were worthy of coaching the New York Hawks."

"Hey, Borden," I said. "Everything okay in Four Percent Land?"

Four percent was his standard cut.

"Jack," he said.

I said to Bobby Bullard, "We stayed kind of long with the first unit in a game we were winning by nine thousand points, wouldn't you say, Coach?"

Bullard gave me an absolutely brilliant fuck-you smile of his own, his teeth looking so white I thought he must be using that new miracle paint. "You're not tellin' me how to coach my unbeaten damn team, are you, Jack?"

"We're only at the quarter pole," I said. "With, and you should pardon the expression, a loose cannon at quarterback. The longer you leave him in there to rub their faces in it, the more there's a chance some defensive end more hopped up than Harm Battles is going to clean his clock for sport."

"I train my horses to run the whole race," Bullard said. "You got a problem with that, take it to the big boss."

Borden Skiles said, "You knew what you were getting."

"Yeah," I said on my way out the door. "Bet the Over Bullard."

This time, I didn't leave the coach laughing.

I shook a few more hands in the locker room on my way back through, noticed that Ty Moranis's clothes were already gone from his locker, walked out onto the field to see if Annie, sent over by CBS to work the sidelines that day, might be doing some kind of stand-up for the new late-night highlight show the network aired on Sunday nights in what was Letterman's time slot during the week.

Annie and I hadn't spoken since I'd yelled at her on the phone about hanging around with Jeff Brewer. She'd called it yelling, by the way. I just called it making a point.

She took what I considered to be good, constructive criticism as well as most women I'd known in my life.

Which meant she reacted as if I'd told her she was putting on weight.

"You're acting as if I slept with the enemy," she said. "All I had was a drink."

"That's how it started with us, wasn't it?"

"What's *that* supposed to mean?" she said.

"Withdraw the question."

Annie said, "Too late, the jury already heard it."

"You can't possibly like that guy," I said.

"Just because he works for Miles doesn't mean he wants to grow up to *be* Miles."

"You're right," I said. "That's because he wants to grow up to be *me*."

"That's really the problem, isn't it?" Annie said. "You can't stand a guy who wants to be just like you."

"Thank you, Dr. Laura."

"It was a drink, Jack. Not a date. Not that you have the right to tell me who to date."

"Do you *want* to date the right-hand guy of the guy you hate me for selling to?"

"None of your business."

"Fine," I said.

"Fine!" she said.

Both of us hot now.

It was hard to tell which one of us slammed down the phone first, but I hadn't heard from her since, and hadn't tried to call her myself.

And I hadn't heard from Carey Nash Miles for three weeks. The only contact with her I'd had since leaving her apartment that morning was a phone message on my machine in Suite 19, saying she was in Los Angeles checking into some things, it would probably take some time, she'd be in touch when she had something more concrete to tell me about.

If I really needed to reach her, she said, I could send her

an e-mail at the AOL address she left instead of a phone number.

Maybe this was a good thing, the two of us not talking; our relationship might last for years.

Billy Grace said his guys hadn't turned up anything in Miles's holdings worth sticking a red flag up anybody's ass, as he put it. But, he said, fishing expeditions like this took time, whether it was the league doing the checking or him, you have to keep putting your rod out in the water and stay patient.

"You hate fishing, and have no patience," I said.

"The shit I do," he said, "for them that I love."

So far, I hadn't noticed anything unusual in the way Miles and Brewer were conducting the day-to-day business of the Hawks, even with Borden Skiles and Bobby Bullard having the run of the place. The only real off-the-field headline had come when our rookie defensive end, Moombasa Basie, had been handed down a four-game drug suspension, for what he swore was over-the-counter allergy medicine and not something on the banned-substance list. As soon as we got word from the league office, I went down to the trainers' room looking for Harm Battles and Hans Nowitzky.

"What did you give Moombasa?" I said to Harm Battles, whose eyes were blinking so rapidly I thought he might be trying to send a message to Hans in Morse code.

"Hans does the defense," he said. "I'm an offensive guy."

When I looked at Hans, he just said, "Hans is FDA approved now."

"Then how did Moombasa get clipped?"

"Ask Moombasa's big-tits girl from The Vitamin Shoppe how he is getting clipped," Hans said. He walked away, talking to himself. "She know everything about Moombasa's big unit, why you are not asking her how come it isn't peeing so good in the bottle all the times."

I turned to Harm Battles then and said, "One more positive test, for anybody, and I'm gonna have the fat boys talk to you."

Battles said, "No disrespect, dude? But how do you think they got so fat?"

The only new front-office business was Miles's tearing up Ty Moranis's contract after we won our first three games.

The incentive clauses, the ones about guns and drugs and restraining orders and any parole violations, all stayed the same; Miles basically just added a three-million-dollar signing bonus to them like a cherry on top of a sundae.

I asked Miles how we were able to manage that, since you weren't supposed to add salary to an existing contract during the season unless you got an injury exception. He said Manny Katzenberg had handled it. I asked how he'd handled it, and Miles said, "Got some guys to defer some shit, that it was for the good of the team." I asked which guys, and he said that Manny and Borden Skiles had worked it out with the three free-agent linebackers we'd added to our 3-4 defense, all of whom were Skiles's clients.

This had been on Friday, before the Patriots game. I said, "You're trusting Mandrake the Magician and a thief like Skiles to manage our salary cap? What, you couldn't get any of the guys from WorldCom?"

Miles said, Christ-o-mighty, I should lighten up, we were a lock to be 4–0 by the time we handled the Patriots, the fucking Patriots couldn't beat Cornell.

Now we were 4–0. And I was the latest guy, but not the last, to be reminded that winning, especially in sports, seemed to put a bow around everything. Especially winning in the National Football League, only the biggest game going. One that had gotten bigger while I'd been away, the way the fat boys in the line had. More coverage on television, more coverage on the Internet. A whole new channel, like The Golf Channel, devoted solely to the NFL. There were more columns, more information everywhere on how to bet, in the papers, on your computer, with 800 numbers, handicapping next Sunday's games like some kind of wall-to-wall football *Racing Form.* I had read somewhere that one hundred million dollars had been bet on the last Super

Bowl game. That meant bet *legally.* The amount that had gone through bookies was probably big enough to buy Beverly Hills.

Nobody really gave a rat's ass about how many 9–7 teams there were, about all the parity in the league, that was just space-filling and hand-wringing from sportswriters, something more for all the screamers on the TV and radio talk shows to act indignant about. Most fans just came to Sunday afternoon looking for what Dick Miles had come to me for in the first place:

Action.

Same old same old.

High-speed video-game action on the field as everybody kept getting not just bigger, but faster. Action with the Vegas books and with your friendly neighborhood bookie and even in your office pool. You couldn't even follow the puck in hockey. Try staying awake for one of those four-hour baseball games that sometimes had about as much action as an empty Senate floor on C-SPAN. The NBA? More and more it had become three six-eight guys standing over there while the two six-eight guys over there ran another pick-and-roll. All the other sports seemed to be playing about two hundred games a night and our games were still on Sunday, one on Monday night. Everybody else had seasons that seemed to go on forever. We didn't even take five full months from the first game of the regular season until the Super Bowl. You got the idea sometimes that people were more interested in watching football pregame shows in October than they were in watching this year's Cuban sensation pitch to the new guy from Japan in the World Series.

My friend Charlie Stoddard, a pitcher who'd made a big comeback with the Red Sox the year before, told me one night at The Last Good Year that I'd never properly appreciated the nuances of baseball.

"Here's the nuances of baseball," I said to him. "Another pitching change."

I cooked myself some pasta, poured some Rao's marinara sauce all over it, opened a bottle of red wine, made a more serious pass through the Sunday *Times* than I had in the morning, watched *Alias* to see if Jennifer Garner's lips had gotten even poutier from last week's episode and if she was wearing any new skintight secret-agent outfits, then turned on the second half of the ESPN Sunday-night game between Seattle and the Giants, listening to Joe Theismann, whom I used to take care of in Vegas, analyze everything except the mouthpiece hanging from the quarterbacks' helmets.

And wondering this all of a sudden:

Did I really want the Hawks to win now that Miles was the one calling the shots?

Or did I want them to somehow go into the shitter the rest of the way because that would give me a better chance of getting them back, even if I had no plan about how to do that?

Real question being this:

By rooting for my team, the way I had my whole stupid life, was I rooting against myself?

I was pondering all that when my phone made its chirp noise a few minutes after eleven.

At first I couldn't hear a voice at the other end of what sounded like a cell call from outer space.

I was about to hang up and wait for whoever it was to call back, the way they always did, when I heard Elvis Elgin, apparently trying to keep his voice low even over the snap-crackle-pop, say, "Boss, you better get your ass down here *now.*"

"Down where?"

"Hundred-and-sixteen and Third," he said. "Behind that new dance club we all go to? Be A Wolf? South side of one-sixteen I'm talkin' about. Walk through the alley next to the club. We're back there in the basketball court they built, underneath one of them bubbles. It's like their version of the VIP Room at House of Blues."

"Elvis," I said, "you know how much I love you. But what's going on at Beowulf—"

"*Be* A Wolf."

"—that requires me coming down to the new Cotton Club at this time of night?"

He said, "Understand, I tried to talk Ty and them out of it."

"Out of what?"

"Once the Patriots showed up to the club, I mean."

"Elvis," I said, starting to get exasperated. "Talk Ty and the Patriots out of *what*?"

"Gunfight at the O.K. Corral, I guess that's one way you could look at it," Elvis Elgin said.

PART THREE

Bet the Dog

14

Little Ray and Sideman were the two top lieutenants from Elvis's posse, which meant they got to sit in the front seat of his new Hummer 2. They were waiting for me at the door to the indoor basketball court behind Be A Wolf. And even from the outside, I could see it really did have one of those white-bubble tops like you got with indoor tennis courts around the city, or the practice field we'd built in one of the parking lots at Molloy Stadium, for when we had to move inside because of bad weather.

Little Ray was wearing an orange, No. 99 Warren Sapp jersey that went down to his knees. I couldn't see the gun I knew was underneath the jersey somewhere—Little Ray always had a gun on him somewhere. It was harder to tell with Sideman, who was tall and ripped and wore his T-shirts and jeans so tight I assumed the only place he could be carrying was in his unlaced, kick-ass Timberland boots.

As Little Ray walked me in, I asked him what Elvis had meant by Gunfight at the O.K. Corral.

He said, "You know the kind of standoff you get on the

field, one brother in a diss-down with another? We got a situation like that there going, just with live ammo."

"I don't suppose anybody has called the cops."

Little Ray and Sideman both laughed. "Good one, Jack," Sideman said.

I said to them, "Don't let anybody else in, okay?"

Little Ray said, "Are you shittin'? Nobody in they right mind *wants* to get in."

"So what's Elvis doing here?"

Little Ray raised his shoulders underneath the Sapp jersey, dropped them theatrically. "Man never stops protectin' his quarterback."

Inside, I discovered a full basketball court, with buffed hardwood, free-throw lane, pro-length three-point arc, the whole deal, even a wolf logo painted into the center-jump circle at midcourt. Across the way was a scoreboard, dark right now, up above what appeared to be a disc jockey stand with giant speakers at each end of it, presumably for the postgame party and dance contest. Next to the disc jockey stand was a small bar area, also dark. It occurred to me that I had read something about this place once, maybe in *Sports Illustrated,* about how the rappers and hip-hoppers and homeboys, all of whom thought they could have been Kobe or Iverson or McGrady if given half a chance, would slip back here with their VIP cards and have pickup games in front of the shimmy bar girls who came with them to watch, especially if there were some celebrities in the game.

But right now there was no basketball being played behind Be A Wolf, just Ty Moranis in his Eminem wool ski cap and two of his buddies in their caps, the two slit-eyed buds both wearing Moranis No. 13 Hawk jerseys—maybe as part of a dress code—underneath oversized windbreakers, unzipped and open in the front. Ty was bare-chested underneath a satin Snoop Dogg windbreaker of his own, filling out his outfit with carpenter's pants and his own unlaced Timberlands.

Facing them at the other end of the court, spread out

across the three-point line, were three members of the Patriots' secondary who had clearly not taken the team plane back to Boston: free safety Acie Dobbs, strong safety Caldwell Barker, cornerback O-Dell Irving. They were all in zooty-looking suits, worn over matching white T-shirts.

Acie, Caldwell, and O-Dell all had their hands free at their sides, their double-breasted jackets open.

They were even wiggling their fingers occasionally.

The Eminems, including my star quarterback, kept doing the same.

I went over to where Elvis was standing at the halfcourt line and said, "Sharks against the Jets."

Elvis said, "I thought Winnipeg was out of the NHL now."

I said, "I assume they've all got guns on them, even though I can't see guns on them."

"Oh, they got 'em, don't worry on that," he said. He nodded at Ty. "You white boys and your Westerns," he said. "Guns and holsters on Christmas morning."

"What about the brothers over there in their zone defense?"

Elvis said, "They's just the unfortunate products of a dangerous environment."

"How long has this been going on?"

"Hour."

"Like this?"

"Occasionally one of them will mo-fuck the other, but it hasn't led nowhere."

"Yo?" O-Dell said now on the court. "Got a question."

Ty nodded. O-Dell put his hands out, took a couple of steps forward, as though speaking for the group.

Caldwell Barker said, "Don't worry, baby, I got you covered."

Elvis said to me, "Oh, I get it, *now* the brother wants to cover somebody."

O-Dell said to Ty, "We gonna stand here all night or find a way to settle this shit?"

Ty said, "Make your play."

I said to Elvis, "He didn't really say that, did he?" Elvis shrugged.

O-Dell said, "Tell *me* somethin': We really gonna take this all the way over a Cincinnati Bengal?"

I said to Elvis, "What the hell is a Cincinnati Bengal?"

Elvis said, "You know how they got those sharp uni-forms with the ugly-ass helmets? The helmets look like snakes crawling all over them?" I nodded, keeping my eyes on the court. Elvis said, "A Cincinnati Bengal's what we call a homely girl with a great body. Ty was chattin' one up at the bar, except then Acie comes back from the men's saying he had dibs on her. One thing led to a lot of bitch-fag back-and-forth, and now here we are."

"Oh yeah," Elvis said, "I almost forgot myself, you got to factor in the lingerin' emotions from the game, and all the tequila they had already digested."

"Not good," I said.

"Oh, we way past not good. Was all the way to oh-fuck when I dialed you up, thinking you're always the top idea guy around." He looked at me. "Got any?"

I winked at him and called out to the group, "Hey, Ty. Jack Molloy here." Ty gave me a quick head-turn, then his eyes went right back to O-Dell. "I thought we had sort of an agreement about guns?"

"They're not my guns, dog."

O-Dell said, "We don't need no help on this."

"Hey, O-Dell," I said. "Know your owner, Barry Teitle-baum? Great guy. You think he really wants you to end up in the hospital tonight? Or jail?"

Caldwell Barker said, "They called us out, yo."

"Listen, guys," I said. "There isn't a single bar dispute I can ever remember that couldn't be solved with more drinks and more girls. Am I right?" Out of the side of my mouth, I said to Elvis, "Jump in any time."

"Man's got a point," Elvis said. "You might want to shoot a bitch occasionally. Not get shot *up* over them."

I said, "Why don't we go back inside and the drinks are on me? What do you all say about that? And everybody forgets this ever happened."

O-Dell wasn't quite ready to let go. He said to Ty, "You wanted to act like a big shooter on the field today. You sure you don't got somethin' you want to show us now? Now that we down to it?"

Ty said, "I'm here, dog."

As tight as I felt, it actually made me laugh. "Yeah, man," I said, and this time I couldn't help myself when he said it, I finally did make a woof-woof-woof noise. "Baaaaddd dog." Deciding on the spot to make my own play now. "I don't want to act like a teacher at the prom, kid, but if I walk out of here right now without getting gunned down, I will go back to the office and when I get there, the only thing I'll have to decide is whether I want to violate your parole first, or your contract."

"We're unbeaten," he said.

"So everybody tells me."

Ty said, "You'd do that?"

"Yeah, I would. So here's how I think we should play this: You and your two friends from the luge team, you walk out first. And Ty? Hand your gun over to Warren Sapp there at the door. O-Dell? How about you and your boys and me head over to A.T.M.'s place? I know you've heard of it. Yum? No Cincinnati Bengals there, trust me on that one. All they got there is the prettiest hats you've ever seen in your life."

O-Dell said, "No lie?"

"Prettier than those lightning bolts on the old Charger helmets."

Acie Dobbs said, "I *love* those."

Ty and his knit caps waited about another minute, then filed past me, Ty leading them in the slouch and head bob, none of them making eye contact. I watched Ty reach into the belt of his baggy jeans and hand his gun, some shiny make out of my realm, over to Little Ray and then disappear with his boys down the alley, nobody looking back. O-Dell and his boys stood with Elvis and me and watched them go.

Like a public address announcer, Elvis said in a big voice, "Ladies and gentlemen . . . *your New York Hawks*!"

I told him my old man would be so darn proud.

I got O-Dell, who turned out to be a cool dude, squared away at the spa at Yum along with Acie and Caldwell, had one drink at the bar—quiet on a Sunday night, low-key—with Elvis, telling him I didn't know how much longer I was going to be able to hang in there with the Hawks.

"But we're goin' good," he said. "Tonight notwithstanding, of course."

"Well, I'm not going so good."

"Used to be one and the same, as I recall."

"Not anymore." I drank some Scotch, said, "Shit, having to let it ride on a punk-ass like Ty Moranis. Needing to put up with him to win."

Elvis said, "You and every other owner in sports." Gave me one of his smiles with all the gold in it. "You know, he's not so bad, once you got him disarmed. Guy at least wants to win. A lot of these rich punk-asses these days don't, they just want to add on to a fuckin' house already looks like it needs its own campus."

I said goodnight to Elvis, spotted A.T.M. over near the door, gave him a quick rundown on the evening's festivities. He gave me a high five and said, "Like I always say, they can't make enough *Lethal Weapon* movies to suit me." Then he said don't bother with a cab, let his driver take me home. I said I was good with that, got into the backseat, told A.T.M.'s driver to take it all the way up Madison and then over the Madison Avenue Bridge to the Deegan, I was in no rush, I needed to think.

What I really needed was something to happen. I just didn't know what.

No: That wasn't it, either.

I *did* know. I needed Dick Miles to decide he really didn't want to be in the pro football business as much as he thought he did, sometime before the sale came up for the final vote. Decide on his own, or with some help from me. Have him call the whole thing off, at least my half of it, let me have my part of the team back. And my control of it.

But how did I make *that* play, especially now that he considered himself the king of all football?

I had always considered myself the luckiest bastard, all things considered. That didn't mean things always broke right for me. My mother had died too young, the old man had left the party way too early, I'd busted up my knee at UCLA. But mostly I'd gone through life, or so I told myself, falling out of trees and landing on my feet. And I knew most people saw things falling for me that way again, at least from the outside. People looking at the sale and the Hawks and thinking that I had done it again, kept his old job and made the score of a lifetime at the same time.

Jackass Molloy?

Are you kidding?

They thought I was Jack*pot* Molloy.

Only I didn't feel that way.

This time I felt like I'd fallen out of a tree and landed on my goddamn head.

The car dropped me off near Gate A at Molloy, and I walked through the manicured gardens that the old man had planted there, past the new statue of the old man Ken and Babs had commissioned while I was away, the one we'd unveiled two Sundays before, at our home opener, a pretty good likeness of him in his topcoat, hat in his hand, his free hand pointing to the sky.

Thinking that I needed more than my own luck now, that I needed luck bigger than that, which meant some of his.

I got it when I got upstairs to Suite 19, the bowl of pasta where I'd left it, half a glass of red wine sitting there next to it, *SportsCenter* on the television. Green message light on the phone machine blinking away.

Two new messages.

The first one was from Billy Grace, one of his long ones, telling me he was going to be up late, he was going to watch his tape of *Alias* as soon as Oretha went to bed, so he could enjoy the show properly.

Then his gravel voice said, "Turns out somebody fronting for your Dick has been betting pretty big on the Hawks lately. Like a couple of mil a game, you add it all up. I'll tell you about it when you call."

Message two, one that had come in about fifteen minutes ago, was from Carey Nash, telling me she was about to get on a plane, she'd call when she landed.

"Don't start spending that money just yet," she said.

I thought that might be it, more mystery from her, and reached down to jab at the Stop button when her voice said, "Guess who's not the richest guy in the world anymore?"

15

Billy asked if I'd already watched *Alias*. I told him I'd seen most of it. He told me not to tell him anything about the conclusion of the story that had started in last week's episode. I told him I was more interested in his story tonight. He said we'd get to that in a minute, but back to *Alias*, without telling him what happened, just tell him this: Did she wear that black bathing suit when they all got down to the Bahamas looking for the mole and the missing hard drive?

"Oretha must really be in bed," I said.

"She even looks cute sleeping, this kid."

"Not as cute as Jennifer in her two-piece."

"Fuckin' ay," Billy said, "my secret-agent girl is going to the beach."

Then he told me what he knew, the guys at his sports book having noticed slightly bigger action on the Hawks than usual the first couple of weeks, nothing crazy, but when extra play came in on anything, they immediately started tracking it, just to see if it was a one-shot deal out of the stars, or the start of a trend they needed to watch. He explained to me that everybody's limits on how much could be bet on one game were different, at least for somebody walking off the street, varying from book to book, casino to casino. Some places wouldn't let you go past twenty grand, some places fifteen, some ten. Like that. At Amazing Grace, they'd let a stranger go as far as fifty, high number for the whole Strip. We both knew the rules were different for whales—high rollers, the comp players. They could bet a million or more if they wanted, they had lines of credit to the moon, Billy reminded me of a couple of names out of the Fortune 400 who would occasionally bet that much on some kind of big football game, even a regular-season game. Most of the time with players like that, no money ever changed hands, win or lose, it was just markers, the book either added or subtracted the amount bet from their accounts when the game was over.

And, Billy reminded me, if some whale bet a million at Amazing Grace, it didn't take long for them to know it at Caesars and everywhere else.

"Our way of giving back to one another," Billy said.

I said, "It takes a village."

"You always were the one with the words, kid," he said.

Anyway, he said, long story short, one of his favorite expressions, it turned out that a kid fronting for Maurie Grubman—the guy from the movies? The one who put everything except the sand in Coronado up his nose when he owned the Chargers?—came in last week and put down two hundred grand on the Hawks to cover against the Titans. This week he makes the same play on the Hawks against the Patriots, even though it was the nuttiest spread of the season, you had to lay twenty-eight if you wanted the Hawks.

"Maurie's got that kind of credit still?"

"Don't worry about Maurie, he's back to being a pussycat, now that he did the rehab thing at the place in Malibu. You know, where the President's kid went."

You had to have cracked Billy's conversational code to know who he meant. And who he meant was Martin Sheen, who played the President on *The West Wing*. And his son, Charlie.

Now that Billy had settled down with Oretha and was staying in more at night, he really did watch a frightening amount of television.

"So he could be one of your million-dollar players on Sunday?"

"He can drop a million here," Billy said, "any given Sunday he wants."

"You say it was a kid fronting for him?"

"Some young guy from his studio. Implant Productions? Kid's got one of those development jobs I think used to mean developing good contacts for Maurie's dope. Now I actually think he has to read scripts without moving his lips."

You had to let Billy Grace tell these things at his own pace, even when you sometimes wanted to scream for him to get to the fucking point.

"But this Sunday, the kid goes two hundred with us, two with Caesars, and three more twos until it's a million. When he comes to collect, one of my kids asks Maurie's kid how come he's spreading Maurie's play around like this, and the kid says, 'Oh, it's not really Maurie's play, he's not really into it, he's just doing a favor for a friend.' So the kid fronting for Maurie tells us Maurie's fronting for somebody else."

"He volunteered this?"

"I think he'd had a few, waiting for this hostess he likes, Andrea, to get off work."

"Somebody from the book called you."

"They know the rules—if they even think it's something I should know, then I should know."

"Words to live by."

"I don't want my whales fronting for other whales, it's

not the way it works, I get to decide who I hold markers on, who I don't. Long story short? I put Vinny Two and Johnny on it."

"Boy," I said, "you never want to hear that."

"So they talk to the kid and he tells them that Maurie's doing it as a favor to Dick Miles, Miles advanced him some big change once when Maurie's studio was in some trouble. Vinny and Johnny tell him that's very interesting, but if he tells Maurie or Miles that they came to visit, there'll be another visit. And also, they promise, that Andrea will take those dual airbags of hers someplace else."

"Because you never make threats," I said.

"Promises," Billy said. "Anyway, the kid's story is that Miles always liked to bet, still likes to bet, maybe still *has* to bet, if you catch my drift. But doesn't want the league to get wind of it while he's waiting to be approved."

"Makes sense, actually."

"And have I mentioned that I didn't get to the good parts yet?"

"Probably not," I said. "But then, you have a tendency to jump around like Tarantino."

"It turns out the million the kid, whatever the fuck his name is, is betting in Vegas, is half of what Miles is betting in New York."

"With bookies?"

"Man, you're quick," he said. "The point man in New York is none other than Jeff Brewer, whose chestnuts you want to roast on an open fire. He moves it around with about five guys we know, works out to be about the same play Miles is making through Maurie in Vegas. Usually with the spread. One time, this week, he gets down on the over."

"How'd you find out so fast about New York?"

Billy said, "Ferret."

"Ferret *Biel*?"

"I thought I mentioned I had him on staff now. Like my East Coast liaison."

"Don't you mean lesion?"

Ferret was a shifty little operator who'd mostly been based in Vegas, a scammer and hustler who'd worked his way out of card shows and the sports memorabilia craze, miraculously escaped doing any jail time, and had somehow wormed his way into the good graces of Billy Grace.

I reminded Billy on the phone that it was Ferret Biel who'd tried to set me up with some fake betting slips—on an Orange Bowl he'd somehow managed to fix—when I was the one trying to get approval from the league after I'd inherited the Hawks from the old man.

"You sure you want to trust this rodent now?" I said.

"Remember—Jesus Criminy, that was a cute caper—how he helped us set up the God guy right before they voted on you?"

It happened the night before the vote. Donnie Mack Carney, then the head of the Finance Committee, was the owner of the Baltimore Ravens, and bigger in Christian broadcasting than Pat Robertson. Loved Born Agains on the field of play, black hookers the rest of the time. We got Oretha to play the part. Of a hooker, not Born Again. Annie burst into the room and we got him on tape, and when the Finance Committee finished with their show of hands the next day, Donnie Mack was ready to do everything except carry me around the conference room on his shoulders.

"Yeah," I said, "I remember."

"Ferret gets it now."

"Does he?"

"I told him this was like one of those twelve-step programs," Billy said. "Only there's just two steps. He steps outta line again, I step on him. He's gonna call you in the morning, explain the whole setup to you."

In the background, I could hear the sound go back up on his television set, a commercial ending, meaning Billy must have unpaused Jennifer Garner.

"Oh, yeah, that's it," he said. "One little dip before you go for the drop with bad Vlad. . . ."

Ferret Biel's rap sheet included masterminding a half-season's worth of point shaving at Notre Dame. Somehow Ferret beat the whole rap when a mistrial was declared, the jury hopelessly deadlocked because some of Ferret's old Vegas friends who'd cleaned up on the Orange Bowl had bought one half of the room and some wealthy Notre Dame alums, hell-bent on revenge against Ferret, had the other.

"I think we'll just call it a six–six tie, skip the overtime, and move on," the judge in the case finally said.

Ferret swore at the time that he'd be going straight after that, even if he was later caught trying to steal sports bras from the World Cup–winning U.S. soccer team at the Rose Bowl in 1999. And then, of course, he'd tried to set me up with those fake betting slips. They weren't his idea, as it turned out, the whole thing had been orchestrated by Allen Getz, billionaire computer nerd, the one who'd decided he wanted the Hawks to be his newest toy. When it became clear that I planned to do everything I could to hold on to the old man's team, Getz did everything *he* could to sandbag me with the owners who'd eventually be voting on me; one way was making it look as if I was in on the fix at the Orange Bowl, thereby putting one more black mark on my permanent black-sheep résumé.

Ferret and I had eventually resolved our issues on that one through what I considered a rather creative intervention: I had him get into a car one night with Elvis's posse, not just Little Ray and Sideman, but Elvis's cranky bodyguard, Twenny Five Cent, who was a martial arts specialist despite being nearly as big as Elvis.

Ferret was on his best behavior after that, at least when I was around. Billy said it was just a variation of having the guy on the inside of the tent pissing out, instead of vice versa. Vice, Billy adding, always being the key word with Ferret Biel.

I'd lost track of him after leaving for Europe, just assumed that he was back scamming in Vegas and living with Inger, an on-again, off-again girlfriend who had worked her way up from escort services to spinning the roulette wheel on a game show they taped at Amazing Grace, *Problem Gambler.*

That was the one, way ahead of the curve on reality television, where you had to prove you'd cleaned out your checking and savings accounts and were willing to let everything you had ride on one night of various casino games. If you won, you had the choice of keeping the money—hardly anyone ever did—or coming back the next week and letting it all ride again.

You lost, straight to the next Gamblers Anonymous meeting.

I'd arranged to meet Ferret at the Pierre Hotel and my favorite breakfast place in the city, called the Rotunda Room because of its high, ornate ceilings, though it looked to me more like the library at the Rockefellers' house. I figured there was no point in meeting him in my office at Molloy, knowing how often Dick Miles and Jeff Brewer just ignored Susan Burden and came walking into my office.

Because anybody who had ever taken one look at Ferret always thought the same thing:

Perp.

And I knew from experience that once he started talking, he was a little like Dick Miles, you sometimes had to stick a rolled-up sock in his mouth to stop him.

He was wearing his usual outfit on this morning: black lightweight suit, black silk shirt, black tie. His face was as white as copy paper, thin lips almost as white, what hair he had left slicked back, starting with a Phil Collins strip that seemed to have moved about another inch up his forehead since I'd seen him last. As usual, his small, pig eyes were looking everywhere in the Rotunda Room except at me, Ferret going through life as if he were sure that somebody he owed money to was about to come through the door.

I'd waited until 8:30 to hear from Carey Nash. When she said she was getting on a plane, I'd assumed she meant a red-eye to New York. But then I played back her message and she'd only said she was getting on a plane and she'd call me when she landed. So she could be anywhere, knowing whatever she knew about Miles, everything she'd found out in the month or so since she'd seduced and abandoned me.

I left a message on my machine saying where I'd be for the next couple of hours, and a note for Susan on her desk telling her the same thing. Now I was having my first cup of coffee with Ferret, making small talk while we looked over the menu.

I said, "How's Inger?"

"Funny you should ask," he said. "She got spotted on *Gambler* and moved to L.A. last month for that new Fox show? *Blackout Drinker?* It's the one where they get the three drunks together the morning after a big bender and then you and the audience try to guess if one of them actually did it with one of the girls on the show. Inger's on every third Tuesday."

"Does she?" I said. "I mean, actually do it with one of them?"

"No, Jack," Ferret said. "While you were away, she had an Ingerectomy." Then he closed the menu, placed it on the table, leaned forward, and said, "Listen, before we talk about what we're here to talk about, I want to tell you something: I am on your side now. This comes from the heart."

"You don't have a heart," I said. "There's a cash register where yours is supposed to be."

"At some point, Jackie, you have to trust me."

I said, "You can't even begin to imagine how many people in my life who I really don't trust tell me that these days."

He gave it up then, as we both ordered our eggs, and then gave me a short preamble about the ten or twelve big sports books in Vegas, about how the online, offshore books, so many of them based in the Caribbean, had become such a booming business in the last few years, and now those were the main outlets for high rollers, unless they wanted to go to the New York bookies handling the most serious action.

And, Ferret said, even though everybody was in competition with everybody else, there was always a lot of intelligence-agency chatter going back and forth.

"The CIA talking to the FBI and the FBI talking to the NSA," Ferret said. "Just with a vig."

"So even people who think they're being cute moving money around are being monitored most of the time."

"*All* the time," Ferret said, "For a very simple reason: If the play gets big enough, somebody's always looking to lay it off somewhere else."

"Banks protecting other banks."

"I forget sometimes that you were an honor student at the University of The Strip."

"Ferret," I said, "my grandfather was a bookie, remember?"

"Anyway," he said, "come to find out through my brilliant network of information—"

"Your fellow snitches."

"—that your Jeff Brewer has been making a play of about a million or so every Sunday on the New York Hawks."

"This you have nailed down."

"Jesus' hands."

"So Miles is betting a million here, a million in Vegas."

"He might be doing something offshore, but that's harder to track."

"Brewer's betting to win?"

"So far. Always laying the points, except for last Sunday, when he bet the over."

I said, "Really."

Ferret may have smiled. "If Brewer bet the over, your coach sure played it for him, didn't he?"

I pushed some scrambled eggs around on my plate.

Ferret said, "Nothing they're doing is moving the line very much. What makes the smoke alarm go off is when somebody that they know is on the inside goes against his own team."

"You're sure they haven't?"

Ferret was attacking a second order of hash browns like a guy at a shelter on Thanksgiving. Mouth full, he shook his head, no.

I said to him, "You think Brewer and this kid in Vegas betting for Miles—you think *they* think they're flying under the radar?"

"I think they don't give a shit. Whether the bets are coming off Maurie Grubman's credit or Miles's, they know the books and the casinos and all like that don't want to lose either Maurie or Miles as whales. What makes this all so interesting to Mr. Billy Grace is that they're doubling up back here."

"I don't care who you are," I said. "That's a lot of bet."

"The kind somebody makes when he needs the money," Ferret said. "Except the guy they're fronting for doesn't need it. Does he?"

I could hear Carey's message again, about Miles not being the richest guy anymore. And shook my head, no, at Ferret. Whatever was happening with his other businesses, there was no way Miles could be in so deep that he needed to put his hands on six or eight million in a hurry.

Maybe it was as simple as this:

Maybe Miles was the one who was the problem gambler.

Ferret said, "So where do we go from here?"

"*We* don't go anywhere. *We* don't want Jeff Brewer to know we're watching him. You stay on him, though. I'm going to the office."

"How about a little love for Ferret?" he said.

I said, "Thank you, Ferret."

He must have had his cell phone on vibrator, because I

didn't hear anything before he jumped in his seat as if a bee had stung him.

Ferret unclipped the tiny phone, looked at what must have been the caller ID, and nodded.

"Inger," he said to me.

Into the phone, he said, "Slow down, baby." Nodding. "With *both* guys next Tuesday?" Nodding again and then saying, "C'mon, kid, relax, we're talking about your *specialty.*"

Carey Nash never called that day.

Annie Kay did, right after I got back from watching practice.

"Who's Carey?" she said.

"Carey who?"

"Don't play games with me."

I said, "It's too late to stop now, I'm an addict. I'm still not over the one where I'm the college professor and you have a C-minus3."

Annie said, "I called while you were at practice and said, 'Hey, it's me.' On your private line, the one that doesn't go through the switchboard. Susan must have been in your office, because she picked up and said, 'Carey? He's been waiting all day for your call.' So who's Carey you've been waiting all day for her call?"

"A friend."

"Oh, no, don't give me that. You don't *have* girl friends, Jack. Two words. Girl friends. You have Vegas friends, drinking friends, fat friends from the team. You have Bubba, Mo Jiggy, Pete Stanton, Brian Goldberg. And Susan doesn't count, she's not your friend, she's your mom, and I will kill you if you tell her I said that. But no girl *friends.*"

I took one swing at keeping things light. "You're my girl friend, girlfriend."

"I *was,*" she said, and hung up.

Then I wandered out of my office to where Susan Burden

was still at her desk, a few minutes before six, working away on her computer. "Tell me that Annie Kay is spreading malicious gossip about you. Tell me that you didn't call her Carey."

"Busted, as you like to say, dear. Rookie mistake. You kept asking me all day if Carey had called, and I had it in my brain when I picked up that line that she was finally calling. Not to worry," she said, "I'll fix it when Annie calls back."

"I have a feeling she's not going to be calling back anytime soon."

"Sure she will. She loves you and you love her."

"If she loves me so much, how come she's seeing Jeff Brewer?"

"Don't know," Susan said. "But you still love her. And she still loves you." She pounded a fist gently on the desk and said in a slight southern accent, "That's my story and I'm sticking to it."

An old Bubba Royal line.

I said to Susan, "When was the last time I was going good, I forget?"

She said, "When Annie was your girl, Bubba was your quarterback, Josh was your coach, Pete was your general manager, Brian was your p.r. man. And Mo Jiggy was around to watch your back."

"The only one still around is you."

She gave me her best smile, a sweet smile, and said, "And I'll be around until you figure a way out of this."

"How do you know I will?"

"Because you're your father's son," she said. "Blood is thicker than water, Molloy."

I kissed the top of her head and said, "Even Dewar's and water."

16

A week later, I still hadn't heard from Carey Nash. No news from her, no word from Ferret on which way Jeff Brewer was betting. No Annie. Just us against the Jets at Molloy Stadium, early fourth quarter, Hawks and Jets tied at 17; we'd been ahead 17–0 after our first three possessions of the game, but over the last hour and a half our offense had been working about as well as a bad marriage.

Corky DuPont IV, the Jets' owner, had wandered over from Dick Miles's suite, asking if I minded if he watched the fourth quarter of what he actually called this fine contest with me. I said fine, but where was Hadley? Mrs. Corky. He said he'd left her in deep conversation with the little blond hellion who'd replaced his dear friend Kathie Lee with Reege.

Corky DuPont's father, some kind of third-string DuPont, had made most of his robber-baron fortune late in his life, but in the early days of cable television on Long Island. From the time Corky IV had graduated from Princeton, he had held the title of vice chairman of IslandVision, but everyone knew he had spent the bulk of his adult life sailing, and waiting for Corky III to die so he could sell the company to whichever Rupert Murdoch made him the highest offer. Which is exactly what he did when Corky III finally kicked, at the age of eighty-nine, at the apartment of his executive assistant, mistress, and former core-conditioner, Kelly Liu.

It was why everyone who had ever known Corky IV, from prep school on, was shocked when he bought the Jets from the Leon Hess estate, telling the press he thought owning his own team would be "rollicking good fun."

Now he ran the Jets in about the fashion you'd expect from a rich kid who'd never been on the line for a minute of his life, apart from making an occasional risky tack in weekend races on Long Island Sound.

He was tall, all-Wasp, wore a green knit tie on Sundays because green was the Jets color, did that preppie thing where a frayed collar of your Brooks Brothers blue shirt is considered the height of fashion, never seemed to have his blond-gray hair all the way combed, and in the times I'd been around him, seemed to be like a lot of pleasant, rich-boy owners I'd met in the league, which meant he didn't have a clue about whether the ball was blown up or stuffed.

The best thing about owning the Jets, as far as I could tell, was that it gave Corky something to do, an excuse to get out of the sixteen-story town house he owned in the Seventies between Madison and Fifth, reported to be the biggest private residence in Manhattan, and get the hell away from Hadley, at least during the week.

"I just told Had I needed some quality time with that old rascal Jack Molloy," he'd said upon entering Suite 19, but I was fairly certain the quality time he was really looking for was with this week's collection of Yum girls, with whom he'd made the elevator ride up to the suite level at Molloy.

Corky DuPont IV wasn't halfway through his first gin and tonic when Ty Moranis threw a slant pass to Sultan that became a spectacular seventy-six-yard catch-and-run touch-down, and put us back in the lead, 24–17.

"I was assured by all my football men that this year's collection of defensive backs could do more than their hair," Corky said, looking sadder than if New Zealand had taken the America's Cup.

The Jets hadn't had a winning record since he had owned the team, hadn't sniffed the playoffs.

"You'll get this thing turned around eventually," I said, just to say something.

I wasn't sure he'd heard me, because his attention had shifted from the ensuing kickoff to where the Yum girls were watching the rest of Sunday's one o'clock games on all the television sets at the back of the suite, having a contest to see which of them had slept with the most out-of-town players.

A.T.M. Moore was back there with them, A.T.M. now an official regular at Suite 19 for Hawks home games, saying he just liked the general ambien of the place. When I'd pointed out that I was pretty sure ambien was a sleeping pill, A.T.M. had said, "Well, fuck French, then."

Today he'd been joined by some NYPD detectives I knew from The Last Good Year, and Butterball, who'd sustained a high-ankle sprain on Wednesday.

Butterball's story for the trainers was that it had happened on the last play of practice, the thing just swole-ing up real bad on him when he got home. Elvis and the rest of the fat boys had a different version, telling me it had happened during some hijinks with the spa girls at Yum later that same night.

For most of the game, Butterball had sat on the couch with a Yum girl on either side of him, drinking beer and eating the delicious Philly cheesesteak sandwiches the catering staff always provided for me, saying the same thing over and over again, no matter how the home team was faring down on the field:

"This is my favorite daytime place ever."

Corky, eyes not leaving one of the Yum girls, a spiky-haired blonde seated to Butterball's right, said, "It's nice to see that you and The Dick have worked through that rather rocky patch in your relationship, by the way."

"I think it was the counseling."

Corky somehow seemed to nod with his jaw. "Just between us blokes, I've suggested counseling for Had and me. She prefers going to the gym and, being so generous, taking our players around in our extensive outreach programs."

I didn't see any point in mentioning to Corky that it was well known around pro football that Hadley DuPont was so frisky around Jets players that some of the veterans had formed the "Had Had Club."

Instead, I just said to him, "Can I ask *you* something between the two of us blokes? Since you and Dick Miles travel in the same circles?"

On the field, there was just over eight minutes to go in the game and the Jets had just turned the ball over to the Hawks on downs.

"I consider being an owner in the National Football League a darned sacred trust, you know that, Jack-o. Mum's the word."

"Is everything all right in his world?" I said. "Meaning his business world."

Corky's eyes had traveled back to the other side of the room, where Butterball was bouncing the spiky-haired blonde slowly up and down on his knee. Sometimes around.

"The girl with the church-spire hair? Do you happen to know her name, Jack?"

"Squirm," I said.

"Oh *yes*," he said, "she certainly can," coloring a bit in the process.

"No," I said. "I meant that's her name. Squirm."

"Sorry, misunderstood," he said. "What were you saying about Dick?"

"I know a lot of guys have taken hits the last few years. I was just wondering how he's doing."

Corky said, "We all assumed there'd be a normal drop-off for him, just because there has been across the board. The darned economy and all. Then you have to factor in Bill Francione up and dying on him. Good man, that Bill. Certainly one of the nicest Italians *I've* ever met."

"Never had the pleasure. Heard a lot about him, though."

"They were a perfect team. Cheney to his W, if you will. The power behind the throne. Almost like Dick's daddy, if you want to know the truth. Once he was gone, the boys downtown all predicted Dick would become a little more impetuous, more of the risk taker and gambler he always wanted to be. And he was for a time. I don't know if you remember, but he took an especially nasty hit in the telecommunications field, with an outfit of his you may have heard of, called You Talkin' To Me."

Knew the company, I told Corky, but had missed that particular hit, maybe I could catch it on the highlight shows.

Corky said that one certainly caused an uproar on what he called the big street, someone with Dick Miles's track record misreading the immigrant market for cell phones as badly as he did, God man, it was like missing the fourth green at Shinnecock.

"Bounced right back like the trouper that he is, of course," Corky said. "But I remember him taking the whole thing pretty hard at the time. Just because he loves being a winner."

"Doesn't he, though."

"In everything," Corky said. "Even women. Have you ever met Carey, his last ex? Good God, man, she could straighten an octogenarian's rope."

I said I'd run into her once or twice, she wasn't bad-looking.

On the field, our rookie punt returner from Virginia Tech, Najah Dampeer, took a low spiral at his own thirty-yard line, eluded the first would-be tackler down the field, cut back to pick up his wall of blockers, sprinted into the clear and all the way down the sideline until he was doing his zone crotch-grab dance. It was 31–17, Hawks, and we were three minutes and change away from our first 5–0 start in ten years.

Butterball jumped up, a new Bud Lite in one hand and a giggling Squirm in the other.

"Nagahhhhhhhh," he yelled at television screen. "God-damn, boy, I take back everything I said in camp about that little surprise you dumped in your girlfriend's closet."

Corky said, "Is that the lad from Tech accused of tak-ing—"

"It was apparently an ugly breakup," I said.

I turned him around so he was facing the field again and said, "So the phone deal cost Miles a ton of dough."

"It did. Only he knows how much, because of the se-crecy around his companies. You're aware that every em-ployee, whether under contract to him or working with him, has to sign a confidentiality agreement about the com-pany's finances? Under penalty of prosecution?"

"Old affable Dick does that to the hired help?"

"Sometimes," Corky said, "the most public people de-fend their privacy most fiercely. I think Dick Miles might be like that. Only letting us *think* we know everything there is to know about him."

"But you think he's generally okay?"

"Jack-o," he said. "He's Dick Miles, for God's sake."

Now he said if it was just the same with me, he'd watch the very end of the game with Butterball and the girls, this after calling Hadley on her cell and telling her he'd meet her at Bemelman's Bar at The Carlyle later.

So I was alone in the front row of Suite 19, in my favorite seat, when Ty Moranis, who should have been running out the clock again, threw an absolutely dead-brain screen pass to Bobby Camby right before the two-minute warning that was picked off by the one star the Jets had on defense, outside linebacker Harper Lee Peck, who returned it twenty yards for the touchdown that brought the Jets to within a touchdown.

I was still alone in the front row, sitting on the edge of my soft blue leather seat, when the Jets recovered an onside kick as soon as CBS was out of commercial break, drove down the field with a series of short passes, and scored with six seconds left in the game to make it Us 31, Them 30.

"Goddamn overtime," I said to Butterball, who was standing behind me, not drinking now, just watching.

"Our coach doesn't know whether to shit or go blind," Butterball said.

Except there wasn't going to be an overtime.

Because the Jets decided to go for the win right there. Because Jets coach Kevin Rafalski shocked everybody in Molloy Stadium—especially Coach Bobby Bullard, who didn't call time-out to change his defense when he saw the Jets hadn't sent out their kicking unit—by running his quarterback, Edgerass Coles, on the draw play that won the game for his team by a point.

"This is better than Princeton beating those pesky Quakers from Penn!" Corky DuPont IV yelled from where he was getting an enthusiastic victory hug from Squirm.

I was still in my seat in the front row when Suite 19 had emptied out, staring at the TV people doing their standups all over the field, smoking and sipping on a Scotch, wondering whether Ty had called the screen pass on his own or if it had been sent in by our genius coach, when Ferret Biel walked in, apologizing all over the place for not calling sooner, saying he didn't talk to the guys he needed to talk to until he was in the cab on the way over to the stadium.

Ferret saying he thought he better tell me in person, on account of how the game turned out, that this time Jeff Brewer hadn't bet the game.

"He didn't take the points?" I said.

Ferret shook his head, then said, "But an awful lot of people did."

"Meaning?"

"Meaning that a fucking boatload of late money came in on the Jets today, Jammer."

"Well," I said, "they certainly must have been happy about the way the last two minutes went."

"Happier than pigs in shit," Ferret Biel said.

I watched on the closed-circuit feed as Bobby Bullard said in his press conference to put it all on him, dad-gummit, it wasn't nobody else's fault, that sometimes when you're hellbent on putting the rubber to the damn road you blow a damn tire.

"I'm the lead dog," Bullard said, pushing his visor back and rubbing his hair like he'd developed ticks. "But that don't mean I can't be a horse's ass."

By the time I got down to the locker room, Ty Moranis had dressed and left in world-record time, even for the kind of media-hater he was.

I walked through the room and down to Bullard's office, wanting to ask him myself about the screen pass, but was told by Vance Hopewell, Jr., that our head coach had gone straight from his press conference to his car.

Dick Miles, I was told, hadn't made it down to the locker room today.

When I came back from Bullard's office, Jeff Brewer was standing near the locker room door looking like a greeter at a funeral home.

I didn't know how I was going to use the information Ferret had given me about the late money on the Jets, just basically knew I wasn't going to use it quite yet.

So I said, "Welcome to the NFL."

"Where," Brewer said, "it ain't over till it's over and the fat lady's sung."

"And, to quote our monkey-ass coach, until the hay is in the barn."

Brewer started to smile, but then saw the weekend sports anchor from Channel 7 walking toward us and put his sad face back on, and a hand on my shoulder, like he was consoling me.

When Channel 7 was out of earshot, Brewer said, "Hey, don't be too hard on Coach Bobby. They were expecting us to run, he just crossed them up and threw."

"Guys who took us and laid the points probably threw *up*," I said.

There was just the slightest pause, like the little glitch-freeze you get when the feed from your satellite dish breaks up, and Brewer said, "To tell you the truth, I don't even know what the point spread was."

"Ten," I said. "Not that it matters, right? What matters is that we lost the frigging game."

"My first loss," Brewer said. "Dick's, too. He said upstairs it was harder than he thought it would be."

"Well," I said, "I'm a silver-lining guy, look at all the happiness we brought today to the people who covered."

"I guess so," Brewer said, and started to walk away.

As he did I said, "Hey, where you are going to be later? Maybe I'll buy you a drink."

Now Brewer gave me his class-president smile. "*You* want to buy *me* a drink?"

"You're always telling me we're all in this together. Maybe we should get to know each other a little better. I mean, didn't you tell me you think of yourself as an apprentice Jammer?"

He said, "Actually, and please don't bite my head off, I had asked Annie to meet me for a drink at Elaine's later, if she finished taping whatever she needed to tape for her highlights show."

"Great!" I said. "Maybe I'll see you guys there," and walked out the door before he could tell me that maybe that wasn't the best idea he'd ever heard.

Telling myself that by the time I wandered down to Elaine's later to check in with the happy couple, maybe I might have come up with something resembling a plan.

Information was power, Billy Grace liked to say, but not if you just let it fucking sit there.

I'd always thought I could talk my way through anything. Or out of anything, if I had to. Annie called it the power of positive bullshit.

When I didn't have the votes to get the Hawks, when nobody thought I'd ever get the votes, I believed I'd come up with them the way I'd always come up with two tickets to see the Stones in Los Angeles, or two on the fifty for Notre Dame–USC at the Coliseum.

Or that game of five-card stud for the leader of the Free World.

Or a way to introduce the Senate majority leader to the cover of the *Sports Illustrated* swimsuit issue.

The Senator's aide had called and said, "He said if anybody could get him fixed up with the white mesh girl, you could."

The aide was right.

In the cab on the way into the city, I thought about what I had, imagining them as corner pieces to a big puzzle. Carey telling me there was a game within a game. Carey saying Miles had money problems, even though we both knew what he was going to have to lay out to buy the Hawks. Brewer and Maurie Grubman's boy betting on the games. Late money coming in on the Jets today, as if somebody knew something.

Bullard calling for that screen pass today and Ty Moranis throwing it to the wrong team and changing the whole day.

I had the cab take me all the way down to P. J. Clarke's, at Fifty-fifth and Third, always the old man's first stop after a game, win or lose, sitting there in the back room with Danny Lavezzo, the owner, Lavezzo a Giants fan, and the two of them thrashing it all out, into the night, all the way into Monday morning sometimes. Now the old man was dead and so was Lavezzo, but Clarke's was still there, after a renovation that seemed to have taken the same five years everything else took in Manhattan, still looking like a saloon from the outside, a squat redbrick joint at the corner of Fifty-fifth and Third standing in there with all the high-rises around it, like some tough little middleweight who wouldn't quit, even if there was a new upscale dining room upstairs.

I ducked into the back room, which was still dark enough, which they hadn't turned into some kind of fern bar, took a table in the corner and ate a couple of Clarke's cheeseburgers, feeling as if I wanted to order a couple more as soon as I was done, decided against doing that, decided to walk all the way up to Elaine's, a good thirty-block walk, instead.

Maybe the big city would smarten me up.

I didn't know for sure that Dick Miles or anybody else had gotten to Bobby Bullard. Even if it sure looked that way.

I couldn't make myself believe that anybody on our side actually wanted us to lose the game, even though that screen pass was dumber than one of those bachelor shows on television.

I told myself, Play the whole thing out.

Losing the game didn't change the outcome of a Jets bet once they were going to cover. More likely Moranis did what he was told, sold it as a lousy pass, and then watched along with everybody else as the game turned completely around on us in the blink of an eye.

Which was supposed to be the beauty of it all in sports, even when your team lost.

A TV guy I knew from hanging around, a guy named Steve Bornstein who'd run ESPN for a while in the '90s, was talking once about some interview he'd given. The reporter asked him why sports and sports television had exploded the way it had in the last twenty years. And Bornstein said, "Because you can't go to Blockbuster and rent tonight's game."

It was never over until it was over and the fat lady sang.

So what did I believe?

I believed that somebody didn't want the Hawks to cover today. Miles or Bullard or both. Whether Miles bet the game himself or not. Bullard called for that pass after the punt return, but he still needed the Jets to intercept. Which meant that Moranis had been told to throw the ball up for grabs, or that somehow the Jets knew what was coming.

But if Miles *wasn't* betting the game, then why?

Whose action was this now?

Shit.

I walked past all the Gaps and Banana Republics that dominated the high Sixties now on Third Avenue, walked past Grace's Market on Seventy-first, which used to be a branch of Balducci's, the great Balducci's all the way down in the Village, a couple of blocks from NYU. Only that Balducci's was gone now.

Walked past Melon's, another old saloon hangout, thought about all the hangover Sunday brunches I'd had there, back when everybody on the Upper East Side knew Melon's had the best Bloody Mary around.

Asking myself why I didn't just go to Wick Sanderson with what I had already, or what I thought I had, on Miles. But what did I have, exactly? A Hollywood gofer putting big money down for the boss. And a lot of bullshit from Ferret Biel about what sports books and bookies and the money Miles had laid on the Hawks early and then all the late money on the Jets today.

I imagined walking Ferret into Sanderson's office and saying, Tell the commissioner what you told me.

Knowing Ferret the witness would make the cockroaches who took down Pete Rose look like they were from the National Council of Churches.

I walked right past Yum without even looking in the window—good boy, Molloy—and crossed over to the west side of Third to where my joint, Montana, used to be. They'd turned it into a Korean grocery after I left town for Vegas. Now it was a Starbucks, crowded even on a Sunday night, everybody in there speaking Starbucks, the smokers out in front with their half-cafs and cappuccinos and grande mocha drinks and vente espressos.

A new romance language, for people in love with themselves.

Smiling to myself about that now, getting ready to take a right and walk east on Eighty-eighth Street to Elaine's. Knowing I wasn't going to turn Dick Miles in, because I didn't have enough yet.

When I did, I wanted to nail the bastard myself.

17

I had been back at Elaine's a few times since returning from London, sometimes just to sit at the bar with Tommy, the number one nighttime bartender, a hip black dude with earrings and one neck tat and an attitude who'd worked for me once at Montana. I'd listen while he joined the ranks of people beating me up for selling, telling me one night that I had to be the dumbest white man who'd never owned Madison Square Garden.

The place was fairly crowded for ten o'clock on a Sunday night, most of the tables along the right-hand wall, Murderers Row at Elaine's, occupied with the usual collection of writers, producers, flacks, good and bad girls, cops, television personalities, two disc jockeys who'd gotten fired for putting mikes on a couple while they had sex at the Temple Emanuel synagogue, a couple of Yankee relief pitchers, the mayor's chief of staff. Halfway down, two tables before you got to the door to the men's room, was the table where Dick Miles and his faithful companion Jeff Brewer were sitting. No Annie. Maybe she wasn't here yet.

Or, better yet, wasn't coming.

But there was a woman seated between Miles and Brewer, the woman waving me over to the table, a mischievous smile on a still-pretty but too-thin face that was a tribute to superior genes and the very best plastic surgeons on both coasts:

My darling stepmother, Kitty Drucker-Cole Molloy.

I walked straight over to their table, bent down to kiss her cheek hello, then said what I always did when I wanted to see how many frown lines she had left.

"Mommy!"

Somehow the smile held. "Jack, darling," she said. "Dick said you might stop by. How lovely to be here with both the current and former owners of your father's football team."

Miles said, "Sit your ass down, Jack. I was just telling my dear friend Kitty what it's like to lose your first one."

I sat down to his right, on the outside, directly across from Brewer, who reached over, probably for Kitty's benefit, and shook my hand.

"I wish I could tell you there's something in the owner's manual to cover games like today," I said to Miles. "But the only thing that really works is whiskey."

Miles lifted his martini, a big one with lots of olives. "How about gin?"

"That, too." To Jeff Brewer, I said, "Annie's not here?"

"Not finished working yet. I just talked to her. She said she'd stop by if she could."

Kitty, who liked having a younger, prettier woman at the table about as much as she liked people knowing that she'd been born when Give 'Em Hell Harry Truman was president, said, "Well, maybe I'll stick around and keep all you handsome men company."

I said, "What are you doing here, by the way? I thought you and your boyfriend spent most of your time in Palm Beach now. Or is it Palm Desert?"

"Allen's plane is still on the ground in West Palm," she said. "Some sort of silly thunderstorm thing. Or maybe it was a hurricane, it seems like we spoke *hours* ago. I was just sitting around the apartment, bored to tears and—would you believe it?—the phone rang and it was Mr. Dick Miles himself asking what Allen and I were doing tonight. As soon as I told him what a sad girl I was, he told me his car was on the way."

She'd started up with Getz a few months after the old man died. That was her story, anyway. My sister Babs believed they had to be seeing each other behind the old man's back well before then, even if nobody could prove it. What I could prove, just because I had the stab marks in my back as evidence, was this: Once Kitty found out I'd inherited the football operation and that she was officially out as First Lady of the Hawks, she did everything she could to have Getz in place as a potential buyer if the Finance Committee voted me out on my ass. When it didn't happen that way, I'd just assumed that would mean the end of her relationship with Getz, who seemed to own all the goodies in the computer business that Bill Gates and Paul Allen didn't.

But despite the difference in their ages—if Getz was forty, he'd just turned—they were still together two years later, and I'd finally come around to the realization they were made for each other:

She was one kind of bitch, and had somehow turned the sixth-richest man in America into another.

"Is Allen Getz a friend of yours?" I said to Miles.

"You know how it is, Jack. If we're not running into each other at the same parties, we're trying to screw each other out of a merger or acquisition."

"It's the big-guy version of short-sheeting each other's beds at the frat house," Brewer said.

Kitty Drucker-Cole Molloy said, "Now, don't start talking about sheets with a sexy man like Dick Miles sitting so close to me." And put her diamond hand, both bracelet and ring, on top of Miles's. She was also wearing a diamond necklace that reminded me of a chandelier. I knew the hip-hoppers called necklaces like that dog collars. This one looked as if it could wrestle a St. Bernard to the ground.

I said to her, "Didn't you and Dick go to college together?"

"Dear, dear Jack," she said to Miles and Jeff Brewer. "Never quite as funny as he thinks he is."

Miles took another healthy swallow of gin. "Well, that sucked the big one today."

"The French have a phrase that covers it," I said.

"I can't wait to hear," Miles said.

"Your coach is a fucking asshole, *s'il vous plaît*."

Miles sighed. "Bobby told me that he told Ty that if there was nothing there, he was supposed to throw the fucking thing away."

"Is that what Bobby told you?"

Jeff Brewer said, "Oh, come on, Jack. You know Bobby. Overdrive is the only speed he knows."

I said to Brewer, "Well, you'd know, wouldn't you, Jeff? You've been around this game a long time."

Brewer didn't say anything back. Kitty wasn't listening, of course, she was telling Miles to discreetly look over to his left, no, no, the table in the middle, apparently Martha *had* posted bail.

Miles turned around, but I saw he wasn't looking at Martha's table, he was checking out the new Uma from *The Producers*.

I said to no one in particular, "You know, if a guy was cynical, he might think that whoever decided to start throwing the ball around with two minutes to go had bet the Jets today."

Miles managed to take his eyes off Uma and put them on me. "Not funny, Jack."

Kitty said, "I told you he wasn't funny," and then announced she was going to the little girls' room.

Jeff Brewer leaned forward, trying to keep his voice underneath the usual dull roar of the place, and said, "You're kidding, right? You can't possibly believe Bobby is betting on our games."

I told them I was just making an observation, and then asked if either one of them remembered an old Bears quarterback named Chipper Jenks, who'd come out of Wake Forest and played in Chicago in the '60s. Brewer said that was before his time, but Miles said, of course, everybody remembered Chipper.

Chipper had been a throwback character like Bubba Royal, just not as good. Drank too much, never had the arm, but somehow managed to win the game. And the bet. It didn't make him much different from a lot of players in those days, the ones who thought gambling was a cute idea, the same way later players would think recreational drugs and guns were cute ideas. That was until Pete Rozelle, the commissioner, got the goods on a few high-profile players, most notably Paul Hornung, then the golden boy of Vince Lombardi's Packers. Rozelle made an example out of Hornung, suspending him for a year, even though there was no evidence Hornung had been betting on Packers games.

"Notre Dame," Miles said of Hornung. "Old Number Five. Hell of a competitor."

Anyway, I said, I was drinking one night with Chipper Jenks, in those years when what was known as the Old Quarterbacks Tournament was being played at God's Acre, and everybody stayed at Amazing Grace. And when Chipper got shitfaced enough, he asked if I wanted to hear about the best goddamn call he ever made. I said, sure. And he proceeded to tell me about a game not a whole hell of a lot different from the one the Hawks and Jets had just played, when he and about half the guys on the Bears' offense had bet on a bad Browns team to cover at old Municipal Stadium. Only thing was, a punt returner the Bears had just moved up from the taxi squad, one Chipper described as Rasmus Somebody, didn't know what the deal was. And late in the game, the guy caught a punt on his own ten-yard line when everybody in old Municipal Stadium was sure he was going to fair-catch the sucker, turned into Red Fucking Grange, finally took the thing ninety yards for a touchdown. Just like our kid today, I told the table. Suddenly the Browns weren't going to cover, even though no one in that old dump by the lake thought they could actually come back and win the game.

But now the Bears needed the Browns to score another touchdown if everybody was going to win their bets. Only the Browns couldn't even make a first down on their next possession. They had to punt again. The punter kicked it out of bounds this time. Bears' ball on their thirty. Chipper ran his fullback, a good old boy from Georgia Tech named Stephen Hands, up the middle on a play that was guaranteed to get one yard, because, according to Chipper, the fucker'd only been getting one yard all day. On second down, he called for a short pass in the flat and hung it just enough for the Browns' Hall of Fame–bound corner, Cotton Randolph, to pick it off and run it in for a touchdown. The Bears ended up winning, 30–21, the Browns covered with the twelve points they were getting, Chipper and his buddies all won their bets.

"And *that*," Chipper Jenks told me that night in the bar, "was the greatest goddamn call of my goddamn career."

I asked why.

He said, "'Cause it was only second down, Jammer. If that cotton-pickin' Cotton had dropped the ball, I could have called the play again on third down!"

Dick Miles said, "Cute story, Jack, no shit. But I'd appreciate it in the future if you'd keep your cute stories and your suspicions about our coach, and our quarterback, to yourself."

"All I'm saying," I said, "is that what happened today reminded me of Chipper, that's all. I'm not accusing anybody of anything." I sipped on my Scotch. "I know you used to bet a little, Dick. You know, before you owned the team. You have to know how suspicious people can get, whether there's really anything there or not."

"Bobby Bullard's not going to blow his last chance at coaching because of some stupid bet," Miles said, dismissing the whole thing with a wave of his hand. "Ty Moranis isn't going to blow his last shot at the brass ring. Or blow more money than he ever thought he'd make when he was still a guest of the state."

"You're not going to tell me players still bet," Jeff Brewer said. "Not with the kind of money we're paying them."

I didn't see any need to tell either one of them about how much Bubba Royal bet on himself, with my generous backing, in our dramatic Super Bowl victory over the Bangers.

"Of course they don't bet," I said. "They also don't use drugs to get bigger and faster. And they've all stopped screwing around on their wives."

Kitty came back from the ladies' room then, saying, "There are *far* too many lesbians in this city, if you ask me."

I laughed, just because I couldn't help myself.

"I'll drink to that," Dick Miles said, "but then, I'll drink to anything at this point."

Jeff Brewer said, "Hey, there's Annie."

Kitty said, "You know something, I was starting to get a little tired, but I do believe I could be about to rally. That's what you're always telling people late at night, isn't it, Jack? How they have to rally?"

Annie was still wearing her blue CBS blazer and had a leather purse slung over her shoulder that I knew from experience weighed more than a bowling ball.

She stopped to say hello to Tommy, then to Pepe, one of our favorite waiters, and to Jeremy Schaap of ESPN, who'd been at the Hawks–Jets game to do postgame interviews and was drinking with some friends at the bar. It bought me a little more time to think of something clever to say to her when she got to the table.

I was still watching her work the room, not paying attention to anything else, just because I hardly ever did when Annie, even a hostile Annie, was in the general vicinity, when I heard Dick Miles say, "Well, you can forget about rallying, Kitty. Because here comes the old rally killer herself."

Not talking about the fabulous Annie Kay.

Looking past Annie to the spot near the front door at Elaine's where his ex-wife, Carey Nash, was standing.

There wasn't the kind of hugging you got at family reunions.

Brewer got up to greet Annie. She said hello to him and sorry she was late, the show came up light and instead of just tagging her feature on the Giants–Colts game with a voiceover, she had to chat about it on the set with Jim Nantz. Brewer was already pushing a chair back for her, so he didn't notice that she was looking at me the whole time she was explaining the vagaries of show business to him.

She also seemed to be deciding whether she was glad to see me, or planned to continue her recent ball-busting festival.

"Jack" was what she said.

"Annie" was what I said back.

"Nobody told me—"

I said, "I thought I'd surprise you."

"Nobody's more full of surprises than you," Annie said.

Dick Miles was completely oblivious to the rest of us, devoting his attention to Carey, the only one smiling on this whole side of the front room at Elaine's, standing next to the pay phones in the open area where the cigarette machine used to be in the old days, waiting for Annie, who still didn't know Carey was behind her, to sit down next to Jeff Brewer.

"Well" was the best Miles could do.

"Hail, hail," Carey Nash said, "the gang's all here."

Annie turned around to see where the voice was coming

from. Carey extended a hand to her. "I'm Carey Nash," she said.

. Now Annie smiled, at me, then her. "No shit," she said. Back to me. "*The* Carey?"

"In a manner of speaking," I said.

Kitty Drucker-Cole Molloy came around the table herself now and said, "Carey, dear, I don't believe I've seen you since . . . you know."

"The divorce, Kitty," Carey said. "It's all right, you can say it. Dick says it's really only a dirty word if you're paying both lawyers."

Kitty air-kissed her and then patted Annie on the shoulder and said, "And while we're on the subject, I'm sorry to hear about you and Jack."

Annie said, "I'm actually starting to feel much better about everything."

Dick Miles said to Carey, "I didn't know you were back in town."

"Just got back tonight," she said.

"Off spending a little more of my money?"

"Oh," she said, "who's to say anymore where yours ends and mine begins?" To Annie, she said, "Aren't men adorable?"

"Once you get them housebroken," Annie said.

Miles said to his ex-wife, "Are you meeting somebody?"

"Jack?" Annie said.

Annie looked at me as if she wanted to say something about Carey and me, but chewed a bit on her lower lip instead.

"Beg your pardon?" I said.

Annie said, "I was just going to say that I think you need to get us a couple more chairs here. And a waiter."

Kitty clapped her hands together, like it was officially a party now, and said, "Let's do boy-girl."

"Let's," I said.

Annie was already in place to Brewer's left, facing the rest of the room. I moved over and sat next to her, which put

Carey next to Miles. As I pulled back her chair for her I said to Carey Nash, "Let the games begin."

Miles, who I'd noticed was slightly hard of hearing, said to me, "What?"

"I was just telling Carey we had a tough game today."

He said, "I didn't know you and Carey knew each other."

"We've just run into each other here and there," I said, and felt Annie give me a slight kick under the table. "Oh," she said, in what was a dead-on silly-girl impression of Kitty. "Jack knows soooooo many people."

I could only guess that Carey had gotten the message I'd left about being at Elaine's. Ever since her late-night phone call, I'd changed the tape at Suite 19 and in my office every time I'd gone out, never saying the new message was specifically for her, just announcing where I planned to be if somebody needed to find me.

It would have been easier to carry a cell phone, I knew, just because of the special circumstances, but I wasn't going to give in on cell phones now, them or one of those new hand-job BlackBerry computers.

"*Are* you meeting someone?" Miles asked.

"I'm a big girl now," Carey said. "Sometimes I go out to bars by myself and everything."

She was sipping a Cosmopolitan. So was Annie. Carey was wearing a black jacket that reminded me of a windbreaker, a red pullover underneath it, blue jeans. Annie'd taken off her blazer to show off a tight blue turtleneck, either because she thought it was hot at Elaine's or because she wanted to show she could outsweater Carey.

Nothing fancy from either one of them, and they still looked like a couple of showstoppers about to fight for the title.

Kitty, scoping out the female competition the way she always did, tried to focus her attention on the men at the table but kept looking at Carey and Annie, first one, then the other. Younger and prettier no matter which way she turned. It was clear that she wasn't having nearly as much fun as she thought she was going to.

But she was a game girl. And was going to get her licks in, one way or the other, just for bitchy sport.

"So," she said to Jeff and Annie, "are the two of you really an item?"

Brewer decided that was a good time to move his chair noisily back from the table. Annie said they were just friends. Kitty said, well, that's not what she'd heard on the Rialto.

The Rialto was an expression the old man liked.

I said, "You're dating yourself there, Mom."

"Well, Jack dear," Kitty said, "at least I'm dating *some-one.*"

We all sipped our drinks at once, as if in formation.

Carey said to Dick Miles, "So it really was a tough loss for you guys today?"

"Only about as tough as a goddamn kidney stone."

She said, "I remember how Sunday nights used to be when you were just betting on your favorite teams. I can only imagine what it must be like now that you own the team."

"I'm not a good loser," he said. "So shoot me."

"You know what I always used to say, sweetheart. Only if I could get away with it."

Annie said, "You all must have wanted to shoot your stupid coach today. Or your quarterback."

"Or both," I said.

"What were they *thinking?*" she said, just asking me now. "If you still want to be throwing it around there, throw it down the field. Right?"

Only wanting to know what I thought now, like it was just the two of us doing a postmortem on the game, and everybody else had suddenly gone home.

Carey noticed it, too. She was looking at Annie now, as if really noticing her, the force of her, for the first time.

"I can't wait to tell my coach the same thing," I said, "first thing in the morning."

"Now, c'mon," Jeff Brewer said, "let's remember this did only count for one loss in the standings."

Kitty said, "When the Hawks would lose in the old days, Jack's father would close the door to his study for what he called a club meeting."

"Canadian Club," I said, a little too quickly, cutting her off before she could deliver the punch line herself.

She had gotten enough money out of the old man, I figured the good lines were mine.

It occurred to me I'd never asked what Carey Nash had gotten out of her old man, the one seated now to her left.

Miles said to her, "I heard you were out visiting the You Talkin' To Me office a couple of weeks ago."

Even I had to admit it was a cool name for a cell phone company.

"You know I still have friends there," she said, "from the start-up. I just wanted to see who'd survived the carnage."

Miles gave her a palms-up shrug and said, "Phone cards for Mexicans who didn't want to punch in nine thousand numbers. . . . I still think it should have been a goddamn home run."

"What did Bill used to tell you? If the pyramid comes down, make sure you've already left town."

Like it was just the two of *them* now.

"Bill said a lot of things."

Carey said, "Almost all of them smart."

Miles speared his last olive. "It's like football. Get 'em next time."

Carey ran a finger around the top of her glass and licked it. "Before they get you."

"Thanks for your support."

She said, "Remember, I've got a lot riding on you, big guy."

"Sometimes I feel like I should have spur marks in my sides," he said, "I've got so many people riding me."

It was here that Carey Nash held up the wrist with her big-faced, big-numbered wristwatch on it and said, Wow, look at the time, a magician distracting you with one hand while doing some sleight-of-hand trick with the other.

In this case, the trick was Carey Nash putting her other hand under the table and in my lap and fishing around down there as if she planned to pull a rabbit out of my stonewashed jeans.

Then she stood up. "It's been fun, everybody, but I've got to get some sleep. Kitty? You never change. Annie? Nice to meet you. Guys, I'll see you around campus." She put a hand on Dick Miles's shoulder. "You look tired, sweetheart. Still taking your fountain-of-youth pills?"

He stood up, too, mostly as a way of moving her hand off him. "It's nice to see you still care."

"Always," Carey said.

She left. A few minutes later, Miles asked if he could drop Kitty somewhere, since it appeared Allen Getz wasn't going to make it back from Florida tonight.

"Tell your driver to take the Park," she said. "We really do have soooo much to talk about."

Now it was Annie, Brewer, me.

Waiting each other out.

I thought of a line from Counting Crows, about the last one out of the circus having to lock the door.

So we all had one more drink, bullshitting a little more about the hideous game, and then it was Annie who seemed to get tired all of a sudden, like all her engines shut down at once, saying she had to get up in the morning and do the stupid morning show again.

Brewer started to say something and she cut him off, answering a question he didn't get to ask. "Thanks, anyway," she said. "I'll just get myself a cab."

Then, looking at a point between Brewer and me, she

said in a quiet voice: "I don't want to play this game anymore."

Jeff Brewer probably thought she meant Hawks vs. Jets.

When she was gone and Brewer was gone, I went to the pay phone and called Carey Nash and said I was more than willing to let her trade me information for sex.

18

Carey Nash and I were sitting in the small alcove off her living room, one she'd turned into a cozy dining area, the morning sun seeming to come out of the sky and off the East River and make it feel more like summer than October. I was wearing an oversized Tom Petty T-shirt she'd given me and an undersized pair of gray sweatpants that she swore didn't belong to Dick Miles or his short stupid hairless veiny legs. She was in a white robe. She'd been wearing only her red pullover when I got to the apartment from Elaine's, and her hoop earrings.

"This clinches it once and for all," I said at the time. "Less is more."

"You're sure you don't feel as if you're cheating on Miss Kay?" she said, leaning against the door frame, hand on bare hip.

"I don't think it's technically cheating," I said, "if you and I already know all the answers."

Then we'd kissed in the open door of apartment 21 N, neither one of us too worried that 21 O, right across the narrow hallway, was going to bother us very much at two in the morning.

I said, "I'm really not this kind of boy."

"Sure you are," she said. She pushed back a little and said, "I really had started to think you might have left with Annie."

I told her Annie and I weren't playing that game anymore.

"Sure you are," Carey said.

We didn't get to the information before finally falling asleep inside some thick quilt she'd thrown down on the living room floor. Now we were in this sunny corner, bookshelves all around us, and she was trying to get me up to speed, jumping around the way she usually did, getting into it by telling me what a buying frenzy Dick Miles had been in since his partner had died.

"Bottom line on Mr. Bottom Line Miles?" she said. "In the year and a half since Bill Francione died, he's managed to get himself sideways."

"Sideways meaning he really does have money problems?"

Carey said, "Sideways as in the banks have been running him for about the last six months, and have him on the kind of tight budget he used to joke about putting me on when we were married."

"I'm not doubting you," I said. "But how the hell can that be possible?"

"Because it was possible for Murdoch once, that's why. It was possible for Trump, when he was nearly out of bullets, and out of bank covenants. Now it's happened to our Dick. Sideways isn't entirely accurate, by the way. He's actually gotten himself upside down, even if nobody outside the banks and his most serious investors, here and in Europe, know it. Bill's gone and there's been nobody to rein him in, and now he's terrified that people are going to start finding out."

"How big a fall are we talking about here?"

"The Roman Empire."

I shook my head, smiling at her. "No way."

"Way."

"Before you explain how he got himself into this fix, without making it harder to understand than geometry, explain something: How do the Hawks figure into this? You must have a better fix on that now than you did before you went off and did your Nancy Drew thing."

"It's the part I still haven't figured out," she said. "The best guess of my guy—"

"Time-out," I said. "What guy?"

"A banker who wasn't supposed to talk, because none of them are supposed to be talking about Dick Miles's business, but sort of did."

"I don't suppose you traded sex for information," I said. "Because that would be wrong, wrong, wrong."

"Yes, it would," she said, pouring herself more coffee. "And none of *your* business."

I told her not to worry either way, I wasn't jealous.

"Anyway," she said, "my Los Angeles banker friend thinks that even if Dick can make it through the season without going under—going under meaning he humiliates himself by asking for bankruptcy protection or having to sell things off left and right—he's still going to have to bring in a new partner on the Hawks if he wants to hold on to them."

I said, "Which could be anybody."

"Or my guy thinks that between now and when the league votes on him, he might try to use the Hawks as collateral against some other kind of deal. His main problem, as I see it, is that the banks aren't going to help him. On top of that, his investors have shut him off." She sipped some coffee out of a Museum of Natural History mug. "All of this, of course, is playing itself out in an economy that refuses to correct itself."

"So there really is a game within a game."

"How sweet," she said. "You remembered."

I told her to back way up. She did. Asking me if I knew how secretive Miles was in business. I told her about my conversation with Corky DuPont, and how strict he said the confidentiality agreements were. She said that's the way Bill Francione had always wanted it, always resisting the temptation to take MF, Inc., public, preferring to have a handful of big investors, all of whom MF had made boatloads of money for in the firm's glory years, moving them from deal to deal, only Francione himself really knowing where all the money was coming from, from whom, how much. It's why even in the best of times, no one knew exactly how well Miles and Francione were doing, just that they were boomtown boys, especially in the Clinton years, operating within a boomtown market.

"You remember how your father used to own the Hawks?" she said.

"No, I forgot."

"That's pretty much the way the banks own my ex-husband these days."

I nearly laughed, saying, "How can people not know this? Everybody knows everything about everybody else these days."

"The banks don't want anybody to know," she said. "They don't want people to know how much money they've given him, they don't want them to know how much trouble he's in."

"So you're telling me that Dick Miles is broke?"

"Rich-guy broke," she said. "Not *broke* broke. He has enough money from the banks for now. They let him sign a coach, and a quarterback. They didn't want it to look as though America's number one fan had bought the New York Hawks and then turned into some cheap nickel-and-dimer. He's not going to have to put his houses on the market like Ken the Dipshit from Enron did."

"Well," I said, "thank God for that."

"But the banks know what he knows: that he is running out of time to find the money to pay you and your sibs."

"The league's vetting him, and doesn't know this shit?"

"He used to joke that he's got more books than the Library of Congress."

"And he wasn't in this kind of shape when he bought the Hawks?"

"It's mostly fallen apart lately," she said. "I'm getting to that." She bit off a piece of blueberry muffin. "He probably knew he shouldn't be laying out that kind of money for a football team. But he was Dick Miles, remember. He wants what he wants when he wants it. And he believes he can bullshit his way through anything."

I told her I knew the feeling.

"I imagine you would," she said.

I said, "Why are you doing all this?"

My cigarettes were on the table. She took one out and lit it, not even bothering to open the terrace doors. In addition to so many of the truly wonderful qualities Carey Nash had exhibited on the quilt that was still on the living room floor, she also smoked in the house.

"I'm protecting my investment," she said.

"C'mon," I said. "You had to have done great in the divorce."

"I got greedy in the divorce, is what I did," she said. "I could've taken a lump-sum payout and walked away free and clear. But then the sonofabitch gave me the option of getting much more, over time. Playing me like an investor, really, telling me to hang with him, there was a bigger score to be made down the line, as long as I was patient."

"You went in on that."

"With both feet." She opened the side of her mouth and blew smoke to the side and somehow looked cool doing it. "Now if he goes down, I go down. I've done all right, don't get me wrong. But I planned on doing better than all right."

"Betting on the come," I said. "Gets them in Vegas every time."

She said, "Two days after Christmas, Dick and I will be divorced two years. At that point, I have the option of cashing out with a fraction of what he promised me. Or gambling that he can pull out of this. But I need to know where I stand."

"And where he stands."

"If he's still standing at all," she said.

She told me the rest of it then, explaining that Dick Miles had really dug this hole for himself in three areas: health care, energy, and telecommunications. I said, "Aren't those the things that dragged down Bush the First?" She told me to shut up and listen. She said her ex-husband hadn't just taken the nasty hit Corky DuPont IV had talked about with the You Talkin' To Me deal, he'd been run over. Even though he'd convinced his money guys it *was* a surefire home run, especially considering the way the immigrant market was growing. He figured he could buy the phone cards from the telephone carriers, resell them through a network of investors, each person along the chain making a solid profit.

"On this one," she said, "he fronted most of the money."

"Until the pyramid you mentioned at Elaine's collapsed."

"They could have run it on television the way they do when they blow up another old stadium," Carey said.

Then there was his hospital deal. Carey said that most hospitals got their money from insurance companies, or individual private payments from people who don't have insurance. But about ten years ago, she said, a bunch of companies went to hospitals and said, don't wait six to nine months for your money, we'll pay you at a reduced rate and then wait ourselves to get paid at the full rate.

"It sounds like a spin-off of *ER,*" I said, "just with loan sharks."

Carey said it all worked fine as long as the insurance companies did their jobs and everybody paid. What nobody could see coming, not even Bill Francione, who didn't make many mistakes, was the flood of Medicare and insurance fraud over the last five years, particularly the last year. All of a sudden, people were saying, Hey, we're not paying, this is all a scam. Then Francione was gone and Dick Miles was eventually left holding the bag.

She started to explain how Miles's energy deal fell apart because of a block of western states and deregulation, but I begged her to stop, this was all starting to make my bad knee hurt.

"We need to know how the Hawks fit into all this," I said.

"I believe that's where I came in."

She crossed her legs, the way she had the first night at The Last Good Year, only this time she did it in her apartment, wearing a white robe that I knew for a fact had nothing underneath it, making no attempt whatsoever to cover up.

"I want my team back," I said. "You want your money."

"And we've got what's left of the season to make it happen."

Carey Nash came around the table now, pushed the table back slightly, sat herself down on my lap. "Don't you find the union of two selfish agendas a turn-on?" she said.

"I have more questions."

"They can wait," she said.

19

It was the second weekend in November. We'd won two more games, against the Steelers and the Bills. In between, we'd gotten our doors blown off by the Raiders; we played the Raiders at Network Associates Coliseum in Oakland, in front of that home crowd of theirs I'd always thought looked like a cross between a bad-ass biker convention and a leather bar in the West Village.

So we were currently 6–2, tied with the Bills for first place in the AFC East, two games ahead of the Jets, who had won three in a row and turned their season around after carjacking that game from us at Molloy.

If Dick Miles had bet any of our last four games in Vegas, nobody knew about it at any of the big sports books along The Strip. Or any of the smaller ones, for that matter. Jeff Brewer hadn't gone anywhere near the New York bookies Ferret had been using to track him and his play.

I'd had my sit-down with Bobby Bullard after the Jets game, and he'd rubbed his hair and gotten all dewy-eyed and told me that calling that screen pass had been the lamebrainest damn thing he'd done since he'd knocked up his first girlfriend in high school.

When I asked him if he'd bet the game, I thought he might cry.

"Jack," he said, "it makes my heart ache even hearin' you suggest somethin' like that."

"Anybody said that about me, Coach," I said, "I wouldn't have worried about heartache, I would've put him up against a wall." And left him there, scribbling his ball plays and getting ready for the Steelers.

Billy's accounting firm in Vegas, House Money, had sent a couple of its troubleshooters out into the field to look discreetly into the actual state of Dick Miles's finances, see if there was any hard evidence that things were actually as bad as Carey Nash said they were.

"I talked to the guys myself," Billy said, "told them to pretend they were undercover with Jennifer on *Alias*. And Jesus H. Christ, did you see that black evening gown last week? I'm sitting there in front of the high-def, throwin' designer water on myself. Even with my chocolate bunny waiting for me in the bedroom."

Annie Kay was still being seen around town occasionally with the hated Jeff.

Carey and I made it a point not to be seen anywhere together, spending most of our time together at her apartment, doing a lot of takeout, watching old movies on television, occasionally going for a walk on the jogging path between the FDR Drive and the river, then going back to the apartment and jumping on each other as if she'd just discovered boys and I'd just discovered girls.

Occasionally, she would fly off to the West Coast, saying she'd gotten a new lead from the MF office in Los Angeles or the one in San Jose.

She didn't mention her banker boy, and I didn't ask about him.

In addition to everything else I liked about Carey Nash,

she didn't need to analyze our relationship every time we changed positions under the covers.

"Think of it as a wartime romance," she said one night as we were watching one of my all-time favorite black-and-whites, *The Americanization of Emily*.

I told her, okay, but that meant sooner or later I was going to have to ask her to get into uniform.

Since the Jets game, Dick Miles had been spending less and less time in the office, and when I'd ask either Ms. Thorn or Jeff Brewer where Miles was, they'd explain that I'd just missed him and he was in transit again.

Our next game was on Sunday in Los Angeles against the Bangers. Brewer assured me that Miles planned to be at the Coliseum by kickoff. The game had been getting a big buildup, both in the newspapers and on CBS, for a couple of weeks, because it was our first game with the Bangers since the Super Bowl, and because they were 9–0. CBS's number one game crew, Greg Gumbel and Phil Simms, was working the game, and they'd even decided to bring out the whole *NFL Today* crew and do the pregame show from the Coliseum, which meant that even the fabulous Miss Annie Kay would be in L.A. for the weekend.

The Hawks were staying at the Four Seasons Hotel on South Doheny, just past Beverly Hills. I had set up my personal headquarters at the Hotel Bel-Air along with Billy Grace and Oretha, who'd flown over from Vegas on Friday afternoon. Now it was Saturday morning and the three of us were sitting at the Bel-Air pool along with a special guest attraction, Neville Hayward, who'd arrived unannounced in New York a few days before for what he called "R and R," which he said for him meant recreation and rough trade. When I told him I was headed for L.A. and the Hawks–Bangers game, he decided to come along on the team plane, saying this would make it an even better holiday for him, an opportunity like this to cruise upscale Hollywood gay bars and track down closeted leading men.

We'd all just ordered more coffee. I was still trying to decide whether or not to drive my cool rented Mercedes convertible over to the Coliseum and watch our Saturday-morning walk-through, see for myself how Ty Moranis looked throwing the ball; he'd taken a late hit on his throwing shoulder against the Bills, and had been officially listed as questionable for the Bangers game.

Oretha was waiting for it to be ten o'clock so she could go shop at Fred Segal.

She said to Billy, "I'm gonna buy up some retro jeans, tight tops with those sparklies all over them, maybe even some of those underthings you liked so much from last time, big man."

"Underthings for you, or underthings for Billy?" Neville said.

He'd been swimming in a black Speedo that looked like a guy version of a G-string. When he got out of the pool, Billy told him to put a robe on for Chrissakes, he was scaring the straight people.

Billy's position on homosexuals had always gone something like this:

They were basically harmless as long as you didn't make any sudden moves.

Oretha said, "Why don't you come with me, Neville? My big man says he won't get caught dead at Fred."

Neville, who'd been queening himself up for Billy, said, "I'll model for you if you'll model for me."

Oretha said, "You got a deal, boyfriend."

"Jack says Queen Elizabeth here already has a boyfriend," Billy said.

Neville laughed and said he was going to take a shower, he'd meet Oretha on the swan bridge in fifteen minutes.

Just about everybody at the pool, male or female, watched him leave in his Speedo.

Billy said, "That guy better be queer."

I told him if Neville Hayward wasn't, he had a hell of a scoop.

Over time, they'd expanded the bar at the Bel-Air, my favorite bar west of the Hudson River, but somehow managed not to change the character of the place, other than giving in to the smoke Nazis and making you go outside if you wanted to light up. But the lighting inside was still just right, the drinks were big, the bartenders knew when to talk and when to shut up. All the basics.

And, as I pointed out to the group, you still couldn't tell whether that was a well-dressed pro at the end of the bar reading *The Hollywood Reporter* or somebody married to a studio head.

"Wife or hooker, what the hell's the difference?" Billy said to Oretha, Neville, and me. "I mean, if you're being objective."

"Whoa, big dog," Oretha said.

We were taking our time, in no rush, knowing that when it was time to have dinner, we had to just walk out of the door here and into the restaurant right across the way. It was always that way with the Bel-Air. Once you got there, you didn't want to leave the premises without a very good reason.

Oretha wanted to know what was going on with Annie and me, and I told her it was all status quo. Then she asked about Carey Nash, because Billy had told her about Carey Nash, and I said that wasn't romance, it felt more like business.

Billy said, "Not everybody can be as involved as me."

Neville said, "Don't you mean evolved?"

Oretha said, "Oh, we still got a way to go on evolved."

Our dinner reservation was for eight-thirty. We were getting close, but Billy had just ordered another round. The waiter brought the drinks and said that Ralph, the bartender, had a phone call for me.

I went over and picked the phone up and said, "Molloy here."

Bobby Bullard, sounding a lot less redneck-folksy than he usually did, sounding strained, said, "I, uh, need you to get over to The Four Seasons if you could, bud. Sooner the better, if it's all the same."

"Is there some kind of problem?"

"Why don't you just get over here, Room Six-oh-four, and I'll, uh, tell you in person."

"Bobby," I said. "Tell me what's going on, or I'm not going anywhere."

I heard what sounded like the receiver being dropped, then some muffled voices in the background, then heard Ty Moranis saying to me, "I told him he could have one phone call. You're it, dog."

"Ty, what the hell's going on over there? Put Bobby back on."

"He's tied up."

"I just want to talk to him for one second."

Ty said, "Dog, like he's *really* tied up."

When Neville and I got to the lobby of The Four Seasons, Elvis and Butterball were there, along with Sultan McCovey, who was dressed up like the opening act at the Grammy Awards: Kobe Bryant No. 8 white jersey with blue trim, one more in a rapper, replica-jersey world, this one going almost to his ankles, baggy jeans hitting the top of old Adidas Superstar sneakers, high-top white, Foot Locker white, with the three blue stripes. And, of course, a Yankee baseball cap turned sideways, apparently pointing toward the ocean.

Or Japan.

I said to Sultan, "Nice look. You on your way out?"

"Chillin'," he said. "I go out, I go with my Tracy Mc-Grady."

"No doubt," I said.

"Straight tip, Gee."

I quickly introduced Neville, then pulled Sultan and the fat boys away from the concierge desk, quickly told them about my call from Bullard and Ty, asked if they knew what was going on. Elvis said, fuck man, all kinds of shit was going on, but they thought it was over now. Telling me that Bullard had told Ty at practice that the doctors thought he should rest his shoulder one more week, Ty getting more and more pissed off about that as the day wore on.

Elvis said, Like somebody told him that the gun show was in town and he couldn't go.

After practice, Ty and his boys had gone over to the House of Blues, had a few beers, came back to the hotel, decided to have a few more in the bar here. Which, Elvis said, is where they ran into Bobby Bullard and Vance Hopewell, Jr.

Having a drink they ownselves, Butterball said, picking up the story, the two coaches kicking back, watching the Oregon–USC game, fondling waitresses.

"What happened then?"

"Ty walked over and said, Hey, Coach, and sucker-punched his booger ass," Sultan said.

Elvis said, "Me and Butter was on our way out when we hear people yellin' from the bar, what sounds like glass breakin', so we get in there and break it up. I got Ty under one arm, his two posse boys in the other."

"Pussy boys, you ask me," Butterball said.

Elvis said, "Butter takes the coach, who I got to say is happy to be taken at that point."

"No doubt," Sultan said. "Punked by his own QB, bam bam bam, laid out like 'Pac 'fore he knows what hit him." Nodding. "Bitch laid out *nice.*"

Neville turned to me. "Is Sultan speaking in some sort of code?"

"Sul-*tan,*" Sultan McCovey said.

"Bobby said he'd be in his room, ice on his face, so's he didn't show up for the game tomorrow look like he went a few rounds with Roy Jones, Jr.," Elvis said. "I thought Ty took off with his hobbit boys, dressed up in L.A. like they lookin' for a snowball fight."

"Apparently they hung around," I said.

I told the others Neville and I were heading upstairs. Elvis asked if we needed backup, if not, he and Butterball were on their way to Lucy's El Adobe to see who could eat the most chimichangas. I told him Neville and I could pretty much take it from here.

"Boy looks a little *light,* you ask me," Sultan said, nodding in Neville's direction.

Neville said looks could be deceiving and asked if Sultan wanted to feel his muscles. Sultan looked at Elvis and Butter and said, "Motherfucker must be trippin'." Neville said to Sultan, All right, then, how about if I feel *your* muscle? Before Sultan could motherfuck him again, the elevator doors opened and we went upstairs to say howdy to the coach and quarterback of the New York Hawks.

We got out of the elevator on six, and I could see one of Ty's L.A. boys, looking like the road-company version of his New York boys, seated in a chair outside 604. Another young white guy trying way too hard to be black, you could see it before he even opened his mouth.

Yo.

Black knit cap with a Hawks logo on it. Ridiculously big Hawks hooded sweatshirt. Black motorcycle boots. A sixteen-ounce bottle of Mountain Dew on the carpet next to him.

"What it is?" he said.

"Boy," I said, "that one has troubled the existentialists from the beginning."

"Say what?"

"We're expected," I said. "I'm Molloy."

"Down with that," he said, getting to his feet.

Neville said, "Before long, this entire country will require subtitles."

"Uh-huh," I said, leaning slightly to one side, making a motion with my hands as if trying to raise the roof. "Uh-huh, uh-huh, uh-huh."

Neville said he'd pay me to stop.

The kid gave the door two quick raps, and it opened. There was another toy soldier inside, this one in a sleeveless parka. The parka let us in. As I passed him, I said, "Aren't you hot in that?"

As soon as were in the suite's foyer, I could hear somebody inside making *mmm mmm mmm* sounds.

Neville and I came around the corner and saw it was Bobby Bullard.

Ty hadn't been kidding. He had Bullard tied to one of the chairs in the dining area, a colorful and patriotic-looking do-rag, the kind Ty Moranis liked to wear under his helmet on Sunday, stuffed in the coach's mouth.

"After we called you," Ty said, "I couldn't listen to more of his Gomer talk."

"I hear you," I said.

Bullard said, *Mmm mmm mmm.*

I noticed he had the beginnings of a pretty good shiner going around his left eye.

I said to Ty, "Is this about you not playing tomorrow?"

Ty said, "Was like I remember that other Gomer— Vance? his defensive coach?—used to say when we were all at Tech. Was just the straw that broke the coffin's back."

He was wearing a T-shirt with the sleeves cut off and black jeans and black sneakers, the sleeveless shirt showing off the tattoo parlors up and down both arms. He was smoking an unfiltered cigarette in a jittery way.

"The shrink says I have these delayed-rage issues and whatnot," Ty said.

"You're seeing a shrink?"

"Part of my probation," he said. He shrugged. "Whatever, dog. She says that's what made me go over to my old man's house that night, all the shit I had been building up in me just finally exploding."

Making, I thought, his rage issues sound somewhat like the operating principles of a septic tank.

Bullard kept making his gagging noises, hair and eyes wild.

"We're going to have to untie him soon," I said. "Or at least take that thing out of his mouth."

"Not until I finish," Ty Moranis said. "Now, no doubt, I bring it with him in the bar because he tells me he's sitting me down when I'm good to go tomorrow. But then I go back to the room and call my shrink . . ."

I said, "You got her on a Saturday?"

". . . she tells me that it's all because of unresolved shit from the Jets game. And maybe some other unresolved shit I've had blocked since he coached me in college."

Bobby Bullard quieted down all of a sudden.

I said, what would the more recent unresolved shit be, exactly?

"Dog?" Ty said. "Like you don't know?"

"Humor me."

Ty said, "The shit where he told me to throw it to them there at the end."

"What it is," I said in a quiet voice.

Ty and I sat across from each other at the dining room table, smoking. Neville was over on a long couch in the living room area, watching television. There was a video camera set up at the end of the couch, on top of a pile of magazines, facing the folding chair Bullard had set up near the television; I'd noticed the equipment when we came in, briefly thinking Ty Moranis was going to have Bobby Bullard make a hostage tape. Then I remembered that Bullard had been keeping a video diary of his first season with the Hawks for HBO's *Inside the NFL,* the show wanting it to have a home-movie look, Bullard taping himself and mugging for the camera every Saturday, telling them how he thought the game would go.

Ty told me that Bullard had pulled him aside, Bullard trying to make a joke of it after we'd scored the punt-return touchdown, saying, well sumbitch, wasn't this worse than a limp dick at the orgy. "Asshole won't speak English," Ty said to me in 604. "You know?"

I said, "Hear you."

Ty picked the story back up, saying that on the sideline now, Bobby Bullard laughed, Ho ho ho, and said, You know, this shit goes on all the time. Ty said, What shit? Bullard said, Guys betting the dog, even when they want their team to win. Ty said, No, he didn't know that shit went on all the time. Well then listen up, Bobby told him, getting serious then, it turned out he had some good-old-boy friends who'd put some big green down on the Jets to cover today, just for the hell of it, and it wouldn't exactly be the worst thing in the world if maybe the Jets got another touch before the game ended so everybody could put a damn bow on the whole occasion.

Ty said to me, "I told him no fuckin' way. He told me it wasn't no big deal, he was just asking this one time. And besides, he says, it's not like I had the best job security in the world, if I got his drift? I said, I'm winning games for you. He gave me that asshole grin of his and said, Son, all due respect, it's the *system* winning these games as much as it is you. I told him that no matter what kind of fuckup I'd been, I'd never fucked with the game when I was on the field. Coach said he knew that, he *respected* that, but if I wouldn't do it, he'd have Down Low do it. And that by next week, he had this funny feeling a gun would turn up some-where, my car or my locker or my apartment, and that ol' Down Low Malufalu would be the one calling his ball plays." Ty said, "Smiling at me the whole time he was say-ing all his shit."

Just call the screen, Bobby Bullard told him, throw it over to that old No. 81, swearing on his momma and *her* momma he'd never ask Ty to do anything like this ever again.

He squeezed his eyes shut, not looking like a rough-tough rapper boy now, just like a kid. "So I did it."

"And then we ended up losing."

"Fuck."

"It's been eating you up ever since."

"Yeah."

"And now you got me over here . . . tell me again why did you get me over here?"

"I'll tell you why," he said. "You could've busted me that night at the Be A Wolf, and didn't. And I know you played, dog. And on top of all that, I don't trust any of the rest of the other assholes in charge of this team."

Ty said, "I wanted you to hear this shit from me first, *then* him."

"Why didn't you want Dick Miles to hear?"

"You trippin'? He owns Coach the way Coach thinks he owns me."

"You think he told Coach to do this?"

Ty Moranis shrugged. "He won't say that to me, maybe he'll say it to you."

I said to him, "You really feel like you're good to go to-morrow?"

"No doubt."

"Then you play."

"Like that?"

"Like that," I said.

"You can still do that?"

"Yeah, dog," I said. "I believe I can."

I told him to take the Backstreet Boys and get lost and stay out of trouble between now and the kickoff. He said he was down with that, and left. It was me, Neville, Bobby Bullard now. I went over and squatted in front of my coach. I told him I was going to take the gag out of his mouth and then I was going to ask him a question, but that if he yelled at me—or worse, lied to me—I was going to leave him alone with Neville.

"And you never want to be left alone with Neville," I said.

"Give us a kiss," Neville said from across the room, where he was watching what looked like an old Wham video.

I said to Bullard, "Is Ty telling the truth?"

I took the do-rag out of his mouth and Bobby Bullard said, "I can explain."

"You can explain later," I said. "First tell me if he's telling the truth."

Bullard's shoulders slumped, and suddenly he wasn't so folksy.

"Yeah," he said.

He told me the rest of it then. When he was done, I turned to Neville and said, "That thing work?"

Bobby Bullard's video cam.

"You know what they say," Neville said. "The camera never lies."

"Aw shit, pards," Bullard said. "You taped this?"

"It's a variation of a scam I ran on somebody else one time," I said. "It's a play a lot older than one of your ball plays. Called the Bump-and-Run."

Before we left, I told Bullard what the deal was going to be from now on. I told him that if anybody asked him to do anything funny from now on, he called me. I told him not to tell anybody about the little meeting of the minds we'd just had. If he did, then I'd have to tell on him.

I had untied him by now. He was sitting, beaten, at the dining room table himself.

"Bobby," I said, "I think I just found myself a football coach."

He said he needed more ice, and walked out of the room.

At the elevator, Neville Hayward said, "Just tell me one thing: Is every weekend like this in your football?"

20

By the next day, the fight in the bar at The Four Seasons had gotten enough play on television and the Internet and in the local papers that Bobby Bullard, black eye and all, had to address it in an on-camera with Annie Kay for *The NFL Today* before he even left the hotel.

"Hey," Bobby said, looking straight into the camera. "I figure I got off easy with a coon's eye. You might be too young to remember that time Billy Martin, God bless his pickled soul, got jumped on by one of his pitchers in the old days. But that old boy showed up at the ballpark the next day with his broken arm in a damn sling."

Annie said, "But, Coach, considering Ty's record, hasn't he violated several clauses in his contract by taking a swing at his *coach*?"

Bobby pushed back a Hawks visor I was starting to think he must sleep in, ran a hand through his hair, and said, "That's what you say, hon. I just look at my QB and think, There's a dog wants to be in any kind of fight. Give me his kind over some of the bitches and poodles I've coached anytime."

I knew I was watching a taped version by the time they aired it on the West Coast, but noted that in a reality-TV world, CBS elected to leave in "bitches."

Annie said, "Can I ask you what Dick Miles thinks about all this?"

Bullard said, "Mr. Dick Miles wasn't around yesterday. And when Mr. Dick Miles isn't around, I take my marching orders from my man, Jack Molloy, who isn't gonna get his Jockey shorts tangled over boys bein' boys in a bar."

We were watching all this in Billy's suite.

"*My man* Jack Molloy?" Billy said. "Jesus, kid, you still got it."

"I told you," I said, "the coach and I have an understanding now."

Neville held up the cassette we'd brought with us from 604, one we'd just shown Billy and Oretha, and said, "The power of television."

I said, "The medium is still the message."

When it was time to go over to the game, we went in Billy's personal limo, which Vinny Two had driven from Vegas. Vinny driving was the reason I didn't get lost trying to find the Coliseum for the first time in my life. It had been a while, but the place hadn't changed much, reminding me more and more of the Roman Colosseum, which meant imposing and historic and in about the same shape as South Central L.A. But Vito Cazenovia, the Bangers' owner, was still being forced to use it, same as the hated USC Trojans; it was his trade-off for getting the second-biggest television market in the country back into the league. And, I thought, his punishment for believing the mayor and the governor were actually going to deliver on the stadium they'd promised him if he'd do that. But now Vito was in the *L.A. Times* every few days making veiled threats about bailing out the way the Rams and Raiders had before him, the

Raiders having moved down the coast from Oakland in the
'80s, during that period when their owner, Al Davis, gave
you the idea he planned to tour them like Holiday on Ice.

Al wanted a stadium, too, never got one, went back to
Oakland. The best the city council had done for Vito
Cazenovia so far was build him some luxury suites, sharing
the cost with rich USC alums. That's where our group
watched the game. Dick Miles was supposed to be in the
one next door with a bunch of Hollywood assholes, which
is why I kept poking my head in during the first half to see if
he'd shown up yet. I finally gave up and assumed he wasn't
coming. Jeff Brewer wasn't in there, either. I also hadn't
seen Brewer on the field before the game, or in the press box
when I made a quick pass through there.

By halftime, Ty Moranis had thrown three touchdown
passes, two to Sultan, and we were ahead of the unbeaten
Bangers, 24–10.

I noticed Sultan had made some variations in his touchdown dance, losing most of the old Michael Jackson stuff
in the middle of his number—"Sul*tan* McCovey," he explained, "ain't coppin' some brother who brags on TV
about his bed being a class *trip*"—and gone with some old-
fashioned break-dancing instead. Neville watched him after the first touchdown, on a slant pattern, and said, "We
need more of this back home in the First Division."

It was after the second touchdown that Sultan pretty
much ensured, I thought, that he would lead most of the
prime-time highlight shows. His jersey had been out of his
football pants from the first series of downs. Now he reached
behind him, pulled out a cell phone that didn't look much
bigger than his thumb, and called up to the CBS booth and
asked Phil Simms and Greg Gumbel if they had any questions that couldn't wait until after the game.

The television set we had on in the suite verified that
Sultan's Nokia did provide amazingly good reception.

"Touchdown brought to you by Nokia," Sultan said,

when they were through chatting. "And by Sul*tan* Mc-Covey, who *always* provides the best receptions."

At the end of the third quarter, by which time the game had become an official blowout at 34–10, Annie and her cameraman, Duff, knocked on the door to the suite. Vinny answered it, gave Annie a kiss, and showed them in.

"I'd like to ask you a few questions," she said, all business. "On air."

"I'm all yours."

Duff had us set up in the front of the suite, the field visible through the big window we'd kept open. Before we were rolling, Annie said, "How about one off-the-record question?"

"I don't think so."

She asked anyway. I knew she would.

"Why are Bobby Bullard and Machine Gun Moranis so sweet on you all of a sudden?"

"If I were to give in to your relentless probing, which I'm not, because you obviously plan to go a whole season being mean to me, I would just point out that my immense personal charm wears down everybody eventually."

"Almost everybody."

"You say."

"Something's going on here."

"Actually," I said, "there's a lot going on. But given the current political climate, I'm just not going to share it with you."

Annie said, "I had lunch with your former team president, Ms. Liz Bolton, yesterday. She sent her love. Though not as creatively as she used to, of course."

"How's she doing?"

"She says clawing her way to the top of the movie business is taking more time than she thought it would," she said, "but that Hollywood's about what she expected, just with more lying."

Duff said, "Speed, kids."

Annie said, "Jack, are you planning any disciplinary action against Ty Moranis for his fight with Bobby Bullard
yesterday?"

I gave her a straight answer.

"I think any disciplinary action would have to come
from Mr. Miles, the managing partner of the Hawks."

"Coach Bullard said that with Mr. Miles not around, you
were the one who elected to play Ty today, despite the advice of the team doctors. And you were the one who basically decided to ignore the two of them having a brawl in a
hotel bar."

"Well, Annie," I said. "I guess old habits die hard."

"Which habits would those be?"

"I'll give you a line from my father," I said. "He used to
tell me that this wasn't the Boy Scouts of America. That if
you were going to show up on Sunday, you might as well
win the game."

"But—"

"Ty told me he was good to go. I believed him. The only
people who would've wanted him to sit this one out are the
Bangers. And now, if you don't mind, I'd sort of like to get
back to this ass-whipping."

We stood there for a moment, looking at each other, before Duff said, "They're telling me in my ear they need us
downstairs with ten minutes left."

To him, Annie said, "Okay." To me: "How did we end
up here?"

"Ask Vinny," I said. "I always get lost as soon as I get off
the freeway."

"I wasn't looking for smart-ass."

"Then try this," I said. "I'd rather be with you."

"You're with somebody else."

I saw Oretha on the other side of the room, watching us
instead of the game.

"You're the one with somebody else," I said.

"Not the way you are."

"I'm just trying to get my team back."

"And Carey Nash is helping you?"

Actually, I told Annie, she was.

She and Duff left. I stood at the window and watched the end of the game, which we ended up winning, 41–17. When it was over, I told Billy and Oretha I wouldn't be long, made the walk down to the locker room. The writers were still outside. A few of them asked me what I thought about the events of the last eighteen hours or so, and I told them, well, the New York Hawks considered it our obligation to provide some kind of Hollywood ending to the weekend. Then I walked past them and showed the guy at the door my pass and went inside to find Ty Moranis.

He was in the trainers' room, with an ice bag the size of a beach ball attached to his right shoulder, and a smaller one on his elbow.

He'd sat out most of the fourth quarter once it was 41–10, Bullard giving some time to Down Low Malufalu.

"Good game," I said.

"They come out so bad, then we get up on them and they just stuck their candy asses up in the air and said, Give it to us."

I told him that was probably the way Jim Nantz had described the action on the extended postgame show.

"See you in New York," I said, and started to leave. When I was at the door, Ty said, "Yo?"

I turned around.

"Thanks," he said.

I said, "You stay out of trouble from now on, and I got your back."

"Hear that."

"No guns," I said.

"Day at a time, dog," Ty Moranis said. "Day at a time."

Dick Miles didn't show up in the office on Monday. Neither did Jeff Brewer. When I did see Brewer on Tuesday morning and asked where Miles was, he said, "Amsterdam."

"Amsterdam Avenue?"

"The one in Holland," he said. "Something to do with transponders."

"Any idea when he'll be back?"

Brewer said, "I'll bounce the question off one of the satellites he already owns and get back to you."

Mr. Open Door went into his office then and shut his door, maybe to send dirty e-mails to Annie.

Billy called later in the day, wanting to know if I'd had my sit-down with Miles yet, the one we'd talked about in L.A. I told him Miles was in Amsterdam.

"Legal hookers in Holland, who would've figured," he said. "Can you imagine what a growth industry that would be in Vegas?"

I said, "Have you found out anything more about Miles making any friends from what you like to call an alternative financial lifestyle?"

"I'm workin' on it," Billy Grace said. "These things take more time than they used to. One of the reasons being that a lot of my old contacts have passed."

We played the Colts the next Sunday, at Molloy.

It only became the worst home loss since the team had moved from Memphis to New York.

At halftime, by which time it was 27–3, Indianapolis, Boomer Esiason would suggest on CBS that he was almost positive we had qualified for federal disaster relief.

Boomer was talking about the three injuries, not the six turnovers we'd already had.

Bobby Camby, who'd already rushed for a thousand yards and had the media talking about another shot at two thousand, tore up his anterior cruciate ligament early in the second quarter when Zeke Widger fell on him. You could tell by the way Bobby, a tough kid, started writhing on the field that it was bad. They brought a golf cart out for him, which is never good, took a look at the knee in the X-ray room we had at Molloy, then took him straight to Columbia Presbyterian. I'd end up getting a call early in the fourth quarter. They were going to have to wait for the swelling to go down to do the surgery, but he was gone for the season and maybe for good, you never knew with knees, especially when you moved into the area where the injuries required initials.

While they were taking Bobby to the hospital, Redford Newman, our fullback, took a late hit on the sideline and broke his collarbone.

Then, right before halftime, cherry on top of the sundae, Ty Moranis took a helmet shot to his sore right shoulder. He went to the X-ray room, the doctors said the pictures were inconclusive and they'd have to do an MRI in the morning. But Ty was through for the day, too.

The final was Colts 44, Hawks 3.

A.T.M. and this week's Yum girls left at the half, one of the girls saying this was more depressing than running out of weed. I watched the rest of it by myself. Neville had taken the morning American back to London, reminding me before he left that he wouldn't need much notice if I needed him to come back. Like the kind of notice where all I had to do was ring the flat or the club and he would throw some clothes in a bag and be on his way to Heathrow. I told him I appreciated that, but to get back over there and continue to make Scratch the hottest club in town because, who the hell knew, maybe he might end up a partner someday.

He answered with a lot of smashing and jolly good.

Ferret called with about five minutes to go in the game and said there'd been no unusual action on us, either in Vegas or New York, which made it five games in a row when nothing had happened to make the needle jump.

I'd left messages for Carey Nash all week, with no response.

When the game was mercifully over, I called Wick Sanderson over at Giants Stadium, where I knew he was getting ready to watch the Giants play the Cowboys, and asked if he and Carole Sandusky would like to meet me at Yum later and watch me drown my sorrows.

"Carole is back in L.A.," he said. "Some deal where they injected the wrong stuff between her eyes."

"Well, then," I said, "if the old commish thinks he can handle the temptation, why don't we meet up there about nine?"

"Let's sit in the back," he said. "I think Ginger's on tonight."

"Who's Ginger?"

"A girl who loves pro football, Jack."

We sat in the back. Ginger had our table. She was the tall redhead I'd seen there before, one who clearly had no future with Victoria's Secret, she actually looked as if she liked a hot meal once in a while.

Wick Sanderson called her Ginger the big red girl.

Elvis and Butterball, who'd both left the Colts game with ankle sprains, limped over to our table when they saw us come in, paid their respects to the commissioner, bitched that some of the painkillers Harm Battles and Hans Nowitzky had given them before the game had done too good a job of masking the pain.

Wick Sanderson did what he usually did when players started talking about drugs:

Put his hands over his ears and starting singing show tunes, in this case "All I Need Is the Girl" from *Gypsy,* currently in revival on Broadway with Madonna.

They said they'd stay and have a drink, but they both had spa appointments starting in five minutes.

Butter said to Elvis, "And for the last goddamn time, I get that Eva. On account of, I got that thigh bruise to go with my ankle."

Elvis said, "What about my groin?"

"You said he gave you a shot for that shit, too."

Wick Sanderson sang louder. ". . . got my best vest . . ."

Elvis said, "Wore off. I'm getting that old tingle back right now."

They walked toward the stairs, still bickering.

"Liar," Butter said.

"Deep thigh, my ass."

"Faggot."

We sat there for a while, sipping our drinks and looking at Ginger and the other goddess women in the room, and then I said to Wick Sanderson, "What happens if some guy buys a team and then when it comes time to pay he doesn't have the money?"

Just like that.

He looked at me through orange-tinted glasses.

"What are you really asking me, Jack?"

"You heard me."

Ginger brought us a new bowl of mixed peanuts, leaning over to take the empty bowl between us. Wick Sanderson looked as if he wanted to jump into her arms like a kid jumping into Santa's lap.

"You can't possibly be asking me about Dick Miles."

"Work with me here," I said. "What happens?"

"Okay," he said. "I'll give you a serious answer to a ridiculous question, if the question really is about Dick Miles. If in the course of our vetting—which we take pretty fucking seriously, by the way—we discover that a probationary owner doesn't have the financing we thought he had, or that he might not have the money when it comes time for what is essentially a delayed closing, we begin to take steps to blow him out of there." He sipped his white wine. "Which means, we let him know that he's not going to have the votes, and prep him on what we want him to say to the media. How it wasn't what he thought it was going to be, or that his life was moving in another direction. Blah blah blah. The whole time stressing that he better be a good camper and do what he's told, or we tell the world he's a fraud."

"Has it ever happened?"

"About ten years ago," he said, "when Paul Tagliabue was still commissioner. Jack Kent Cooke had finally kicked, the son was selling the Redskins. This was before Danny Snyder came along with his eight hundred mil to save the day. The Cooke kid had originally agreed to sell to somebody else, a rich guy from Long Island, I forget his name. I think from the North Fork, could've been the South. Anyhow, he said he'd pay the eight hundred mil, and then it turned out that he didn't have anywhere near that kind of money, even though he was scrambling around to get it. This was in the days before we even had the probation period, or the Maurie Grubman rules. They just told the Long Island guy to get lost, moved on to Snyder, case closed. But as I recall, that whole thing played out during the off-season."

I lit a cigarette.

"What if something like that did happen with somebody like Miles?"

"Jack," he said, "cut the shit. We're talking about Dick Miles here."

"Who you have thoroughly checked out."

"Yes, as a matter of fact. Who we have thoroughly checked out." He leaned forward, lowered his voice, though I didn't think Ginger was some sort of security risk, not dressed in her spank-me outfit with the black see-through cape. "Is the guy as flush as he used to be? No. And, by the way, who the hell is these days? But he's still Dick Miles. He called me the other day, from some goddamn place in Europe, and said he was planning to divest himself of a couple of his loser companies, streamline his situation a little bit, maybe even sell a couple of houses now that he says he's a permanent bachelor. And you know why? Because he wants to concentrate on the Hawks."

"That's just it," I said. "He's *not* concentrating on the Hawks. I am. The bastard is never around."

"Yeah, he's the first camper ever to behave that way."

"Wick, listen to me. I've been debating whether or not to go to you with this. Now I have. You're not just the commish, you're my friend. Miles is in trouble. He may still think he's one of the sharks, but the sucker is swimming in red ink."

"Bullshit. I'd know. Hell, *everybody'd* know."

"You know that's not true. Remember that guy Robert Maxwell, owned all those newspapers in Europe, even had the *Daily News* for a while? He finally went over the side of his boat and then everybody found out that not only was the fat bastard nearly broke, he'd been stealing pension money."

"What you're suggesting about Dick Miles," Wick Sanderson said, "you can prove this, of course."

I leaned back. "Not exactly." I blew some air out of me. "Not yet, anyway."

"Oh, good, Jack, I'll run straight to the Finance Committee with this. Tell them we need to run a benefit for Dick Fucking Miles before the sale can be approved." He smiled up at Ginger and said, "Hey, big red girl, how about two more," watched her walk away, smiling at him over her shoulder.

"Miles says he's waited his whole life to own his own team, and now, in his first season owning his own team, he disappears for weeks at a time. You don't find that unusual?"

"I told you, he's reorganizing shit."

"He's grifting around for money!" I said, loud enough to make people at the other tables look around.

"Jack," Wick Sanderson said, "you know I love you. I know it must piss you off to no end that this prick has your team. But give this up. The other owners want Dick Miles in the club. He's one of them. And if he's got the money when the time comes, they're frankly not going to give a shit where it came from."

I sat back, closed my eyes, wondering what the commissioner of the league would think of my Bobby Bullard home movie, the coach of the Hawks admitting he had Ty give it up for the Jets.

Knowing at the same time I couldn't show it to him, because it would mean the end of both their careers.

"All Dick Miles is trying to do is win a Super Bowl, same as you did," he said.

"It's not the same."

"Sure it is. You just won't admit it."

I saw him give a little wave. Turned and saw Ginger taking off her cape in a slow way, like she was stripping for him, untying the little black apron she was wearing underneath it, waving back at him.

"I don't want you to think the conversation has started to drag," Wick Sanderson said. "But Ginger's shift is ending a little early tonight."

"Miles shouldn't own my team," I said.

"You should have thought about that a long time ago," Wick Sanderson said.

I should have gone home when the commissioner and the much taller Ginger—their relationship already looked like a mismatch in the low post—went off into the night.

Instead I took a cab down to The Last Good Year, always a good quiet Sunday night place.

When I walked in, Joe Healey looked up at the end of the bar and said, "Nice outing today. No shit, I think the Colts just scored again."

Healey and I stayed at the bar until one in the morning. I still wasn't drunk, despite all the Scotches I'd had since showing up at Yum, still wired about the way we'd played, all the injuries, my conversation with Wick Sanderson, the last thing he'd said to me about Dick Miles.

I said goodnight to Healey, decided to walk a little bit before getting into a cab and heading home to Suite 19.

I could have walked over to Third from The Last Good Year, which was between Second and Third on Fiftieth, walked uptown so I could eventually get into an uptown cab, not that it mattered very much.

I walked up Second instead, thinking about everything Billy and I had talked about in Los Angeles, how he thought this thing might play out.

I got a pretty good track record of betting right, Billy said.

I told him that nobody knew that better than I did.

Including betting on you when you first come out to Vegas with your tail between your fuckin' legs, Billy said.

I told him I'd been an out bet all the way. A sure thing.

Sure you were, he said.

I walked up Second and took a right at Fifty-sixth by habit, and found myself standing in front of Pete Stanton's building. I knew he wasn't there, having talked to him last week, knew he was still in Florida with Pam, giving his marriage one last big shot.

You miss it? I'd said to him on the phone.

Only every day, he said.

Pam sick of you yet?

No comment.

I said, you find the food as tasty at the early-bird specials?

He said I should go fuck myself.

I sat on the low brick wall that was the boundary of the circular driveway at 300 East Fifty-sixth and smoked a cigarette and thought about Pete, and everybody else who was gone: Josh, who was struggling with the Packers, either 4–7 or 5–6 now, I didn't even know if he'd won his game against the Lions; Brian Goldberg, who'd called the Bel-Air from Detroit when he heard about Bobby Bullard and Ty Moranis, laughing and telling me I was on my own now, I didn't have the little Jew to clean up messes like that.

Sat there and did the math on my ticking clock, how many more weeks and months I had before Dick Miles closed the deal on the Hawks, if he could.

Closed the deal, closed me out.

I walked the block over to First now, not thinking too much about it, thinking about my guys, realized I was across the street from Carey Nash's building. The last time I'd talked to her, before I'd left for L.A., she'd said something about needing some "me" time, that she might sneak off to someplace warm, she wasn't sure what else she could do with her ex-husband, now we just had to wait and see if he had one more trick up his sleeve.

Maybe she was back, maybe she wasn't. Even if she was, I'd never been the type, even after a few drinks, to show up unannounced in the middle of the night.

Not my style.

Except with Annie.

But Annie was different.

Goddamn I was tired.

There was a bus-stop bench on the west side of First. I sat down, told myself one more cigarette, Molloy.

Then home to Molloy.

Maybe I was a little drunk.

I sat there and smoked, and when I finished, I stood up and crossed First Avenue just as the Lincoln Town Car that had been idling in front of 400 East Fifty-sixth, on the street near the circular driveway that looked exactly like the one in front of Pete's building, slowly eased into the driveway and toward the front door.

I saw the doorman come through the revolving doors first, laughing as he did, waving at the driver of the Town Car to stay where he was, then opening the back door nice and wide for the guy behind him, the one making him laugh, the self-proclaimed young Jammer, Jeff Brewer himself.

21

Big Tim Molloy, who bragged that he had more theories about things than China had Chinamen, had this theory about what to do when you started to feel like you were surrounded, in business or love or any damn thing.

"Molloy," he'd say, "when in doubt, look busy."

The first time he ever used the line on me was when I was on my way out of the restaurant business, and on my way out of New York City, just not knowing that last part at the time, still thinking I could make my joint, Montana, the hot place on the Upper East Side all over again. The old man and I weren't getting along then, hadn't been getting along for a long time, were giving off no signs that we ever would again. But I knew he was trying to help, and so I told him that was such brilliant advice he ought to write one of those color-code-your-life books.

"Seven simple plans my ass," he said. "Sometimes any plan will do."

By the time I got to the office on Monday morning, having drunk a little more when I got back to Suite 19 and slept as late as I used to in the old days, back when a hangover was like my second job, my plan was simple: fix the Hawks before trying to figure out if Carey Nash was the latest woman in my life who might possibly be sleeping with the enemy.

Basically what I decided was that job one for the upcoming week was to get a running back to replace Bobby Camby, who was having surgery on his knee later that afternoon at the New York Hospital for Special Surgery. The surgery had originally been scheduled for Columbia Presbyterian, where they'd brought Bobby C. after the game. But he'd decided to make the switch at the last second, explaining it had nothing to do with a preference for the orthopedic surgeons at either hospital, it just turned out by sheer coincidence he had intimate knowledge of a whole floor of candy stripers in the orthopedic wing at Special Surgery.

"Once they stop cuttin' on you," he told me on the phone a couple of hours before they put him under, "then it's just pain pills, downtime, and askin' the wash-up nurse to come in and lock the door."

I told him I was good with all of it.

I had more options replacing a star like him in midseason than I used to, the new collective bargaining agreement having dramatically relaxed the salary cap rules, at least as they related to injured players. Meaning that if somebody like Bobby C. did go down once your roster was basically set, you didn't have to feel as if the cap had you pinned when you started looking for ways to replace him. If you lost your best runner in the old days, or your quarterback, you were basically fucked, having to promote from within, or pick up some guy, usually with more baggage than baggage claim, off waivers.

In-season trades were as rare as an honest back judge.

But Wick Sanderson, who fancied himself a visionary when you could get him out of places like Beef or Yum—or out of Ginger, for that matter—had noticed how over-

heated everybody got in baseball right before the midseason trading deadline, and how the same thing happened in
pro basketball, as if everybody in those sports were getting
ready to swap wives. So now in the NFL you could make
trades up until the twelfth week of the regular season,
which meant with four games to go before the playoffs.
The big thing was, you could add salary in cases where you
were replacing an injured player. If a team going nowhere
had a big-ticket stud it wanted to unload, trying to dump
salary or pick up draft choices or both, you could make the
deal, as long as the guy you were picking up had a salary
that matched the one belonging to a Bobby Camby.

Bottom line on all this dizzying high finance?

Bobby C. was making five million a year, and if I could
find myself a five-million-dollar running back, I could go
for it.

As soon as Susan Burden handed me the morning giant-
sized Starbucks she always had waiting for me—I refused to
describe them in Latin—I started working the phones. My
first call went to the hateful Borden Skiles, agent to the stars.
I had one question for him. He gave me the answer I wanted.
It meant that before they even wheeled Bobby C. into the operating room, I'd already settled on his replacement:

Priceless Braxton.

"Isn't he still off doin' one of them spiritual ass-wipe
deals?" Bobby Bullard said when I told him the good news
about Priceless.

"Ashram," I said. "But I think he's back in the country
for a card show."

"Aw, shit, Jack," Bullard said. "You know I've never
been scared off by no flakes. Look at Ty. Hell, looky here at
me, I'm a bowl of damn Frosted Flakes by myself. But
you're not serious about makin' a run at that old twisty-
hipped Dolly Lammer, are you?"

"He's the best guy out there. He's still one of Borden's
clients. And if we can make it work with a project like Ty,
we can make it work with him."

"What's that mean, *we,* white man?" Bobby said.

Priceless Braxton of the St. Louis Rams was the only running back in NFL history who'd gained two thousand rushing yards in a season twice. He'd played his college football at Iowa, had moves that made people call him a combination of Gale Sayers and Barry Sanders, had most football fans in general agreement that he was the fastest thing to ever come out of an NFL backfield. But with Priceless, there was also agreement on one other point:

He was a Psychic Friends Network all by himself.

Even Barry Sanders, another one who'd walked away from football in his prime and seemed to disappear into thin air, admitted in an ESPN Classic interview one time that he thought Priceless was even more weird than Sanders himself was.

"After that," Sanders said, evoking the name of another old Detroit athlete, "you're moving into a Dennis Rodman area."

Priceless Braxton really had started making off-season pilgrimages to see the Dalai Lama when he was still playing. Had traveled all over the world, to countries even *National Geographic* had never heard of, protesting everything from whales to wars to human rights to holes in the ozone. Had gone on a famous hunger strike to protest the imprisonment of the boyhood friend—Reverend Rashidi Kareem Jones— who'd started the Church of Privileged Brothers in St. Louis, and later had been accused of embezzling twenty million dollars, half of it from Priceless himself.

Priceless had gone his entire football career without speaking to the media, but four days into his fast did make a rare comment outside the jail in Columbia, Missouri, the last official public statement he'd made anywhere:

"Redemption. Forgiveness. More bottled water."

He'd retired the same year we won the Super Bowl, disappearing off to India or Nepal or someplace; now the only way to track him, if you could call it tracking him, was through his weird drop-ins at card shows, which had now become his main source of income. Priceless remained a big attraction for promoters despite his refusal to make eye contact with the patrons, his meditation breaks in the middle of his sessions, and his frequently showing up wearing his Discman headphones. But I knew Borden Skiles had been sending out feelers since the start of the season that his client might be willing to return to the game, describing a spiritual man now free of his contractual obligations to the Rams—they'd won five games in his last two seasons and apparently Priceless had decided they were never going to be any fucking good in his lifetime—and ready to cut a new deal for himself.

Preferably guaranteed and long-term.

As close as he was to our coach, Borden Skiles hadn't discussed bringing Priceless to the Hawks, because we already had Bobby Camby.

That was then. Now Bobby C. was gone for the year, Redford Newman was gone for the year, and Ty Moranis was going to be out for at least two weeks with a slight tear of the labrium in his throwing shoulder.

"I think Mrs. Elvis had that one time," Elvis Elgin said when informed of Ty's sore labrium, "when the two of us got a little overstimulated and this and that."

In Bobby Bullard's office now, I said, "Borden says it'll take a five-million signing bonus, which we don't have to count against the cap. And then two million for the rest of the season."

"That's not a contract, Jack, that's stick 'em up."

I reminded the coach that Skiles might be a thief, but he was his thief, too.

"You think Frank and Jesse James didn't have their differences?" Bullard said.

But he said he'd walk the idea down to Dick Miles before practice, since Miles was scheduled to make a rare Molloy Stadium appearance later. I told him I'd either see him at practice or still be in my office when practice was over, working the phones about quarterbacks in case Ty Moranis's shoulder was slow coming around.

This was all part of the new spirit of cooperation between the coach and me, forged as soon as I'd left his suite at The Four Seasons with the tape Neville had made. Our deal was that I was making personnel decisions for the Hawks now, at least behind the scenes, with Bobby Bullard claiming them as his own in public, and especially in the presence of Dick Miles.

I'd decided that whatever happened between Miles and me, I couldn't get around the fact that in my heart, my team was still my team. And if I could save the season while Miles was trying to save his sorry ass, I had to do it.

My own game within a game.

Making myself busy, the way the old man said I should.

We were practicing late that day, four o'clock. About a quarter to four, Bullard poked his head into my office and told me that Dick Miles had said no to Priceless Braxton.

"Why?" I said. "He knows how much we could use him."

"Just said he'd spent all the money on this year's edition of the Hawks he was gonna spend, and for me to work it out with what I had."

"Did he really say this year's edition?"

"That he did, pards."

"Fuck him."

Bobby Bullard took off his visor, pointed it in the general direction of my old office, now Dick Miles's.

"Have at him," Bobby Bullard said. "You're the boss."

"Yours, anyway," I said.

Dick Miles said he didn't have a lot of time, he had to be somewhere.

"You just got here," I said.

"Out-of-the-office meeting."

"Which European country is it this time?"

Miles said, "I said out of the office, not out of the country."

"You can tell me where it is, we're partners."

"New Jersey."

"Management," I said, "or waste?"

He said we were the ones wasting time here, what did I want to see him about?

"Why won't you sign Priceless Braxton?" Before he could answer, I pointed out something I'd noticed as soon as I'd walked in the door.

"You're wearing a tie," I said.

"There are exceptions to every rule," he said.

He reluctantly motioned for me to sit down on the other side of the desk, asked if I wanted coffee or a soft drink or water. I told him I was fine. I was still standing, looking at the view behind him through his bay windows, seeing the players on the far side of the field warming up for practice.

I tried to remember the last Hawks game Dick Miles had attended in person, much less the last time he'd been at practice. The first month of the season you couldn't keep him away from the practice field during the week, mostly because that's where the cameras and microphones were.

Sitting down now, thinking to myself: The number one sports lover in America didn't seem to love sports too much these days.

"You are aware we get a big, fat salary-cap exception on Priceless," I said.

Miles said, "Where's he been working out lately, by the way, the planet Dipshit?"

"Borden says he's never out of shape, and it would only take him a couple of weeks to get into game shape."

"Borden doesn't know what kind of shape he's in," Miles said, drumming his fingers on the desk. "Borden just knows what four percent of seven million is without even using a calculator."

"We need him."

"We can get by without him."

"No," I said. "We can't."

Miles stood up and put his hands behind him and stared out the window at the field at Molloy. Back-talking me.

"I thought you understood something, Jack," he said. "There's a new sheriff in town." Turning around when he delivered that one, maybe to see if I'd somehow managed to keep a straight face. I thought even he might have smiled at how stupid that sounded. But he didn't. "We don't throw money around the way you and Pete Stanton did in the old days. We're paying Bobby Bullard half what we paid Josh Blake—and how's he doing in Green Bay, by the way?— and we got Ty Moranis on the cheap compared to what guys who don't have numbers close to his are getting. If Bobby wants a new ballcarrier, tell him to go bargain hunting."

"If we don't get Priceless, some other contender will."

Miles sat back down, drank something out of a New York Athletic Club mug, just like one the old man used to have.

Or maybe it was the old man's.

Miles said, "We'll just have to take that chance, won't we?"

I took a nice deep breath, one of those cleansing breaths Annie used to talk about when she'd do her yoga in the morning while I was watching *SportsCenter,* and said, "Why don't we just pay Priceless with a couple of Sundays of winning bets." Now I was smiling. "Manny Katzenberg'll be thrilled, you know how he loves money that doesn't come off the books."

Miles was cool about it, I had to give him that. He punched a button on his intercom, telling Ms. Thorn to hold all his calls, even though I was pretty sure she was already holding all his calls. Then he walked over to his bar setup, threw some ice into a tumbler, poured some gin over the ice, came back and sat on the edge of the desk closest to

me, dangling one of those tassled loafers that for some reason always reminded me of golf pros.

"Is that all you've got?"

Like I'd hit him with my best shot and he'd taken it.

"Nah," I said. "That was just moving my pawn up to
rook four, or wherever you move your fucking pawn."

Miles shrugged. "I placed a few bets for old times' sake.
I wanted to see if I needed to pile action on top of action.
Turned out I didn't. I quit. Case closed." He ran a finger
around the rim of his glass. "You think I'm the only owner
who bets on games, Jack? You know better than anyone.
Because you're the one who fronted Bubba Royal all that
money that he bet on himself in the Super Bowl that time."

Then: "Sure you don't want a drink?"

"Have fun trying to prove it," I said. "About Bubba."

"You prove I bet on the Hawks."

"We seemed to have reached an impasse," I said. "And
not just on Priceless."

Dick Miles said, "Let me give you some free advice,
Jack. Don't *ever* underestimate me."

"I just came in to talk about a running back, then the
conversation took this wrong turn."

Miles looked at his watch. "You're the one who took a
wrong turn," he said. "But if you want to continue down
this path, let's go, I've still got a few minutes."

I walked over and leaned against the windowsill and
watched Down Low Malufalu throw a sideline pass to Sultan McCovey, who caught it with one hand the way A.T.M.
used to. Remembering how I loved to stand here when this
was my office, watch practice from here, realize later that
I'd been standing in the same place for an hour. Or more.

I said to Dick Miles, "You can't be such a bitch to the
banks that you can't come up with the money for a player
like Priceless Braxton."

Miles said, "Now we're turning cards over."

"Chess was a bad example," I said. "I'm a blackjack guy."

"Blackjack Molloy," he said. "Always thinking he's smarter than he really is."

"Who's underestimating who now?" I said. "Or is it whom—I never could keep that Strunk and White shit straight in college. I always thought they sounded like a couple of pulling guards."

He stood up, put himself on the other side of the windows. I wondered what some of the players would think if they looked up and saw us facing each other, pointing at each other sometimes like it was *Crossfire*.

"If you're such a smart guy, Jack, how come this is my office now?"

"Yours," I said, "or the banks'?"

"Somebody's giving you bad information."

"I don't think so."

I wanted to tell him he should go easier on whatever cologne he was wearing. Instead I walked around to the other side of the desk, hoping the urge to smack him would pass.

His office now.

Miles said, "If you're listening to my ex-wife in addition to screwing her, well, that's the price you have to pay for screwing her, I'm afraid. She's a lot like you, now that I think about it. Another one who thinks she's a lot smarter than she really is."

"You're in trouble," I said, "and we both know it."

He grabbed his glass again, toasted me with it, drank some gin.

"Even if I am, that's part of the fun of *being* who I am," he said. "I'm Dick Miles, Jack. And I do get into trouble sometimes. But I always get out of it. I thought I explained that to you the night we met in London."

"Why don't we put that trouble in the papers and let the readers decide?"

"You're not going to do that."

"Try me."

Miles said, "What are you really after here? You want

me to admit to you that I'm getting squeezed a little bit by the economy and by a few banks? Okay, you got that, Jack. I put myself in a position where I need a few good men who are a little more loyal than some of the ones I've made rich and now don't want to play. That's it. It's happened to a lot of guys, some you know about, some you don't. Now it's happening to me. Big fucking deal."

"Nice speech," I said. "Tell it to that hot chick on CNBC someday. I just want my team back."

He laughed.

The urge to slap him was back.

"What is this, the playground? I'm supposed to give you a do-over because I took something away you want back? Sonofabitch, Jack, they're right about you, you never did grow up."

"If you don't have chump change for Priceless Braxton, how do you plan to come up with the money for my sibs and me?"

"I'll come up with it. I told you, I always do." He looked at his watch.

"It's obvious your situation has changed since London," I said. "So explain to me why it's so important to you to hold on to this team."

"You really don't get this, do you? Getting out now would be losing. I'm a bad loser."

"Not as bad as I am," I said.

"Right," he said. "Now I'm supposed to go all jelly-legged because you're threatening to run to the papers."

"You're a big man about town, Dick. So you must know it only takes one blind item to start a shitstorm."

I was thinking again how much better we got along at The Savoy.

"You're not going to call the papers," he said. "Or have any of your people call the papers."

I had to admit to him that I really didn't have many people around here anymore.

Miles said, "Because if you do, you'll pick up the *Post*

or *Daily News* the next day and read about how Annie Kay has been sleeping with Hawks players."

"She's not sleeping with players, and we both know she's not."

Dick Miles said, "Well, as a matter of fact, I've got players who are prepared, and already extremely well-compensated, to say differently."

Miles smiled his come-on smile now. As if we were back at The Savoy. "You said it yourself," he said. "It only takes one blind item."

He stood up, smoothed out his slacks, reknotted his tie. "I may be behind sometimes," he said. "I never lose." He walked past me, opened the door, started to walk out, then stopped and turned around.

"You think the team needs Priceless Braxton that much? Pay him out of the money you already got off me."

"Maybe I will," I said.

"Now you know something a lot of smart guys know," Dick Miles said. "They don't call the company MF for nothing."

22

Billy's lawyer and mine, the great Oscar Berkowitz, set it up. I didn't even have to use the money Miles had paid me when I signed over the Hawks, we just took out the same kind of bridge loan on Priceless Braxton you'd use to buy a house.

Oscar said, "If any of his make-goods kick in, we'll do what Billy used to do, which means figure it out later."

Oscar was an old-time Vegas guy, which means he had a lot of clients who hadn't died of anything close to natural causes. He also thought the town was a lot more interesting before they turned it into a church social.

"I do find it somewhat fascinating that the New York Hawks nearly have to hold a tag sale to sign ballplayers," he said. "Can I ask why?"

"No," I said.

His voice had a wistful tone.

"Now, there's a client response that brings back memories," he said.

I said that the big boss had had a few reversals lately and we left it at that. When I was done refinancing my backfield with Oscar, I walked down to the office of Miles's accountant and the Hawks' de facto salary cap-ologist, Mandrake the Magician Katzenberg, and told him we'd changed our minds and were going to sign Priceless Braxton to a rest-of-the-season contract.

"Before Mr. Miles left town," he said, "I was under the impression we were promoting from within."

Manny was either naturally bald or had shaved his head so that there would always be another bald guy in the room with Miles. He always wore blue shirts with spread white collars and French cuffs, expensive ties with thick, old-man knots. He looked as out of place around a football team as a ballet dancer.

I told him Miles had left it up to me, it was my money, I hadn't stopped by to negotiate with him, start the fucking paperwork.

"Okay, okay," he said. "It's your money."

"Well, not exactly," I said. "But you know all about that, don't you, Manny?"

Borden said Priceless would be in New York by Thursday night at the latest, he had obligations to do card shows in Spokane and Portland before that. Then, Borden said, he wanted to stop in St. Louis and see his fiancée.

"Get out of here," I said. "Priceless is finally gonna get laid?"

Priceless Braxton was the most famous public virgin since Mary Kate and Ashley were in their show business primes.

Borden Skiles said, "He and Shakeera are very much in love."

"I'll bet they're doing it already," I said. "It's probably just screwing on a more spiritual plane than the rest of us have ever known."

Borden said, "Cut the check, he'll try out on Friday."

"Don't let that minx Shakeera take his edge off," I said, but I was pretty sure Borden had already hung up.

I still hadn't confronted Carey about Jeff Brewer. I thought briefly about doing it once I'd finished with Manny, just showing up at 400 East Fifty-sixth, telling her door- man I wanted to surprise her, the way I'd decided not to surprise her the night Brewer got into the limo.

But I knew that as much as she'd been traveling around since I met her that night at The Last Good Year, she wasn't going to leave town permanently, she was going to play this all the way out.

Same as I was.

I decided to have a pace night instead.

You stayed in on a pace night. You consumed no alcohol of any kind. You either cooked something up for yourself or ordered in from your favorite takeout place, you got on the couch eventually, put your remote-control switcher in your switching hand, and then spent the entire evening try- ing to wear the sucker out.

You went from the screamers on Fox News to NBA bas- ketball to some *Untold Story* exposé about some former child star on E!

You watched old Nebraska–Oklahoma games on ESPN Classic, or the new *Ocean's Eleven* again if you were any- where near the part where Julia Roberts tells Andy Garcia that in Vegas somebody is always watching and dumps him. You watched actors doing the best jobs of their lives: acting as if they cared about the kids asking questions on *Inside the Actors Studio* on Bravo. Or watched an old *Cheers*. If you were really lucky and the veg-out stars were per- fectly aligned, you could not only catch a reair of *Alias* on one of those JV channels that ABC had started up, but have it be one you had missed because you were sitting around with the commissioner of the National Football League at

Yum while he waited for Ginger the big red girl to get off in more ways than one.

All in all, you were a guy.

A guy who didn't want to talk to Carey Nash right now even if he did want to talk to Annie Kay and tell her to watch herself with a shitweasel like Jeff Brewer.

As hard as it was for me to see Annie Kay, who was smart and hip and cool before she became a star, who was that way even when she was a bartender at Beef, being used by anybody.

Especially a guy.

I thought briefly about having a glass of red wine to go with the linguine I'd cooked up and smothered with Newman's Own.

But it was a pace night, and rules were rules.

I read through the papers I hadn't had time to read in the morning, coming out of the gate all fired up about Priceless, reading now all about what the writers thought Miles and Bobby Bullard might do to replace Bobby Camby.

Treating me like the invisible man again, after I'd briefly been good copy for them again, acting as the public point man for the Hawks after Ty and Bobby Bullard got into it in L.A.

I saw I'd taken another glancing blow from Gil Spencer in the *Daily News*:

"It wasn't so long ago that a Molloy, father or son, would step in with some flare at a time like this. Or at least send up a flare to let you know they were still in the game. We know what happened to Big Tim. But whatever did happen to Jack Molloy?"

"Eat me," I said to the sports section of the *Daily News*.

I thought of something Pete Stanton had told me on the phone the last time I'd talked to him.

"I know that you've at least considered the possibility that it might be better for you if the season suddenly went further south than Havana."

"I have," I said. "But I can't let it happen if I can possibly stop it."

"You still want to win real bad," he said, "even when it's real bad for you."

"You were the one who told me once that there's no such thing as a bad win."

"Or a good loss," Pete said.

I just knew that Priceless would give us a better chance to win in the short run. That was on the field. And if things didn't start falling into place the way I wanted them to off the field, it wouldn't matter how the Hawks finished.

I fooled around with the switcher a little more, watched Charlie Rose talk to an Arab for a while.

It was about ten after eleven when the doorbell to Suite 19 rang.

Sometimes the guys from security would check in with me, their version of turndown service at a hotel.

In a lame, high-pitched Dame Edna voice, I said, "Who is it?"

A female voice, clipped, said, "Me."

I started to say something smart to Carey Nash as I opened the door with a flourish, maybe ask if Jeff Brewer was parking the car.

But for once in my life, the smartest thing I did was keep my mouth shut.

When I opened the door, there was Annie.

"I know you hate surprises," she said.

I told her it was funny she should mention that, because Mr. Dick Miles himself had been saying just the other day that there were exceptions to every rule.

I was in jeans and my Homestead Grays T-shirt; you could buy Negro Leagues stuff now because you could buy just about everything on the Internet except happiness. And maybe there was a website I didn't know about where you could buy that, too. The way you could buy football teams even if you didn't have the money. Annie had bought me the Grays T-shirt for Christmas along with a New York Cubans cap and a jacket from the Baltimore Elite Giants. She said she knew I'd love it all, T-shirt, cap, jacket. She was right, as usual.

She was wearing a gray leather jacket that was almost black, a red flannel shirt underneath, black jeans. I asked if she wanted anything and she said a diet soft drink. I was glad I'd cleaned up after dinner, already having put everything into the dishwasher, and especially glad my cleaning woman, Imparo, who came down twice a week from Yonkers, had been in that morning; it was why Suite 19 didn't look as if it had been searched.

When I'd helped Annie take off her jacket I'd gotten a whiff of her hair, a smell I'd always told her drove me insane with desire.

She said she'd be sure to put it with the other things that drove me insane with desire, on the world's longest list.

We were in the living room part of 19, next door to the bigger, game-watching, Yum-girl part of it. I got her a drink and placed it on the coffee table in front of her, even using a coaster.

"We need to talk," she said.

I thought about what Dick Miles of MF, Inc., had said about her earlier in the day and said, "Do we ever."

"I'm serious."

"This may shock you," I said. "But so am I."

"First I want to spell out exactly why we're not together."

She liked to talk about things. It's the girl version—or just the grown-up version—of guys not wanting to talk about things. Guys preferring to have the remote in their hands when girls wanted to talk.

That way we could switch channels and try to find a game.

She said, "We have to be clear on this."

She kicked off her Skecher sneakers and tucked her legs underneath her on the couch. One, I might add, where I thought we'd done some of our best work.

"You didn't stay behind in London because you loved Scratch all that much. You'd talked yourself into believing you were oh so committed to the Hawks, and to me, but you weren't. But going back to New York would have meant a real commitment to both of us. London was still just play."

She stopped and looked at me with beautiful eyes.

Beautiful girl.

I told her she was doing fine.

"We've talked enough about how dumb selling the Hawks was. Especially knowing what Billy and I thought. Dumber than dumb. You'd fought so hard to keep them. You know all this. And they belonged more to your dad dead than they did to you alive."

I lit a cigarette. "They still do."

Annie motioned for the pack, and I tossed it to her. There was another pack of matches on the coffee table. She was the type who could smoke one in November and then not want another one until spring. She lit up, inhaled deeply, said, "Then as soon I was through Customs you slept with Fiona, and when you got here you slept with Carey Nash."

I could hear Ben Webster playing "Blues for Mr. Broadway."

I said, "You didn't sleep with Jeff Brewer."

It was in there between a question and something else.

"This isn't about me," she said, "but no, I did not."

That was it. She never lied, about anything.

Ever.

"You and Jeff came up when I had it out with Dick Miles today," I said, and then told her all of it. When I finished, she laughed. I said, "You think I'm funny even when I'm being serious."

"Frequently," Annie said. "Can you really imagine somebody like Sultan standing up like a wide receiver scorned and saying, 'She used me'?"

"I thought maybe it could be one of those Page Six things where they say the ballplayer's gay and have the guy deny it."

"So you've been worried about protecting my honor."

"And your career."

"You're sweet," she said.

"Not really."

"Well," she said, "you have your moments."

I decided to have a Scotch. Once an Annie showed up, your pace night was all shot to hell anyway. When I came back with it, she said that from the start it felt like some game she and Jeff Brewer were playing. He had to know she was using him to piss me off, and maybe get some inside skinny on what he and Miles were doing with the Hawks.

And Brewer, she said, wanted to know everything about me except which side of the bed I liked.

"But why?" I said. "I wasn't a threat to them. From the jump, Billy said they only wanted me around as a goddamn hood ornament."

"I know. It's like they wanted you around, but they didn't. Because they knew from the start what a loose cannon you are."

"Now you're the one being sweet."

"They tried to get you with that one article in the *Post,* just to see how you'd react. Then, before they could try anything else, the team got going good. I was getting ready to back off with Jeff after that night at Elaine's when I ran into you and Alimony Slut. But it was about that time I could tell from Jeff that something was going on with them." Annie waved a hand in front of her, saying, "Them meaning him and his boss."

I went over and sat at the other end of the couch from her, knowing that *she* knew I wasn't making a move, that this was important. "There is," I said. "Miles is as close to busted as a big guy can be. He doesn't have the money to buy the team."

"You're kidding," she said.

Knowing I wasn't.

"He's getting punked by the banks. Most of the guys he could count on when he was flush have lost his phone number. So he's scrambling around like crazy, as far as Billy and I can tell." Leaving Alimony Slut out of it. "And he doesn't particularly care who they are."

Annie said, "Well, that explains something."

"What?"

"Why he's been sucking around Allen Getz, trying to get him to come in as a partner."

I thought of Kitty Drucker-Cole Molloy, my evil stepmother and Getz's sweetie, being at Elaine's that night for no real good reason; that's why Dick Miles had called her.

"Allen Getz is after the Hawks again?" I said. "And he's willing to help get Miles out of the shit to do it?"

Annie said, "Revenge of the nerds."

"How do you know this?"

"Remember in L.A., when I told you I'd had lunch with Liz? Sort of our version of the Jack Molloy Ya Ya Sisterhood?"

When Liz was still president of the Hawks and I'd just taken over, we'd had a brief fling. Which had unfortunately occurred in the midst of my initial flinging with Annie. I didn't know at the time that not only was Liz an old girlfriend of Getz's, but had started out on his side when he was trying to sabotage my chances of holding on to the Hawks first time around. But she came around, became one of the good guys. She and Annie even became friends before Liz went off to Hollywood.

A couple of weeks before the Hawks–Bangers game, Getz had called her and asked if he thought the Hawks were still worth having.

"It turns out," Annie said, "that Allen Getz was a bad loser."

"Boy," I said, "who isn't these days?"

Getz had sworn Liz to secrecy, said that if she told me about his negotiations with Miles then he, Getz, would back out of some movie financing he'd promised her.

"Why'd she tell you?"

Annie said, "She heard we'd broken up." Shrugged and said, "And girls talk."

"Tell me about it."

"I told her she didn't have to worry, I was mad at you and was going to stay mad and I wouldn't tell."

"But you are."

"Allen Getz is a spooky little geekface," she said. "I don't like him, I don't like that he could back-door you out of the Hawks."

All fired up now.

"You think Miles is going to do it?"

"I asked Jeff and he laughed it off, saying why would somebody like Dick Miles give away control of a team he's always wanted?"

Yeah, I said, what kind of an asshole would do that.

Allen Fucking Getz, I thought. Allen Getz What He Wants. Coming at me again like one of those Freddies in the horror movies.

"The plot certainly do thicken, Sapphire," I said.

"You can't do Kingfish," Annie said, "while wearing a Homestead Grays shirt."

Ben Webster was now working his way through "The Ghost of Dinah." Even at the other end of the couch, I could smell Annie Kay's hair.

It would have been insulting, I decided after a brief debate, not to make a pass, and so I leaned over quickly and kissed her. Annie, surprising me again tonight, kissed back. The way she had right out of the blocks on this same couch once, our first night here in the old days, what seemed like way too long ago, when she was still bartending at Beef and taking her classes at NYU and I told her she had to come back to Molloy Stadium with me and see this place, not to mention my etchings.

When we finally did a pullback, she said, "What about Carey?"

"Old news."

"Or just old."

Same old Annie.

"Well, then," I said, "youth must be served."

She said, "I'm just a girl with a C-minus trying to improve my grade."

She woke me up at about five in the morning to tell me she was leaving. She said she didn't want to be seen by anybody who might mention seeing her to Jeff Brewer. I called the car service I used, the guy picking Annie up on the far side of the practice bubble.

The next night we were at her new place on Horatio Street in the Village.

Priceless Braxton passed his physical on Friday, signed his contract, issued this statement through Borden Skiles to the media:

"The game is truth."

It was probably a coincidence that Nike, his shoe company, would start featuring that slogan in new commercials, built through old clips of Priceless during Sunday's NFL games.

He scored a touchdown on Sunday as we beat the Ravens by a field goal in Baltimore. He scored two the next Sunday at Molloy, but the Bucs scored two touchdowns of their own in the fourth quarter, both set up with interceptions of Down Low Malufalu, and this time we lost by a field goal.

It was at Yum the night after that one that Ferret Biel showed up in the back room to tell me that he'd heard from a friend of a friend that Dick Miles had been seen having dinner in New Jersey a couple of weeks before with Joseph Nacero, at Nacero's club, Baby Doll.

Or Joe Necktie, as Nacero was known in his younger years.

If it was the day I thought it was, it at least explained why Miles had been wearing a tie.

For business meetings, Joe Nacero insisted you dress up.

I went into A.T.M.'s office and called Billy Grace, and he said, "Well, isn't this a blast from the fucking past?"

Tony Soprano meets the NFL, I said. Then Billy said, "You know something, kid? This is starting to get interesting."

PART FOUR

Red Zone

23

Billy gave me the crash course on Joe Nacero. Some of it I knew because of the newspapers, and what passed for the public record these days. Most of it I didn't.

Nacero, he said, controlled a good chunk of the casino business in Atlantic City, even if you couldn't find his name on much paper there.

But then, Billy said, that was the same way Nacero quietly controlled several mayors around New Jersey, the head of the New Jersey Sports Authority, a state senator, and at least one former governor. And most of the good racketeering and loan-sharking on the East Coast, not that anybody had ever been able to charge him with anything that stuck in those particular areas, no matter how hard the government kept trying.

It had reached the point over time when it was impossible to tell where his illegitimate business enterprises ended and the legitimate ones began.

"Joey has cleaned up over the years," Billy Grace said. "But there's still some dirt left under those fingernails."

He wasn't ever an official tabloid mob guy, the way Gotti had been. He had been investigated from southern Jersey to southern Manhattan like a mob guy, been under surveillance like one, been charged a few times by the RICO boys and named in a few other RICO cases. But he had never done any jail time, though he seemed to have plenty of relatives who had. Sometimes, Billy said, even the United States government acted as if it was afraid of Joe Nacero.

He grew up in Newark with the mob all around him, and when he was still a kid he had been the kind of runner and bit player Billy had been when he was a kid, running hard, same as Billy had, operating on the fringes of the bad-guy world of the '50s.

He had gotten the nickname Joe Necktie because of a fight at a clip joint in Hoboken called Not for Nothin'; when the police arrived, they found the guy who'd lost the fight to Nacero nervously standing on a chair in the men's room, afraid to move, hands bound behind him with the cheap flowered necktie he'd been wearing. The much more expensive silk tie Joe himself had been wearing, because he was a snappy dresser even as a kid, was noosed around the guy's neck and tied to a sturdy hook near the ceiling.

The hook was just high enough off the ground that Richie Petrocelli, the guy attached to it, a low-level hood from one of the New York families, didn't want anything to happen to the chair.

It was a slow news day, the local cops didn't like Richie's attitude very much, and so they left him there long enough for a photographer from the old *Newark News* to show up and make an instant character out of Joe (Necktie) Nacero, turning him into the hero of the piece after it was determined that Richie had given one of the waitresses in Not for Nothin' a good slap right before the fight started.

After that, he began a long career in business operating inside and outside what Billy had always called "the god-damn life." And no matter how much legitimate business he did have and no matter how many charities he funded, people had still connected him over the last forty years to everybody except the Dixie Mafia.

Billy said Nacero used to come through Vegas once in a while, usually during football season so he could sit around at the sports book at Amazing Grace on Sunday and watch all the games he'd bet on. Later, they'd sit around and tell lies about the old days, and laugh about how the movies and TV still wanted to glamorize the mob, and how the newspapers did the same thing.

"He always got a kick out of how they used to call Gotti the Dapper Don," Billy said. "Joe always said the guy looked like he was modeling what he called the Gambino clothing line."

In his late twenties he had started his own construction business—Joseph and Mary, after his wife, Mary—with one crew and one truck.

Then it was a whole fleet of trucks, and Joseph and Mary was getting the biggest bids on the biggest road contracts in the state; Joseph and Mary that was supposed to be the official centerpiece of his own business empire. And, over time, as both his fortune and his legend grew, it became difficult to determine what was fact about Joe Nacero's dealings, and what was just legend. And according to what Billy told me and what I'd read in the clips, Nacero did nothing to discourage the printing of the legend.

Billy said Nacero still wanted people in business, all the way to Wall Street, to think they could end up on a hook if they crossed him.

No one was exactly sure how much control Nacero had over New Jersey's toughest labor unions. Or how many pols he really had in his pocket. Or how much property he really owned in Jersey, on his own or through his various holding companies.

Or how much money he'd really made in the market, after apparently having a second career picking stocks that rivaled his hero Warren Buffett's.

These days Joe Nacero sightings were increasingly rare.

Mostly they occurred at Baby Doll, the old-fashioned night-club he owned just outside the city limits of Ridgewood, New Jersey, so as not to scare the decent people, or on Sundays at the Roman Catholic Church he'd built with his own money in Hawthorne, a few miles from the Nacero estate that had been described by one Newark *Star-Ledger* columnist as "a shrine to the old Flamingo Hotel."

That was right before the columnist left New Jersey suddenly for a job with the *San Jose Mercury News,* something else that just added to the Nacero legend.

"I don't give a shit what business you're in," Billy Grace said, "the power they think you have is better than the power you do."

Over time, Nacero really did diversify, with not only his holdings but some of the deals Joseph and Mary brokered in other parts of the country, sometimes as far away as the Middle East. I frankly thought that what he'd done in business reminded me an awful lot of what Francione and Miles had done with MF when they were starting out:

Being creative with alternative financing.

Even with all the guesswork about his total net worth, the consensus was that Joe Nacero was now richer than Kuwait.

And extremely attractive to Dick Miles all of a sudden.

What made him so attractive to me was this:

Of all the favors Billy Grace had done for people on his way up the old ladder, the most significant—at least in terms of current events—turned out to be that he had once saved Joe Nacero's life.

"It's kinda cute how these things turn out sometimes," Billy said on the telephone, before telling me he was on his way to New York in a few days. "Sometimes the guy you tell not to wait for his entrée at the steakhouse turns out to be *this* guy."

But Billy said I shouldn't get carried away, there was a protocol to follow with somebody like Joe Nacero, and part of it was to never act as if he owed you anything.

You always conducted any kind of important business with him in person.

"People who really know him know he's not big on middlemen," Billy said. "And he likes you to dress up."

I'd heard about the dressing-up thing, I told him.

Billy said he had some business he had to clear up with the clowns from the Gaming Commission, so he probably wouldn't be in New York until the end of the week, maybe not until the beginning of next week, and I should sit tight until then. I asked if he was bringing Oretha, and he said her and both Vinnys. We were playing the Giants on Sunday, this being one of those years where we played them in the preseason and then again in the regular season, and I asked if I should leave tickets for him. He said he'd try to make it, even though the Giants broke his fucking heart by leaving the Stadium, had he ever mentioned that?

I told him, usually right before he got weepy about the Giants leaving the Polo Grounds.

I had been putting off calling Carey Nash, as much as I still wanted to know about her and Jeff Brewer, jammed up now trying to get with Joe Nacero.

But after practice later that day, she called me for a change, saying she wanted to have a drink that night. Her place, she said. I lied and said Pete Stanton was in town for the night and I was having a late dinner with him.

"How late?" she said in a husky voice.

"Late," I said. "Boys' night out," then asked what about lunch tomorrow at The Last Good Year.

She said, "We're going to be seen in public? And in the daytime?"

I pointed out that it was technically never daytime in the back room of The Last Good Year.

We sat at the same table we'd had the night I'd met her. By two in the afternoon, we were the only people in the back. As soon as we'd ordered our drinks I said, "I've been meaning to ask you something."

"If it's where I've been, it's the same old same old," she said. "Still keeping my eye on the prize, though."

I said, "What was Jeff Brewer doing coming out of your building a few nights ago?"

Sipping my Diet Coke. Smiling my Chamber of Commerce smile.

She smiled back. She was a beautiful woman. But now that Annie kept suggesting that she was older than subways, I was starting to wonder how old she really was. "Spying on me, Jack?" she said.

"I'd just left here," I said, "and then I started walking and then I thought about just showing up at your place the way you showed up here that first night. You know, before all the rapture and whatnot."

"And you saw Jeff come out of the building and assumed . . . what exactly did you assume?"

"Well," I said, "I thought it was pretty late for you two still to be discussing how you thought the Hawks had played. And awfully early to start game planning for next Sunday."

Carey moved her glass of white wine about an inch to the right. "What if I told you Jeff was an old friend?"

"I'd probably ask how the friendship was holding up now that you were divorced from his boss and had been sleeping with somebody trying to take the boss down."

She was quick. "Had been sleeping?"

"I can't lie to you," I said. "I feel we're starting to drift."

"Annie," she said, nodding, like that closed the case.

On it just like that. Another girl thing. There's some kind of spooky radar, almost paranormal, they have about other girls.

I didn't say anything.

"They said it would never last," Carey Nash said, and now she took a sip of wine.

The waiter, a kid I didn't know, another one from Ireland, probably waiting to get his papers, asked if we were ready to order yet. I said we were going to need a little more time. "You don't trust me," Carey said, when the kid was gone.

"More than you think, actually. I came into this knowing you were on your own side."

"I thought I made that clear." Smiled again. "Bad intentions, good sex."

"Getting back to Jeff Brewer would be good for now."

"You're not going to believe this," she said.

"Try me. You won't believe how good I've gotten at suspending disbelief lately."

"Jeff came to me asking for help."

The rest of it, according to Carey Nash:

Brewer knew the deal she'd cut with Miles in the divorce. Laid it out for her that night as if he'd written it himself. Or as if he were reciting it from memory. Didn't go into much specific detail about what kind of sinkhole Miles had fallen into, just put it to her this way: "There isn't nearly as much in the kitty as there used to be."

"His exact words," Carey said.

Carey said she played it with what she thought was just the right amount of shock and surprise, making sure not to overplay it, she said, because she was afraid that might tip him that she knew more than she was letting on.

Or so she was letting on with me now in The Last Good Year.

Then she asked Brewer how she could possibly help Dick Miles out of any jam he might be in.

Brewer said that with Bill Francione gone, there were fewer and fewer people they could trust to make sound decisions.

Carey: "Making it sound as if he and Dick were some kind of team now."

And, Brewer told her, there wasn't anybody who could control Miles lately, that he was becoming an easier and easier mark if the plan was for fast, big money, running around like a rat in a maze.

I asked her if Brewer really said the part about the rat. She said it was just colorful paraphrasing, Jeff Brewer went through life acting as if Miles might have the room bugged, just waiting for him to say the wrong thing.

But, Brewer told her, there had always been one person after Bill Francione who had not only been a clear thinker, but who had established some of the more interesting contacts MF had made since Miles and Francione had begun their partnership, when they had hit the big street running and started finding ways to outmaneuver the big boys.

"You," I said to Carey Nash in The Last Good Year.

"The former little woman," she said.

Then Carey Nash was telling me about something that had happened about a year after she'd gone to work for Miles. Telling how the financing for what she called this certain venture had started to fall apart at the last second, but how she had acted as a liaison between MF and an interested third party, and how it turned out that the interested third party had shown more than a passing interest in her, and how she had used that to save the deal.

"I'll bite," I said. "What was the deal?"

"It was that casino just over the Pennsylvania border from south Jersey," she said. "The one on land they found out belonged to an Indian tribe nobody had ever heard of."

Billy Grace always said that the head of the tribe ought to be called Chief Guido.

Or Chief Carmine.

"The chief had the hots for you?" I said.

"It was actually a different kind of chief," she said.

I knew before she told me. I don't know why I knew, exactly. But I did.

"I'm sure you've heard of Joseph Nacero," she said.

Now I was the one who didn't overplay the reaction.

"Hasn't everybody?" I said.

"MF had the state," she said. "He was with those fine Native Americans from whatever their tribe is. We all worked it out. When it was over, Dick said it was the one

and only time he was getting into business with that greaseball, quote unquote."

"Until now."

"Jeff told me I should make the phone call, it was really
in my best interest."

"Though not necessarily mine," I said.

"Just because Joe Nacero might provide some financial
aid doesn't mean Dick holds on to the Hawks."

"But you made the call," I said.

"I cannot tell a lie," Carey Nash said. "I did."

We sat there for a moment looking at each other. Finally
she said, "What are you thinking?"

"That it really is a small world, after all," I said.

We lost to the Giants.

Ty Moranis had finally practiced with the team on Friday, and had quarterbacked the offense during Saturday's
walk-through, but then felt something pull behind his shoulder warming up, and we all agreed to sit him again. Now the
doctors were saying that even if he did make it through the
season, he was going to need surgery before next season if
he wanted to keep playing.

Sultan had caught a late touchdown pass from Down
Low Malufalu to bring us to within six points against the
Giants, but that was it for the home team. Priceless Braxton
continued to look like a bargain, even with the five million
signing bonus, scoring two more touchdowns. After each
one, he did what he always did, and handed the ball to Sultan instead of the nearest official; then Sultan offered the
kind of cool, self-contained dance he thought Priceless
should be doing in the end zone.

"Man won't f——ing dance himself," Sultan told Ken
Verdi of the *Post*. "How freak is that?"

Billy and Oretha arrived on Tuesday. Billy said he'd
placed a couple of calls to Joe Nacero, but that he was at a
bridge tournament in St. Bart's and wouldn't be back until

late Thursday night at the earliest. I asked Billy how long he and Oretha planned to stay and he said he was here now for the duration, at least now that the new guy running the Gaming Commission had turned out to be much more open-minded than he'd originally been.

He and Oretha decided to stay at the Sherry-Netherland this time, on my recommendation. They had passed on dinner their first night in town, staying in and ordering room service from Harry Cipriani, the restaurant downstairs.

"Jesus Christ," he said the next morning. "I looked at the bill and couldn't decide whether we'd had two orders of risotto with the house salad, or broke a fucking chandelier."

Then he told me he'd spoken to Nacero's secretary, who said that Mr. Nacero had left specific instructions not to be disturbed, but that she was going to make an exception for his old friend Mr. Grace. She called back fifteen minutes later and told Billy we were supposed to meet Nacero at Baby Doll on Friday night.

"You're the best," I said.

"But you need to understand something going in," Billy said. "Joe Nacero is gonna do what he's gonna do. You don't play him, you don't even let him get it into his head that you might *want* to play him."

I said I was good with that.

"You do *not* play him," Billy repeated.

Got it, I said.

"Anything else before I go back to running my team on the sneak?"

"Yeah," Billy said. "He might not think you're as much of a sparkling wit as you think you are."

"Is something like that possible?" I said.

Then Billy Grace told me something I already knew, that I might be screwed even if Nacero wasn't going to give Dick Miles some kind of bailout money or bailout deal. Or put him with somebody who could do the same thing. Because there was still nothing to prevent Miles, as a last resort, from running to Allen Getz.

"He might think Getz is the same kind of no-account cocksucker we do," Billy said. "But if it gets down to nut-crunching time with the Finance Committee and he thinks Getz is the only one who can save him . . ."

Billy's voice trailed off.

"If you can't be with the one you love," I said.

"Give it up for the one you're with," Billy said.

In the background, I could hear Oretha yelling at him to wrap it up, he spent more time talking to me than he did to her, it was time for him to get his ass out of the suite and walk the damn reservoir.

I hung up and took the elevator all the way down to the locker room. It was still early, so most of the players hadn't shown up yet for treatment. I thought: I'm the one who needs treatment. We were in second place now in the AFC East, tied with the Jets. And suddenly we were in danger of missing the playoffs, even as a wild card, especially if we couldn't get a couple of more games out of our quarterback's right shoulder, and what used to be the golden arm attached to it.

When I got downstairs, Ty Moranis was on his back in front of his locker doing some stretching exercises, Price-less Braxton standing over him.

"Dog," Ty Moranis said with a grunt.

Priceless nodded at him and said, "Art."

As usual, I had no goddamn idea what he meant by that.

Ty sat up and said, "He doesn't mean any, like, Andy Warhol art. Or the other big artist."

"The other one?"

"Did the fruit."

"Picasso?"

"Him," he said. "Anyway, Price is talking about this active response technique he got me fixed up with. A-R-T."

"Got it," I said.

"Shit breaks down scar tissue. Price took me to this guy in the city, Chang, he's like the lord high prick of ART. Hates sports doctors, hates surgery, hates everything and everybody, far as I can tell. But he's the one cured that old baseball pitcher."

"Charlie Stoddard," I said. "Friend of mine. And don't call him old. I remember that was a big part of his comeback story, him hooking up with some Chinese voodoo guy."

Ty said, "Bottom line? I think I can play on Sunday without taking the shot Harm and Hans wanted me to take."

"I told Harm no shots," I said.

"Dude said it would be our secret," Ty said, and stretched out again. "Tell you the truth, I think he shot up Bobby C. before he hurt his knee."

"I didn't know that," I said.

"Dog," Ty said. "You're like everybody else thinks they know all this shit about sports. If you're not in the room all the time, you don't know half what you think you do."

"Got it," I said again. Then turned to Priceless Braxton and said, "By the way, you've been great, man."

"The game is truth," he said.

I said, "You know, sometimes you're so spiritual, I can't believe you don't play the game for free."

Priceless Braxton leaned over, no change of expression, maybe just a little fun in his eyes, and whispered something in my ear:

"Fuck that."

I felt myself smiling.

"Priceless," I said, "I had a feeling you weren't a total virgin."

He shrugged. "Comes and goes," he said.

I left the two of them there and walked down the hallway to Harm Battles's tiny office. When he saw me standing in the doorway, he came bounding around the desk as if he wanted to lead us both in a cheer.

"Bring on the bitch-ass Bills!" he said. "Right now." He grabbed his crotch and gave it a big squeeze. "I got their playoff possibilities for them right here."

"Did you give Bobby Camby a shot of something?" I said. "And then try to give one to Ty before the Giants game?"

He blinked in slow motion at me. Fish eyes that seemed to get bigger every time he opened them back up. "I thought we were doing whatever it takes to make the playoffs," he said finally.

"*We* are," I said. "But *you're* fired."

"You can't do that," he said.

"Let's just go ahead and find out."

"You're serious," he said.

"Clean your Rite Aid shit out of here," I said, gesturing at his office. "If you're still around in an hour, I'm sending the fat boys back here."

I took a step into the hall, then poked my head back into Harm Battles's office.

He was where I'd left him in front of his desk, cracking his knuckles like it was some kind of precision drill.

"One other thing, Harm," I said. "Your assistant, Dr. Mengele? Take him with you."

24

"**Welcome to Baby** Doll," Billy Grace said once we were inside. "Please set your watches back fifty years."

The only thing I knew about old New York nightclubs, the high-end ones, was what I'd seen in the movies, and in some pictures the old man had saved of him and my mother, the two of them sitting with other swells at places like the Copa and El Morocco, the table in front of them filled with glasses and champagne bottles and a sea of ashtrays, everybody dressed to what Big Tim Molloy had called the nines and tens and elevens, smiling for the camera. This seemed to be Joe Nacero's vision of all that, the lights down low for the blond singer at the other end of the main room, a four-piece band behind her, the men in the place wearing dark suits, the women, even the younger ones, looking as if they were in their best party dresses, as if this were some kind of formal occasion in the city, instead of a private club owned by somebody who went through life scaring the shit out of people the way Joseph Nacero did.

There was a lot of smoke, and even a tall girl who reminded me of a Rockette passing through the room selling cigarettes and cigars.

There was valet parking out front and a tough-looking tuxedo at the door, checking his list of members and invited guests.

The singer was working her way through "Someone to Watch Over Me."

I said to Billy, "What time do you think the rest of the Rat Pack shows up?"

"I'm going to tell you something one last time from the heart, because you really are like a son to me," Billy said. "This is not the night to have a smart mouth."

Joseph Nacero looked as if he could pass for Billy's older brother. He wore a dark suit of his own with lapels a lot thinner than were in fashion or had been in fashion anytime lately, a thin dark tie, a white shirt with a starched collar. His gray hair was brushed straight back from his forehead, streaks of white showing in amazingly, I thought, straight lines. He had a thin, straight nose, thick black eyebrows that didn't have any gray or white in them, a small pinky ring on his left hand with what looked like his initials on it, out of the time when tough guys wore rings like that instead of tattoos, or rings in their ears.

He came around the table when Billy and I were escorted to his table up near the stage area, set up above two steps higher than the rest of the room, one that even had a velvet rope the maître d' unhooked with a flourish when he presented us to Joe Nacero.

Nacero came around the table and kissed Billy on both cheeks, smiled and shook my hand, and in a deep voice devoid of any accent, Jersey or New York or anything, said, "I see your father in you, but believe you favor your mother more."

I said, "She was the best part of both of us, to tell you the truth."

"I know," he said, motioning for both of us to sit. "Then he married that *donnicciola*."

"I'm just going to assume that means gold digger," I said.

Joe Nacero said, "Close enough."

The singer received polite applause, having finished her set with a smoky version of "Young at Heart." I had started to say something near the end of the song, and Nacero made a motion that told me to wait until she finished. When she did, he said to Billy Grace, "Remember the movie? Frank and Doris Day? It was all over for poor Gig Young as soon as Doris opened the door and Frank turned around in his snap-brim hat." He shook his head sadly. "Whatever happened to snap-brim hats?"

Billy said, "What happened to gold cigarette cases?"

"And Toots Shor's after a big fight at the old Garden?"

"Those were the days," Billy Grace said, not just playing along, really meaning it.

I watched the cigarette girl, a six-footer even taller than Ginger the big red girl, and found myself wondering how the New York Hawks' season had ended up here.

Nacero got right to it as soon as our drinks came, Scotch for me, a bottle of red wine for him and Billy, both of them backing that up with espresso.

The waiter stood at attention until Nacero tasted the wine and gave him the nod. "My old friend here informs me you have a situation with your father's team."

"I'm trying to get back the family business," I said. "Which I was stupid enough to sell away." I grinned at Nacero and said, "Is there an Italian word for dope?"

He said something Italian that sounded like an appetizer.

"That works," Billy said.

Nacero said, "Explain exactly how your business involves my business?"

He knew and I knew and Billy knew and maybe the cigarette girl did, too. But this was all part of the protocol, and I certainly knew that. His rules, his turf. So I gave him the bumper-sticker version of my relationship with Miles, all the way back to when he'd flown over to London, what I had learned about his finances, how I knew he was scrambling around looking for money. Finally, respectfully as possible, making it sound as if Dick Miles had finally wised up, I said that I was aware that Miles had finally come to Joe Nacero himself.

I lit a cigarette without asking if he minded, since Baby Doll was clearly a shrine to secondary smoke.

Nacero sipped red wine, wiped his lips with the linen napkin next to him.

Said, "So."

"We're trying to get a feel as to whether you're of a mind to help bail him out," Billy said. "Doing it yourself, or putting him with somebody else." Billy had his hands clasped in front of him, and I was struck again by how big they were. "Whether this is something that you think makes sense for you, old friend."

"So we're talking about everybody's business, then," Nacero said. "Mine, yours, Mr. Miles's."

"Yeah," I said, "we are."

He looked at me, his face completely calm. Kind, almost. Waiting.

"Mr. Nacero," I said. "I'm going to tell you something we all know, in the interest of not bullshitting you. Or having you bullshit me." I looked at Billy, shrugged. "You know that if you help Miles out of this mess he's in, it's the same as you getting my team. Because it's the best asset he's got right now, even if it doesn't officially belong to him yet."

"You don't want me to bullshit you, I won't, I will be completely honest with you," Joe Nacero said. "I've always wanted to do more than bet on football.

"I've always wanted my own team," he said.

Sounding exactly like Big Dick Miles.

He gave Billy and me a history lesson then, telling us about the discreet inquiries he'd made about buying NFL teams; the most serious was about the Tampa Bay Bucs, mostly because he had a winter home in Tampa. The first was when Paul Tagliabue was commissioner, then again after Wick Sanderson had replaced Tagliabue. And how he had finally been told something straight-up by Wick Sanderson himself:

Don't even start the process, you have no shot, why embarrass yourself?

"Joe had finally found people who said no to him," Billy said when Nacero paused for a sip of espresso. "He doesn't get a lot of no."

I said, "I'll bet."

Nacero said, "I was told, as respectfully as possible, of course, that while professional sports is filled with owners who want to act like bosses, they couldn't have someone in the club that most of the public had decided long ago was a real boss.

"I am more successful than just about all of them," he continued. "But at the same time, I'm not good enough for them. I have the last name I do, the ancestry I have, the reputation I have. The family I have. I'm just another goomba. A table like this, even in a semipublic place, I could not sit at a table like this with Mr. Buffett, at that modest office of his in Omaha, the one at Kiewit Plaza. If people found out . . ." He closed his eyes, shook his head. "Imagine the consequences for him." He smiled then. "As much as we would have to talk about."

Nacero said, "I watched every move Mr. Buffett made at Berkshire Hathaway, long before the rest of the world did. I purchased *Washington Post* stock before he did in the seventies. I stayed in textiles in the seventies the way he did, despite all the prevailing wisdom to the contrary. And by the time he got out of textiles and saw the future of insurance companies, I had done the same." He drank red wine and said, "I never ran with the dot-com boys, and neither did he." He looked at me, almost embarrassed. "Some of this must bore you, Mr. Molloy."

"Not so long as you go slow," Billy said. "When it comes to business, his focus tends to come and go."

Joe Nacero said, "I even started playing bridge when I learned that Mr. Buffet was a championship bridge player. And now consider myself of that caliber myself."

I listened to him and thought of all the little cartoon tough guys I'd seen around the NFL in my life, and owning teams in other sports, Steinbrenner with the Yankees and little Danny Snyder of the Redskins and Bobby Finkel of the Saints, who had bodyguards wherever he went; even guys I liked, like Al Davis, who'd always carried himself like the last don, who was one of the toughest guys I'd ever met in any business.

It was ironic, I thought, listening to Joe Nacero, that they wouldn't let him into the club when so many sports owners wanted to act just like him.

"What about Vito Cazenovia?" I said. "Didn't he rocket to the top of the construction business when he ran over his brother with a cement truck or something?"

"So he wanted people to believe," Nacero said. "The way Vito wants everybody who won't give him his new stadium to believe he's vaguely connected. He's not."

Nacero smiled again, small this time. "Trust me."

I thought: Now, *him* I trust.

"How can they keep you out if nobody's ever been able to actually prove you're connected?" I said. "With all due respect."

"The perception becomes the reality." Nacero sighed. "Billy knows from the casino business. We don't think of it as being connected. We think of it as networking, just without conventional boundaries."

"I found out a long time ago," Billy said. "Money's money."

"So they kept you out and you let them," I said to Nacero.

"If you fight too hard, they think they've won," he said. "And I hate to lose."

Then he told us about his old friend Edward DeBartolo, Sr., who'd made the bulk of his fortune building and operating shopping malls, and who wanted to buy the White Sox in the early '80s. Except the people who ran baseball didn't want him, even though the old man had bought the San Francisco 49ers for his kid, Eddie, Jr., a few years before that. And the reason that baseball didn't want him to own the White Sox or any other team wasn't that he owned racetracks, and racetracks meant gambling and gamblers. The reason was that baseball had decided he was all mobbed up. "He used to say that there would not be these rumors if his last name were Carnegie or Mellon, and of course he was right," Nacero said. "But they just saw another rich greaseball who couldn't possibly have made all of his money legitimately." I saw him clench and unclench his hands on the table in front of him. "I hate that word. Greaseball. Like our nigger."

So DeBartolo the father was considered dangerous to baseball owners, Joe Nacero said, to all the rich boys with their inherited money who looked at him and saw gang wars breaking out all over the American League.

"But the NFL did let his kid in, even though the old man was the original buyer, and the money flow started with him," I said.

Nacero said, "Eddie Junior. He won all those Super Bowls with Mr. Montana and then lost his team because of some licensing deal for riverboat casinos in Louisiana, the boy caught paying four hundred thousand dollars to the governor. He eventually pled out on failing to report a felony, and his sister ended up with the 49ers." He lifted his shoulders, dropped them, sighed again. "Children," he said. "The boy got greedy and eventually lost his football team and would have broken his father's heart if the father were alive to see all that."

Nacero was looking at me when he said the last part, at me and through me and all the way to the Lincoln Tunnel.

I found myself wanting to loosen my tie.

"I remember that deal," I said, "just because it made a liar out of my old man. He'd always told me that any problem in life could be solved with a suitcase full of money."

"It was the ultimate irony, if you think about it," Nacero said. "The son loses his team because of the kind of thing they were all afraid the father was into but could never prove."

Picked up his wineglass, put it back down gently, without drinking, telling us that it turned out that DeBartolo, Sr., was the last of what he called "our kind" allowed to own an NFL team or have one in the family, the door slammed shut forever after DeBartolo's son got into trouble in Louisiana. No matter how much the son cried, Nacero said, about being the victim.

"But now I could have your team," he said. "I could own it and Dick Miles and the league wouldn't be able to do anything about it."

The singer was back, doing an Ella medley.

"Nobody wants to be a silent partner in sports," I said. "Even when they say they do. The whole object of owning a team is to be the opposite of silent. You can trust me on that one."

"I'll manage," Nacero said. "That's if I decide to enter into a relationship with Mr. Miles. I'll manage the way I have in other areas of business that would surprise even my friend Billy Grace."

"Joe," Billy said. Not judging, just curious. "You'd really help out a *bischero* like Miles?"

"I could tell myself I'd be helping out my old friend Bill Francione."

Fuck, I thought.

It *was* a small world.

Getting smaller all the time.

Billy said, "I didn't know Francione was your friend."

"Sometimes even people I like," Joe Nacero said, "know only as much as I want them to know. But yes, he was a friend. Like you."

"But Miles isn't."

"Sometimes they have to prove it," Nacero said. "By passing a test."

"And Miles passed?" I said.

Nacero smiled. "Screen passed, actually," he said.

I stared at him.

"The Jets game?" I said. "You were the friend?"

Nacero looked at me, then Billy, gave us one more little lift of the shoulder. "What are friends for?" he said.

Then he told us that when he made up his mind about Miles, he would let us know, stood up, told us to have a nice ride back to Manhattan, this was his regular bridge night.

In the car I said to Billy, "That was interesting, in a Scorsese film sort of way."

"It didn't go exactly the way we wanted," Billy said. "But I'm going to be straight with you, kid: I miss sit-downs like that."

"Maybe you can tell me what really went on back there. Other than us finding out his fingerprints are all over the Jets game?"

Billy said, "That was just everybody establishing a negotiating position."

"You think he really hasn't decided what to do about Miles?"

From the semidarkness next to me, Billy Grace said, "Fuck no.

"This is just business," he said. "He's got something we want, we need to find something he wants."

"What could Joe Nacero possibly want that he doesn't already have?" I said.

"It's like wondering whether it's the bra or the girl," Billy said. "Sometimes the fun's in the finding out."

Sultan twisted a knee in the second quarter against the Bills, had to come out of the game, never went back in.

Now we had to play without him, even though Ty Moranis was back in the lineup, thanks to whatever black-magic manipulation his new Chinese friend had working for him. So this time we were trying to win a game without Tucker O'Neill, who was supposed to have been our starting quarterback this season, and without Sultan, Bobby C., and Redford Newman, the three best guys we were supposed to have on offense. We hung in there against the Bills anyway, kept coming back after they'd get ahead, sent the sonofabitch into overtime but finally lost on a field goal by the Bills' thirty-seven-year-old rookie placekicker, Milos Vujanic, somebody Buffalo had signed out of the Croatian army after a series of worldwide tryouts, the Bills desperate to finally find a guy who wouldn't kick the ball wide right every time they had a chance to win a big game.

"Forget all those other nancy-pants sidewinders we've had in years gone by," Bills coach Pooch Downey said. "I've got me a hard case now's been shot at by a bunch of Herbs."

As soon as the ball went through the uprights, the announcers immediately started telling their viewers that if the season ended today, the Hawks would be out of the playoffs. It was the kind of insight from TV sports twinks that always made me talk back to the television set.

Which I did now in Suite 19, telling this to my high-def:

"And if they ended the broadcast now, nobody would have to listen to any more of your bullshit."

"There it is, Snap," Oretha said. "Let all that anger go."

I had watched with her and Billy in the suite, just the three of us, no Yum girls or A.T.M. this time, since A.T.M. Moore would fake his own death to avoid being in the same room with his ex-wife.

Before they left to go back to the city, they asked if I wanted to join them for dinner afterward. I told them I was just going to hang around here and ponder what a magical and festive season this had turned into.

That was Sunday night.

The next morning, Dick Miles had Jeff Brewer inform Susan Burden that she was fired.

She was already cleaning out her desk by the time I got downstairs, saying she knew I'd be down soon, there was no point in waking me with her news. No point to any of it, she said. And kept packing. Carefully putting brown paper around the picture of the old man she kept on her desk. Another picture of her and the old man and me. And one of her and Pete Stanton I'd never even noticed, the two of them sitting on the Hawks' bench at Molloy. Susan Burden: red-eyed but refusing to cry or let anybody passing by and watching her pack up her life into these boxes see her wobble for one minute.

She told me the letter had been waiting on her desk when she came in, the language all very formal, Miles's signature at the bottom, telling her that since she wasn't a contract employee or a member of any union, she was being terminated immediately, what was described as part of a new cost-cutting around the Hawks, and oh, by the way, please be off the property as soon as possible.

If not, the letter said, she would be deemed in violation of the terms of Miles's arrangement with the Molloy family and the National Football League.

Telling me this as she placed her Montblanc fountain pen into its hard black case, the pen I'd given her on her last birthday even though I had been told in her strict, classroom voice that she wasn't having birthdays anymore.

"I was waiting for them to say they thought I was a flight risk," she said.

"So there was no real reason given," I said.

She shook her head.

"But you're working for me," I said. "If I can come up with the money for Priceless Braxton on my own, I can certainly keep you on the payroll. In the whole grand stupid scheme of things, you're probably worth more than he is.

Certainly to me." I put a hand on her shoulder. "But then, you were worth more than any football player when you were still teaching at McBurney."

"I mentioned the first part, that I worked for you, when Jeff Brewer came by to see if I'd received the letter."

Stopping the packing now. Tall and elegant and beautiful, in a white blouse and dark blue skirt and flat shoes so she'd be tall but not too tall. No jewelry. Hardly any makeup. Still holding it all together.

"He said that he was terribly sorry, but Mr. Miles's contract was quite specific in these matters. Nothing personal, he said, across the season they'd gone over the books and started to do some general belt-tightening, that this was the beginning of a series of layoffs, they'd done it with other companies and now they were being forced to do it here."

"It isn't personal with you," I said. "It's personal with me."

"So I've gathered."

From the bottom drawer of her desk, she pulled out a game program from Charles Keating Stadium, the one from our Super Bowl win over the Bangers. Underneath it, kept there since we'd made the move down the hall, was the framed front page from the McBurney school paper, the year she announced she was leaving to come work for the old man:

GOODBYE, MS. CHIPS

"I was going to leave at the end of the season anyway," she said. "I didn't know I was going to get caught in one of those games you've been talking about."

I told her to not go anywhere until I got back.

Brewer must have been back to his open-door policy. Maybe he was just afraid I might kick it in. He was standing behind his desk, using his hands-free phone.

"Hang up," I said. "Or click off. Whatever you do in a cellular world."

"Gotta run," he said to his phone. "Call me on this number later."

He took the headset off and placed it on his desk. I shut
the door behind me, feeling the way I'd feel in football
sometimes when it was my turn to hit somebody, when the
other team would intercept and all of a sudden it was me
chasing down the ball in the open field with a chance to level
somebody the way they were always trying to level me, not
hearing the crowd or anything except a high, singing sound
in my ears.

Then I realized there was one other person in the room
with Brewer and me.

He was a squat, hard-looking guy in a crew cut seated on
the couch to my left, wearing a short-sleeved white shirt,
probably to show off forearms that looked like the fat part of
a baseball bat, and what I was pretty sure was a clip-on tie
that didn't make it past the fourth button of the white shirt.

"Meet Carl," Brewer said.

"Who's Carl?"

"Carl works for us."

"Us?"

"Mr. Miles and me. Kind of an all-around troubleshooter
sort of guy. A little driving, a little security, a little body-
guarding. Lots and lots of muscle."

Carl nodded, keeping his amazing arms crossed in front
of him. As cool as it was in Brewer's office, I noticed little
beads of sweat on Carl's forehead. And that his face was a
little flushed.

I said, "That a clip-on, Carl? You don't see a lot of clip-
ons anymore."

He just sat there, red-faced and sweating, as if just the
anticipation of beating the crap out of me was wearing him
out.

"Carl has practically no sense of humor," Brewer said.

"I'm running into a lot of that lately," I said. "Bad attitudes, bad losers. No wonder there's so much stress in the
world."

I stood a few feet inside the door, talking with Brewer just
to talk, knowing that if I got any closer to him the impulse to

go over the desk would be stronger than my concerns about how fast Carl could get off the couch and get to me.

"Why'd you do this to Susan?"

"Wasn't my decision."

"Sure it was, you punk. Miles barely knows the players' names, much less the people who work around the office. He asked you to pick out somebody close to me to hurt, and you picked her."

"It was just business," Brewer said, then grinned and said, "though I could see how you might take it personally, since she is the person here you've known the longest, the one you're closest to, like a member of your family."

I took a couple of steps inside the office and Brewer said, "Before you come any closer, I want you to know that Carl has this deal, from a previous life from when he used to collect money from people who didn't pay their gambling debts? He can break things and not leave a mark on you."

"You can't force her to leave."

"I went over this with her already."

"Tell Miles to leave her out of whatever the fuck this is."

"Can't do that, I'm afraid," Brewer said. He sat down and sipped some of his coffee. "In fact, if you fight this in any way, we'll be forced to tell the press the real reason for her dismissal."

"And what would that be, asshole? She sexually harassed you?"

"Punk. Asshole. You're really going to have to make up your mind."

"You'll run to the press with what?" I said. "And just a heads-up? When you do make that run, make sure that Carl here is right behind you."

"Are you threatening me?"

I thought of Billy Grace.

"Promising, actually," I said. "To knock you on your ass one of these days."

"Whatever," he said. "But in answer to your question

about Ms. Burden, it seems that she's been selling your weekly allocation of game tickets for quite a bit more than face value and pocketing the money. And if there's one thing Mr. Miles won't abide, it's people stealing from him. Stealing big or stealing little," Jeff Brewer said.

It actually got a laugh out of me, though not the kind *M*A*S*H* reruns generally produced.

"Susan Burden, master thief? Even a punk like you must be able to do better than that."

I'd settled on punk, it just felt right.

"Sad to say, Jammer, but it's true." Grinning at me again, giving me a palms-up shrug. "We put Manny Katzenberg on it, and he's got deposit slips, and people who'll come forward and say they were wondering why she was charging them more for primo seats. What's the computer version of a paper trail? Unfortunately, that's what we've got here."

"You set her up," I said.

Brewer leaned forward now, gave me a hard look he must have learned from his boss, and said, "Who knows, it might be somebody like Annie Kay next."

Braver than the 101st Airborne with Carl in the room.

"Miles already ran that one up the flagpole," I said. "You've got nothing on her and you know it."

"Manny just proved how easy it is to make something out of nothing."

"What do you want?"

"What makes you think we want anything? We're just two concerned people trying to run this company the best way we see fit. And, really, we'd only go to the newspapers as a last resort."

"Unless?"

"Well, Mr. Miles did mention one thing."

I stood there, waiting.

"He did mention that maybe you and Billy Grace should stay out of New Jersey for the time being."

"You heard we went to see Nacero."

"I have no idea what you're talking about, I'm just passing on something Mr. Miles mentioned."

Before I could say anything else, Jeff Brewer said, "Oh, and by the way, Jack? Remember when you told me your dad could beat up mine? Well, it turns out I can beat up the woman who acts like your mom."

25

Billy's response to Susan's firing was fairly straight-forward, I thought:

He asked which Vinny should have the talk with Jeff Brewer.

Then I told him about Carl. Billy barked out a laugh.

"You have no idea how many Carls the Vinnys have met along the way," he said.

I told him I'd handle Jeff Brewer when the time was right, that we had other things to handle first, starting with Joe Nacero, whose career I was researching like it was for a term paper at UCLA I actually planned to write myself.

"You sound like you're back at the casino," he said, "all revved up to handle whatever the hell needs handling."

Yeah, I said, the Jammer was back, older, richer, just not any wiser, unfortunately.

I said Suite 19 was going to serve as my office from now on, my way of serving myself with a restraining order on Brewer. My thinking was that the less time I saw him, the less chance there was of my hands ending up around his neck.

I was even getting a cell phone, just in case Miles thought he could have somebody listen in on any of my private lines.

Billy said, "I thought cell phones were less secure than landlines."

Not the cell phone Ferret hooked me up with, I said.

"Make sure he gets you those unlimited free hours on weekends," Billy said.

I told him I'd meet him in the city later for a drink—as soon as Ferret delivered the phone I had a bunch of calls to make.

"No shit, you really do sound like you did when you were my director of logistics," Billy said.

I told him, yeah, but if you looked at it that way, my career wasn't really progressing the way I'd hoped it would.

I called Wick Sanderson at the end of the day and asked if he could meet me at Yum later, I'd already checked with A.T.M. and found out Ginger the big red girl was working tonight.

I'd called on his private line, not going through his secretary, and as soon as he heard my voice at the other end, his became very formal, as if I were calling about a new strain of steroid, or had come up with a new way for owners to screw injured players out of their guaranteed money.

"Yes, Jack," he said, "I can see why you'd consider that an urgent matter."

"You're not alone, are you, Commissioner?"

"Exactly so."

Then: "Just one second, dear. The car should be downstairs in about five minutes."

I smiled to myself. "Hollywood Tits gets to come to the office now?"

"Excellent point."

"But I'll bet you'd rather meet me at Yum so you could look at Ginger's hooters."

"I can't disagree with you."

"That's really more urgent than anything I want to discuss, am I right?"

"I understand: Just the two of us."

"Would eight o'clock be all right with you, Commissioner?"

"I know you wouldn't have called if it wasn't important. Eight o'clock at your office would be fine."

"Our special table, okay?"

"We'll take as long as we need to get her done," Wick Sanderson said.

A.T.M. Moore had designated Monday as what he called Assisted Living Night at Yum, closing off the bar area and restricting it to players from the Hawks, Jets, and Giants, knowing they all had Tuesdays off, the way just about all NFL players did. Unless your team was in the Monday night game, players traditionally had Tuesday as their day off. It was different for coaches; Bobby Bullard and the rest of them bunkered down all day Tuesday and into the night, getting ready for next Sunday's games, drawing up game plans for their players to get their dicks knocked off all over again, to the extent that they'd need something exactly like Assisted Living Night at a place like Yum the following Monday night.

It was a visit to Bobby Camby's hospital room after his reconstructive knee surgery, A.T.M. said, that had given him the idea for what he shorthanded as A.L.N. at A.T.M.'s.

"Walk in there with my fruit basket and pain pills and reefer and what not," A.T.M. said, "and the room is just filled with Bobby C.'s candy stripers, givin' off a wellness groove like you couldn't believe."

So now on Monday nights, the Victoria's Secret wannababes wore candy striper outfits of their own—though significantly smaller than the real thing, and with much bigger heels—right up to the little hats that I was sure could get a rise out of a parish priest. They served mostly sweet, umbrella-type drinks on hospital carts, and A.T.M. had worked out a deal with a Hawks fan who operated a local hospital-supply store to let him rent recliner beds that even had television remotes built into the armrests.

He also opened up extra spa rooms upstairs.

"I want us to get one of those on-time seals of approval," he said, "not have the boys think they got bullshit appointment times like you do at the real doctor's."

The Giants got the six-to-eight shift in the spa rooms, the Hawks got the eight-to-ten, the Jets went from ten until midnight. A.T.M. said that after midnight, it was every man and caregiver for themselves.

When Wick Sanderson walked into Yum a little after eight, he had the same kind of reaction he'd had the first time I took him down to Beef, the commissioner arriving in the middle of a floor show down there we used to call "Venus and Serena."

"I'm dead, aren't I, Jack?" he said when the hostess on Monday night, Candy Striper Valerie, brought him to the table. "I've died and gone to what heaven is going to be like for horny guys like us."

I'd worked it out with A.T.M. that Ginger the big red girl would be working the eight-to-ten shift, just to ensure the commissioner had the proper motivation.

When she brought us our first round of drinks, Wick Sanderson said to her, "Honey? Do *not* lose the hat."

The players were allowed to make movie requests on Monday night, strictly by popular vote. The winner right now was some kind of director's cut version of *Unfaithful* that A.T.M. had managed to put his hands on, the one with Diane Lane playing the frisky suburban housewife who gets involved with the hunky downtown bookstore owner.

"That's it," I heard Butterball Morton say from his recliner bed a few feet away. He was already wearing his lemon-colored Yum spa robe. "Put down your Starbucks and get on the couch, you bad *bad* soccer mommy."

"Well," I said to Wick Sanderson. "Two weeks until the vote on Miles."

"She's got some miles on her," he said. "But she can still go."

I couldn't tell whether he was still fixed on Ginger's hat or what was happening with Diane Lane on the huge flat screen above the bar.

I said, "Stay with me for just a couple of minutes, and then you and Ginger can go upstairs to the Magic Kingdom."

"I don't think of it as two weeks to the vote, I think of it as two weeks until Molloy's big score."

"Whatever," I said. "I was hoping you wouldn't mind taking me through the process, just so I'll know what to expect."

He said it was pretty straightforward, a two-day outing for the owners, usually someplace warm, this time Longboat Key in Florida, near Sarasota, a resort known as The Colony. The Finance Committee met the first morning, got to interview the prospective owner one last time if they wanted to, talk the thing around the room one last time if they wanted to, like it was a jury room. They voted in the afternoon. If the guy passed, the way Dick Miles was certain to pass, he emphasized, there was a conference-call vote with the full ownership later; the next morning there was the NFL equivalent of a closing. Lawyers for the buyer and seller, the league lawyer, the commissioner himself, just to make the occasion as formal as possible. The final papers were signed, and then the check—three checks in this case, one for my brother, one for my sister, one for me—made their way across the conference table.

"Big-ass checks," I said.

"Oh, yeah," Wick Sanderson said, "we also have representatives from the banks involved there as well." His gaze shifted again to the big screen. "Look at her on the train, trying to act ashamed. Like she ever got it that good from Richard Gere."

"Wick, come back to me," I said.

"Sorry."

"So the banks know right away that the checks are good and everything is in order."

"Got their PowerBooks, or whatever the hell they are, right in front of them," he said. He gave me an oh-right look. "You know, Jack, just to make sure that somebody like Dick Miles isn't kiting checks for three quarters of a billion dollars."

"There's always a first time for everything."

"Not this time, kiddo. I talked to the guys we've had checking him out again the other day. They said all Miles has been doing lately is restructuring."

I thought: Like the airline industry.

I said to Wick Sanderson, "Let me just ask one hypothetical, for the hell of it. What happens if something *does* go wrong with the money on the day of the closing?"

He took off his glasses, the kind that automatically turned into sunglasses outside, rubbed his eyes hard, said, "Why are you asking me all this?"

"I'm a curious little monkey."

"Okay," he said. "If the money's not there, the deal's off. We don't fuck around. The deadline is the deadline. Our thinking is that the buyer has usually had, like, six months and sometimes more to get his shit together. So there's no extensions. End of the business day. That day. There's a problem, the deal's off. Nobody stops the clock."

"Even if the problem turned out to be with Big Dick."

"At that point, it wouldn't matter who he was, no matter what kind of p.r. hit we'd take."

"So no matter who it is . . ."

"Fuck him, he's out."

He leaned across the table, his big cuff links with the NFL logo on them making a noise like rocks, and shook a cigarette out of my pack, explaining that Carole didn't like him to smoke, she said it made a yuck out of his breath, but that Ginger was a much better sport.

"I know we've gone over this before," he said. "But you can't possibly believe that Dick Miles is going to have a problem coming up with the dough in two weeks."

I shook my head. No problem. I said, "I'm screwed and I know I'm screwed. I went up against the wrong big guy and lost."

"I should get screwed like that sometime, all due respect to Big Red."

"I want my team back."

"Find something else to want. Or go back to London. Or sell the rest of your stake to Miles and double your money and I'll find you another team someday. Maybe the Bangers. If they don't give Vito a stadium soon, he keeps threatening to sell. And I might not even try to stop the cocksucker."

Yeah, I said, maybe that's all I needed, one more change of scenery. Changes of scenery had always been my solution to everything.

"This is a done deal," Wick Sanderson said. "Leave it alone."

"I'm done," I said.

We drank to that. And to the health care profession in general. And then to Ginger the big red girl, who came over to the table with another round of drinks and asked if I wanted to meet her sister, who'd just started working upstairs.

I said that was certainly tempting, but took out my new cell phone instead and called Annie Kay at her apartment, describing the scene at Yum and telling her about Ginger's sister.

Annie said to come on over, extended care had always been one of her specialties.

I brought her up to speed at breakfast, which for her meant the last few contraband Krispy Kremes from the deli.

She picked the donuts up on her morning run, over to Washington Square Park from Horatio, then a couple of brisk laps on the surrounding streets where most of New York University was located. About twenty minutes ago, or so it seemed, she had been taking classes there by day and bartending at Beef by night, getting any kind of entry-level intern job she could at the local stations; even getting coffee for a no-talent hair-care junkie like Vicky Dunne.

Now every smart girl at her old school and maybe all the schools, every one who knew she was smarter and more talented than most of the boys, wanted to be Annie Kay.

Susan Burden, I told Annie, was in the screenwriter's flat at Lennox Gardens, having a splendid time for herself in London, hitting the theaters, bringing Harrod's to its knees, even, she had said the last time I'd talked to her on the phone, inviting a friend over.

No word from Joe Nacero, who seemed perfectly willing to let the thing play out all the way, to the end of the regular season.

"More than anybody you could ever meet in your life," Billy said, "don't call him, he'll call you."

Carey Nash was off my personal radar again, had been since our conversation at The Last Good Year about Jeff Brewer, and her realization, as I now pointed out to Annie, that I had been welcomed into the open arms of my one and only sweetie pie.

"That is gross," she said.

She took a big bite out of a raspberry-filled and said, "I should have made you come crawling the way Dick Miles did with Joe Don."

It was what she called Joe Nacero. Making him sound like a good-ole-boy running back out of the Big 12 Conference instead of the last don.

"But you're better than that," I said.

"You don't still trust the slutty whistle-blower, do you?" Annie said, out of nowhere.

Carey.

"Only to look out for herself. And her money."

"And she really thought you could help her somehow?"

I said, "I don't think she knew anything specific when she came to me."

"Came on to you."

"As I was saying. I don't think she knew that this could turn into Enron-buys-a-football-team or anything like that. And I still think there's a part of her that wants him to go down, even if it costs her big-time."

"Don't count on it," Annie said. "He gets out of it, she gets everything coming to her."

"He needs Nacero to be his new bank, or Allen Getz to be his new bank, at least in the short run. Carey told me over at Joe Healey's that her snitch friend guy out in California says that when Miles realized how much trouble he was in early in the season, he even tried to pull a Bert Lance. Remember him? He was the secretary of the treasury with Jimmy Carter who got nailed later for using the same asset—in Miles's case, the New York Frigging Hawks—to get three different loans with three different banks."

"And still he doesn't get turned in . . . why?"

"Because they're all into him for so much," I said.

"Loan sharks with better credit ratings."

"Who are out of patience with him being this far in the red."

"Wait, I get it," she said, "a different kind of red zone."

"Same part of the field," I said. "He's trying to score, I'm trying to stop him."

"You still believe you can stop him."

"I could be wrong," I said, "but I just don't see him giving it up for Getz. Which means I've got a couple of weeks to figure out a way for Joe Don to like me better."

Annie gave me a long look and said, "And if you don't?"

"If I don't," I said, "then I do what Carey Nash is looking to do, and cash out, all the way."

"Does all the way mean sell the other twenty-five per-cent?"

I nodded.

Annie said, "Even to Miles if he wins?"

"Even to him. Wick Sanderson says the Bangers might be for sale. I'll get Pete out of retirement. I'll find a way to get Josh back. We'll turn the Bangers into Hawks West."

Annie gave me an even longer look than before and then got up and leaned all the way across the table and kissed me. Then we finished breakfast in bed. I told her sex had a way of clearing my head. Annie said that in my world, sex also cured cancer and world hunger and straightened out the dollar against the yen.

Ty Moranis, Butterball Morton, Elvis Elgin, Price-less Braxton, and I were in my office the day after we'd beaten the Bengals, 23–20. Ty had only attempted nine passes for the whole game, but Priceless had rushed for two hundred yards and two touchdowns and Benito Siragusa had kicked three field goals and we were still alive for the playoffs, even though both the Bills and Jets had also won the day before, making the Bills 10–5, the Jets and the Hawks both 9–6.

If we beat the Dolphins at Molloy on Sunday, the worst we would get was a home wild-card game the Sunday after the owners' meeting at Longboat Key; we had the tiebreakers on the Jets in the event of a three-way.

If we beat the Dolphins and the Bills lost, we won the AFC East from the *Bills* on tiebreakers, and got a bye the first weekend of the playoffs, whatever Corky DuPont's Jets did.

If both the Jets and Bills won and we lost to the Dolphins, we were 9–7 and out of the playoffs. Because they were both playing one o'clock games and we had a four, we'd know the deal by the time we took the field.

The league, of course, loved even moderately complicated higher math like this, fans thinking that everybody except Harvard and Yale had a chance coming into the last weekend.

Ty had taken another hit to his shoulder in Cincinnati, a cheap shot from their All-Pro tight end, Gelfand Dupay, who was so hopped up the whole game I started to think Harm Battles and Hans Nowitzky had somehow hooked up with the Bengals after I fired the two pill dispensers. Butterball was still hurt and Elvis had briefly had to leave the game with a dislocated shoulder, which the rest of the fat boys popped back in for him on the bench.

They all sat in my office and said, fuck it, they were playing against the Dolphins no matter what.

Priceless Braxton didn't say much of anything, just sat in some kind of yoga position on my carpet and methodically, almost trancelike, flipped through *Crain's Business Daily*.

As far as I had been able to tell, Priceless Braxton didn't get hurt, didn't get tired, hardly ever changed expression, didn't fumble, didn't miss blocks or assignments, just waited for one of our quarterbacks to call his number and hand him the ball, at which point he made us the toughest out around on bad-weather days like yesterday; made me think that if we did manage to get into the playoffs we might have a chance to do something.

In my office, I said, "Priceless, have I mentioned lately that you're the best fucking football player I've ever seen?"

Priceless looked up from *Crain's Business Daily* and said, "Truth is still beauty."

Butterball belched and said, "Nothin' against Bobby C., but if I coulda blocked for you my whole damn career, I'd have more cars and a better-lookin' wife."

Ty said, "You're, like, *married,* dog?"

"I keep Darlene back in Oklahoma during the season, on account of the school system."

Elvis said, "Darlene ever act curious about that shit, since you two don't have any damn *children*?"

Butterball said, "Once I got her out of that double-wide, Darlene's never been one to rock the boat."

They had been talking about the Bengals game and who we might get in the first round, drinking beers, talking about how you might not be able to tell it by our record lately, but that Bobby Bullard had actually been coaching his ass off.

Even Ty Moranis had come around on him since the hostage crisis at The Four Seasons.

Ty said, "Coach keeps saying he didn't know running the damn ball could be this much fun."

"Said it was like finally bein' faithful to a wife," Butterball said. "Once you get the hang of it, it doesn't suck nearly as much as you thought it would."

Elvis Elgin was stretched out on one of my couches, wearing a mammoth, hooded Hawks sweatshirt and gray sweats. He said to me, "Enough about ball. What about you?"

"Yeah," Butterball said, and let out another belch, this one sounding like a garbage disposal.

At least we all hoped it was a belch.

I said, "What about me?"

Elvis said, "You gonna pull this deal of yours out?"

"It doesn't look that way."

"But you the house, baby," Elvis said. "Don't the house always win?"

I said, "In theory."

Ty said, "You can't let that fucker beat you out of your team."

"I'm running out of time."

Elvis said, "You just got to come up with one of your ideas."

"I'm surrounded by pricks," I said. "Present company excluded. If one of them doesn't get the Hawks, I'm afraid the other one will."

Meaning, the comedy team of Miles and Getz.

I got up and walked over to the refrigerator and got myself another Samuel Adams. The rest of them said they were fine. "You know something, boys?" I said. "I did this to my own sorry-assed self."

The fat boys started to talk about ordering in a bunch of pizza and watching *Monday Night Football* right here in Suite 19, if that was all right with me. I told them I had the number for a place called Fiero's, a few miles up the Deegan in Yonkers. Ty Moranis went into the next room to play the blood-gore video game he'd brought with him, and attached it to the television set over there.

Nobody said anything for a few minutes. There were just the sound effects every time Ty would make another vicious kill with his game controller and say something like, "Die, motherfucker."

Then Priceless Braxton changed positions for the first time since he'd put down *Crain's,* recrossing his legs into a new pretzel position. "There's a Chinese proverb that goes something like this," he said. "Sometimes the least of your enemies can become the greatest of friends."

We all stopped and looked at him. Even Ty looked up from his video game. Just because Priceless spoke so rarely.

"More wisdom from Chang the trainer?" I said.

"Jet Li. His new movie." Priceless closed his eyes and turned his head slowly to one side, then the other.

"I just thought I'd throw that shit out there, anyway," he said.

Ty went back to his game. The rest of us drank beer. Priceless seemed to have fallen asleep. I sat with my cross-trainers up on my desk and thought about what he'd said and tried to rank my current enemies, somewhat like the Associated Press weekly college football poll.

Finally, I got up and walked into my bedroom, telling them to go ahead and call Fiero's, sometimes they got backed up on Monday nights before the football game, I had a phone call to make.

"Who to?" Elvis said.

"Bad girl."

Priceless opened his eyes and said, "Friend or enemy?"

"That's the beauty of a good bad girl," I told him. "Sometimes it's hard to tell."

The next morning, Bobby Bullard came into my office as I was drinking espresso from the machine I'd finally brought down from Suite 19, trying to figure out whether the fucking film critic in the *Times* liked the new Mel Gibson movie or not.

"There's somethin' I've been meanin' to say to you," he said.

He looked hungover, but then he always did at this time of day. I knew about all the coaches in football who liked to brag about showing up for work at five in the morning, but my coach always looked as if that's when he got home from the bar.

I told him that I'd just brewed up some espresso stronger than paint cleaner, and he said, "Thank you, Jesus," and poured himself some into a regular coffee cup, then drank down about half of it.

"I'll choke down a couple of those diet pops after this and a couple of those dietary supplemental pills Harm and Hans left behind," he said, "then we'll see whether or not the old coach is gonna need a nap before he meets with his perky coordinators."

He stretched out on my couch.

"Where were you last night?"

Bullard said, "I heard about this new country bar down in Chelsea or SoHo or some goddamn place, and they had a kick-ass band and dance floor full of kick-ass girls in tight jeans and, shoot, after that it was still the same old story, a fight for love and glory."

"I thought you were being faithful to your wife these days."

He drank up the rest of his espresso and said, "Know what, Jack? Until last night I thought the exact same thing."

"You said there was something you wanted to talk about?"

He pulled himself up with the kind of effort you see when power lifters try to jack their own weight. "I don't know what the ten worst things I ever did are," he said, "just that most of 'em have to do with sex or lyin' about sex."

The two certainly did seem to go hand in hand, I agreed.

"But the worst I ever did was let Mr. Dick Miles talk me into fuckin' around with the Jets game the way I did, and having Ty throw that damn screen pass."

I went over to the refrigerator and pulled out an ice-cold Samuel Adams and brought it over to him. Sat down in the chair closest to the couch. I said, "Ty says the two of you are cool now. And just about everybody on the team is talking about how you've been coaching your ass off."

He took a pull of beer and I thought for a second he might cry at the sheer joy of the experience. Bullard grinned instead. "The last couple a months, coachin' ball has been better'n sex. Least until last night." He took another big swallow and said, "And that ain't no lie."

I told him to just keep coaching his ass off until he'd coached us back into first place. He said he'd justly try. I told him I knew pretty much the whole story now on the Jets game, and even who was behind it. He said that Miles had never even told him that much, just that it was some big greaseball who liked to bet football.

"You know who it is?" Bullard said.

I told him his description would do just fine.

The coach and I talked a while longer, then he said that he just remembered, he had to stop and look at some god-damn game film in our high-tech video room before he met with his coordinators.

I asked if I could tag along. Bobby Bullard said fine, but

that looking at game film was even more boring than marriage counseling.

"Actually," I said, "I've always wanted to direct."

"Whatever," the coach of the Hawks said, then clapped me hard on the back and said, dad-gummit all to grandma's house, I was a funny old mullet. I told him to call me in Suite 19 after practice, it was time for us to hit this little club I knew and have a drink.

26

The funny thing, I finally decided in the days and nights before the Dolphins game, was that Dick Miles was no better or worse than a lot of owners I knew.

Maybe if he still had Bill Francione around, he could have become a star owner the way Francione had helped make him a star with MF, Inc. But Francione was gone and so was a lot of the money the two of them had made, so there was no way of knowing about that.

But then, you never knew how it would go for the newest rich guy buying the team.

Maybe if Miles had more time—and the resources he was supposed to have—he could figure it all out, shoot right to the head of the class.

You had guys who spermed their way into being owners, inherited the family team the way Ken and Babs and I had.

You had others who'd done the same thing with the family fortune, and decided they wanted to have a sports team as a new toy, like a new Gulfstream.

You had owners in hockey who ended up going bankrupt, and one, the fat baseball-card collector who used to have the Los Angeles Kings, who ended up doing more jail time than Joe Nacero ever had.

I kept thinking of how Joe Nacero really should have a team of his own—the Jersey Loan Sharks? Racketeers?—how he'd be as successful as a sports boss as he was being a real boss; how he'd probably be smarter, run his team better, than any of them, starting with Dick Miles, world's greatest fan.

You had rich owners in baseball who acted like they wanted to spend more on lawn care than they did on their teams.

You had Disney owning the Angels when they won the World Series and a hockey team, the Mighty Ducks, that they'd spun off from a Disney movie.

You had the television nitwits who bought the Dodgers from the O'Malley family, and you had guys like Steinbrenner and Davis and Jones and Jerry Buss of the Lakers, all of whom actually knew how to make money and win.

You had the Corky DuPonts of the world, who did really think the whole thing was fucking sailing.

You had Marge Schott, who blew her team by basically being such a dumb-ass.

You had me, who could have done better selling his team on fucking eBay.

I thought about all those things all week long as I kept moving around like a moving target, and then on the last Sunday of the NFL regular season as I watched the New York Hawks play themselves not just into the playoffs but back into first place in the AFC East on the coldest day at Molloy Stadium that anybody could remember.

We made it back into first place because the Bills lost to the Rams, and the Jets got upset by the Houston Texans, and because Ty Moranis, who shouldn't even have been on the field because he had no arm left, rolled out on a field that had turned to black ice by the early evening and threw a touchdown pass to Sultan McCovey with five minutes left. Sultan himself was playing on one good leg and still outjumped half the Dolphins' secondary for the score that tied the game once Benito Siragusa kicked the extra point.

After his catch, Sultan gamely managed an understated touchdown dance, even on his injured knee, a program I thought fit the day perfectly, incorporating some of the best figure-skating moves from girl gold medalists of the past several Olympics.

"I've been waitin' for just the right moment to try out my Kristi Yamaguchi," he said in the locker room after the game. "She come up a little short on her triple jumps, but that girl was *nice*."

The Hawks beat the Dolphins even after Miami's rookie quarterback, Percival Montage, took his team right down the field after Sultan's touchdown, too quickly as it turned out, for the field goal that put his team ahead 16–13.

The Hawks came back again. They did that with snow starting to fall at Molloy and blow around like a nor'easter; did it because in the end we had something the Dolphins sure did not.

Priceless Braxton.

Pete Stanton was in Suite 19 to see that last drive, having called the day before to tell me he'd just gotten back into town. Susan Burden was back from London, saying that she had to be here on just the chance that it was the Hawks' last game of the season. And mine. Billy and Oretha were there, and so was A.T.M. Moore. I told him that this was a day when I wanted to be surrounded by my loved ones, that I knew he could manage to stay away from Oretha and be a good boy.

When I'd called him in the morning, he'd said, "I'd rather sit down in the stands and have my dick fall off like a fuckin' icicle."

"Do this for me," I said.

"All right," he said, "but don't let her start up with that

mouth of hers in front of people. You go back and look it up, yo, she's the one *invented* that 'masculation shit."

"She's much more of a lady now that she's with Billy."

"Man must be deaf and not lettin' on. Or he just puts on his Miracle Ear when it's time to get his pipes cleaned."

So he was there and so were Allen Getz and Kitty Drucker-Cole Molloy, who certainly weren't considered loved ones, but had dropped by from Dick Miles's suite next door to sit with Carey Nash, who was only in 19 on a special dispensation from Miss Annie Kay.

For one more day, Pete was back where he belonged, on my left.

Neville Hayward, who'd taken his own British Airways flight from London a few days before Susan Burden had, was on my right. After Priceless Braxton had picked up our second first down of the last drive, Neville nodded in the general direction of Getz and my stepmother and Carey.

"So that's the dragon lady," he said.

I told him he was going to have to be a little more specific.

"The younger one. You believe she's really going to take his deal?"

"That's what she says."

"What does she know about our Mr. Nacero?"

"What she thinks she knows," I said. "Now watch the game."

"Bitch, bitch, bitch," he said.

"You wish."

We all watched as the Hawks, in the snow and against the wind, went seventy-eight yards on fourteen plays. Priceless Braxton carried on eleven of them. The Dolphins knew what was coming and couldn't do a goddamn thing to stop it. Ty Moranis threw the ball once to Sultan on the sideline, spiked it two other times.

The rest was Priceless.

He ran off-tackle and behind Elvis and Butterball on sweeps. Everybody else looked to be moving in slow motion on the icy field. Not Priceless. Not when he saw his hole, or his opening, or even the hint of an opening. He ran for six and eight and four and then one time for sixteen, the one they'd still be replaying when he'd gone off to whatever Holy Land was working for him after he retired from football for good. On that one, he took the handoff from Ty and ran to his right and dropped the ball and had it come right back up to him like it was a basketball he was dribbling. When he had control of the ball again, all he could see in front of him were green Dolphin uniforms and so he changed directions, reversed his field, slipped, went down, got back up again, ended up all the way over on the left sideline, finally ran all the way down to the Dolphins' eight with thirty seconds left.

He carried it down to the four from there, Ty called our last time-out, then the fat boys opened up one last hole and Priceless ran through it like it was his turn in the spa, and we were in first place.

And for the first time Priceless Braxton danced in the end zone, a smooth little soft-shoe that ended up with him jumping over Elvis and Butterball, still on their backs at the two-yard line.

"That's the move Fred Astaire used when he went over the little picket fence in *Swing Time*," Neville said.

Ty Moranis stood at the five-yard line, where he'd handed Priceless the ball, looked up through the snow at where he knew Suite 19 was, pointed with his right finger, and fired an imaginary gun at me.

Billy asked if I wanted to use the Amazing Grace plane for the flight to Florida. I thanked him and said Delta would be just fine. Then, for about the twentieth time, he asked if I was sure I didn't want him to come with me. I said I was bringing Neville, in case I cried, he was used to girly men.

Oretha Keeshon offered to come, telling me I should re-member the last time I was in a jam over the Hawks, she played the part of a hooker so well when we'd set up Donnie Mack Carney we all thought she should have been the first black woman to win Best Actress and not Halle.

I told Oretha I appreciated the offer but all the good parts were taken this time.

She said, "That's the shit always happens once an actress gets past a certain age."

Then she kissed me on the cheek and gave me a long hug and said, "And, Jammer? Me and the boss daddy will be thinkin' on you."

Neville and I took an afternoon flight to Tampa and dealt with modern air travel, which meant getting snapped at by flight attendants every time we asked if they might possibly, sometime before the plane was hijacked to Havana, think about freshening our drinks and bringing more frigging peanuts. Ty Moranis was on our flight, too; there was a week off before the first playoff game and the doctors told him they didn't just want him to rest his arm, they wanted him to do that somewhere warm. So he decided to come with Neville and me, explaining that there was a girl he knew from Texas Tech who now ran some kind of upscale yoga school in Bradenton.

And, he said, it was a chance for him to catch up with some of his Florida homeboys.

When we were walking through the terminal, Ty said that if I needed anything to call, and gave me his primary cell number, the one, he said, he gave out only to homeboys.

"I've achieved homey status?" I said.

He gave me his sleepy-eyed nod.

"Remember," I said. "This is supposed to be a healing time. No gunplay."

"Dog," he said. "I, like, *told* you, I'm tryin' to quit."

Neville and I rented a Mercedes convertible because Neville insisted, then drove an hour or so south on I-75, where our designated Sarasota exit turned out to be Fruitville Road.

"You paid someone to do this," Neville said.

"Fruitville Road," I said. "Maybe God is sending us a message."

"If it's directed at me," Neville said, "then it's probably the same kind of mixed message He usually sends to us queers."

We passed signs for a Ringling Museum and a Sarasota Arts Center and went over two bridges and finally found ourselves in a part of Sarasota known as St. Armand's Circle, filled with restaurants and old-fashioned ice cream shops and old people crossing the street slower than leg-irons. Then we were through St. Armand's Circle and going over the huge drawbridge that put us on Longboat Key, finally taking the left into The Colony. I had somehow managed to book what passed for their Presidential Suite, one the current president had actually stayed in once, or so we were told when we checked in.

"I'm getting chills," Neville said, "just thinking about being in the same bed as a real God-fearing *Republican*."

I told him not unless I was the one giving off the mixed message, I had the master bedroom, he was upstairs.

The woman at the front desk told me Dick Miles and Jeff Brewer had a two-bedroom bungalow right on the beach, with the same view of the Gulf we had. Ours was just higher, and better.

Wick Sanderson and Ginger the big red girl were in the suite across the hall from ours, with a spectacular view of Har-Tru tennis courts, and a partial water view beyond that.

I knew the commissioner didn't care, he was just interested in any view of Ginger.

"Carole wanted to come," he said, when I saw him in the elevator. "But I made this whole thing down here sound more tedious than the Yalta Conference."

He said that Carole (Hollywood Tits) Sandusky then asked if that was the conference with the Browns and Steelers in it.

I had an early dinner that night with Ken and Babs at a corner table of The Colony's main restaurant, one with the best view of the sunset and the Gulf.

I hadn't seen either one of them since I'd come back for the season. The biggest change was my brother Ken, who'd divorced Ashley, permanently retired from being an ass-hole, turned into an official guy's guy. He'd spent most of the season, he said, traveling the world looking for the best places to fish and get laid.

Babs and her family, the children and what's-his-name, had moved to Scottsdale. The first time she'd gone to the ladies' room, Ken had informed me that she was spending more time than ever on her passions:

1. Southwest art.

2. Good causes.

3. Tennis.

4. Tennis pros.

She informed us herself upon her return that Arizona was much *much* safer from terrorists than lower Fairfield County.

"My feeling," she said over her second after-dinner brandy, "is that those people just aren't going to *bother* with another old desert."

Ken and I said we'd both drink to that, then waited for Babs to call it a night before I told him how I thought the next thirty-six hours might play out.

He listened without interrupting and then said, "What if there's a player in the game you don't know about?"

"I am royally and thoroughly screwed once and for all."

"Then what?"

"Then I root for the home team for as long as we last in the playoffs and then quietly sell the rest of my share when the season is over."

Ken asked where Miles and Brewer were; I told him they were probably next door at the Longboat Key Club, where I happened to know both Joseph Nacero and Allen Getz were staying, just at opposite ends of the property.

Miles probably willing to negotiate all night if he had to, with one or the other.

Or both.

Ken said, "It's like the end of a close game."

I said, a *bad* close game.

My brother asked if I wanted to slide over to the bar, known as the Monkey Room, and have a nightcap. He said he'd just seen a big redhead who looked like a free-agent tight end walk in there wearing a dress the size of a cocktail napkin.

I told him to forget it, she was with the league office.

He said he was going to have one more anyway. I told him I was going to take the last of my Hennessy and go out on the beach and smoke for a while and maybe have a talk with the old man.

Ken said, "You'll be fine with this, either way. You were always fine, even when you'd been busted down to buck private by the restaurant business. It's why I always wanted to be you."

"It hasn't been so hot lately, being me."

We were at the entrance to The Monkey Room. We saw Wick Sanderson sitting with Ginger the big red girl. Ken asked if Ginger was really with the league office. I told him the deal, that she was the girl on the side to the commissioner's original girl on the side, Carole Sandusky. But, being a good brother, I also felt it would have been wrong of me not to tell him where Ginger worked in the city.

And which nights.

I took off my sneakers and walked to the end of a row of palm trees, away from the bright lights of the swimming pool, and stretched out on a lounge chair. Big Tim Molloy had never been one for the west coast of Florida. He had always been Miami Beach in the old days, back when the biggest acts, even Sinatra, used to play at the Eden Roc and the Fontainebleau, and all the clubs down there felt like the East Side of Manhattan in the winter. Later on, when he was with Kitty Drucker-Cole Molloy, his winters, or big chunks of them, had been spent in Palm Beach, in the oceanfront palace Kitty still owned, one right down the street from Trump's place.

The old man liked what he liked, and when he found something he liked, he stayed with it no matter what.

He had no use for the twins, not really, and they both knew it, even if none of us talked about that, even now. He wasn't proud of that fact. There it was, anyway. I don't believe he ever had much use for his second wife, she was just a pretty companion for him, someone he didn't have to take seriously, a vanity grab by a sixty-five-year-old man, maybe one who even got him going in the bedroom without meds.

When you got down to it, the things he'd truly cared about in his life were my mother and making money and football.

And me.

He loved my mother even when she was gone, and he loved me even when we were fighting and even after that, when I had gone off to Vegas. He loved football even in all the years when he couldn't find himself the right general manager or the right coach or enough good players, when he was the one who looked like one of those owners who would never get it right, who could be a genius in every business except the sports business.

"Molloy," he used to say, "I carry a picture of the way it's *supposed* to be. I can *imagine* it. But I just can't seem to make it happen, no matter how hard I imagine."

Then it happened five months after he died, the one truly rotten piece of luck the old man had ever had.

I thought about that on the beach, imagining the way things were *supposed* to be, the way they were supposed to work out. I lay there and smoked and looked up at the stars and wondered which one the old man was riding on tonight;

which star was carrying the smartest son-of-a-bookmaker who ever was.

I finished my drink and left the glass in the sand and started walking barefoot down the beach, sneakers in hand, toward the Longboat Key Club, feeling light-headed and jazzed at the same time.

Suddenly imagining something that had nothing to do with anything.

Imagining a long-ago game at UCLA, us against Arizona State, the one that ended with me running down the sideline on the last play of the game and us behind by five points at the Coliseum, running down the right side by myself because Bubba Royal had sent all our receivers down the left side.

Seeing Bubba throw that Hail Mary pass high up over everything, because they had become Hail Mary passes by then, miracle plays in football having gone Roman Catholic after Franco Harris made his Immaculate Reception against the Raiders that time.

Seeing myself jumping over the one safety who'd reacted to the play about two beats late—"Jumped yourself Afro-merican that day," Bubba had always said—and catching the ball and holding on to it when I landed on my ass in the end zone of the Los Angeles Coliseum at the same moment I heard the gun go off to end the game.

The members of the NFL Finance Committee met the next morning in a second-floor conference room in the main building at The Colony, three floors below what Neville kept solemnly calling the Bush Suite. There was Chairman Vito Cazenovia, Barry Teitlebaum of the Patriots, Al Davis, Jerry Jones, Bobby Finkel of the Saints, Corky DuPont, my old friend Donnie Mack Carney. Donnie Mack had given up the chairmanship while I'd been in Europe, sold most of his Christian broadcasting empire, ended the Ravens' policy of signing only Born Agains, di-

vorced *his* wife the way my brother had, married a twenty-
five-year-old singer from one of his TV choruses, a hot little number whose mother had been one of those knockoff
Supremes you used to see after Diana Ross left the group.

"Had an epiphany there in Phoenix when you caught me
with my Saint Peter out," Donnie Mack had said to me that
morning in the breakfast room. "And here it is: The Lord
loves sinners, too, Jack."

"I'm hoping," I said.

Jeff Brewer represented Miles, introducing himself
to the members of the committee, then telling them that
nothing had changed from when Mr. Miles bought the
team, that owning the New York Hawks was a dream come
true, and that he looked forward to the official closing tomorrow.

I represented the Molloy family.

When Brewer finished, Wick Sanderson asked if there
was anything I wanted to say.

"My brother and sister and I look forward to tomorrow
as well," I said.

Wick Sanderson, who looked as if he'd forgotten to use
any sunblock yesterday—parts of his face were as red as
Ginger's hair—looked at me, frowning.

"That's it?"

"I'm talked out," I said.

"Then you and Jeff can go," the commissioner said. "The
rest of us will discuss this for a little while among ourselves,
along with a few other matters that you'd be shocked to discover have nothing to do with you, and then we'll convene
here for the vote after lunch."

In the hallway, Jeff Brewer said, "I've got to meet Mr.
Miles over at Longboat. But I have to say, big guy, you're
taking this much better than I thought you would."

I'd noticed Carl standing between the two elevators as
soon as we'd stepped outside the conference room. His outfit looked like Early Gold's Gym: dark nylon shorts with
two white stripes down the side, sleeveless T-shirt showing

off his array of tattoos, a flowered bandanna that somehow fit all the way around his fat head, socks up to his knees, Nike cross-trainers.

"You know what I was thinking in there?" Brewer said. "Wouldn't it be something if the Hawks got on a roll now and Wick Sanderson ended up handing the Lombardi Trophy to Dick Miles? I mean, would that be a picture?"

"Wait, I've got a better one," I said. "Why don't you fuck yourself while Carl watches?" I grinned and said, "You like to watch, Carl?"

"Huh?" he said.

Jeff Brewer said, "Don't be a bad loser, Jack."

"Okay," I said. "I won't."

Later in the afternoon, Wick Sanderson called the Bush Suite and said that the committee had voted 6–1 in favor of Dick Miles.

The only dissenting vote, he said, came from Donnie Mack Carney.

"Said he owed you one for helping him see the light," Wick Sanderson said.

"Amen," I said.

Then I went downstairs and popped the top on the convertible and drove up to the Tampa Airport to pick up Annie; *The NFL Today* had sent her down to cover the closing, for a piece they planned to run before our first playoff game. She had called from La Guardia before her plane took off and said that I didn't need to come all the way up to the airport to get her, she could drive to The Colony with her crew.

I told her it was a turn-on for me to watch her hair blow around with the top down.

"Oh," she had said on the phone, "*that's* the turn-on I'd forgotten," then wanted to know how it was all going down there.

I told her I was trying to behave myself and had promised Jeff Brewer not to be a bad loser.

27

Annie and Ty Moranis and I had lunch in the suite on Thursday. The closing was scheduled for two o'clock. Chang had somehow hitched a ride on somebody's private plane and arrived at the Sarasota Airport, only about ten minutes away from Longboat Key, the night before. The two of them had spent the morning working out at The Colony's new training facility—"Whoa, dog," Ty had said when he described it, "like a *real* spa"—then gone out to the beach to stretch, swim against the current a little bit, run in the sand, and, from what I could see from my balcony, come on to bikini-wearing towel girls, some of whom showed Yum potential.

Annie did an official interview with me that she planned to run with the piece, even though I told her she should put off talking to me until after the closing if she wanted some gritty human drama and the chance to see a grown man cry on camera. She said that she'd seen me cry plenty of times, and I said, I did *not* cry at any of those Meryl Streep movies. Yeah, right, she said, and then she and her crew went over to the other side of the grounds to interview members of the Television Committee about what kind of sick, depraved numbers they were asking for from CBS, Fox, ABC, NBC, and ESPN this time.

She asked me when she should be back, and I told her about five.

"It is the opinion of this reporter that you're not being completely forthcoming," she said.

"Of course I'm not being forthcoming," I said. "I'm a guy."

I looked her over, smiling because sometimes I couldn't help it with her: Annie the TV star, with her new short haircut, in her green sundress with the thin straps on her shoulders, wearing some kind of cool white sandals.

"I like your hair," I said.

"Oh, that's the ticket when you don't want to really talk, talk to *me* like I'm the set of knockers with the commissioner."

Ty said he was going back down to the beach so that he and his homeboys could hang with the towel girls; I told him I'd call him later when it was time for us to meet.

At five minutes to go, I gave myself one more look in the mirror: blue blazer, blue buttoned-down from Brooks Brothers, rep tie. Khaki slacks. Even loafers instead of my New Balance 609s. Put my face up close to the mirror and told myself that it was being in the sun yesterday that had put more gray in my hair; an old girlfriend had told me once I looked a little bit like Harrison Ford without the hat.

Now I was starting to look like Ford when he stood next to Ally McBeal.

Then I went down to the second floor, running down the stairs like I was running out of the tunnel for the big game.

Darnell Whitfield, the hip black lawyer who'd represented my stepmother at the reading of the old man's will, a guy who told everybody he was set up to out-Johnnie Johnnie Cochran if he could just find the right brother and the right murder, was sitting with Ken and Babs, representing them now. Oscar Berkowitz was there representing me. Oscar the Great. Wearing an elegant summer suit, perpetual tan, thinning hair brushed straight back, looking fresh despite having flown all night on Billy Grace's small backup Citation. He was next to Darnell. Oscar's fat worn leather briefcase, what he called his million-miler, was on the table in front of him, chock-full, I was certain, of all sorts of goodies.

Wick Sanderson was there with with the league's top attorney, Gus Laggos, who I knew was Greek but looked as if he belonged with Joe Nacero.

And at the other end from me, head of the table, in a starched white dress shirt, his own blazer draped over the chair in back of him, checking his watch every few minutes and looking jumpy as a lookout man outside a bank, was Jeff Brewer.

"Where's the buyer?" I said to him.

It was a rhetorical question, even if Jeff Brewer didn't know that. I knew where Dick Miles was. He was next door at the Longboat Key Club in Joe Nacero's vulgar suite, one that made the rooms I had upstairs look like public housing, trying to close his deal with Nacero.

And Nacero's people.

"I just talked to him on his cell," Brewer said. "He's going to be a little late." He ran a hand through his thick, tangled hair, trying to act casual.

Like the winner in life he believed he was.

"The end of today is the absolute deadline, right, Commissioner?" I said.

"Five o'clock, as stipulated in the league contract," Wick Sanderson said. "But I was under the impression we'd be able to wrap this all up before that."

We all sat around and made small talk then. The room-service guy brought more chips and dip and soft drinks and beer for anybody who wanted beer. Wick Sanderson stepped away from the table and made a cell phone call of his own, keeping his voice low, trying to make it sound like official business. I couldn't tell whether he was talking to Hollywood Tits or Ginger.

I asked him where the bankers were and he said they were next door, cable-modemed to the max and ready to hook up with their home offices as soon as Miles arrived.

Babs was doing what she had done her whole life, filling every available pause in anybody's conversation with more babble about herself, talking now about her social life in the Valley of the Sun.

"We get a lot of string ties there," she said. "Belt buckles the size of hubcaps. New wives with new breasts, and old wives still hanging on and who frankly need to spend less time in the sun."

The older my sister got, the more she sounded like Kitty Drucker-Cole Molloy. It had begun to occur to me that in some weird way, the old man had married his daughter the second time around.

Ken said, "Check me on this, Babs, but what else do they have out there besides sun?"

Babs said, "Shopping. Hellooooooooo."

I said to Darnell, "My sister has always thought shopping could get stroke victims turned around."

"Tell me about it, dude," he said. "Our office pays her credit-card bills."

At two-thirty, I said to Jeff Brewer, "Why don't you and Carl and I take a ride and see what's holding Dick up?"

"Excuse me?"

"Relax," I said. "I know where he is, I know who he's with, I know what they're doing."

Wick Sanderson said, "All due respect to the lady present, but would you mind telling me what the fuck is going on here?"

Ken Molloy said, "Why, the sale of the Hawks, Commissioner. Isn't that what we're all here for?"

"If everybody will just be a little patient, this shouldn't take long," I said.

Babs said, "I'm going downstairs to finish having my nails done."

Darnell said he'd go with her, he'd been having some cuticle issues his own damn self.

I said to Jeff Brewer, "Before we go? You really ought to run over to the bungalow and get a tie."

When we had gotten out of the elevator on the penthouse level of the Longboat Key Club's main building, one of Joe Nacero's bodyguards—a Vinny of his own—was standing there to tell us we were expected.

There was another Vinny posted at the door.

Maybe there was a service that guys like Billy and Joe Nacero used.

The second Vinny gave a rap on the door, opened it, Jeff Brewer and I walked in. Carl waited in the hall.

Joe Nacero was in a summer suit that looked even softer than the one Oscar Berkowitz had been wearing. Dick Miles was standing on the other side of the room. He wore his usual crested blazer, white shirt, a pink tie that matched the handkerchief in the front jacket pocket. And despite what I knew had been a long night for him, he squared himself up when he saw me. Stuck that jaw out. Bring it on.

"Hey, partner," I said. "Glad to see me?"

"No."

I said, "Now, what the hell kind of language is no?"

I gave a jerk of my head toward Miles and said to Joe Nacero, "Where's his lawyer?"

Nacero smiled thinly. "I told him we'd call him if we need him."

There was a long dining room table behind him, and beyond that, out the sliding glass doors, was the Gulf. There were two laptops on the table, piles of paper, thick

books that had ANNUAL REPORT written big enough and
bold enough on the covers for me to see from twenty feet
away.

There was one person still seated at the table, clicking
away at one of the laptops like a Kelly Girl:

Neville Hayward.

In his low-key, mobbed-up Jersey accent, the one he
used at Scratch sometimes, depending on how rough a
customer wanted to play it, he said, "Anybody here intro-
ducin' me?"

Miles made a dismissive gesture with his hand. "This is
Mr. Nacero's lawyer, Hagen Thomas."

It made me smile. Tom Hagen had been the name of the
Corleone *consigliere* in the *Godfather* movies.

"You, sir," I said to Neville, "are a very attractive man."

In his normal voice, more English now than Bucking-
ham Palace, he said, "I try to keep myself up."

Miles looked at him, then at me, then at Joe Nacero.
Then back at Neville.

"What's with the accent?" he said.

I said to Dick Miles, "He's with me."

Miles looked at Joe Nacero. "Joe?" was the best he
could do.

Nacero didn't waste any time. He walked over to the
television set in the living room, hit the power switch, then
hit the Play button on the VCR attached to it.

He must have cued it up before anybody got here, because the face of Bobby Bullard came up right away,
Bullard sitting there in the Hawks' high-tech video, Bullard
saying ". . . all he told me was that he was about to do a
deal with some greaseball from Jersey who obviously didn't
have any balls, he wanted a sure thing . . ."

Joe Nacero hit the Stop button.

In a voice that was softer than snow hitting the ground,
Joe Nacero said, "It was never about sure things. That was
never the point. I own most of the bookmakers you placed

those bets with. It was not about me winning a bet. It was about you showing loyalty. Showing me how much you could be trusted."

I thought of Butterball Morton, standing next to me that day in Suite 19 when he thought we were about to go into overtime against the Jets:

Because now Dick Miles was the one who didn't know whether to shit or go blind.

"Hey," he said. "Hey, Joe. I was just kidding around with that redneck."

"No," Nacero said. "No, you weren't. People like you never are."

Neville Hayward said, "Probably makes antigay remarks as well."

"He *is* the type," I said.

Miles's head whipped around. He said to Neville, "Who *are* you?"

"I can explain," Nacero said. "I'm not a very good liar. Maybe you'd expect me to be. But I actually have a terrible poker face. It can be a problem in bridge, you have to bid sometimes without any points in your hand." He said to me, "Poker face, bridge. Am I shuffling cards here, or metaphors?"

I said, "Knock yourself out."

"Anyway," Joe Nacero said, "Jack suggested Neville might be useful."

Neville brightened. "I can lie like one of those bitch lawyers anytime," he said.

Joe Nacero did most of the talking. Occasionally, I talked. Occasionally, Dick Miles would try to talk and Nacero would tell him to be quiet. That's what we said, anyway. Be quiet, please. What we heard in the suite was this:

Shut the fuck up.

Now.

"It's amazing how many I meet just like you," Nacero said at one point. "Won't listen."

"Why?" Miles said. "Can I at least ask why?"

"Why you refuse to shut up?"

Miles said, "Why you're doing this?"

Nacero said, "I could present it to you in a number of different ways. But mostly it came down to this: The more I looked at this thing, and the more I looked at you, there was just something about you that pissed me off, Mr. Miles."

Miles said to me, "You turned him against me."

I smiled, big and wide. Having saved my best fuck-you smile for the biggest prick in the room.

Like father, like son.

"I wish," I said.

I didn't really need to make a tape of Bullard, the way Neville and I had made the hostage tape at The Four Seasons. I just wanted it in case I could not only persuade Nacero to shut down Miles, but torture him a little bit the way he was being tortured now at the Longboat Key Club.

So Bobby Bullard and I made the tape that day in the video room, me interviewing him from off camera, me using what I modestly thought was almost Bergman-like lighting. Then that night the coach and I took a ride over to Jersey and sat at Joe Nacero's table at Baby Doll and he told Nacero his version of why the Hawks–Jets game ended the way it did that day.

I knew I'd have to give Nacero more than that. And did. But he was a good listener, and so he listened that night as Bobby Bullard said he'd take a dad-gummit poly-damn test if Mr. Nacero wanted him to.

"I believe you," Nacero had said. "People don't normally sit at this table and try to tell me something that is not true."

"Havin' sat here myself, sir?" Bobby Bullard said. "And

all due respect? People at this table would tell you the truth about jerkin' off."

That was when we decided that Nacero would string Miles along all the way to Longboat Key. He told me that after having his real lawyer and his very real accountants go over Miles's books, he thought it would be easier to re-build Iraq than rebuild Miles's business empire, at least in the short run.

"I could own him," Nacero said. "But I keep thinking: Who'd want to?"

He told me that he'd be willing to come down to Florida, but knew enough about himself at this stage of his life to know he didn't have the energy to sit in a room with Miles and have to listen to him for as long as he knew he'd have to. Then I told him about Neville. All about Neville. Nacero said he didn't know a lot of homosexuals, if you didn't count several members of the Giamberella family.

I asked who they were.

"In my world," he said, "think of them as one of the top teams in the other conference."

"Don't worry about Neville," I said that night at Baby Doll. "He's one of the greatest bullshitters you'll ever meet."

Nacero grinned. "Better than you, Mr. Molloy?"

"No," I said. "But he's close."

"Then he'll do."

Now here we were.

In the suite, Miles said, "How many times do I have to apologize? It was a figure of speech. Like faggot."

Neville whistled, then said in his Jersey accent, "Not for nothin', Dick? I would *not* go there if I was you."

It occurred to me that I couldn't remember Jeff Brewer, seated next to Miles at the dining room table now, having said a single word since we'd walked in.

"I'd like to make a phone call," Dick Miles said to Nacero. "With your permission, of course."

Nacero slowly shook his head. "When we're finished." Miles said, "I'm running out of time here."

"Well, no shit," I said.

Joe Nacero stood up. "You're a fool, Mr. Miles. Maybe my dear friend Bill Francione chose to ignore it. Or maybe he had a higher tolerance for suffering fools than I do. Or thought he needed you to be the public face and the public voice of MF if he was to take the company all the way up-town." He went and stood and stared at the water. "But I would be the fool if I chose to throw my good money at you, even if it would have meant controlling Mr. Molloy's football team."

"It's not his team anymore," Miles said, hot. "It's mine!"

"Well, for like another hour," I said.

Miles suddenly picked up what I'd discover later was the You Talkin' To Me annual report and slammed it down on the table, scattering papers like they'd been swept up in the breezes off the Gulf.

"Mother*fucker*!" he said.

"Yes," Neville said, looking at him over the tops of his adorable prop reading glasses, "that is the name of the company, after all."

It was interesting then: Dick Miles suddenly seemed to remember who he was. Or who he had been before he started rolling down the hill. He stood up from the table, walked around it, yanked his tie off as he did, shook Joe Nacero's hand, walked over, and stood in front of me. "You don't think I came here without a backup plan, do you?"

"I would have expected nothing less."

"One call is all it's going to take," he said. "And then we're still going to pull this baby out of the fire, aren't we, Jeff?"

Jeff Brewer didn't seem so sure.

What he did say was "Yes sir," looking happy that he still had the ability to speak.

"Two phone calls, actually," Miles said. "One to Wick Sanderson, one to a friend staying here."

•

He was in the middle of the room now, rocking back and forth on the balls of his feet, reminding me of Harm Battles. "I'm the asshole here, is that the deal? Okay, I'm the asshole. You guys have had your fun. But your brother and sister are still gonna want their money. And I'm still the asshole who can get it for them, even if I have to go to another suite to get it."

"I've already got somebody to buy their half," I said. "Because you're absolutely right, they do want their money."

"And who's going to put up that kind of money?"

I said, "Allen Getz."

Said to Dick Miles, "He's not waiting for a call from you. He's waiting for one from me. The one telling him that Neville and I are ready to drive him over to The Colony."

Dick Miles opened his mouth and closed it. And suddenly looked older than the water stretched out behind him, as far as the eye could see.

"Sometimes the least of your enemies can become the best of your friends," I said. "You ever hear that one?"

At long last, Miles couldn't get his mouth to work.

Mine still did.

"Trust me," I said to Dick Miles.

There was no point in telling Miles how Ken and Babs had agreed to take less money from Allen Getz. My brother and sister *did* want their money, but they knew that the difference between what Miles had offered in the first place and what they were about to get from Getz was just a way of keeping score.

Only modern athletes kept score that way.

And agents like Borden Skiles.

And guys like Joe Nacero and Dick Miles.

There was also no point in telling Miles about how my aging bad-girl stepmother had set up the meeting for me with Getz, and how I had then explained to him that he could finally get a piece of the Hawks at a good price, with the chance to be the kind of happy, out-front partner to me that a guy like Robert Tisch was to the Mara family with the Giants.

The deal was this: He got forty-nine percent. He could sit on any league committee he wanted, starting with the Finance Committee, and be doing me a huge favor in the process. He could run everything on the business side except the actual football operation. Which was mine. Now and forever. But even with that, I told him that if the Hawks ever won another Super Bowl, he could have it in writing that Wick Sanderson would present the Vince Lombardi Trophy to him in front of the whole wide world.

In other words, he could have all the perks of being a sports owner, half the profits, none of the responsibilities.

It would be my Irish ass on the line, the way it had been with the old man.

I told Allen Getz that day in the city that I even had a rather inspired choice to run the business side of the Hawks for him. Inspired, I said, just because of who was going to be the loser in this game.

Who's that? Getz had said.

Carey Nash, I said.

"Golly," he said to me in Suite 19, the day he'd sat with her. "She's as smart as you said she was. And quite a looker, too!"

I said, "I'm sure she and Kitty are going to be great friends."

Now Getz was at the Longboat Key Club, like a relief pitcher about to come out of the bullpen.

In the suite, Joe Nacero said to me, "We'll be in touch."

He left. It was Dick Miles, Jeff Brewer, Neville, and me. Miles was like a fighter who'd quit on his stool.

Miles said, "What are you going to tell them?"

"That you'd had a change of heart, there was too much going on right now in your other businesses," I said. "That you'd been thinking about this for the last week or so, and that's why you had Getz waiting in the wings."

Dick Miles said, "None of this happens if I don't have a run of bad luck."

I told him I used to get a lot of that in Vegas.

He started to say something else. Nodded at Brewer instead. Miles headed for the door Nacero had left open. Brewer got up to join him. I told him to stick around for a minute, I had one more thing to discuss with him.

Brewer put his hands up. "Hey," he said. "This was never between us."

Miles left. I told Neville to call Allen Getz when he got downstairs, and have somebody bring the car around.

Jeff Brewer and me now.

He said, "I really need to get back to The Colony myself. Let me just tell Carl I'll be right out. Is that okay? I promise not to try anything."

"Be my guest."

He opened the door to the suite, stuck his head outside in the hall.

"Shit," he said.

I went and stood next to him. Carl was on the couch just across from the elevators. He was sitting between two of Ty's Sarasota homeboys. Who looked exactly like his Hollywood homeboys. And the ones I'd met that night at Be A Wolf.

The guns they were holding also looked pretty darn familiar from where I stood.

Ty was standing by the elevator doors. When he saw me, he reached into the pocket of his jeans as if reaching for his own piece, then pulled his empty hand out fast and fired an imaginary gun at Carl, who went up in the air like the part of the couch between the homeboys had turned into a trampoline.

"Relax, dog," Ty said to Carl. "I'm just playin'."

To me, Ty said, "We done?"

"Almost."

I stepped all the way out into the hallway, turned, and hit Jeff Brewer with a short right hand, knocking him back into Joe Nacero's suite and on his ass.

"That was for making Susan Burden cry," I said.

28

I **had made** some extra work for my friend Wick Sanderson, of course. But that extra work did give him an excuse to stay over at The Colony, along with the Finance Committee members, for another day.

Allen Getz passed the committee with flying colors, then the full membership in the conference call a few hours later. Right after the Finance Committee vote, he gave an exclusive interview to Annie Kay on what he called "this nutty audible Jack Molloy called," for the *CBS Evening News with Ed Bradley*.

The commissioner then issued a statement saying that as much as Dick Miles loved the Hawks and the NFL, he had decided to devote all of his energies toward the restructuring of MF, Inc., and that he was stepping aside in favor of his dear friend, Allen Getz.

"The two of them go way back," I told Annie later.

Neville, sipping champagne with us on the balcony, said, "I've had deeper relationships with some of the dear boys I used to meet in bathhouses."

By then, Wick Sanderson had dropped by the suite to inform me that the Finance Committee, with his approval, had amended the Maurie Grubman Rules again, and that the league was waiving the probation period in Getz's case, and that his ownership of the forty-nine percent of the New York Hawks was effective immediately.

"How did you do that?" I said.

"We're the National Fucking Football League, Jack. We do whatever we want to do."

I asked him if he wanted to hear the whole story.

"Hell, no," he said. "Sometimes running this league is a lot like bed. I just want to skip the small talk, have the earth move, then move on."

On the balcony, Neville said there was a little bar he'd heard about in Clearwater he thought he might check out, and that we shouldn't wait up for him. When he was gone, Annie said, "I probably should have asked this sooner, but what does our old friend Carey Nash get out of this?"

"She's already got the last of her settlement with Miles, even if it turned out she had to settle a little on the settlement."

Then I confessed that Carey was probably going to get a variation of Liz Bolton's old job with the Hawks.

Her champagne flute stopped inches from her gorgeous lips.

"She's going to *work* for you?"

"Getz, really. Business end of stuff, not football. She got pretty fired up when I told her that Liz had gone from the Hawks to Hollywood."

Annie sat there for a minute, quiet, then smiled. "This is definitely not a good thing for your stepmother."

"Probably not."

"Wasn't she the go-between for you and little Allen?"

She was, I said, but we were just going to have to let nature take its course, and then told her A.T.M.'s philosophy of life, that you either wanted to compete or you didn't.

We drank champagne and looked at the stars and the

lights on the water and then left the sliding doors open as I
led her toward the bedroom, telling her how tired I was all
of a sudden, Annie telling me that I was in luck, maybe it
was because I had mentioned A.T.M. before, but welcome
to Assisted Living Night at The Colony.

The next Saturday, the day before Hawks vs. Raiders,
I met Joseph Nacero at Teterboro Airport, not too much of
a drive from his home in Hawthorne, and we boarded the
Gulfstream that NetJets had provided and flew to Omaha,
arriving at the Omaha Airport around noon.

Nacero tried not to show it during the flight, but was
clearly as excited as a kid making his first trip to the ballpark.

"I didn't know he was a friend of your father's," he said
when we were up in the air, about the man we were going
to see. "I thought I knew everything about him. But I didn't
know that."

"Grad school," I said. "Columbia. The funny thing was,
he barely graduated Fordham. I think my grandfather might
have pulled a few strings on that one. I mentioned that my
grandfather was a bookie, right?"

Nacero said, "It only enhanced my opinion of you."

I said, "It really was a challenge coming up with the
right gift for the man who has everything."

"Almost everything."

"It's funny how these things turn out," I said. "He even
owns this airline."

"That I know," Joe Nacero said.

When our plane landed, we taxied over to a private runway away from the main terminal and parked right along-
side another Gulfstream, gleaming in the sun, looking like
the twin of the one we were in.

The cabin door opened and the stairs locked into place.
The same happened in the plane parked next to us, where
Warren Buffett was waiting to play bridge with Joe Nacero.

"Do you know who the other two players are?" Nacero said.

"I told him to surprise you."

Joe Nacero shook my hand. "Thank you for this."

I said, "Thank you for everything."

I reached into my pocket and took out a brand new deck of playing cards and handed it to him.

"Remember what I told you about how to bluff," I said.

"I told you," Nacero said. "We don't call it bluffing in bridge. We call it psych bidding."

"Call it whatever you want. It's the same in every game."

The first person to arrive in Suite 19 for the playoff game was Mr. Mo Jiggy himself, somehow wearing a retro version of my old UCLA No. 19, wide brushed denim jeans just a shade darker than the jersey, and toothpaste-white sneakers that looked like they had platform heels.

He had ended his world tour in Hong Kong two nights before, and said that was it for him, no more touring, sports was his life, the international situation was much too unsettled these days and he was staying in the US of mama-lovin' A.

"God Bless America," I said to Mo.

"Tell you somethin' else, Jack Molloy: If I want a Muslin from now on, I'll have Montell or one of them other boys in the posse change his name to Mohammed."

Sounds like a plan, I said.

"I got to be honest with you," he said. "Allah's about done worn out his welcome with old Maurice."

Maurice being his real first name.

Then he wanted to know if we were still serving those little Philly cheesesteak deals he liked so much, and I told him they should be arriving any second. He went over and dropped himself down on the couch and started watching nine pregame shows at once.

Pete Stanton and Susan Burden arrived next. Both of them smiling.

Smiling and holding hands.

Susan said, "There's something we've been waiting to tell you, just because you've had so much on your mind."

I said to Pete, "You look like a teenager about to ask me if you can use the station wagon tonight."

"I promise to put gas in it," he said.

"Am I allowed to ask what happened to Pam?"

"I'd forgotten something about Pam," he said. "And the something was how much she liked going to the Palm Beach Gardens mall. Or any mall. At which point I made one of those executive decisions I used to make around here all the time, and decided not to spend the rest of my life over the cap."

"He needed a shoulder to cry on," Susan said, "and you were kind of busy."

"When she went to London, I asked if she wanted some company."

"I did tell you," Susan said, "that I'd invited a friend over."

Then she looked at Pete the way I used to catch her sometimes looking at the old man. "Hey, friend," she said to him.

"Holy . . ." I said.

She leaned over and kissed me on the cheek and said, "Thank you for not saying shit, dear."

"Where's Dick Miles these days?" Pete said.

"About to roll an eleven, I hear. As in Chapter Eleven."

Then Billy and Oretha were in the suite, and so were A.T.M. and about half a dozen Yum girls. Carey Nash showed up and said that Allen Getz was going to be late, that Kitty was a little under the weather.

"I'm starting to think Allen might have a different idea about our relationship than I do," she said. "And I don't want him to. Been there with the last boss, you know? Done that."

"I'm sure you two will work it out."

Mo Jiggy was standing with us then, having watched Carey Nash walk in. "And this is?" he said.

"Carey Nash. Our new team president."

"Well, I'll be damned," Mo said, taking her by the arm. "C'mon over here, baby, and watch Jimmy Nantz with me. Let Mo tell you about this fantasy he's always had about him and a wo-man pres-i-dent."

Wick Sanderson and Ginger the big red girl arrived about a quarter to twelve. When he came over to the bar to fix himself a Bloody Mary, I asked what had happened to Hollywood Tits.

"It's like they say in the doctor shows," he said. "We did everything we could. But we lost her."

I told him I'd be back before kickoff, walked out to the elevators, went down to the field level, got something out of my office, then walked down the runway and out the tunnel and onto the field at Molloy. It was after twelve now. Officially Sunday afternoon.

The old man was right, I'd always known it, even if I forgot for a little while.

Let the rest of the bastards have the rest of the week.

I saw Ty Moranis and Sultan McCovey over near the Hawks' bench, jostling each other, pointing into the stands, laughing about something.

Priceless Braxton sat on the bench, already fully dressed for the game, helmet included, in the lotus position.

And then, maybe because there was so much Molloy Stadium sun in my eyes at this end of the field, I looked up at midfield and was sure I could see Big Tim Molloy standing there, back to me the way it was in that old photograph, looking up, his head full of sky, wearing his old camel topcoat.

But I knew that was impossible.

Because I was wearing the topcoat.

I walked up there anyway, looking around, noticing the stands were pretty full already. Already full of the day. Remembering something Joe Namath had told me in a saloon once, about how as much as he loved trying to win the game, he loved the time right before Sundays at one just as much.

When I got to the fifty, I turned and saw Annie over by the Raiders' bench, probably getting ready to do a live feed to the pregame show. The sun was high in the sky over Molloy, but the temperature was around thirty degrees, and so she was wearing a long winter coat, and the kind of hat I remember Julie Christie wearing in *Doctor Zhivago*.

I started for her and she started for me, and there would be some question, much later that night, about whether or not I had mouthed the words "I love you."

On the field, she said she was about to tag her taped piece, and asked if I wanted to hear her kicker. Sure, I said, and she went right into her anchorperson, breaking-news voice.

"Jack Molloy, remember, came here from Las Vegas, where they tell you the house always wins," she said. "But this one time, it seems as if Molloy won the house."

I told her it was a good line, but then made a gesture with my right hand as if introducing her to Molloy Stadium and told her she might be wrong.

"This house *always* wins," I said.

Then I said I had a line for her I wanted to share, one I'd heard from the commissioner of the National Football League.

"Do *not*," I told Annie Kay, "lose the hat."

FROM THE *NEW YORK TIMES*
BESTSELLING AUTHOR
MIKE LUPICA

0-515-13364-7

"A hilarious satire of the NBA."
—*Orlando Sentinel*

**A THREE-RING CIRCUS ENSUES WHEN A
WOMAN PLAYS IN THE NBA FOR THE
FIRST TIME—AND FOR THE WORST
TEAM IN THE LEAGUE.**

"Sportswriter Mike Lupica takes you on a
wild, witty ride."
—*Lexington Herald Leader*

**Available wherever books are sold or at
www.penguin.com**